Lady Ambition's Dilemma

THE SCOTT-DE QUINCY MYSTERIES

BOOK THREE

Published by Aspidistra Press

This book is a work of fiction. Names, characters, places and incidents either are products of the author's imagination or are used fictitiously. Any resemblance to actual events or locales or persons, living or dead, is entirely coincidental.

Created with Vellum

BOOKS BY JANE STEEN

The House of Closed Doors Series

The House of Closed Doors

Eternal Deception

The Shadow Palace

The Jewel Cage

The Scott-De Quincy Mysteries

Lady Helena Investigates

Lady Odelia's Secret

Lady Ambition's Dilemma

Lady Ambition's Dilemma

THE SCOTT-DE QUINCY MYSTERIES

BOOK THREE

JANE STEEN

'For there is no friend like a sister
In calm or stormy weather;
To cheer one on the tedious way,
To fetch one if one goes astray,
To lift one if one totters down,
To strengthen whilst one stands.'

— FROM *GOBLIN MARKET* BY CHRISTINA ROSSETTI

1
HAWTHORN HALL

August 1883

Dearest Helena . . .

"It's from Lady Hastings," I said to Guttridge.

The remark was somewhat redundant since my lady's maid was certainly familiar with my sister Blanche's handwriting and had handed me the letter I had just opened.

"How delightful, my lady." Guttridge arranged the rest of my post into a neat pile on the rosewood escritoire in Whitcombe House's morning room. "Should I leave you alone for a short while to read your letter? We were going to discuss your half-mourning wardrobe, but we can do that later."

"I suppose you could come back in an hour."

I abandoned the dress and fashion journals Guttridge had assembled for me and tried to focus my gaze on Blanche's difficult handwriting. But my mind was full of dresses: lavender, a soft gray that would bring out the color of my eyes, and every glorious shade of mauve. Anything but black. After two years in that depressing hue, I had been looking forward to discussing silk, lace, and the sort of jewelry suitable for a young widow. Still, a sister was a sister, and I hadn't had a letter from Blanche for a long time.

Michaelmas . . . lease . . . retrench . . . A few words of the letter floated into view as I turned toward the retreating Guttridge. "I hadn't heard from Lady Hastings for so long I was beginning to think I'd insulted her somehow. Or that she's so cross over the business with Lady Odelia she couldn't bear to write."

"It's not my place to comment, of course, but I'll admit I was wondering why there were no letters from Lady Hastings." Guttridge gave a small, expressive sniff. It certainly wasn't her place to comment on Blanche's habit of sending me long letters full of criticism and unwanted sisterly advice whenever the opportunity arose, and the sniff meant she was restraining her baser instincts. But Guttridge, who had been much involved in the final, harrowing episodes of what had become known in the gutter press as the Scandal of Sir Geraint's Darlings, knew as well as I did that Odelia had certainly provided an excuse for Blanche's most strenuous censure. There should have been at least six letters by now.

Guttridge departed quietly, leaving me alone in the soft golden glow of my yellow-painted morning room. It was a hot day, and patches of sunlight were already shivering on the ceiling, filtered through leaves above which I glimpsed a deep blue sky. I used Blanche's letter to fan my face for a few moments, sighed with regret for my departed morning of comfort and entertainment, and read:

Dearest Helena,

I hope—indeed, I am sure—you can do me the favor I am about to ask of you. It is within your means, and as you will see, is of the utmost importance to me.

I sighed again, more deeply. The phrase "it is within your means" meant Blanche's favor involved money. It would be nice if this sister of mine, fourth in order of birth in our family but first in rank since she'd married a marquess, could write merely to inquire how I was faring after the tempestuous events of the last few months. But Blanche was nothing if not self-centered.

"Although, to be fair, self-centeredness is a Scott-De Quincy trait," I said out loud to my empty room. It was undeniable that none of my siblings had much regard for other people's feelings, including mine. Why was I alone cursed with concern for others? It made me far too compliant—too generous, perhaps—and Blanche was particularly fond of exploiting this weakness.

I would like you to take out a lease on my behalf, Helena, dear.

My eyebrows rose; this was without a doubt to be Blanche's most expensive request to date. Buying her a new dress was one thing; renting an entire house for her was generosity on quite a different scale. Of course, I alone among her siblings could afford such an expense.

I wish you to rent Hawthorn Hall for me, preferably to start at Michaelmas.

"Mystery upon mystery," I murmured. Blanche loved Hawthorn Hall, which was in Broadmere, less than three miles from my house near Littleberry, but it belonged to friends of hers. Was she really proposing to live there from the end of September?

That way I will have a few weeks to find a tenant for my house here in Tunbridge Wells. Dederick will take over the lease of Hawthorn Hall from you once he is married . . .

Heavens. Was Blanche writing to me to announce her only child's marriage? Perhaps she'd been too busy to write to me because she'd been securing a wife for him. I read on, faster than before.

Dederick will take over the lease of Hawthorn Hall from you once he is married, but until he finds the right young lady, I am keen to secure the Hall for my use and his before anyone else rents it. Until I have found a tenant for my own house, I do not, as I am sure you know, have the ready cash to take on a new lease, and there is some urgency. The dear Whetmores are devoted to me, but they are eager to leave the country before the cold weather, and I can't be entirely sure they will wait if they receive another offer.

Now my interest was very much piqued. Why were the Whetmores leaving? But Blanche's next sentence supplied the answer.

I am the first to know, I believe, that they have decided to spend the winter abroad for dear Fiona's health, which has taken a turn for the worse. You know she has always been delicate. Furthermore, Dederick feels that if he <u>*must*</u> *rusticate himself, Sussex—near you and the rest of the family—is as good a place to do it as anywhere. He is not fond of Tunbridge Wells.*

No, and he wasn't fond of Sussex either. My nephew Deddy, when not visiting some other member of the exclusive Marlborough House set, lived at his club in London. "This looks not like a nuptial," I said aloud. "Deddy wouldn't be retreating to the country if he'd found a rich wife, would he? This looks more like creditors."

I sighed for the third time, even more heavily than before. We all knew Dederick's debts were mounting. The last thing our family needed was more trouble.

But I needn't have worried. *Dederick has sufficient funds for the time being, but he has finally agreed that he absolutely must retrench this winter and is willing to spend some time in the country with his Mama. More importantly, the notion of preparing to look for a wife next Season is beginning to appeal to him at long last.*

Well, desperately needing cash might induce a man to listen to his mother, and Blanche had been telling him for some time that his only solution to the monumental expense of being part of the Marlborough House set, that extremely high-living social elite connected with the Prince of Wales, was to acquire a rich wife. A *very* rich wife. Only the wealthiest aristocrats could live on that exalted pinnacle for long without ruining themselves. It was Blanche's fault for encouraging the boy to aim high; no wonder Odelia's nickname for her was Lady Ambition.

Position and fortune would be best, but fortune alone, and an amenable temper, might make for a good wife, if she is sensible enough to value the advantages of a match with a nobleman blessed with youth and good looks in addition to his excellent connections.

I nodded. Dederick was certainly blessed with youth and good looks. He had not yet attained his twenty-fourth birthday; he had been gifted with the legendary Scott-De Quincy "air"; moreover, he had inherited the title of marquess, only one step down from a dukedom, at the age of eighteen when his father had died. With that impressive title adding to his personal allure, it wasn't surprising he had readily been accepted into a social set that lived in an endless, expensive whirl of travel, parties, and amusements, and his youth perhaps excused him from being so easily drawn into living above his means.

A pretty country house in our beautiful county, the family nearby, and my own title and connections will show Dederick off to his best advantage when we invite prospective brides to visit us in the balmy summer months, when all Sussex is bright with flowers and quaint charm.

So Blanche wanted a house where she and Dederick could entertain properly. Well, that made some sense.

There is, of course, the scandal, but Dederick and I are blameless when it comes to Odelia's behavior, and I have done my best to distance myself while our shameless sister remained at your house. You naturally understand why this is important.

"Hmph." But now I grasped the main reason why I hadn't heard from Blanche.

Your own behavior appears to have been eccentric in the

extreme—"Lady Helena Investigates" indeed, the very idea—but I have a notion that having the "investigating lady" nearby will add a certain piquancy, and it is well-known you were unaware of Odelia's scurrilous behavior until the truth was forced upon you.

I groaned. How well-known? And it was like Blanche to throw that newspaper headline in my face. Still, Odelia had done the right thing and gone abroad, and I supposed the gossip would die down eventually.

And then there is the matter of the paintings for your drawing room, which are the object of curiosity of a different kind. Sir Geraint is looked upon more kindly than Odelia, as might be expected, and this crowning work of his career is eagerly anticipated.

"Yes," I said to my terrier, Scotty, who was snoozing at my feet. "What's sauce for the goose is definitely *not* sauce for the gander in society." It rankled somewhat that Sir Geraint, just as culpable as Odelia, was still received almost everywhere, while our sister had been obliged to retreat to Rome for the family's sake, lest we too found doors shut in our faces. Why were men always so more readily excused? Yet I too received him, and had not canceled the half-finished commission for a splendid set of paintings for Whitcombe House's drawing room.

I hope to hear from you by return that you have put matters in hand with your man of business and that he will deliver an offer to the Whetmores shortly. I know it is a lot to ask that you should advance such a sum of money on my behalf, but I also know my request will cause you no hardship. I am sure, being the good sister you are, you will readily agree to help your loving,

Blanche

I FOLDED BLANCHE'S LETTER AND PUSHED IT DOWN INTO A pocket, then took a moment to remove a speck of something or the other from the fine black wool of my dress, now edged with black satin ribbon to indicate I was in the last three months of my mourning. Black, I had found, showed absolutely everything.

Not that I resented showing my grief for my late husband, Justin, of course. I rose, pressing my fingers to my lips and touching them to the photograph on my desk, a rather nice one Justin had had taken before he proposed to me a mere five years ago.

The morning room was becoming increasingly warm. Perhaps I should go to the library and summon Guttridge to discuss dresses? But I had lost interest in clothes. Where could I go? The sun would not be on the drawing room this early, and the artisans and workmen would not arrive to continue their work there for another forty minutes, so I could be private and cool. I needed to think.

I took the drawing room key from a drawer and turned my steps toward the room destined to become Whitcombe House's showpiece, followed by the click of claws as Scotty trailed behind me, sniffing into various corners as he proceeded.

Yes, I could think here, within sight of the sea, brilliant turquoise in the summer sunlight. Within sight of the French coast, which showed as a vague bumpiness and haze on the far horizon.

The large room was quiet and cool, stripped of its furniture and finishings, smelling faintly and pleasantly of sawdust and linseed oil. I sank onto the long window seat, now bare of its cushions and covered with sheeting, and caressed Scotty as he sprang up to settle near me, his head on his paws.

"I'll do what Blanche wants, I suppose. After all, what else do I have to do?" I asked my dog. "Wait for Fortier to come back to Sussex, if he ever does? Perhaps I'd be better off with something to keep me busy. I think I'm brooding."

Deep brown eyes stared back at me from a whiskery face, and I laughed—at myself as much as at my beloved terrier. "Yes, you're right. I have some peace at last, so I ought to be able to settle down in it. But I can't."

It was only three weeks since Sir Geraint's son, Edmund, had been hanged by the neck until he was dead. Ten days since Odelia had departed for Paris, then Rome, for an indefinite period. A month since I had said goodbye to Armand Fortier in his father's house in London, and he had kissed me.

"Oh, for heaven's sake." I realized I was running a finger back and forth across my lips while my other hand had found Blanche's letter and was squeezing it as hard as I could.

I pulled out the folded paper, the muscles of my jaw tightening. I had no claim on Fortier. He would leave for France as soon as his father died—and almost certainly bring back a woman who had passed as his wife in that country since the war with the Prussians thirteen years ago. *And* a boy who called him "Father." Would he even want to introduce these people to the scandal-smeared Scott-De Quincys? He might remain in London. After all, he would inherit his father's house there and could hardly live any longer with his sister and brother-in-law in Littleberry when he had a wife and child to look after.

The light reflecting off the crystalline sea hurt my eyes. No doubt that was why my head ached and my eyelashes were wet when I closed my eyes to escape the glare.

I could hear voices, one of them that of Dunnam, my butler. Scotty made a gruff noise to show he was alert to the new arrivals. I rose, running my fingers quickly over my eyes.

"It's Dunnam and the workmen, Scotty. He's come to let them in."

I patted my dog reassuringly, deciding to improve the shining hour by questioning the foreman at length about the work accomplished and yet to be done. I would then write to my man of business, as Blanche had asked, instructing him to make an offer to the Whetmores to lease Hawthorn Hall. Perhaps I would summon up a shred of gratitude toward Blanche for giving me something to do. Family should come before foolish hope, before brooding on the past, and before fretting about the future. I turned my back on France, squaring my shoulders to meet the demands of the day.

2
AN UNEXPECTED GUEST

The Whetmores seized upon my offer with alacrity. Before ten days had passed, I had visited Hawthorn Hall to refresh my memory of the property and commiserate with Fiona Whetmore on her failing health. The Hall was a pretty Jacobean manor house close to the center of Broadmere, an odd little town composed of a picturesque central area inhabited by such gentry as had not moved away, with a collection of crumbling cottages farther out, some military dwellings from the Napoleonic Wars, and an assortment of ruins poking out from the outlying fields. It was near enough to Littleberry that I could see it from my house, perched secretively on its tree-shrouded rock, mourning the loss of the harbor that had once assured its prosperity, its once-great church a half ruin.

I had known the Whetmores, and Hawthorn Hall, since my childhood. Sir Andrew Whetmore had improved the Hall considerably in the last fifty years, and it looked sound and comfortable, arranged by Fiona with good, if rather staid, taste. It was set well back from the road on four acres of land, with a lodge—reserved for the Whetmores' use should they return to England—and a walled kitchen garden, in addition to an orchard and adjoining field, both rented by a local farmer for his sheep. The Whetmores were fond of Blanche, who was far closer to their age than I was, and would, I was sure, be good landlords. They were the center of Broadmere's small circle of aristocratic society, and Blanche, as a marchioness, could easily step into their place in the little town.

"The Hall will do well for Blanche," I told my nephew Thomas as we took tea in the green drawing room. This large room had been Thomas's domain ever since he had moved in with me at Whitcombe, but since he was more of a brother to me than a nephew, I sought him out whenever I needed company. "She and Dederick won't exactly be able to entertain on a grand scale since there are just eight bedrooms, but they can make a reasonable show. The reception rooms are quite large. I suppose I'll help with the arrangement of them."

Thomas grinned. "I imagine Aunt B-Blanche is counting on that. You have the knack of getting the most out of a p-property. I hear from M-Mama that Uncle M-Michael is p-pleased with what you've done to Scott House."

"Yes." I smiled ruefully. "I have improved Michael's London house for him, and in doing so have lost his wife, my closest confidante, for the entire parliamentary session. How very ironic." My brother Michael had decided that, since Odelia no longer lived at Scott House and I had improved its comforts, he would bring Julia and the children to London instead of staying at his club, bachelor-fashion.

"And you've lost your new friend, Mrs. D-Dermody, to London as well. I suppose she'll be b-back once her father p-passes?"

"She says as much in her letters." I heard far more from

Gabrielle Dermody than from her brother, Armand Fortier, and that bothered me. I changed the subject.

"Tell me about your forthcoming career as an undergraduate." Thomas had decided to become a clergyman, which involved a belated attempt to earn a degree. "Isn't Prince Albert Victor going to Trinity College this year?" I watched as Thomas heaped more sandwiches onto his plate. "Gerry *will* be pleased to have you at the same college as the Prince of Wales's son."

"I d-don't know why; I have no intention of c-cultivating his acquaintance." Thomas frowned. "Besides, I'm n-n-not going up this Michaelmas term."

Having only one good hand, Thomas was in the habit of putting his plate on his lap to eat; I clicked my tongue at Scotty, who was eyeing it rather too closely, and waved my dog back into the far corner of the sofa.

"After Easter, then? You must be nearly ready." Thomas had been learning Greek and Latin with a tutor.

"M-maybe. Perhaps M-Michaelmas next year. Winship says a little more study w-w-would help me g-get the most out of university."

I sipped my tea, gazing at my handsome nephew. "And every delay extends Winship's term of employment."

"Cynic." Thomas's beautiful smile lit up his face. "As a m-matter of fact, P-Papa wants Winship to spend a t-t-term or two at Trinity with m-me. Just until I settle in."

"Very grand. A private tutor, just like the prince." I suspected the delay, and possibly the tutor, had more to do with Gerry's tendency to underestimate her son, but at least the prince would set a precedent.

Thomas took a healthy gulp of tea. "So I'll be here to see Aunt B-Blanche become the châtelaine of Hawthorn Hall. M-M-Mama says she's already sent letters of self-congratulation to all the b-bores of B-Broadmere."

I snorted with amusement. "Gerry didn't really put it that way, did she? If you're going to be a clergyman, you had better learn to speak more tactfully. See if you can rephrase that sentence as if you were already in holy orders."

Our conversation became rather foolish for a few minutes as we imitated the kind of clergyman who appeared in novels, and we ended up in a fit of giggles. Scotty, never one to pass up an opportunity, brought an end to our frolics by stealing two sandwiches from Thomas's carelessly abandoned plate.

"All joking aside, Gerry will be glad to have you close a little longer, I think," I said as I returned from banishing my dog to the floor, taking his place on the sofa next to Thomas. "She's grown more fond of you lately, I swear. She's beginning to cluck over your future ecclesiastical career like a broody hen. She probably imagines you as a bishop."

"Heaven forfend." Thomas put his good arm around my shoulders and hugged me briefly. "D-don't you start thinking I'll have a splendid c-career. I really d-don't want one. Just a small church, a simple vicarage, and p-p-p-perhaps, one day, a wife who won't mind half a m-man for a husband. After all, Mr. C-Collins was a complete fool, b-but he readily found a wife."

I smiled in appreciation at the reference to *Pride and Prejudice*, but it saddened me to hear my handsome, kind, intelligent nephew refer to himself as half a man. I opened my mouth to refute the assertion, but Scotty's whine of welcome made me realize a footman had entered. "Yes, Robert?"

"Lady Hastings has arrived, m'lady." Robert ignored Scotty, who had raced to sniff enthusiastically at his well-shined shoes. "Mrs. Eason is having her ladyship's things taken to her usual room. Lady Hastings says to tell you she will be with you as soon as she's taken off her hat."

Thomas waited until Robert had left before expressing his surprise. "Were you expecting Aunt Blanche?" he asked me.

"I was not." I rose to my feet, dusting myself down with my hands and instinctively patting my hair to make sure it was in place. With Gerry and Blanche, more than with my other sisters, I always felt the need to present myself as well as possible or risk their criticism. "I thought Blanche was staying in Tunbridge Wells till nearly the end of September."

"Perhaps she's decided to attend your birthday dinner for M-Mama after all." Thomas began stacking plates and cups on the tea tray, eating some more of the remaining sandwiches as he did so. "Will she upset your seating arrangements? She'll make us an odd number, won't she?"

"That doesn't matter. It's only family, and there are already more women than men." I turned. "I think I can hear her. Goodness, it's not like Blanche to come downstairs so quickly."

I moved toward the door, followed by Scotty. The green drawing room was long and relatively narrow, and we had been sitting in the middle of it, in front of the empty fireplace. Out of the corner of my eye, I saw Thomas rise to his feet, a movement that caused him a little difficulty because of his lame leg and withered arm.

The door opened, the footman announced "Lady Hastings," and the tall, rather stout figure of my sister swept into the room. Ignoring my barking dog, she kissed my cheeks—or rather, saluted the air beside them—before stepping back.

Blanche, Marchioness of Hastings—a title she would hold until Dederick married—had eyes of a somewhat cold pale blue. As always, her critical gaze assessed me from head to toe before she passed on to Thomas, to whom she gave the tentative embrace the family so often bestowed on him, as if he might break. Thomas showed her to the most comfortable seat, where she ensconced herself without paying much attention to him.

"I'm having them bring more tea," I said, and at my nod the footman stepped forward to take the tray. "Perhaps some little cakes?" I smiled at my sister. A sweet tooth was one characteristic we shared.

Blanche did not smile back. Indeed, there was something tense about her whole bearing. We made small talk as the footman left, but I found myself making most of the effort in the conversation without garnering any clues as to why she had arrived so unexpectedly.

It didn't take Thomas long to deduce his presence was the problem. After a few minutes, he announced he had things to get on with and took his leave, taking Scotty with him. There was then another delay as the footman brought fresh tea and petits fours, but finally the door shut and we were alone.

I poured tea in silence. Outside, I could hear a peacock's mournful cry, the raucous calling of seagulls farther off, and bees buzzing among the flowers. A slight breeze stirred the air from an open window; the green drawing room, being on the north side of the house, was pleasantly cool.

"There." I used the small silver tongs to add a slice of lemon and handed Blanche her cup. "We won't be overheard." I had correctly interpreted her glance toward both ends of the room to see the doors were properly shut. "Would you like me to have them close the window? Or perhaps you could try. The handle's rather high for me to reach."

Blanche raised her eyebrows at the suggestion that she, a marchioness, might close a window, but in a moment she appeared to forget my error. She leaned forward, speaking in an undertone.

"I'm going to need your help with a . . . a dilemma, Helena. I don't know whom else to ask—and, after all, you helped Odelia." She frowned. "Although I'm not at all sure you didn't make things worse, interfering as you did. I have very *mixed* feelings about your drawing room, given its connection with the scandal."

"As do we all." She meant the principal drawing room, of course. "But in my defense, the work was already well underway, and undoing the commission would have been highly complicated and probably just as much remarked upon. We all—the whole family—thought, in the end, that we had better just make the best of it."

"Hmmm." Blanche shrugged. "It doesn't seem to be doing a great deal of harm, from what my friends say. A little disapproval here and there, but of course Sir Geraint is a man of such genius everyone seems inclined to forgive him."

"There will always be gossiping tongues, whatever we do," I reminded her. "Ignoring them is the Scott-De Quincy way, isn't it? In any event, O formally broke with Sir Geraint before she left, and as far as I can tell, he's leading a monk-like existence at Edenholme. That's his house in Lower Broadmere."

"I *know*." Blanche frowned again, in annoyance this time.

"Of course you do." I sighed inwardly. "Work on the paintings is advancing well, as is the construction of the special frames. Does your visit today involve O or Sir Geraint or—or the decorative arts?"

"Don't be facetious." Blanche's plump lips pursed into an expression I knew well, one she might not make if she realized how it made vertical lines appear around her mouth. She would turn forty-one in November, and as with Gerry, I had no memory of her living at Hyrst with us. I had not yet reached the age of three when she married her marquess, Francis, and Dederick had been born before my fourth birthday. In many ways, I barely knew either of them.

"I'm not trying to amuse myself at your expense," I said with as much patience as I could muster. "Something's worrying you, and I do wish you'd get on and tell me. I'd be happy to help if I can. It's not Hawthorn Hall, is it? I have matters well in hand there."

"It's not the Hall." Blanche's face seemed to crumple for a moment. I caught a glimpse of a different woman—older and more anxious than she usually looked—but then she appeared to get a grip on herself. "The Hall will allow Dederick to make a good show of it before and after the Season. Several of my friends in Broadmere have promised good hunting for his guests, even if they're new people. They probably *will* be new people; I'm thinking of Americans, of course."

"Of course." Americans, as Gerry so often remarked, were everywhere these days, fueled by fortunes from the grain and cattle that had taken away so much of England's trade and by the railway and property money created by their own fabulous expansion westward, an entire country building itself before our eyes. They came to Europe to buy up its clothes, its art, its grand estates, and, increasingly, the heirs to its noble titles.

"If Dederick stops moving in exalted circles for a little while," Blanche continued, "he should be able to afford a decent carriage and a matched pair of bays. He already has two excellent hunters and two beautiful horses for cutting a dash on Rotten Row during the Season."

"He's certainly handsome, and one can't fault his title." I smiled encouragingly at Blanche. "From what I hear, he's an expert rider and a good shot. Does he dance well?"

"Like an angel." At last, a real smile spread over Blanche's face. "I'm hoping to find a girl who's in London for her first

Season, perhaps one whose parents are looking for an aristocratic lady to present her at court. Apparently, that's a marvelous way to get oneself acquainted with the Americans. Her parents will often buy this lady a new dress or two as a sort of thank-you gift. A new arrival, who hasn't yet formed any opinions, will be the best catch. Dederick can dazzle *her* with his personal attributes and her *parents* with his connections to the royal family."

Her voice had risen to its usual stridency as she set out her plans, but then the quite different look stole back over her face and she leaned toward me. Her next words were spoken so softly I had to pay close attention to catch them.

"But there's a problem, and this is where I need your help. I daren't tell Gerry."

3
LADIES DO NOT USUALLY KNOW SUCH THINGS

"So tell me." I also lowered my voice and leaned in confidentially. "You know I'll be discreet."

"It's too horrid. I can't think where to begin." To my surprise and dismay, Blanche's eyes suddenly brimmed and tears trickled down her cheeks. "Oh, I can't—I can't. If Gerry were ever to find out . . ."

For the first time, I felt genuine alarm. "What does it have to do with Gerry? And what would she do anyway? She loves you. The two of you have always been closer to one another than to any of the rest of us. The twins may be a little closer in age to Gerry, but they were always in their own world; Mama said Gerry was like a little mother to you." I smiled tremulously, hoping I could make Blanche feel better. I had never seen her so upset, not even when Francis died.

"Gerry would be so cross." Blanche sniffed. "You know what she's like. The shame of telling her . . . Worse than anything Odelia's done . . ."

Blanche's words had become indistinct as she dissolved into tears again, but that was the gist of it, I thought. An idea was forming in my mind about what could be worse than

Odelia's behavior. Justin had once said something about Dederick that I'd discounted at the time, but I'd never forgotten it, just hoped he wasn't right.

Blanche took in a big gulp of air and visibly stiffened her backbone. She swallowed twice, and when she spoke again, her voice was more normal.

"I'm not sure if I can even make you understand. Ladies do not usually know such things." She shuddered, her cheeks flushing vermilion. "Dederick had to *explain* it to me. That I should have to hear such a thing from my only boy."

I was becoming more and more certain Justin *had* been right. I put my hand on Blanche's.

"I *am* a married woman, Blanche, dear. Or I was. I'm not blind to the ways of the world. Justin was rather fond of scandals, and not at all hesitant about explaining certain . . . matters . . . to me. He had a theory that, once married, women should not be innocent fools. He felt it was a husband's duty to enlighten them."

"How unpleasant." Blanche's face assumed an expression I knew all too well, disdainful and quick to judge, just like Gerry. "But then . . . we have wondered, Gerry and I, whether you were entirely as *innocent* as a girl should have been. When you were young, I mean, and there was Daniel. We thought at the time Mama was worried about you."

Now it was my turn to redden; Blanche's shot had come near the gold. "I was a virgin on my wedding night," I hastened to assure her. "Daniel and I were impatient to marry; we were very young, and our blood was hot, and we had already talked about eloping if Mama and Papa didn't give their permission, but I was still a virgin. Though perhaps not entirely innocent."

But it was Justin who had made sure there was nothing I didn't at least know in theory. Had he done wrong? Certainly, obeying the Apostle Paul's injunction to think only on pure and virtuous things occasionally required some effort; but sometimes, as now, a little worldly knowledge was helpful. I hastened to bring the conversation back to the subject of Blanche's son and thus deflect her from prying further into my past.

"In any case, we're not discussing me. Are you trying to tell me Dederick . . ." I searched for the right words, "prefers the company of other men?"

Blanche's irises were an even colder blue than usual, in contrast to the tear-reddened whites of her eyes. Now they were trained on me with an expression that would once have made me quail. Clearly hardened by the events of the last two years, I gave her back as good a glare as I was receiving.

"I am *inexpressibly* shocked at your assumption that my son *prefers*—" Blanche choked on her words. "And that you are blaming your dear departed husband, of all people, for your depravity of mind—"

"Would you rather I screamed and fainted?" I was not prone to losing my temper with my sisters, but I could feel myself beginning to simmer with irritation. "You're asking for my help, so I'm making it easier for you by admitting I know something of such matters instead of acting like a hypocrite. Justin told me that such men exist and that they often marry anyway. Although," a new thought struck me, "it would be rather unfair to your putative American heiress, wouldn't it? Is that your dilemma?"

My words appeared to strike Blanche dumb for the space of twenty seconds, but then she recovered. "Dederick's not *such men*." She looked quite distraught, and I began to feel sorry for her again. "He has sworn to me it was with just the one boy—at school—that matters went beyond mere affection." She choked again.

And you believe that? trembled on my lips, but I mastered the impulse to speak my mind. I reached out my hands to

Blanche again, imprisoning her somewhat large right hand between my two small ones.

"I'm sorry I'm making assumptions. I was just trying to help you get over the difficulty of telling me. There's obviously more to it than simply something that happened, what, five years ago?"

"Six." Blanche took a deep breath. "It was the year before Francis died, during the time my poor dear husband was so ill." The hand in mine relaxed a little. "Of *course* there's more to it. The creature is apparently still a friend of Dederick's, or at least is one of the Marlborough House set." She began to speak very fast. "He told him he was planning to marry, and he says he will reveal all if he becomes engaged to a woman, and you *have* to dissuade him."

I mentally worked my way through the *he's* and *him's* before speaking. "So you're saying," I said slowly, "this man has threatened to make their former . . . friendship . . . public if Dederick gets engaged to be married? And you want *me* to somehow ensure he doesn't carry out his threat?"

"Isn't that what I just *said*?" Blanche's voice rose to a strangled squeak.

"I was merely making sure I understood correctly." I frowned. "Why would this man make their . . . their goings-on public and risk scandal for himself? He can't possibly be serious."

"Dederick thinks he is. He says he's reckless—unbalanced—capable of anything."

And how on earth was I supposed to even begin to prevent him? "May I ask his name since we've come this far?"

"It's Arthur Southgate-Haigh." Blanche sniffed. "They always were a terribly *peculiar* family. There was that older brother who shot himself; there was some scandal around his suicide about a servant—a *male* servant. It was a mercy, if you ask me, because Johnnie—the second brother—will inherit the title when his father dies, and he at least appears to be happily married. Six children, I believe."

I remembered the scandal of the older brother; in fact, I remembered being introduced to the older generation of the Southgate-Haigh family shortly after it happened, during my first Season. They had possibly wanted me for Johnnie, a dreadfully dull young man. The Southgate-Haighs were a rather important family with several titles, the one that Johnnie would inherit being very grand indeed. On the strength of such splendid prospects, he had been engaged by September, to my relief. I didn't remember Lord Arthur, but of course he would have been very young then.

"I'm not acquainted with Lord Arthur," I pointed out to Blanche. "It sounds as if you may know him. Why can't *you* talk to him?"

"If I thought myself capable of dealing with such a matter, do you think I would have turned to you?" Blanche spoke in a stage whisper in an effort to control her temper. "If Francis were alive, he'd have horsewhipped the boy. If your Justin were alive, I could have asked him to act on my behalf."

"What about Ned?" Gerry's husband would certainly know what to do.

"I can't possibly ask Ned. He tells Gerry everything, and I just won't have her know." There was an expression of something like fear in Blanche's eyes; as close as she was to Gerry, their relationship had always been an unequal one.

"But what qualifies *me*?" I asked. I sensed I was beginning to weaken.

Blanche's eyes narrowed. "Your recent experiences, of course. You've been gallivanting around, mixing yourself up with suicides and pox-ridden servants and adulterers and that French physician who turns out to be a duke. Your remarks about my dear boy show that this irregular life of yours is coarsening your fibers—and now you tell me poor dear Justin taught you every sin in the book."

"Told me about them—it's not the same thing," I retorted, a little sulkily.

"Be that as it may, you have changed." Blanche stared at me for a moment, then plunged on. "And I'm asking you—*begging you*—to help me. From one widow to another, if you must. You could at least try writing to Lord Arthur for me."

BLANCHE'S WORDS HUNG IN THE AIR WHILE I SEARCHED FOR the right thing to say. I wanted to help Dederick—and Blanche—of course I did. But I saw Blanche's "dilemma" somewhat differently than she did, and I was eager to secure some promises before proceeding.

"I can't, in all conscience, write to Lord Arthur without talking to Dederick first," was the outward conclusion of my inward reasoning. "You'll have to get him to come here. As women, we can't go to his club to talk to him, and I don't suppose you'll want me in Tunbridge Wells with you so busy getting ready to move." Blanche had never invited me to stay with her anyway. "I insist on discussing the matter with him in person—and in private, without you present—and on being sure I'm in possession of all the facts before doing such an impertinent thing as writing to a man I don't know about a most intimate facet of his personality. Those," I continued loudly in the face of Blanche's obviously impending objections, "are my conditions."

"I'm hardly accustomed to ordering my son around," Blanche objected. "He is a marquess—"

"—who has blotted his copybook and needs to be called to account." I spoke over her words and continued without allowing her to reply. "Those are the sole conditions under which I will do as you ask. And if you want me to help you win him an American heiress for a bride once the matter of Lord Arthur is cleared up, I also insist we tell her about Dederick's . . . youthful indiscretion."

"But it's quite usual to gloss over a young man's past." Blanche glared at me. "Of course, I can't expect a barren woman to understand a mother's feelings on such a matter as this. If you had a son, you'd know young men *will* do untoward things—sow their oats, as the saying goes—and if every man had to confess his peccadilloes, there'd be far fewer society weddings."

Or fewer peccadilloes. "This is a bit more serious than sowing a few oats with a willing housemaid," I pointed out. "It's against the law for one thing, if I remember rightly what Justin told me." I squeezed Blanche's hand. "Look, as far as I'm concerned, Dederick's past should be forgiven and forgotten. He's still very young, and from what Justin told me, such things happen at boarding school. But a girl—an eligible young lady in her first Season, as you want her to be—deserves our protection for the sake of our common womanhood, doesn't she? I'll help you put the best face on things, but I won't help you manage the deception of an innocent woman."

There was a long silence, during which I allowed the sting of Blanche's reminder of my childless state to dissipate. I was used to my family imagining I was barren since they didn't know what I—and Fortier, since he'd been Justin's physician—knew.

Eventually, Blanche, who had withdrawn her hand from mine and sat back in her chair, gave a curt nod of the head. "I will tell Dederick to come here at his earliest convenience."

"Thank you."

Another long silence ensued while I struggled for something to say. I absolutely did not want to continue the subject of Dederick for a minute longer before I'd talked to him.

"We should discuss Hawthorn Hall, I suppose, now you're here," I said at last. "But tell me—do you intend to stay for Gerry's birthday dinner on Sunday? It's just family."

"I'll have to stay till Dederick visits, I suppose." Blanche, who had previously told Gerry she was too busy this year, looked apprehensive. "Gerry will think I'm being lazy."

"Then let her. We'll tell her you couldn't bear not to celebrate her birthday with her, and I'm sure that's also true."

I smiled, trying to bring a little cheerfulness back into the summer afternoon; after all, Blanche was my guest. "Let's make a real fuss of Gerry, shall we? We all need some happiness after the last few months."

4
AN UNEXPECTED RELATIVE

"To Gerry!"

My eldest sister's finely molded features did not lend themselves easily to a broad smile, but they were certainly radiant as she nodded her appreciation to the assembled guests. There were nine of us, eight standing with outstretched arms holding glasses of hock, while Gerry remained seated in the place of honor. Thomas sipped his wine and grinned mischievously.

"M-may I say, M-Mama, you are just as beautiful on your forty-ninth birthday as I remember you on your twenty-n-ninth. It's one of my earliest m-memories, you know," he said to the rest of us as we reseated ourselves. "My n-n-nursemaid carried me into the dining room at Hyrst with Lydia and Auntie Helena skipping along in front of us in p-pink dresses, hand in hand. And then M-Michael had a tantrum, and G-Grandmama sent all us children away without a taste of d-dessert. She had some sent to the n-nursery later, but n-n-not before Lydia and Helena had been thoroughly c-cross with Michael."

"Poor Uncle Michael. We were cross with him far too

often," said my niece Lydia, whom marriage and motherhood had mellowed. "I hope he and Aunt Julia are happy at Scott House with the children. How nice to think the old place is being used properly, not just Aunt Odelia rattling around in it with her paintings."

Gerry raised her eyebrows at the mention of Odelia, but Ned, always quick to spot an arch remark brewing in his wife's eyes, headed it off neatly.

"Sensible to use Scott House in such a pleasant August, with no disease in London for once. It'll give the children and Julia a change of scene, and it's time young James at least saw the Houses of Parliament. After all, he'll be in the Lords one day. He ought to know something about his father's work and his own future career."

"I hear Scott House is a sight more comfortable than it was, thanks to Aunt Helena." Lydia's husband, Sir John Durber, raised his glass to me.

"And better run." Ned chuckled.

The thread of the conversation escaped me as I nodded to Dunnam, who made a sign to the footmen to serve the boiled salmon with caper sauce and brill with shrimp sauce. Our second course and entrées would mostly be game, although I had chosen dishes of duck and curried lobster especially for Gerry. The third course would abound with raspberries, peaches, and mulberries, all much to my sister's taste.

Outside the windows, a pink sky glowed, casting its light on the diners and making my sisters look younger, almost as if we had all grown up together. We were a diminished family group without Michael and Julia, not to mention Odelia, and with Michael absent, the conversation was less political than usual. That was fine with me; it was going to be a pleasant family dinner, with little prospect of an argument. I served myself a small piece of brill with anticipatory enjoyment.

We had reached the second course—haunch of venison, leveret pie, and capon à la financière since Gerry liked it—before Gerry broke her news.

"I've received a letter, Helena. From a most unexpected relative. Can you guess who it might be?" There was an oddly expectant look on her face.

"I have absolutely no idea," I said. "Who?"

"Jonathan Murray-Jones."

My heart gave a small, rather painful lurch at a name I had not heard for a decade. Jonathan was Daniel's brother, the elder by three years; they were both distant cousins of ours on our mother's side. I had only seen him once, when he visited Hyrst to take his leave of Daniel before joining his regiment in India, and it was perhaps the sudden, vivid memory of the three of us talking together that caused the pain. I remembered Daniel's voice wavering between gruffness and boyish high notes as he pelted Jonathan with questions.

Those had been happy days for me. Daniel's envy of his brother's imminent departure had not spoiled the excitement of having a hussar in full uniform in our midst. I had thought Jonathan magnificent.

By that time, Daniel had been living with us for almost half a year and had befriended me, a child of twelve, in a brotherly way that fulfilled the yearning within me for a sensible sibling—Michael was anything but—who was, unlike my sisters, close to me in age. Our friendship had been based on a shared love of adventure stories, and after Jonathan had left, Daniel had pulled books about India down from the library shelves and sworn he too would join an Indian regiment as soon as he was old enough. But we had fallen in love by the time I was sixteen, and Daniel had delayed his plans until we could be married.

And then, when I was almost seventeen and our marriage

—perhaps our elopement—seemed inevitable, Daniel had died. The ten-year anniversary of the worst moment of my youth had been in May, when I had been busy with Odelia's troubles. I had marked it with a brief visit to the orchard at Hyrst, to gaze at the spot where Daniel had collapsed onto the rough grass in front of me.

Ten years of being pounced upon by my memories of that time had hardened me, and I was able to reply to Gerry with perfect calmness. "Jonathan? Why was he writing to you?"

"He stayed with us after Daniel died," Ned's voice rumbled out. "They gave him compassionate leave—arrived too late for the funeral, of course. He wanted to pay his respects to you, but Alix sent word you were too distraught and not to be disturbed."

"I never knew."

I realized my sisters—Gerry at the end of the table, Alice and Annette opposite me, and Blanche at my side—were all looking at me with the expression I remembered well from my long days of melancholy. As if I were an object of pity, not only for my grief but for crumbling so completely under the first trial of my life. As if I'd become half-witted. Was something of the Helena of that period showing on my face?

I straightened in my chair and spoke crisply. "Do give him my regards, Gerry. I hope he'll call on me if he visits England someday. Is he still with his regiment?"

Now Gerry looked almost triumphant. "He's coming to stay with us. His request is to come straight here when his ship docks, which looks like tomorrow or the day after, from the shipping reports. He's on long leave from his regiment. It's short notice, of course, but there's plenty of room at Four Square. Won't it be nice to see him? Shall I tell him to call on you whenever he wishes?"

Her tone suggested Jonathan was a special treat for her little sister, as if she'd thought up a surprise for my benefit.

The impression was reinforced by Alice and Annette, who had arranged their identical faces into identical expressions of delight and were clapping their hands.

"You *will* be pleased to see him, Helena, dear!"

"What a treat to have an officer of hussars in Littleberry—"

"—fresh from India—"

"Is he still handsome, do you think?"

"I do hope he wears his uniform."

As usual, I had no idea which twin had said what. I smiled at the gathering in general and made sure to sound enthusiastic.

"Of *course* it will be splendid to see Jonathan."

"He's a captain now." Ned grinned. "Captain the Honorable J.S.T. Murray-Jones. Such a mouthful—took up most of the envelope when I wrote back to him. He was a conceited pup when last seen; I wonder what ten more years of bullying the natives on behalf of Her Majesty's government have added?"

Gerry rolled her eyes. "You always assume the worst, Ned. He says he's traveling alone, without a servant," she informed me, "so he'll be very little trouble."

Another flash of teeth showed between Ned's mustache and beard. "We'll be spared the usual native servant, concocting curries and upsetting the domestic staff. Cook is perfecting her kedgeree as a token of gratitude. We had some this morning; it's rather good."

"Is he not married?" The question came from Blanche, who had interrupted her gossip with Lydia to listen.

"He isn't." Ned dispatched a bite of venison before continuing. "Could be wife-hunting, I suppose, although I thought India was full of young ladies trying to catch an officer. Perhaps not so much since the Mutiny."

He flicked a quick glance at Gerry, who ostentatiously turned her attention to her capon, and smiled at me.

"He'll be in his early thirties now. Just the time of life when a man thinks of settling down, eh? Gerry will be in her element introducing a new young man to the county. I hope he's as presentable as he was ten years ago."

5
CONTRACTIONS OF THE HEART

Gerry's birthday dinner took place on Sunday evening. On Tuesday, I received a note from her informing me Jonathan had arrived safely at Four Square.

I had been keeping myself busy with my herbs, perhaps to distract myself from the odd impression I'd been having that I'd wandered back through the thin veil of time that separated the widow of Whitcombe House from the Helena Scott-De Quincy of the 1870s. Had those girlish feelings really been slumbering so lightly it took the mere mention of a Murray-Jones to awaken them? Of course, I had once spent every day praying fervently for the moment when I would be known as "Lady Helena Murray-Jones" to come quickly . . .

On Wednesday morning, I awoke unusually early and decided to seize the day.

"I'll be fine by myself," I said to Guttridge as she helped me into a loose wrapper. "You and Tilda can help me sort everything later, but I rather like the prospect of an hour or two spent cutting herbs before breakfast, all alone. It's such a glorious morning. I'm expecting a caller this afternoon, so I should make the most of it."

"I'll have your bath and breakfast ready when you come in," Guttridge said placidly. "You're right that we should gather in as much as possible before the weather changes. After all, it's almost September. What about your hair?"

"Just twist it up into a chignon—don't fuss with it. It'll end up full of dust and bits of leaf anyway. We'll wash it today."

"I'll have Taylor send an under-gardener along with trugs and twine."

"Good, thank you." I turned round to look for Scotty. "Stop yawning, you lazy dog. We're going to get a little early morning fresh air and exercise."

It was *very* fresh air, cool and with the tang of the sea, and the light had the beautiful, even quality one associates with September, showing how near that month was now. My walled herb garden was bright with late flowers and the fresh green regrowth from where we had been harvesting over the summer.

The air inside the walled enclosure was heady with the scents of mint and lemon verbena and rosemary, other fragrances arising as I brushed against foliage while working. I snipped and tied industriously, pausing only occasionally to watch a butterfly or hoverfly, while Scotty dashed around after imaginary rabbits. The trugs the gardeners had lined up in rows near the gate filled with bound bundles of leaves and flowers.

A group of seagulls took up residence on the wall as I worked, presumably to observe me in case I showed any sign of having food on my person. Naturally, they soon became embroiled in a bout of what Justin called "competitive shouting"; after about twenty minutes of listening to the racket, I abandoned my scissors and went to the garden gate to find a broom to chase them off. Where was Scotty when I needed him?

I rounded a corner, my head down since I was brushing leaf debris off my wrapper, and collided with a man walking toward me.

"I beg your pardon." I looked up, expecting a gardener.

It took me a moment to realize who it must be. The clue to the mystery resided in the deep, even tan of his skin, a most un-English hue; the hands that were steadying me were strong and square, the fingernails showing white against bronze. At his feet was Scotty, his silver plume of a tail waving happily; why hadn't he barked? Of course, he might have done. I wouldn't have heard a thing above the noise of the dratted gulls.

"I do beg your pardon," I said again, stepping back. "I should have been watching where I was going. Are you—are you Captain Murray-Jones?"

He smiled, his teeth white and straight in his tanned face. "I probably shouldn't be in your garden. For *you* must be Lady Helena Whitcombe, grown up from the little girl I remember."

"Cousin Helena, please." I looked down at my right hand, which was stained green since I had left my gloves somewhere, decided it would have to do, and held it out to him. He shook it and then, with a laugh, kissed it briefly. I became suddenly conscious of my wrapper and the fact that my front hair was losing its curl. Scotty, who generally liked young men, gave the short, sharp bark that was his way of asking for attention.

As Jonathan—Cousin Jonathan—bent to scratch my dog behind the ears, I took stock of him. He wasn't in uniform; in fact, he was quite informally dressed, but in that effortless way that bespoke the gentleman. Clean-shaven, with thick blond hair worn a little long, he had the typical bright blue eyes of the Scott-De Quincy clan and a nose that was perhaps slightly irregular, but nonetheless appealing. Because of my paucity of inches, all men were tall to me, but I supposed he was shorter than some; he lacked three inches of Fortier's height, by my reckoning. He was of a muscular build and upright bearing, as if the uniform he wasn't wearing still dictated his posture.

He wasn't at all like Daniel, of course. Daniel had had russet-colored hair and had been of a small and wiry build, a cuckoo, as Mama had remarked, although I knew Daniel took after his poor, doomed mother. Jonathan was undoubtedly "one of us"—Mama's term again—a true Scott-De Quincy. I, never "one of us" in looks—*a wren among peacocks* had been Papa's preferred phrase—had learned from childhood to view the Scott-De Quincy "air" with a proper degree of awe and reverence. I watched the breeze stir the thatch of straw-colored hair with appreciation.

"Gerry told me you'd arrived," I said as Jonathan straightened up and the blue eyes came back into view. "I hope you had a pleasant journey." Polite platitudes, I thought as the words left my mouth. Boring and conventional.

"It was splendid. I adore a sea voyage, don't you? Shall we sit down?"

Jonathan, seemingly quite at home, looked around us and led me to a nearby bench with the poise of a host in his own house. Once I was seated, he sat next to me, crossing one muscular leg over the other and resting his cheek in his hand, gazing at me with a rapt attention that brought a blush to my face.

"I can see that little girl here and there," was his verdict. "You were such a pretty little thing, and time has been kind to you. You must be—twenty-five?"

"Twenty-seven. I was twelve when we met."

"Of course, Dan was only three years older than you." He

leaned back, relaxing into the corner of the bench. "What a happy accident that we ran into one another—quite literally." He grinned. "I thought I'd get out of Littleberry and walk up the hill to where I could see the sea. I don't suppose you can have any idea of what all this Englishness does to a man who has seen nothing but India for years. And the *air*—" He sniffed the breeze in seeming relish. "At least up here it's marvelous. Littleberry smells of tar and fish and sheep."

I couldn't help laughing as his nose wrinkled in illustration. "Spend any time around here and you'll get used to the smell of sheep. The fields are full of them."

"They're far less noticeable in a field than when they're being driven through town. What a stink." Jonathan waved a hand as if warding off the remembered smell. "I had no intention of disturbing you, by the way. I'd decided to wander down through your gardens—since the main gate was open—and find a way down the hillside to the river. My plan was to call on you this afternoon."

"I hope you'll still do so, and give me a chance to redeem myself as to my appearance." I looked ruefully at my hands.

"I shall. I'm seeing a man this morning about purchasing a horse, and I intend to arrive this afternoon like a gentleman—in fact, like an officer." He indicated his clothes with just as rueful an expression. "At the proper time for calling too."

His smile was charming, his gaze seemed to take in the whole of me at once, and I began to feel quite warm. "But here you are, like one of Mr. Hardy's heroines, beautiful and industrious at an early hour, gloriously capable. Not a spoiled miss at all."

My heart contracted at the old joke—Daniel had been wont to call me "Spoiled Miss" if I showed any disdain for effort—then gave a small thump of acknowledgment that his brother had called me beautiful. But a movement caught my eye, and Jonathan also saw it.

"That looks like a footman searching for you. Do you think he's seen me arrive and is here to announce you have a visitor?" He stood as I did, indicating Whitcombe House with a hand. "You're awfully grand here, aren't you? Gerry said you'd married the local moneybags and lost him two years ago. I'm sorry to hear that, by the way."

"Thank you."

"I'm sorry about the family trouble too." He lowered his voice. "I read about the, er, unfortunate business of Lady Odelia on the ship. Don't imagine I care about any of it, but the point is I saw a certain Lady Helena Whitcombe dubbed the 'Investigating Lady' by the press and knew it had to be Daniel's Helena. That's why I'm here; it made me remember Ned and Gerry's kindness in putting me up at Four Square when I came over after Dan's death, and I thought I'd look them up. I hoped I'd see you. The newspapers made me suspect you hadn't lost your sense of adventure, and I thought it might be rather jolly to meet again. As it is."

I was spared from formulating a reply to this explanation, which mingled compliment and scandal rather confusingly, because the footman had drawn near and was hovering at an appropriate distance. At my nod, he stepped forward.

"Mr. Dermody has arrived, m'lady. He begs the favor of an interview."

My heart—which had not entirely calmed down—now performed an absolute somersault, landing somewhere near my feet. A visit from Gabrielle's husband, Quinn, at this early hour could only mean one thing. I turned to Jonathan.

"Will you excuse me? I absolutely must see this visitor."

Jonathan frowned. "Is it trouble? You've gone pale."

"It's not exactly trouble—he's a friend. Or at least the husband of a friend." Quinn Dermody and I were, by now, on much better speaking terms, but I wasn't sure I could call him "friend" just yet. "He's probably bringing some long-expected sad news." I turned to the footman. "Show Mr. Dermody into the library, please. I'll be right along."

Jonathan made a small bow. "I will take myself off immediately and intrude on you no longer. Should I perhaps not call this afternoon after all?"

"That might be best." I no longer knew what my day would be like.

Jonathan smiled. "There'll be plenty of time. I'm rather footloose at the moment, to be honest. Staying in Sussex will give me a chance to think about how I want to spend my leave. Apart from looking up one or two fellows in London, I confess to having nowhere to go and nobody to see. Believe it or not, you and the Freestones are practically my only acquaintances in England."

I smiled back rather mechanically but then pulled myself together. "Then we'll have to make the most of your visit, won't we? I'll send a note to Gerry to let her know when I'll next be at home."

I held out my hand, and Jonathan again performed the slightly odd ritual of first shaking it, then kissing it. I watched him stride away, confident and sure-footed and quite at home on my land, and then, calling to Scotty, turned toward the house and the news I had been expecting for so long.

6

A STAB OF EMOTION

I found Quinn Dermody engaged in an intense perusal of the rows of books in the library. Gabrielle's husband wore formal mourning that suited his height and black hair, although since he favored dark colors for everyday wear, the change was not startling.

The crape band on the silk hat he'd deposited on a table—it seemed typical of him that he hadn't entrusted it to the footman—was a full five inches deep, the mourning of a son for a father. This struck me as such touching evidence of his affection for Alexandre Fortier that I had to swallow against a sudden lump in my throat.

He must have detected my presence, for he turned around.

"Forgive my déshabille," I said, seeing his eyes widen a fraction. "I was doing some early work in my herb garden."

He shook his head. "Don't apologize. I shouldn't be disturbing you at this hour. But I've promised for so long to tell you as soon as I could, haven't I? I also promised Gaby I would come up on the earliest possible train, and of course I wouldn't want to just send you a note. I heard the news very late last night; Armand sent a telegram."

"You must miss Gabrielle a great deal. And the children must miss their mother."

He shrugged. "I have a pottery to run. And young children are best kept away from suffering and death, in my opinion. They were better off with me in Littleberry."

He came toward me, holding out a large, firm hand, and this time I didn't care about the state of my own palms. I let both his hands envelop mine, looking up at features that were rather softer than was usual with this irascible man. There were some threads of gray now in the thick black locks. Quinn Dermody and I had learned to like each other better in the last year, and now I could read the depth of feeling behind his habitually stern expression.

"Please accept my sincerest condolences," I said softly. "I liked Monsieur Fortier a great deal; I'm glad I had a chance to make his acquaintance. Have you heard much from Gabrielle and—and—Armand?"

It was the first time I'd uttered Fortier's given name in public, and it felt odd. Yet it would have been odder to call him "Monsieur Fortier." "Doctor Fortier" seemed too professional for the circumstances, and it struck me suddenly that he was now, strictly speaking, the Duc de Maival in any event. But any awkwardness I felt dissolved as a smile of surprising sweetness transformed Quinn Dermody's saturnine face.

"I know all the details; Gaby got a letter to me by the early post. They were eager to assure me the end was swift and peaceful. He had been talking, and accepting the occasional sip of wine, at midday, but at four o'clock he lost consciousness. Gaby wrote that the change was so abrupt that by seven Armand summoned her to keep watch with him. He died at a quarter past ten. Probably of a hemorrhage, Armand said, although there were none of the distressing symptoms they'd seen during the crises of his illness. It was well past midnight when Gaby sat down to write. Armand was asleep in a chair in their father's bedroom, so exhausted even the laying-out of the body and the tidying and decoration of the room hadn't disturbed him. He'd been by Alexandre's side almost constantly for the past week."

I sniffed, fumbling in the pocket of my wrapper for a handkerchief to dab my eyes. I felt no shame in giving way to tears in front of Quinn, who suddenly did seem like a friend. I was glad indeed to shed tears for Fortier's father, with whom I'd immediately felt some kind of bond, and my heart was full to overflowing with feeling for the brother and sister who had spent so many weeks in their father's sickroom.

"Please offer both of them my fondest regards." I took a deep breath to still my emotions. "I'll write to them today." I glanced at the library clock, ticking sonorously in the place it had occupied since the last century. "And you had better go if you're to catch the next train."

I ACCOMPANIED QUINN DERMODY TO THE CARRIAGE ENTRANCE and watched him climb into his conveyance, made solemn by black ribbons. Once his carriage was out of sight, I directed my steps toward the staircase and my much-delayed bath.

A fresh stab of emotion assailed me on the way upstairs, and I had to admit to myself it contained several elements. There was relief, to be sure, that Alexandre Fortier's long months of suffering and pain had ended. The remedies Fortier had been asking me to send him had suggested his father was afflicted by many bodily discomforts as the cancer did its insidious work, although Fortier had referred only tangentially to the details of his father's illness in his somewhat impersonal letters. There was regret I had not been able to stay in London and visit Kensington Square more often. There was simple grief for this loss of a good man.

And there was, I had to admit, a nagging worry about those letters. Fortier had said he loved me and was waiting only to be free of his entanglement with his cousin Louise, the nature of which I did not fully understand, to woo me. Then he had become "alarmed," according to Gabrielle, at the whole notion of being in love. But he had kissed me when we had last met, a kiss that had been gentle and yet, I was convinced, deeply passionate.

Perhaps his reticence was due to his promise to bring Louise to England, something she had been asking him to do for some time. He had sworn to depart for France at the earliest possible opportunity. Maybe that was why he hadn't even hinted at love in his recent letters.

In short, I wasn't even sure if I was grieving the loss of a simple acquaintance or someone who might have been my father-in-law. And for all I knew, I could be sorrowing for yet another lost love; whatever crisis was to come between Fortier and me, its coming was now imminent. The feeling of not knowing where I stood was deeply upsetting, now that I was allowing my mind to dwell on it.

My tears flowed freely, and it was several minutes before I could command myself sufficiently to seek the refuge of my bedroom. As I'd expected, it was in perfect order; as she often did when I wasn't having breakfast in bed, Guttridge had laid the small table by the window with the daintiest porcelain. A sparkling crystal vase in the center held a bright nosegay of flowers—Taylor must have sent it up while I was in the garden—together with a large bowl of pinks that filled my bedroom with their clove scent.

The room was quiet and empty when I entered, but

within two minutes Guttridge appeared. Her lips tightened fractionally as she took in my appearance.

"It's hardly my fault I've had two very early visitors when I'd expected nobody." I tried to sound brisk, although I didn't deceive myself that Guttridge had missed my tear-reddened eyes.

"I know, my lady." Guttridge came forward to unpin my hair, which was beginning to fall out of its chignon and dragged painfully at my scalp. "Taylor's had the herbs you cut sent to the workroom, and I've set Tilda to sorting them. I can have your bath ready in ten minutes, and there'll be a pot of chocolate brought up in just a minute or two, so you can sit and refresh yourself first. You must be famished."

"I suppose I am rather empty." I dabbed at my eyes. "You're pampering me to an unusual degree, Guttridge. I take it you've guessed the news."

Guttridge removed the last pin and arranged my hair over my shoulders. She was behind me, so I couldn't see her expression, but the fingers of one hand remained on my shoulder for a fraction of a second longer than was customary. When she spoke, her voice was unusually gentle.

"I have, and I'm sorry for it. I know you became fond of the gentleman, as short an acquaintance as it was."

"Do you think I should go to Scott House?" I asked the question that had been growing in my mind. "Mrs. Dermody is my friend, and she has no sister to comfort her. Perhaps I should be there." The cloud over my heart lifted a little. "It's early. We could be on a train just after noon."

"And what about Lady Hastings?"

To Hades with Blanche, was my first, mutinous thought, but I merely glanced sullenly at Guttridge and said nothing as she, sniffing quietly to express some thought she didn't want to say out loud, went to the door to take a small tray from a maid.

"Lord and Lady Broadmere are at Scott House with the children," Guttridge reminded me as she shepherded me into my chair and poured the chocolate. "Lord Broadmere may not like it if they have to host us."

"Heavens, I'd forgotten about them." I sipped my chocolate slowly, trying to imagine the fuss Michael was capable of making. I imagined Julia would do much to calm him; still . . .

Guttridge spoke again. "You could wire to Lord Broadmere to ask him to pay a call on Monsewer Fortier and Mrs. Dermody. That would be a nice mark of respect. He needn't spend a great deal of time there, just leave a card. Ladies don't go to funerals anyhow."

I looked up sharply at the non sequitur, opened my mouth to protest, and shut it. Had I been thinking of attending the funeral?

"I'll go to Taylor this morning," Guttridge continued. "To see about sending flowers."

"No, I'll do that myself after I've written my letters." This was not something I wished to leave to Guttridge, however well she would do the job. "Perhaps I could stay somewhere else."

Guttridge's eyebrows rose to her hairline. "*Not* a hotel, surely, my lady."

"I wish I had more friends in London." I took another sip of my drink. "Maybe I should join a club. I've read there are women's clubs opening." I frowned. "Or buy myself a house. I don't like London that much, but it would be useful to have somewhere to stay that's mine. Lady Hastings has some plan to get me up to Town next Season."

"She'll want Scott House," said Guttridge stolidly. "A lady of her standing—and yours, come to that—needs a couple of centuries of ancestral brick around her. I doubt Lord Broadmere will be interested in the Season."

"It'll be awkward if he is." I began to feel my spirits revive under the influence of chocolate and sugar. "Although he should get used to it. One day he'll need to bring Annabelle Alice out, and won't *that* be an undertaking?" I smiled at the thought of my little niece as a debutante. "But listen, Guttridge. Mrs. Dermody needs a friend with her. Can't we find a solution?"

Guttridge screwed up her face rather comically, as she often did when I was winning an argument. "You need to have your bath, my lady," she said at last. "At this rate, it'll be noon before you have breakfast. Let me get on, and I'll have a think."

7
BLANCHE PLAYS HER TRUMP

"Don't even think of running off to London."

"Good morning, Blanche," I said evenly. "Would you like some coffee? I can get them to bring another cup."

I was engaged in cutting the top off an egg and was only vaguely aware of my sister's tall, stout form looming over me. She had entered my bedroom without knocking, but when one spends one's life with servants, one is always prepared for interruptions.

"I've had breakfast, thank you." Blanche spoke as if she routinely had breakfast before ten, which was decidedly not the case.

"Then sit down, do." I waved a hand at the chair opposite. "You're up rather early." I forbore from saying I would never walk into *her* bedroom unannounced at what, for her, was practically the crack of dawn.

I dipped my spoon into my perfectly cooked egg, savoring the creamy yolk and eating a few bites of toast while Blanche fussed with the chair. Once she had settled, I finally looked her in the eye. "You've heard about Monsieur Fortier's death, then?"

"Naturally. You know what servants are like."

I did know that when Blanche was in my house, she positively encouraged the more gossipy among my servants. It wouldn't have surprised me at all to know that encouragement occasionally took the form of a coin or two. An under-housemaid arriving to tend a fire was easy prey where coins were involved and the morning's news asked for. Well, I couldn't live as I did and not expect my every movement to be observed and discussed. I breathed a prayer of thanks for Guttridge's ironclad tact about my more intimate moments.

"I *am* thinking of going to London," I said in as neutral a tone as I could muster. "Gabrielle Dermody is my friend."

"Family comes first." Blanche's expression was a mixture of triumph and apprehension. "Dederick will arrive tomorrow; he sent word this morning. Since you insist on talking to him before writing to Lord Arthur, you *must* remain here."

My heart sank. Clearly, I could not go to London and . . . comfort Gabrielle, if that was really what I had in mind. And Guttridge was right. I had nowhere to stay, not without intruding on Michael and Julia's first real chance to be at Scott House with just their children for company. I couldn't —or shouldn't—attend Alexandre Fortier's funeral, and I would probably be in the way and maybe embarrass Fortier into the bargain.

"Very well." I was pleased how unconcerned my voice sounded and admired the steadiness of my hands as I poured myself some coffee. "I will hold myself at your entire disposal. Now, if you'll excuse me, I must write my letters and talk to Taylor about sending flowers to London."

By the time the footman announced, "the Marquess of Hastings," the next day, I was longing for my bed. It was past eleven o'clock, and for the last two hours Blanche's head had been nodding over her embroidery hoop.

I had applied myself to reading *Dr. Edith Romney,* a novel I had asked the bookseller to obtain since it promised to describe the career of a lady doctor, an almost unimaginable personage to my mind. So far, the book had had almost no actual doctoring in it; I found myself dropping the volume at intervals as my eyelids drooped.

We had expected Dederick to arrive before dinner. He was at a shooting party on a very large estate near Sevenoaks, which wasn't so terribly far away, but the dinner hour came and went with no sign of him. Our meal was put back by a full half hour because of Blanche's insistence that he would arrive soon. When I eventually decided it *must* be served, the joint of beef, despite Mrs. Foster's best efforts, was a little overcooked.

My digestion was not at its most efficient that evening as a result, and it still rankled that I could not go to London. So I only breathed an irritated, "At last!" as Dederick followed his title into the small library, but Blanche sprang out of her seat.

"My darling boy!"

"Hello, Mama." Dederick returned Blanche's embrace with a visible lack of enthusiasm.

"How late you are." Blanche smoothed back the thick blond curls that fell over her darling's forehead, a gesture that made him twitch away so the curls fell back into place. "But I suppose you had far more important people to talk to than your old mama."

"I suppose I did. Hello, Aunt Helena."

I felt the briefest touch of a kiss on my cheek, so swiftly

executed I had no time to return it before Dederick stepped back.

"Can we all sit down?" He hid a yawn behind his hand. "I've been shooting and talking all day, and I'm simply done in. And—um—you there," he waved an imperious hand at my footman, "you might bring me some brandy."

He barely waited for me and Blanche to seat ourselves before throwing himself into Justin's armchair.

He'd had more than one brandy already that evening, if I was any judge. Yet he was only twenty-three, and dissipation had not had time to mar his beauty. He had the slim yet muscular build of a youth who spent much of his time in the saddle or the field; his abundant blond hair was exactly the same pale shade as Blanche's and shone bright in the light of the chandeliers. His eyes were like his father's, large and a clear, pale gray with more than a hint of green. He was clean-shaven and wore his hair cut quite short around the ears and nape but longer on top, a definite improvement on the shoulder-length mop of curls and nascent mustache he had sported the last time I'd seen him.

He hadn't changed into traveling clothes, sprawling in his cutaway evening coat, starched shirtfront, and white tie as if he were born wearing such attire. A large diamond pin in his shirtfront, his only ornament other than the signet ring he had inherited from his father, winked expensively at the candlelight.

Blanche seemed to grope for something to say. "Did you bring your valet? What's his name again?"

"Rampling, and one doesn't make small talk about one's servants. Of course he came with me." Dederick looked around him. "What a funny little room. Is this all the library you have, Aunt Helena?"

"We call this the *small* library; I have another." I suppressed a yawn. "We're in here because my drawing room is being decorated. My *other* drawing room is mostly for Thomas's use. You may know he's living at Whitcombe at present."

"Cousin T-T-T-Thomas?" Dederick produced a very creditable imitation of Thomas's stammer. "How is he? Has he found a crippled young lady to marry him?" No doubt seeing my eyes narrow, Dederick changed the subject. "Have you seen the Long Library at Blenheim? Now *there's* a library. You could play cricket in it. In fact, I *have* played cricket in it." He grinned reminiscently. "Broke a window. Ah, the brandy at last."

"Helena's drawing room is going to be the frame for an important series of paintings by Sir Geraint Dorrian-Knowles," Blanche said as I answered the footman's query—whether we ladies needed anything—in the negative.

No doubt that remark was intended to boost the standing of my house in her son's eyes, but I saw the danger. Dederick, of course, didn't miss his chance. He snorted with laughter.

"Aunt Odelia's lover?"

He spluttered on his brandy in his amusement, his face turning a delicate shade of pink as the fiery liquid caught in his throat.

"Odelia has parted from him and gone abroad, as I'm sure you know." I tried not to let my irritation show. "Anyway, I can't match Blenheim and have no intention of trying." I hid another yawn. "I know you've only just arrived, Deddy, but would you mind if I retire? I'm dreadfully tired."

8
UNPLEASANT DUTIES

Dederick spent Friday in bed, ringing occasionally to have food or drink—mostly drink—sent up to him. On Saturday, he managed to get up in the afternoon but gave me the slip by going straight out "for a walk," from which he didn't return until dinner. As we had an invitation to Four Square for dinner and didn't get back to Whitcombe until ten, he then excused himself straight to bed, being tired, as he said, from walking and "too much family."

Sunday meant church. Blanche had a hard time persuading Dederick to accompany us, and by the time the service was over, I wished she hadn't succeeded.

"He spent the entire time staring rapturously at Sir Geraint," I hissed to Gerry as we left the church. "Didn't you notice?"

"Yes, and I'm sure he'll tell all his friends at Marlborough House about him." Gerry sounded as peeved as I felt and took her annoyance out on me. "Helena, do you really *have* to nod at that man?" I had just acknowledged Sir Geraint's salutation from a distance.

"Of course I do. He's still carrying on a commission in my house. I'll have to ask him to dine before too long."

"At least Blanche doesn't—oh, *really*!" The latter expostulation because Ned, detaching himself from us, had walked frankly up to Sir Geraint and shaken his hand. Worse, he was beckoning over Blanche and Dederick to meet the painter. Dederick looked as if Ned had given him a Christmas present.

Gerry quickly steered me in the opposite direction, toward where Alice and Annette were talking with one of their spinster friends. "And Blanche flutters around Dederick like the hen with one chick she is," she lamented. "Still, I suppose once Blanche is at Hawthorn Hall, the County will get to see more of Dederick—and after all, he has a title nobody can fault and is very handsome. And he at least has done nothing scandalous."

Oh dear.

I SPENT LUNCHEON LISTENING TO DEDERICK AND BLANCHE talk about people in whom I was not interested, reflecting that Dederick was perhaps an even bigger snob than his mother, and missed my chance of getting him alone straight afterward because Blanche insisted we apply ourselves to our Sunday devotions. I began to wonder whether she was deliberately preventing me from talking to her son in the hope I'd give up and do what she wished anyway.

But as luck would have it, she was soon asleep over her Bible. I was fairly sure Dederick, who had consumed an inordinate amount of food and drink, had not left Whitcombe, and set out to track down my quarry.

I found my nephew asleep in the small library, a decanter of brandy and half-filled glass beside him on one side and

Scotty on the other, curled up tightly in the small space left on the sofa. I watched him for a moment, steeling myself to my task with the determination of a bather nerving herself to take a "healthy" dip in the cold waters of the English Channel.

"Deddy." I spoke softly but shook his shoulder tolerably hard. He grunted, opened his eyes, and sat up. Scotty growled, burrowing his nose deeper into his rough coat to resume his nap.

"I say, Aunt Helena, you might leave off calling me Deddy." Dederick yawned and reached for his brandy glass. "Makes me feel I'm a sprog of ten. An aunt who's only three years older than a chap has no grounds for giving out pet names, as if she's an ancient crone with whiskers on her chin." He scrutinized my chin with insolent gray eyes. "You're quite pretty, really. Never realized that before."

"And you're drunk." Seeing Dederick's hand move toward the brandy decanter, I grabbed that article so fast its crystal stopper fell out; I caught it before it hit the floor.

"I say," Dederick said again, a little less forcefully this time. For a long moment, we stared at each other; then, clearly admitting defeat, he flung himself back on the sofa with a theatrical sigh, being careful to avoid Scotty.

"You came here so I could talk to you, and talk is what we're going to do."

I reflected that, for all his man-of-the-world airs, Dederick seemed so much younger than Michael and Thomas, who were both only two years older than this wayward sprig of the family. Like Dederick, Michael had inherited his title at the young age of eighteen, but Michael, charmless and annoying as he was, behaved like a man. What I had before me was an irresponsible boy.

"You can't really blame me for having a little drink in the circumstances." Dederick watched as I placed the brandy on a shelf close to me and then seated myself. "Mama says she's told you everything."

"She's told me the bare facts. If you want me to help you, the price I exact is a full confession. I won't make a fool of myself, *if* I write to Lord Arthur, through knowing only half the story. I'm *four* years older than you, by the way."

"I may shock you." Dederick looked at me from under his long eyelashes in a way I thought he intended as flirtatious and which I found faintly repulsive. My rejoinder was swift and sharp.

"For heaven's sake, *Dederick,* stop prevaricating and help me to help *you.* Just answer my questions and get it over with. Do I have to ring for coffee to help you sober up? Because I need you to behave like a man—a peer of the realm—instead of a spoiled boy. Do you realize how serious a public charge of being a sodomite could be? Not only will it completely ruin your chances of finding a wife, but it is, actually, against the law. Odelia's situation, disastrous as it is, would be nothing in comparison if enough fuss were made in the right places."

Dederick flinched at the word "sodomite," and his expression turned sulky. "I'm not really a sodomite, you know. At least, I'm not one of those men who hangs around making eyes at boys, who brings low creatures to parties, who puts his hands on them when he thinks nobody's looking. Even Arthur isn't *that* bad."

"Have you performed the act of sodomy?"

I felt my cheeks go hot and red and inwardly cursed Blanche for putting me in a position where I had to ask such a question of my own nephew.

"Yes." Dederick's face was thunderous. "If you *must* know. Good God—"

"With more than one man?"

Now it was Dederick's cheeks that flamed an ugly red, his

self-assurance turning to bluster. "It—well—no—at least, yes, but that was only when a woman wanted her husband to join in. Arthur was the only—and I was just a boy." He lifted his hands in the air in a gesture that seemed like frustration. "Girls don't get put into a school and left there for weeks—months—on end the way we do, with nothing but boys and men for company. You've no idea how it is."

"No," I admitted, feeling my face cool to its usual tone. It was indeed odd that as soon as a girl became a woman, a great deal of effort was put into protecting her reputation, if not always her innocence, while boys were removed from their families and expected to know how to defend themselves against temptation by some innate virtue. Breaking through Dederick's carapace of insolence and arrogance had suddenly made me feel more kindly toward him.

"Did Lord Arthur seduce you?" I asked.

"Yes." The answer was emphatic. "He became my protector against some of the other boys at first. I was so grateful to him." He flushed again. "A little in love with him after a while, in a silly, romantic sort of way. There were quite a few boys involved in what you might call romances, you know."

"Good heavens." No wonder so few men talked about their schooldays.

"We were all lonely." Dederick naturally sounded defensive. "But one can't say so. It's not the done thing to admit to longing for home."

He swallowed. "After a time, Arthur began talking to me about Greek love and all that. He made it sound pure and noble, and eventually—" He shrugged. "We became lovers. It lasted a few months, I suppose, but he was too . . . overwhelming. In the end, I just wanted my freedom. I stayed away from entanglements at Oxford—I was only there two years, you know—and then, when I started being invited to house parties and so on, I found I liked women well enough."

House parties. I sighed as quietly as I could. I'd been to many, and hosted quite a few, as Justin's wife and was well acquainted with the nocturnal sport of "corridor-creeping." The higher up the social scale, the more likely marriages were to be strategic, so there was more infidelity; Dederick was part of a very high-ranking social set.

"So you've had affairs with women?" This was something I wasn't sure Blanche knew.

The arrogance and derision were back on Dederick's face. "I'm perfectly capable of performing the act with them, since that's obviously what's on your mind. Can't I have some brandy now?"

"Let's get the rest of this horrible conversation over with first. I suppose you're in agreement with your mama's scheme to find you a wife?" I waited until Dederick nodded after a brief hesitation. "Then haven't you found any good prospects for yourself? You must know most of the people who do the Season."

"I know their *wives* pretty well." Dederick smirked. "I like married women. They're game, and they know what to do. I don't see much of the sort of girl Mama has in mind, and frankly, what I've seen hasn't been all that attractive. Don't you think I should feel at least some attraction to a girl if I'm supposed to sire children on her? It's what Mama wants—it's not just the money, you know. She wants to see me settled." He rolled his eyes. "I want a woman with a little character as well as some finish. I don't want some callow girl who won't know how to look after me. I like to be made a pet of; that's my problem. So are you going to write to Arthur? Have you tortured me enough?" He looked hopefully at the brandy.

"There is one more thing." I braced myself to introduce yet another matter a lady shouldn't even know about, let alone mention, but I had learned an important lesson from the unfortunate case of Susan Hatherall. "Can you swear to me you have contracted no disease while you've been sowing your wild oats?"

"What?" Dederick leapt up from the sofa, alarming Scotty, who yelped and bared his teeth. "That's taking interference a little too far."

I put a hand out to my dog, summoning him to sit at my feet, and looked up at my nephew as I stroked Scotty reassuringly. "I'm not going to help you at all if the result is to bring misery upon a young woman. It's as simple as that."

I held up my hand to still Dederick's retort, which no doubt would have been somewhat unrestrained. "It's not as if I'm asking you for details. I'll put you in touch with a medical man if need be, but right now I just want to know—do you have any reason to suspect disease?"

I watched the rapid rise and fall of my nephew's chest as he stood before me, wondering what I would do if he answered in the affirmative or stormed out or became violent, since the set of his jaw and the fury in his eyes suggested all of those possibilities. I kept myself still, waiting until he shook his head slowly.

"Nothing. There's nothing."

"You swear on your father's memory?"

Something changed in his eyes. "I do. Ye gods, you're brave, aren't you? You remind me of Grandmama, the way she used to be."

"I'm not that brave." In fact, my palms were damp with perspiration and I wanted very badly to run away, but I had the answers I needed.

I turned toward the shelf where I'd put the brandy decanter, seeing the reflections from the sun shining through the windows flash in its intricately carved surfaces as I took it down and placed it near Dederick. I watched him bend eagerly—too eagerly—to take the decanter and splash a generous amount into his glass.

"You'll write to Arthur?" he asked once he had taken a large swallow of the liquid, releasing its rich fragrance into the surrounding air.

"Ye-e-e-e-s," I said slowly. "I need a little time to think first, but I believe I have all the information I need."

9
A SUPREME EFFORT OF CONCENTRATION

Blanche interrupted my meditations about an hour later. I was standing on the terrace, looking out over the summer-scorched fields below, my attention divided between the sparkling waters of the sea and the River Ealy and the antics of some gulls swooping and turning on the air not twenty feet in front of me, calling to each other plaintively.

"Dederick told me you spoke with him." She fixed her cold blue gaze on me as she leaned against the balustrade. "He wouldn't tell me anything else."

"It wasn't an easy interview." I turned my attention to the high-pitched barking that meant Scotty had arrived from wherever he'd been—digging, from the look of it—and had seen the gulls.

"But you'll write to Lord Arthur now?" Blanche put a hand on my arm to turn me back to her.

"I'll try. That is, I will write to him; I can only try my best to convince him to leave Dederick alone." I bit my lip. "But I'm not so sure about helping you with the Season, Blanche, if I'm to be completely truthful."

"Why on earth not?"

How could I tell my sister I didn't want to help her only son find a wife because—I had to be honest with myself, if nobody else—I simply didn't like him? That I would pity any young lady who had the misfortune to entangle her fate with his? That I saw nothing but bad coming out of any marriage with this—well, *degenerate* was probably too strong a word—with this misguided nephew of mine, who had certainly gone astray morally and didn't seem at all repentant? I fell back on an excuse.

"I'm not keen on London, especially in the summer. And it's been too long since I was in that kind of society, particularly at court. You'd be better off finding one of your friends to help you."

"I want *you* to help me." Blanche's face assumed an aggrieved expression. "You were willing enough to stay in Town most of the summer to help Odelia."

"Not *most* of the summer, a few weeks. And then I had to return to give evidence at the trial."

"And," said Blanche emphatically, with the triumphant air of someone who knows they have a winning argument, "you were happy enough spending time with that Frenchman in London, weren't you? He might be there next Season as well. Odelia says you're transparently in love with him, and I think she's right. You would have abandoned me and rushed off to London—to him—if I hadn't put my foot down. Think on that. And get that letter written by tonight, would you? Dederick wants to leave."

And with that, she turned on her heel and stalked back into the house. I watched her go open-mouthed, unable to think of a thing to say.

Some twenty minutes later, I was at my escritoire in the morning room, which seemed less welcoming at this time of day, overlarge and somewhat pale and flat without the morning light. Guttridge had, at my request, provided me with Lord Arthur's address, or at least, according to the society directories, the address most likely to result in a letter reaching a man who led the peripatetic life of the very wealthy. I had no more excuses.

There is nothing more tedious and unpleasant than writing a letter one absolutely does not want to write. I had various tricks to force myself to such tasks, such as writing out the date and salutation on the paper with great care—so that failing to continue would waste a sheet of paper—placing my chair carefully in the position I thought of as the "serious seat," making a note of the main points of my letter, and summoning up the image of Mama telling me I must not shirk the task. None of these little aids to diligence were working.

It was Blanche's parting remarks that were disturbing me, of course. Was this the opinion—that I was "transparently in love" with Fortier—Odelia had expressed to the entire family? I wouldn't put it past her. My family were all too fond of passing judgment about each other behind each other's backs, and I knew Michael and I came in for more than our fair share of criticism. In Michael's case, there was some justification—he could be *so* annoying—but there was also an element of resentment that he had inherited the title, Hyrst, and the position as head of the family, while his much older sisters must marry or live on a pittance.

Where I was concerned, I imagined my sisters saw my position as a wealthy widow with a large house, now legally in possession of money and property for my lifetime, as the basis for the sort of envy sisters rarely admit to, even to themselves. Granted, I was "poor Helena" who had lost a husband in tragic circumstances, but I was so *comfortable*, wasn't I? Even what my family believed was my barrenness meant I had no children to inherit Justin's wealth and limit my freedom. The fact I had openly longed for a child of my own was no bar to this rosy picture, I supposed.

I stared at the sheet of paper with aching eyes. I had perhaps forty-five minutes before Dunnam rang the dressing gong. Strictly speaking, the rules of hospitality dictated I should already be in the green drawing room drinking sherry with Blanche, Thomas, and Dederick. I shuddered at the thought of making small talk with Dederick after the excruciatingly embarrassing conversation we'd just had.

Was I in love? What if I was? There was still the thorny problem of Fortier's cousin Louise, whom he may well present to the world as his wife when he returned from France. Gabrielle had written to tell me their father's funeral had taken place and Fortier would depart for France on the twenty-seventh—tomorrow. How many weeks or months might pass before I knew where I stood? Would Fortier write to inform me all was finished?

I put my pen back on the inkwell tray and hid my face in my hands. A groan escaped my lips.

The tinkling chime of the clock roused me from my thoughts. Thirty minutes till the dressing gong. Could I possibly go to dinner not having written this blasted letter? Blanche would be sure to ask me at the earliest possible opportunity. No, it would have to be done now, and I had little more time to waste.

I dipped my pen, shook a drop of ink off the nib, and wrote as neatly as I could.

I have been asked to write to you by my sister, the Marchioness of Hastings . . .

It was only through a supreme effort of concentration that a signed, sealed, and addressed letter lay on my writing desk by the time Dunnam sounded the gong to summon us to get ready for dinner. Guttridge would already be waiting for me in my dressing room. But Scotty had returned, needing a wash, and I paused as I entered the passage that led to the Great Hall to instruct the hall boy to take my dog to the pump. Scotty's alternate growls and plaintive yelps chased me as my footsteps rang on the marble floor of the hall.

I wasn't alone. A man stood in the middle of the Great Hall, staring up at the portrait of Justin's grandfather and the rather fine putti and various Greek gods on the hall's painted ceiling. Who on earth was he? I didn't recognize the tall, thin back and clipped dark curls or know anyone who would have business here this late on a Sunday evening.

Apprehension, and the tension of the afternoon, sharpened my voice, and my "What are you doing here?" rang out through the marble-clad hall more loudly than I'd intended. The man started and turned, and I saw he wore the sober dress of an upper servant.

"Oh." I stared at him. "You must be my nephew's valet. Or are you visiting one of my servants, and are . . . lost?" I suggested. In either event, he shouldn't be standing in the middle of my hall, looking around him like a paying visitor at an exhibition.

For a moment, he seemed lost for words, his dark brown eyes round as he stared back at me. Then he relaxed and smiled. The smile altered his long, thin face from an expression of rather obstinate brooding to one of charm and effaced the unappealing effect of his too-long, overly prominent chin.

"I apologize, my lady." The form of address confirmed my impression that he was a servant. "I got turned around trying to find the service staircase, and then I thought I could run up that way instead." He indicated the ornate staircase in the corner of the hall with a jerk of his head. "I'm afraid the fine painting distracted me. I'm fond of art. I'm Lord Hastings's valet, as you guessed. The name is Rampling."

He had a slight northern accent overlaid with London tones but was well-spoken. Very neatly turned out, as a valet should be; some five or ten years older than Dederick, which was no doubt a good thing. But I didn't like finding him in my hall.

"You've been drinking," I remarked. There was an atmosphere of the alehouse about him, and something about the relaxed, almost dreamy expression on his face suggested more than one pint, although I would not go so far as to say he was drunk.

"His lordship gave me permission to visit a public house." Rampling smiled again. "I promised to be back in time to dress him for dinner."

"There isn't much time for dressing." I moved toward the staircase, indicating with my hand that he should follow. "I daresay Lord Hastings is waiting for you."

I tempered the implied criticism with a brief smile. Upper servants earned their places by hard work, and it wasn't done to dress down a valet as if he were a hall boy. And if Dederick didn't mind the smell of beer about his valet, who was I to object?

"Yes, my lady. Beg pardon, my lady." But as we turned the corner of the staircase, I caught a fleeting smile on Rampling's lips. No doubt he knew how to manage his young employer, despite the latter's uncertain temper and acid tongue.

I quickly gave him precise instructions on how to reach Dederick's room. He thanked me and set off at a controlled stride, not visibly hurrying, but purposeful, not at all distracted by the portraits that lined the wide, well-lit corridor.

I hurried toward my bedroom suite, aware that Guttridge now had only twenty minutes to make me presentable for dinner. Blanche was all very well, and I had to put up with Dederick for her sake, but the matter of Lord Arthur and now this wandering valet were making my sister's visit rather trying. Why, after years of practically ignoring me as the youngest sister, could my family not sort out its problems without reference to me?

10
A FAMILY REUNION

Not only was the letter to Lord Arthur dispatched on Monday morning, but Dederick took himself off to London before midday. He spent precisely five minutes with his mother and me before climbing into my carriage to be taken to the railway station.

Blanche shed a sentimental tear over being parted from her darling so soon, but her darling quenched it with a hug—rather more demonstration of affection than I'd expected from him—and a promise to come and stay with her once she had properly settled in Broadmere and the best of the shooting and hunting was over.

For me, Dederick had no greater show of family feeling than a cool peck on the cheek, and his manner was distant. We were plainly relieved to see the backs of one another after our far-too-intimate conversation.

On Wednesday, Guttridge and I walked over to Hyrst in plenty of time to greet the returning Earl of Broadmere and family. As we drew near the house, the Broadmere carriage—the old-fashioned state coach I remembered so well from my childhood—headed sedately toward us down the long allée of beech trees, on its way to the station to collect its passengers. The coachman removed his hat as the carriage rattled past, and the two footmen on the rear platform let go of their straps with one hand to salute me with a touch of their hats and a brief "m'lady" before resuming their positions. Behind them jolted the cart that would bring the luggage, and the nursemaids if there were enough room.

"Well-timed." Guttridge squinted at the watch pinned to her dress by a ribbon. "Lady Alice and Lady Annette have everything well organized, as usual." She shaded her eyes to look toward the house. "And everyone already waiting; very properly done."

"Mmmm." I lifted my face to the late August sunshine darting here and there through the beech leaves. "I don't suppose my brother will appreciate the effort. I'm glad to see it all so well run, though."

I opened my eyes, noting that the day was so limpid I could see the North Downs clearly in the distance from our height on the wooded hill that gave my family home, Hyrst, its ancient name. In front of the distant range of hills stretched the marsh with its winding river, its drained fields dotted with the tiny white specks that represented Michael's flocks of sheep. It was a peaceful, prosperous scene.

"Hello!" My greeting rang out in answer to my twin sisters' enthusiastically waving hands, and I waved back as we drew nearer. At least Alice and Annette were of a cheerful disposition and quite affectionate, even if I found them a little dull. As we came closer, they called out to Guttridge with cordial friendliness. They were always interested in servants and townspeople, a trait I found endearing.

"Now, Helena, you must tell us how Hawthorn Hall is coming along," said Alice as soon as they had greeted me. "What a shame Blanche couldn't be here—"

"—with Michael and Julia and the dear children away for

so long," finished Annette as she and her sister ushered me into my place in the greeting party. "And Dederick is gone? What a shame we didn't see much of him—"

"—and so much better looking with that silly long hair gone."

My sisters carried on in the same, lighthearted vein as we arranged ourselves in front of the carriage entrance. The tall iron gates were wide open, the flowerbeds within the carriage circle bright with marigolds, lobelia, and begonias planted in neat patterns. Someone had recently trimmed the hedges into sharp, level lines. Now and again the raucous cry of a peacock came from the other side of the house; the birds, their wings clipped to prevent escape, lived in the formal gardens.

It was thanks to my sister-in-law, Julia, and my twin sisters who, as spinsters, lived under Michael's roof, that Hyrst was a brighter, more cheerful house than it had been for some years. The improved income from managing Justin's—my—sheep together with Michael's helped, as did Michael's own laudable efforts to pay off the debts our father had left behind him.

My heart was light. Hyrst was a happy and welcoming place, I would soon see Julia and the children again, the sun was shining, and a fresh breeze blew from the sea, only two miles distant but not visible from this side of the house because of the trees. I made my replies to Alice and Annette's chatter cheerfully, encouraged by their eager interest in the servants at Hawthorn Hall and all the little details of furnishings and repairs in which I was inevitably involved.

The time must have flown because there was the carriage again, returning from the station, dappled with pools and flecks of sunshine as it came toward us under the two rows of spreading beeches. Alice, Annette, and I formed a small knot directly in front of the carriage entrance, my mourning black a deep contrast to the twins' identical light blue dresses. Guttridge stood to one side with Hyrst's upper servants, conversing in a friendly manner, their voices a muted murmur. The younger servants were arrayed in a neat line on the other side of the door, silent under the gaze of their superiors.

The large old carriage rattled through the gates and into the circular drive, coming to a halt directly opposite the door. The footmen sprang from their platform to open the doors and let down the steps. I could see Julia waving happily with her free arm, the other occupied with one-year-old Julius, who was wriggling vigorously.

I felt a delighted grin spread over my face as I spotted Annabelle Alice sitting between Julia and her lady's maid. My little favorite was shouting and waving as she saw me; at three and a quarter she was no less mischievous and opinionated than she'd been ever since she could walk and talk.

I could see James, now six years old, sitting by Michael. Like his father, he did not like travel, and his face, delicate like his late mother Cecilia's had been, was pale. Quentin, a year younger than James and Michael's first child by Julia, his second wife, was clearly sitting on somebody's lap; with a twinge of annoyance, I realized it was the odious Brandrick, Michael's land manager and general factotum. Why did he have to travel with them? But Quentin's lively shouts as Brandrick swung him down from the carriage, and the affectionate smiles of the other children as he helped them negotiate the steps, reminded me that although I might not be fond of the man, Michael and Julia seemed to depend on him as almost part of their family.

I forgot my slight irritation as Annabelle Alice flung herself against me, wrapping her arms tight around my skirts. I lifted her onto my hip, and we exchanged several kisses before I put her down so I could greet the rest of the family. Soon the twins and I were laughing as we were bombarded by the noise of three loudly chattering children; even James, usually quieter than his boisterous siblings, was positively breathless in his eagerness to impart the excitement of seeing the Houses of Parliament, the palace, the zoological gardens, and above all the various soldiers and guardsmen who swarmed London.

"You'll have to visit every day for a week at teatime," Julia said as we embraced. "The boys have so much to talk about; they'll burst if they don't have someone new to tell it to."

She whirled round as the coachman climbed into his seat, relaxing as she saw that one of the maids had picked up the toddling Julius and carried him far back from the carriage. I saw Brandrick was keeping an eye on the boys to ensure they stayed well away from the wheels and felt an unaccustomed prick of gratitude. I was trying to get used to the man since he now managed Justin's—my—estate as well as Michael's and seemed, as far as I could tell from our monthly meetings, to be doing a proficient job. I nodded at him; he returned the salute with a quick lift of his bowler hat and a polite "Good morning, my lady."

"Helena, isn't that your carriage?" The question came from Michael, who had leaned forward for his customary faint touch of lips to my cheek. "It is, isn't it?" He glared at the vehicle that had stopped at the far end of the drive to let the Hyrst carriage take the turn toward the stables.

"If you say so, I've no doubt it is," I said placidly. Michael was rarely wrong about such things. "I imagine it's Blanche come to say hello after all."

I had not expected her, but Blanche was probably bored with nobody but the servants around her and undoubtedly resentful over being left alone, even though she had emphatically declared the night before that she would not be up and dressed in time.

"Well, I'm going in before she gets here." Michael turned toward the door. The boys were already running into the hall; Annette had taken Julius, who was crying, from the maid, and both twins were cooing at him as they walked in.

"Come along, Julia." Michael's voice settled Julia's clear hesitation over whether she should wait for Blanche. "We'll see Blanche once we've changed. I'm not dancing attendance on her."

Julia shrugged one shoulder at me, rather apologetically, and followed her family and Brandrick inside, the rest of the younger servants filing in after them at a nod from the butler.

Annabelle Alice and I remained, watching the carriage as it made its way down the drive. "Pretty shells, golden shells, pretty shells, golden shells," chanted my little niece who, clinging tight to my hand, bounced on her toes as the Whitcombe brougham slowed to a halt. "I like your crest, Auntie Helena. I wish *we* had seashells. Why don't we have seashells? Why didn't Auntie Blanche walk? Did *you* walk?"

"Auntie Blanche doesn't enjoy walking." I picked out the most important question to answer. "But say nothing about that to her, will you? And mind you greet her nicely."

The single footman who had accompanied Blanche on her short ride made a dent in the gravel as he jumped down. Within a moment, he had let down the step and was holding his arm at a rigid right angle to receive Blanche's hand, steadying her as she concentrated on lifting her skirts away from her heels. Her lady's maid, Banham, followed her.

"They've gone in," I informed Blanche as Annabelle Alice lifted her face to be kissed. The little girl had begun her training in how to behave and favored Blanche with a sweet smile, a tiny curtsey—she had no doubt learned that Blanche was a marchioness and thus outranked her own family—and a "Good morning, Auntie Blanche."

"Oh, I'll see Michael and Julia later." Blanche waved a dismissive hand, uncharacteristically unworried by this failure to make her the most important personage of the moment. "I've come to talk to *you*. Banham, take Lady Annabelle Alice to her nursemaid; Lady Helena and I must be alone."

11
LORD ARTHUR'S REPLY

"You've had a letter."

Blanche had waited until we were a little distance from the house, shielded from view by the long, straight hedge, before pulling an envelope out of her pocket.

"The crest on the seal is the Southgate-Haighs', I'm sure," she continued as she handed the letter to me. "It must be from Lord Arthur."

"You went through my letters?"

I frowned. In the absence of Guttridge and myself, any mail would be left on my writing desk in the morning room, and it was a strict rule that the staff never interfered with letters. Blanche had been snooping.

"You know very well how anxious I am about this matter." Blanche watched as I inspected the seal. "I didn't *open* it. But since you were off doing something else, as usual, and probably wouldn't have looked at your post all day because you were hobnobbing with Julia and playing with the children—well! If you were to be negligent of my concerns, I didn't see why I shouldn't just make sure for myself whether you'd received something from Lord Arthur. *And*," she concluded triumphantly, "I was right."

I bit my lip hard, breathing through my nose until I could control my irritation. One of these days I would give Blanche the talking-to she deserved. It was typical of my sisters to think their business superseded my privacy; that assumption had appeared even more marked since Justin's death, as if no longer being a married woman demoted me in their eyes.

Well, I certainly wasn't going to meekly open the letter on the spot. I marched, as fast as I could, along the gravel path that led between the hedge and the shrubbery, leaving Blanche to follow. I took the various turns toward the formal gardens with automatic ease; after all, I'd known Hyrst's gardens all my life. Within moments, I had arrived at a secluded nook Odelia and I had called the "snuggery" in our young days, now used as a kind of playhouse by Michael's children.

I moved the old doll Annabelle Alice insisted live in the arbor out of the best seat, commanding a view of the sea, and made myself as comfortable as I could, my temper somewhat cooled by physical exertion.

Blanche had kept up with my short strides fairly easily; she was a lazy walker, but there was nothing actually wrong with her limbs. She sniffed and tutted over debris as she selected a seat but had the sense not to say anything.

I broke the seal on the small envelope and withdrew the folded paper, then held up a hand. "I will read this through once before I discuss it with you." My eyes narrowed as I looked up at my sister. "It's addressed to *me* after all."

It was, of course, from Lord Arthur Southgate-Haigh. Since that gentleman's handwriting was remarkably neat, even if some letters were rather oddly shaped, it did not take me long to decipher.

My dear Lady Helena,

How nice to receive a letter from you, and how unexpected. We are, as you point out, very distantly related, but I suppose the same can be said of most of the old aristocracy, and we have never run in the same social circles.

It is indeed a strange turn of fate that we have, when all is said and done, what one might call a mutual point of affection, and it is that to which you allude.

I consider it careless of you to have made such an explicit allusion in a letter. One is so easily exposed to unpleasantness in these parlous times. I beg of you, kindly do not repeat that error of judgment, which could almost be considered a grave impoliteness. I have burned your letter.

I am not a man who abandons old ties lightly. You suggest you and I could perhaps meet to discuss the matter in question—but, if you'll forgive my frankness, not only do I find the suggestion highly impertinent, I do not see the point of it.

I recognized your name immediately from the newspapers as a lady who rejoices in a little hobby of investigation. No doubt it was your recent notorious adventures that make you erroneously suppose you may have some success with me, but I assure you, you won't.

I am afraid I am far too busy for a meeting in any case. My entire existence is devoted to His Royal Highness the Prince of Wales, to whom I am considered indispensable by many, and to dear Prince Albert Victor.

Do give my sincerest regards to your sister, the Marchioness of Hastings, whose name you invoke in your letter as a pretext for writing. I know she revels in the title of "marchioness" and will find that of "dowager marchioness" sits uneasily with her, so I conclude by wishing her a long continuation in her current excellent state.

I am, dear Lady Helena, your devoted but very distant cousin,

A.S.H.

I REALIZED I WAS GRINDING MY TEETH AND DESISTED. I SAW IN Lord Arthur's words a pointed reminder that his family outranked ours by a wide margin and a clear hint that he could twist our correspondence to represent *me* as trying to blackmail *him*. Especially if he had destroyed my own letter, of which I had not made a copy. I felt the ground shift under my feet.

Blanche's breathing had become louder and louder as I read the letter. I was sure she was doing it on purpose. Without speaking, I handed the sheet of paper to her, watching her face change color as she read. The vermilion flush that spread over her cheeks, throwing her pale blue eyes into rather an unbecoming contrast, was succeeded by a leaden pallor.

"*What* did you write to him?" There was fury in her eyes.

"The most straightforward plea I could muster that he leave Dederick alone." I glared back; I would not let Blanche intimidate me.

"Which he saw as a grave impoliteness." Blanche stood up. "You may have ruined everything."

"If I have, I'm sorry." My indignation turned to contrition. Maybe I *had* said the wrong thing. Lord Arthur's reference to my "little hobby of investigation" was producing a sour feeling in my stomach. "It's clear Lord Arthur isn't the kind of man who would respond to a plea of any sort. That last remark about your continuing as a marchioness is really rather nasty."

"Yes." Blanche's voice broke, and she made an effort to control her emotions—a real effort for once. "If Dederick fails to marry and have a son, it's the end of our family. The end of the title. Francis was the last of his line—no distant cousins anywhere. Dederick is everything, do you not see that?"

I rose, laying a hand on my sister's arm. "It's likely Lord Arthur's threat is empty. As I've said before, any publicity of his . . . friendship with Dederick would implicate him as well, wouldn't it? Could he risk that? If the Queen knew, would she allow him to remain a close confidant of her son and grandson?"

Blanche pursed her lips. "The dear Queen is certainly very interested in the moral character of those who come near her person and her family. She would not receive Odelia now, for example."

"Then there's hope." I gave the arm I held a gentle shake. "I'm sorry I failed. I promise I'll try to find another way to help. Don't dwell on it, dear. Come home with me to luncheon. We should spend a few minutes with Michael and Julia, but I imagine they would prefer a little peace after their journey."

"But supposing . . . it's not just a threat?"

A spasm crossed Blanche's face. She was frightened. We both knew she was playing a game with high stakes, even without Lord Arthur. Ensuring a child was well married was an undertaking few aristocratic matrons took on without some sleepless nights. A wrong turn in events could also, in Blanche's case, mean a disastrous outcome in terms of her own social and financial status. I didn't in any way approve of her scheme to catch a rich wife, but I could understand it; and how could I, the inheritor of a fortune, criticize a woman whose future was teetering in Fortune's scales?

"That's an eventuality we can only face if it happens," I pointed out. "It could take months—perhaps more than a year—to help Dederick find and woo a bride. Anything could happen."

Blanche was silent for a long moment, slowly turning over her reticule between her rather large hands, crushing the velvet under her fingers as she stared toward the sea. A peacock screeched; my stomach, not being as empathetic as the rest of me, rumbled loudly. A fresh salt smell in the breeze playing over us, and a certain heaviness in the air, hinted at approaching rain.

"You could be right." Blanche's shoulders dropped in a gesture that might have been relief or defeat. "I'll go home on Friday. There is so much to do for my move to Hawthorn Hall. I will send you a list of the help I need."

12

HABEAS CORPUS

"I'll be with you in a moment, Mrs. Eason."

I smiled at my housekeeper, who had arrived at the appointed hour for a consultation about two new maids, hired from the workhouse. "I'm sorry it's been such a busy week, and practically all of it spent on Hawthorn Hall." Blanche had sent me several lists, and apart from a delightful tea with Julia and the children and a less delightful estate meeting with Michael and Brandrick, I'd had no time for anything else.

"I've brought a telegram, my lady. From Tunbridge Wells."

"Oh heavens, what now?" I looked down at the long letter I had just written to Blanche. "Let's hope Lady Hastings hasn't changed her mind about the larger items of furniture Lady Whetmore wants to leave *in situ*." I had spent the day before making a farewell visit to the Whetmores and discussing some final arrangements with Fiona, which I had carefully noted in the letter I had just finished. "They're excellent pieces, but I must have a proper agreement drawn up before the Whetmores depart. Sir Justin always said one should never leave matters involving property to just a handshake."

"He was quite right." Mrs. Eason placed the buff-colored telegram beside my inkwell.

"When we've finished talking about the workhouse girls, would you please stay to help me write up the settlement I made with Lady Whetmore about the servants who wish to remain at the Hall?" I asked her. "And about the ones who will stay on half pay at the lodge to keep it in readiness for the Whetmores. I suggested they could supplement their income by doing occasional tasks for Lady Hastings—or even for you, if you need them."

"I'll consider that for spring cleaning." Mrs. Eason smiled. "Perhaps we can cut the whole business down to three weeks."

"And I'd like you to look over Lady Hastings's letter about the servants who wish to remain in Tunbridge Wells." I touched a folded paper sticking out of a cubbyhole. "Whatever she says, we must give them fair terms for ending their employment. Now, let me just look at this telegram, and then I promise we'll concentrate on the two little maids. I'm eager to know how their first week went."

I opened the telegram and looked up, puzzled. "Lady Hastings has requested—well, ordered—Scott House to be opened up for our use. She's leaving for London this morning and asks me to travel up immediately." I looked at the telegram again. "She uses the word 'imperative.' How odd—she wrote me the letter about her servants yesterday afternoon, and there was no hint of a problem."

"Perhaps she's seeing Lord Hastings about something."

"But he's away for a few days' grouse shooting in Scotland." Blanche had told me about Dederick's departure for Scotland in one of her letters. "He took the train up there the day before yesterday." An idea occurred to me. "Perhaps—"

I stopped short. I could hardly talk about Lord Arthur with Mrs. Eason, but maybe Blanche had somehow maneuvered him into a meeting. I let out my breath.

"I'll have to go."

"I'll send a wire to Scott House straightaway, my lady," Mrs. Eason said calmly. "And I'll send Miss Guttridge to you."

"Thank you." I stood up on legs that were very slightly shaky. Excitement, nerves, or fear? If I had to confront Lord Arthur in person, it was probably either nerves or fear.

GUTTRIDGE, WHO LIKED EXCITEMENT AND ENJOYED TRAVEL, was remarkably quick at packing trunks. We left just after my solitary light luncheon.

Unfortunately, no amount of domestic efficiency could guard against the mishaps of train journeys. A long delay in Kent meant we did not arrive at Scott House until the dinner hour was past. Naturally, Blanche was already in residence; naturally, she was out of temper, notwithstanding the telegram I had dictated at Maidstone to warn her we would be late.

"There was nothing I could do," I told her when Guttridge and I finally arrived. "It took them two hours to get the locomotive that wasn't working onto a siding and get one that *was* working to where we were. Apparently, the train stopped at precisely the wrong location, and they had to puzzle out what to do."

I wasn't in the best of tempers myself. Being pounced upon by an irate sister with complaints about one's lateness, when one had spent hours in train carriages and waiting rooms with little forward motion to show for it, was having a deleterious effect on my patience. I felt as if I had a fine layer of grit on my skin and hair, and the Bath buns we had eventually consumed at Maidstone hadn't so much satisfied my appetite as ruined it entirely.

I tried to forget about myself and think of Blanche, who was almost vibrating with impatience as I unpinned my hat. I heartily wished I could pull the pins out of my hair too and be comfortable. Guttridge took my outer clothing in silence as I shed it, her gaze occasionally flicking to my sister as if to judge her state of mind.

"You'll want to be alone, my lady," she said to Blanche once I had slipped my feet gratefully into delicate slippers while Guttridge took command of my traveling boots. "I've give you a little while and then fetch up some refreshment for her ladyship."

I followed Blanche into Scott House's old-fashioned drawing room, sinking with relief onto a William and Mary settee. "Is it bad?" I asked her.

Freed from the restraint of Guttridge's presence, Blanche's face screwed up like a child's when it was about to cry. It was all the answer I needed. She pulled a crumpled slip of paper—a telegram—from her pocket and handed it to me.

COME TO LONDON STOP TROUBLE STOP POLICE STOP

It was from Dederick, of course. I stared in astonishment at my weeping sister; I had thought Dederick in Scotland.

"Where is he?"

"I don't *know*." Blanche's voice rose to a wail. "This," she indicated the telegram, "was delivered late last night, but that *idiotic* Banham didn't want to wake me. I went to the Carlton Club as soon as I arrived, and of course they wouldn't let me in. But as soon as they knew who I was, they sent a friend of his to talk to me." She sniffed. "Sir Humphrey Fearnley—they were up at Oxford together. He told me two men—he said they weren't in a uniform of any kind but obviously policemen—came to talk to Dederick late yesterday afternoon. They must have let him send that later."

I stared at the piece of paper. Couldn't Dederick have said a bit more about where he was?

"Have you sent for the family solicitors?"

Blanche looked blank. "I sent for *you*."

I sighed inwardly but kept my voice calm. "When you say 'came to talk,' do you mean it wasn't an arrest?" All I could think of was that Lord Arthur had somehow made good on his threat, and Dederick had been arrested on some charge, but what exactly?

"Sir Humphrey said they didn't arrest him, just spoke to him quietly. He grew very pale but seemed quite calm. He collected his hat and so on, walked out between them, and hasn't been back to the club since. It must be something to do with Lord Arthur."

"I suppose so," I said. "I was also thinking Lord Arthur must have said something."

"What do you mean?" Blanche was scrubbing at her face with a handkerchief of inadequate size, which had clearly already seen some tears. "Lord Arthur won't say anything to anybody ever again. He's dead."

"LORD ARTHUR IS *DEAD*?"

I spoke loudly, just at the moment the door opened and Guttridge entered, carrying the promised tray of refreshment. She didn't bat an eyelid.

"If you mean Lord Arthur Southgate-Haigh, my lady, it was in yesterday's newspaper." Of course Guttridge would have no inkling of my very private conversations with Blanche and Dederick; and my Friday newspapers were still sitting on the table in my morning room since I had been too busy with Hawthorn Hall to read them. Nobody would have thought to inform me of the death of a nobleman with whom I was not known to have any connection.

"Miss Banham says Lord Hastings was on the same train as Lord Arthur." Guttridge watched as the drawing room door closed itself in the odd way it had, as if shut by some spectral hand. "And that's why Lord Hastings came back to Town yesterday, the shooting party being called off on the orders of the royal household."

I looked at Blanche for confirmation, a feeling of dread growing inside me. She gave a sort of desperate nod, dissolving into tears again despite Guttridge's presence.

"He was a friend of Lord Hastings," I informed Guttridge. She simply nodded and handed Blanche a clean handkerchief. She always seemed to have one or two about her person.

"I'd like Guttridge to stay," I said to Blanche. "She'll keep everything entirely confidential."

"There isn't much information in the newspaper," Guttridge said, tactfully looking at me rather than Blanche while my sister struggled to regain control of her emotions. "The gentleman somehow died while the train was traveling toward Scotland." A look of enlightenment spread across her features. "They told me downstairs that Lady Hastings went to look for Lord Hastings this morning, but he didn't come back with her." She glanced briefly at Blanche again.

"Lord Hastings's whereabouts are unknown." I quickly explained to Guttridge about the telegram and what Blanche had learned at the Carlton Club. "It sounds as if the police have taken Lord Hastings to—to question him, something of that sort." I looked at Blanche, who was twisting the handkerchief in her hands. "Doesn't that seem the most likely explanation?"

Blanche's only reply was a kind of tragic snort, and it was

Guttridge who spoke. "Perhaps he's being held *incommunicado*." She said the word with a certain degree of relish. "They can't do that for very long."

Guttridge moved toward the tray and began putting sandwiches on plates and pouring cocoa. "If they're keeping him when they shouldn't, you can get a writ of habeas corpus. I saw it in a story. The police have to arrest someone and charge him with a crime to keep hold of him, otherwise you can get them set free. What about those Piper and Wiggins lawyers?"

"Piper, Wiggins, and Showell." Those were our family's solicitors in London. "But I'm not sure Lady Hastings—"

"No, I don't want them just yet, not until we know what's happening." Blanche looked desperately at me. Of course, she was probably terrified of anything at all getting into the papers. "I want you to help me, Helena—and Guttridge too, I suppose. *Investigate*."

I had the nasty feeling that word "investigate" was going to follow me around whether I wanted it to or not. "Very well. But where do we even start?" I asked Guttridge as she handed me a plate of sandwiches and set a cup of cocoa down near me. "Surely, the first thing we must do is simply to find out where Lord Hastings is."

"I could nip round to the Carlton Club with a message for him, telling him to come straight here if he gets back tonight," Guttridge suggested. "That would be discreet enough. I can get the doorman to tell me if he's there or not without suggesting there's any worry. After all, he might be back and just hasn't thought of letting Lady Hastings know." She put a cup of cocoa into Blanche's hands and nodded encouragingly; Blanche sipped obediently, like a sick child.

"Come to that," I said, "I could go there myself." Food and drink were beginning to revive me.

"You'll need to be at your best for tomorrow—both of

you." Guttridge surveyed the two of us with a critical eye, and I wondered if I looked as travel-worn as I felt. "The point is, Lord Hastings is *somewhere*," she continued. "If he's with the police, he's safe. They're not exactly good company, as we've found, but they have to follow rules. If I make sure he's not in the obvious place, which is the Carlton, then tomorrow morning we can go to Scotland Yard and make a right fuss till they tell us where he is. And if they say they're not letting him go, you can get your habeas corpus, can't you?"

"Go to Scotland Yard?" Blanche's voice was faint. "Is that really necessary?"

"It's not that bad," I reassured her. "Guttridge and I are old hands at dealing with the police."

13
HELENA ON THE ATTACK

I gave Guttridge a note for Dederick and hastily scribbled another, instructing a footman to take it to Kensington Square. I had a wild, irrational thought Fortier might, by some miracle, be there and could help us.

As soon as I'd eaten, I rang for the housekeeper to make sure all was in order. It was; our rooms were ready, and Banham had taken it upon herself to help with unpacking my things so Guttridge could attend to us. A few words with the housekeeper ensured a housemaid would be dispatched to make sure Guttridge's room would be ready for her when she returned; that would save her some time and effort since she must be just as tired as I was.

Then I persuaded Blanche she should change for bed and put her into Banham's hands despite her protests that Dederick might still come home. I had a feeling we wouldn't see her son until the morning.

Guttridge returned an hour later with no news, and we all retired. The next morning brought no news of Dederick, only a note from Gabrielle; Fortier was still in France, but she would be in London for at least two more weeks. Would I visit her if that were at all possible?

I wrote back briefly that I would, and then, Blanche having made an appearance, we conferred. Guttridge and I persuaded Blanche—to her obvious relief—to stay at Scott House in case Dederick arrived or sent a note from his club, and the two of us set off for Scotland Yard.

It had rained. The granite setts that paved the courtyard of the London police headquarters gleamed and sparkled in the emerging sunlight as we descended from my carriage. There was no point in any attempt at anonymity; my coachman had driven up to London overnight, and the Whitcombe shells shone gold on my brougham's freshly washed paint, drawing curious stares from the men walking or loitering in the forecourt. Even on a Sunday, the place appeared busy.

I marched, Guttridge three steps behind me, up to the well-remembered desk, announcing myself and our errand in tones worthy of Mama in her prime. Within twenty minutes, a soberly clothed man who introduced himself as a senior detective took us into a small, dreary room, offering us two very solid chairs at a thickly varnished table.

"A pleasure to meet the Investigating Lady, I'm sure." The detective fingered his abundant mustache, favoring both of us with a hard stare. "I've heard quite a bit about you. And Miss Guttridge, of course."

Guttridge merely gave a regal nod and shot me a significant glance. It said, as plainly as if she'd shouted, that I needed to go on the attack immediately. I was absolutely certain that in my place she'd already be berating the officer for keeping Dederick incommunicado. No doubt the words "habeas corpus" would be on her lips at that very moment.

"I believe," I said without waiting for the detective to say more, "you have my nephew, the Marquess of Hastings, in your custody. Incommunicado." I didn't look at Guttridge. "Unless you have arrested him, you must give him up immediately. There *is* such a thing as habeas corpus, you know."

I hoped that would be sufficient. Having absolutely no idea how a writ of habeas corpus actually worked, I didn't want to proceed to threats about how I would use such a device to free Dederick. I had no doubt the procedure was complicated, and to reveal my ignorance would weaken my case.

"*Have* you arrested him?" I asked as the detective opened his mouth to speak.

I had thrown him off balance, figuratively speaking; as he shut his mouth again, I saw a little more respect in his eyes. "We have not," he said eventually, hooking a thumb into the pocket of his waistcoat.

"Then where is he? Why was he not allowed back to his club last night?" *Keep the advantage* was ringing through my mind, and every ounce of my Scott-De Quincy blood was up.

The detective took a moment to reply. He struck me as a man who weighed every word before he pronounced it.

"He was at the Bow Street station during the night," he said at last. "The noble gentleman was kind enough to come with us and answer some questions. We had many matters to go over, and the conversation was a very long one; and then he was tired, poor young man, and we let him rest in a comfortable chair for an hour or two before we continued. He was a bit upset about the death of his friend, of course. His *very close* friend."

Beside me, Guttridge made a tiny noise in her throat. If she had not known about that aspect of Dederick's personality before, she did now; the detective's tone conveyed his meaning better than his words.

"I see Miss Guttridge gets my drift." The policeman fixed me with his gaze. "Were you aware your nephew has *unnat-*

ural inclinations, my lady?" The way he pronounced the word was extremely unpleasant. "And that the dead gentleman shared those inclinations? They were very close friends indeed. We think that might be significant."

He was trying to upset me. *Keep the advantage*. I nodded.

"As I understand it, they were . . . close a long time ago. Five years."

"So his lordship says."

The detective's smile had more than a hint of satisfaction about it as he wrote something in the small notebook that lay before him. I resolved not to volunteer any more information unless I had to answer a direct question.

"So are you charging Lord Hastings with anything?" I asked briskly.

Again, a pause. Then: "We are not currently charging him with any offense."

"Then you must let him go." My spirits lifted. "Where is he?"

The answer came quicker this time. "In another room in this very building." The officer's lips curved up under his mustache. "We're a little worried he might take it into his head to run off somewhere. To the Continent, perhaps. A common criminal we can always find, you see. They stay where they're meant to be since it never occurs to them the world's a big place. But a gentleman has so much he can hide behind and so many places to do it." He shifted in his chair. "Money's a wonderful thing, isn't it? And a heducation."

He pronounced the vernacular *h* with emphasis, as if to prove *he* had not been tainted with education and was therefore a pure specimen of John Bullishness. They recruited police officers from the criminal classes, I had read; such men might be prejudiced against the aristocracy, who all too often escaped punishment.

"You have my undertaking he won't run off," I said firmly.

"I'll sign a paper to that effect if you let him go now. If not, we will go straight to our solicitors."

"And where will his lordship be if he's with you?"

"At Whitcombe House, near Littleberry in Sussex." I waited while the detective wrote the address in the notebook. "Perhaps later with his mother at Hawthorn Hall in Broadmere; Lady Hastings is coming to live near me."

"If he moves away from your address, my lady, we'd like to know about it." The detective made another note. "We'd prefer his lordship to stay in Sussex for the time being—keep himself nice and quiet at home. Just until we've investigated the case thoroughly."

I still had no idea what had happened to Lord Arthur. Had he been shot? But this man was not going to tell us anything, so there was no point in asking. I nodded my agreement. "I'll explain that to him. I'm sure he's innocent anyway."

"Are you?" The lips curved up again, this time revealing a glimpse of teeth. "Well, let me see if the gentleman's ready to leave."

THE DEDERICK WHO EVENTUALLY JOINED US WAS A PALE, disheveled shadow of his usual self. He smelled unpleasantly stale but appeared unhurt.

Guttridge and I had been taken back to the public waiting room, so our reunion took place under the curious stares of some twenty assorted people, some of whom made loud-whispered remarks about Dederick's diamond cravat pin and silk top hat, not to mention my own appearance in somewhat expensive mourning, and the fact that I had a lady's maid, "and a right Tartar she looks too." That last remark earned such a withering glare from

Guttridge that the young man who had made it actually blushed.

The public nature of our meeting made any demonstration of affection unlikely; and indeed, Dederick gave no sign of gratitude on the way back to Scott House. Apart from a feeble request for brandy "if either of you happens to carry a flask"—we did not—he was silent, staring white-faced out of the carriage window as we made the brief journey back to St. James's.

Blanche could not have heard our arrival at Scott House since she was in the front parlor behind the heavy door that somehow would never remain open. Dederick, perhaps drawn by some instinct, headed straight to his mother, pushing past the footman before the latter could open the door and announce him. I followed; behind me came Guttridge, and out of the corner of my eye I saw her shake her head to prevent the footman from following.

A sight I had not seen since Dederick was a small child in skirts rewarded our concern: the vision of him clinging to his mother's neck with her arms wrapped tight around him. Both were weeping.

"I'll go downstairs, my lady," Guttridge said *sotto voce*. "You should talk to his lordship, of course, but . . . not now." Then, dropping her voice to the merest thread of sound: "I see they haven't sent today's papers up, and no wonder. I'll take them to your room, shall I? And start making notes."

"I'm not even sure if I should stay," I murmured, viewing the spectacle of sobs and heaving shoulders with more than a touch of emotion.

"Oh, do. You'll be a comfort once the worst is over. Will his lordship be coming straight back to Whitcombe with us?"

"I suppose he must, given the undertaking I made." I fumbled for my handkerchief to wipe my eyes.

"Then I'll send to the Carlton Club for his valet and his

traps and make sure a bedroom is ready for him here and at Whitcombe."

Guttridge produced three large, clean handkerchiefs from her reticule, putting them in my hand, and then removed herself from the room on silent feet, the only noise being the heavy door shutting behind her with a doom-laden click of its old-fashioned latch.

Blanche recovered her power of speech. "My poor, poor boy." She pulled out a tiny lace handkerchief; I put one of Guttridge's in her palm. "Did they hurt you?"

Dederick ran a shaking hand through his by now rather lank curls. "I'm all right."

He sniffed loudly, then, noticing I was holding out a handkerchief to him, took it with a half-ashamed "thank you" and blew his nose vigorously.

"They said the most horrible things," he began once his tears had ceased. His pale gray-green eyes were rimmed with red; his face, which had been entirely white, was blotched with an angry, ugly flush over his cheekbones. "They shouted at me for hours, Mama. Sometimes they wouldn't even let me speak; they just talked over my words, on and on and on. They wouldn't let me sleep till I broke down completely."

"The beasts." Blanche didn't sound angry, just exhausted. "The beasts."

"They made me feel I was the beast." Dederick looked at his toes. "They used such words. They said what Arthur and I did is punishable by penal servitude—is that true?" He looked at me.

"I believe so."

"They said we'd have been hanged for it once, and they wished the country hadn't gone soft on filth like us." He gulped. "And Arthur's *dead*, Mama." Fresh tears rolled down his cheeks. "Whatever happened between us recently, he meant everything to me once. He *understood*."

He took a long, shuddering breath. "They said they weren't finished with me by a long chalk. I should go away—to France or Germany or something. Now."

"The police have already thought of that possibility." I took my nephew's hand. He started, his hand twitching as if his first impulse was to snatch it away, but then his grip tightened.

"I've given an undertaking that you'll stay at Whitcombe with me for the time being," I continued. "Then perhaps with your Mama once she's settled in Broadmere." I curled my fingers more tightly around his. "The police don't think it was an accident, do they? They'll be watching the ports, or why else would they let you stay so near the coast? Maybe that was deliberate, to tempt you into running. They'll see any attempt to reach the Continent as an admission of guilt."

"Oh God." The full import of my words had clearly dawned on Blanche, who sat down suddenly on a nearby chair as if her legs had ceased to work. "Oh *God*. If they think it's murder . . . They hang people for murder."

I let go of Dederick's hand and flew to put my arms around my sister's neck. She looked as if she was going to be sick. I stroked her brow and murmured endearments and then thought of the more practical step of pouring a little brandy from the decanter on the sideboard. I could hear Dederick helping himself to a measure as I persuaded his mother to take a sip.

"I imagine it's only an idea of theirs," I said once some color had come back into Blanche's cheeks. "Nothing will happen yet, and we'll fight Dederick's corner with every ounce of our strength."

I waited till Blanche's breathing slowed to turn back to Dederick. "What happened on the train?"

I was still imagining Lord Arthur shot through the heart or poisoned, stabbed, or hanged—that last with a very nasty memory of Lucius Hatherall. When Dederick answered, it almost felt like an anticlimax.

"He fell off the train or jumped or something." He finished his brandy in a gulp, putting a shaking hand to his forehead. "Dear God, my head's splitting and I'm so cold. All I know is they realized Arthur was missing at one of the stops, so they wired back to the last station and kept us all waiting for hours. Then they said they'd found him near the line and he was dead, but they didn't . . . give details." He looked a little sick at the thought of those details, and I too had to make an effort to curb my imagination.

"Then the police came and asked questions," he continued. "It was interminable. But then I think somebody got hold of the right person because all of a sudden they said we were free to go. We—Rampling and I—got back to London very late, and I think I slept pretty much the whole of the next day. I'd not long been dressed when they came for me." He frowned. "What day is it now? And where's Rampling?"

"It's Sunday, and Guttridge is arranging for Rampling to come here with all your clothes and things." I kept my voice gentle. "Will you promise me you'll stay here, then come to Whitcombe with me, and not try to run off? You're better off facing this with your family at your side."

I DIDN'T STAY DOWNSTAIRS FOR LONG. THANKS TO GUTTRIDGE, not much time elapsed before a bedroom and much-needed bath were ready for Dederick, and Blanche sought her own room to lie down. I would have plenty of time to talk to Dederick at Whitcombe. Right now, the boy was clearly grieving for his friend and horribly shocked by his interview with the police. I repaired to my own room and Guttridge.

"Plenty about Lord Arthur's death," Guttridge remarked

as I joined her at the small table where she'd been reading the papers. "But mostly speculation. Lurid rubbish about whether he committed suicide or fell off the train—there are some nasty imaginings about how that happened, I can tell you—or was murdered. But no details. Hardly a fact in there." She gestured at her notebook, which was almost devoid of notes.

"Anything about Lord Hastings?" I asked nervously.

"Not a sausage—not a thing, my lady," Guttridge corrected herself. "No list of the people who were on the train neither. I expect they want to avoid speculation—you know what it's like when important people are involved."

"Mmmm." I remembered too well the influence I suspected Buckingham Palace of having on the Dainty Darling case.

"A description of Lord Arthur's family and how distraught they must be and so on. What they call sensationalism. And then a lot of humbug about how the police have matters in hand. If bullying a young man like his lordship is having matters in hand, heaven help the country is what I say."

"Then you don't think he did it?" I knew what I thought, but I had not been certain of Guttridge.

"Do you?"

"Not in the least. I just can't see it somehow. In any case, he's my sister's son and I must stand by them."

"Yes, my lady." Guttridge's dark eyes held an expression of sympathy. "So the first thing we must find out is: Who was on the train?" She drew a thick black line in her notebook to mark the start of a list. "When do you think we'll be able to speak to his lordship?"

"Not for a day or two, I suspect." I leaned over to see what Guttridge was writing. "Are we really 'investigating' this? Just because I appear to have been dropped into yet another family disaster, I don't see why I should interfere with what the police are doing."

Guttridge turned a severe eye on me as I pulled a chair over to sit beside her. "What do the police know?" she asked. "Supposing they get it all wrong and accuse his lordship of murder? The two of us can do more thinking than any number of lump-headed policemen." Her expression softened again. "There's an awful lot at stake, isn't there?"

"There is," I agreed. "The look on Lady Hastings's face when she realized her only child could hang . . ." I had seen that look before, on Millicent Dorrian-Knowles's face, and her premonition had come true; her son had been hanged for murder. Ice slid down my back.

I rested my forehead on my palm, pushing my fingers up into my front curls. "She would die if anything happened to Lord Hastings. It was bad enough when the late marquess died. I remember how it feels to be widowed, of course; the dread of losing a child must be far worse."

Guttridge raised a hand to stop me ruining the curls she had spent twenty minutes creating. "Lady Hastings doesn't seem to have made such a life for herself as you have neither, if you don't mind me saying so."

I shrugged. "She's on a much more restricted income than I am, precisely because she has a son. I am . . . unfettered." I sighed deeply, reflecting how much I would prefer to have the fetters of my own family to this luxurious independence.

"You're right," I said at last, sitting up straight. "One must do what one can to help. For now, it's a matter of allowing my sister and nephew a day or two to recover from the shocks they've had. Rest and peace are what they need, some walks around the parks if the weather permits. And I will see if I can manage a visit to Mrs. Dermody before I return to Littleberry. Surely, I can take a little time out of family matters to visit a grieving friend."

14
FAMILY PRIDE

"Are you certain you don't want to come to Kensington Square tomorrow?" I asked Blanche the next day. "Mrs. Dermody has expressly invited you and Dederick." I smiled encouragingly, holding Gabrielle's recently delivered note like a talisman. "She's looking forward to meeting you."

Blanche was in a more than usually peevish mood. She looked tired, as if she'd had a bad night. "I don't want to meet her, Helena, I really don't. And besides, inviting people to tea when she's had such a recent bereavement—what would the Queen think?"

"I don't see Gabrielle caring much what the Queen thinks," I said mildly. "And I imagine she's quite longing for visitors, with her brother away."

"Ah, the brother." Blanche heaved a deep sigh. "You must do what you like, Helena, but I'm not going. What would I have in common with the wife of a pottery owner? Her husband's a dreadful Irish radical, so Gerry says."

"He's not at all dreadful. And Gabrielle's the daughter of a duke—the sister of a duke now." I passed quickly on to my next remark before Blanche had the chance to say anything more about Fortier. "Of course, if you'd rather I stayed at home with you—"

"I'd like to meet her." Dederick looked up from the sporting paper he was reading. "I need a distraction." With the elasticity of a young man in good health, he had recovered his looks and equilibrium after a night's sleep, all the more so because he'd left the brandy bottle alone since rising. "I know we agreed to spend another day or two here before Mama goes back to Tunbridge Wells, but if I can't go to my club or anywhere that's amusing, Town's deadly dull." He drew a deep breath. "To be honest, I barely know what to do with myself. I feel a little as if my skin has been flayed; I can't bear the thought of seeing any of my friends in case they ask questions. Being charming to a French duke's daughter sounds positively idyllic—if you can bear to let me out of your sight, Mama." He leaned forward to take his mother's hand, kissing it briefly.

A watery smile appeared on Blanche's face. "Of course, if you wish it, you must go."

"And why don't you go back home tomorrow morning?" Dederick asked, his tone coaxing. "You can be sure Aunt Helena won't let me out of her sight, and you have such a lot to do before you move to Sussex." He patted the hand that lay in his, speaking with the firmness of a son who was used to getting his own way. "Let's all get away from this gloomy old pile and make a fresh start."

"Did you really mean it about wanting to meet Mrs. Dermody?" I asked Dederick late the next morning, when Blanche had climbed—not without some tears at the parting from her son—into my carriage, which would take her and

Banham to Charing Cross to catch the train to Tunbridge Wells.

"Yes. Why on earth not? You said she lives in Littleberry, and I may as well begin making acquaintances there." My nephew sighed. "To be honest, I've never felt more like hiding in a corner. Littleberry's certainly that."

I ignored the insult to the little town where I had lived my entire life. "And you don't want to be alone with your mother or me for too long in case we start talking about Lord Arthur."

Dederick stared out at Scott House's garden—we were still standing on the steps that led up to the house—and spoke not to me, but to the empty air. "Something like that. I need to lick my wounds for at least a day or two, and watching Mama fret just makes me feel worse. I'll be ready to leave for Kensington Square at three thirty, and I'm going to imagine my aunt is just making me pay a social call and nothing else has happened."

Dederick was as good as his word, and it was pleasant to see him neatly turned out in expensively tailored but unostentatious morning dress, a perfect example of a young gentleman-about-town. His name had still not appeared in the newspapers in connection with Lord Arthur, so there would be no reason for Gabrielle Dermody to make any connection between him and recent events. He helped me down from the carriage with perfect politeness, and although the wary look so characteristic of him was evident as he looked up at the tall town house, he did not falter as we went through the ceremony of announcing our identities and waiting for the servant to bring us into his mistress's presence.

Gabrielle greeted me with an affectionate hug, which I returned with enthusiasm. Mourning dress suited her far better than it did me; her face was a little thinner than when I'd last seen her, to be sure, but she appeared to be in good spirits.

"You know you have my sincerest condolences." I squeezed my friend's hand hard, my own feelings a blend of sadness over Gabrielle's loss and simple delight at seeing her again after so many weeks. Pulling back a little so I could include Dederick, I introduced him.

Dederick, who had visibly brightened at the sight of the house's elegant interior and Gabrielle's flawless appearance, took her hand with a genuine smile of pleasure. "Please accept my condolences, Mrs. Dermody. And thank you for inviting me; I know almost nobody from Littleberry and am happy to remedy that omission. It's very kind of you to allow me to intrude at this time."

I felt a stab of family pride at knowing that this handsome nephew of mine could, after all, behave himself when he wanted to. Perhaps, with the right influences, he could become the sort of man his father had been, kind and urbane, a man whose company I had always enjoyed on the rare occasions I had seen him.

"It's no bother at all." Gabrielle's expression was merry, her French accent pleasing to the ear. "I am grieving, of course, but I'm the sort of woman who does everything better when I gather people around me. Helena's note that she was in London was such a relief; I promised my brother I wouldn't leave until the house was in perfect order, but I'm so tired of my own company. My father wouldn't want me to be melancholy in any case."

Despite Dederick's good manners, this was not quite the tête-à-tête I would have liked with my friend, I reflected as we settled ourselves in the well-remembered library at

Gabrielle's invitation. I began to understand what I had taken on by becoming a sort of benevolent jailer, or nanny, of this young marquess. But Gabrielle was the most gracious of hostesses, and by the time we were served an excellent tea that was a perfect blend of English tradition and French cooking, we were all disposed to spend an extremely pleasant hour together.

"My husband is bringing the children up from Littleberry next week," Gabrielle told us in response to my inquiry about her family's health. "We have four children," she explained, turning to Dederick. "Mariette, Constantin, and Hugh are getting to that age where they are eager to visit London, and I just want to hold my little one, Sébastien, in my arms." She smiled at me, hugging her arms across her chest in a lively illustration of her maternal feelings. "Oh, Helena, I miss them so. I have done most of my work here now, so we will all have a little holiday together and then return to Littleberry on the twenty-eighth."

"My sister will be with me by then." I smiled. "The Marchioness of Hastings, I mean—Dederick's mother. She's taking possession of Hawthorn Hall—do you know it?—on the twenty-ninth, but she'll be staying with me until the house is completely set to rights. You know how it is when one moves."

"Ah, yes, Hawthorn Hall!" Gabrielle clapped her hands, her French vivacity bringing an echo of animation to Dederick's face. "Quinn says it's the talk of Littleberry that the marchioness is moving back to Sussex to be near the family. Will you be a frequent visitor to Broadmere, Lord Hastings?"

"He's coming back with me for a few weeks as a change from London," I said. I saw Dederick's face fall a little at the allusion to his "rustication," but the story of why he would be in Sussex for so long had to be established, and Gabrielle was a good place to start. "It's time he got to know our part of the country, now that his mother will be living there. I'm planning to introduce him to all the pretty rides I know, and to the hunt master of course, and several friends have offered to provide him with some sport. He can fish in the Ealy and in the sea if he likes, can't he?"

I directed a tiny shrug of one shoulder to Gabrielle when Dederick was looking the other way, and she responded with a quick, sympathetic lift of the eyebrows. The Dermodys, and Fortier, had a low opinion of the English passion for hunting, but I had grown up in a milieu where chasing after a fox, shooting birds, and spending hours in the cold and damp with a rod and line in hand were viewed as a gentleman's highest attainments. I knew exactly what Dederick would expect from his stay in the country. "I intend to keep him busy," I finished.

The conversation paused for a moment, and I wondered where Gabrielle would send it next. Would she mention Fortier? But before any of us could speak again, the still air was disturbed by the musical clanging of the doorbell, muted by the rich comfort of the house around us.

"I think this may be my American lady." Gabrielle rose to her feet, causing Dederick to do the same. "I met her in Paris two years ago, and this morning I had a letter from her to say she and her family had come to London. So of course I asked her to tea." She laughed. "I think you'll find her a breath of fresh air."

15
A BREATH OF FRESH AIR

"I'm so sorry I'm late." A tall, very well-dressed woman with abundant dark red hair and bright blue eyes smiled brilliantly at us, not looking at all sorry as Gabrielle ushered her into the library. "Is it terrible to be late to an English tea? In Paris, they would think me fashionable, but the truth is I didn't realize how the time was flying. There's so much to see in London."

Gabrielle smiled. "You're really not late. Mrs. India Walfort, this is my friend Lady Helena Whitcombe and her nephew, the Marquess of Hastings." She watched as we all shook hands. "They would forgive you, I'm sure, even if you *were* late, but I'm 'at home' all afternoon. Tea is a wonderfully elastic event."

She turned to speak to the servant who had followed her guests in, giving rapid orders in French for more tea and coffee since she was serving both beverages. Dederick, still on his very best behavior, handed Mrs. Walfort to an armchair, saying, "A lady is never late," as he did so.

"How nice of you, Lord Hastings." Mrs. Walfort seated herself, smoothing down the lace on her truly beautiful ensemble, clearly from Paris; next to our sober clothing, she was as bright and gay as an exotic bird. "Of course, I've given myself away as a parvenue by not knowing the rules, but I'm starting again in London—they do things differently here than in Paris, I'm sure. And I suppose I don't mind being a parvenue in this company. All Americans must seem like new money, as we'd say in the United States, to you British aristocrats. But one must start somewhere. I will not dissemble; I will admit straightaway that we're new money from New York, tired of Fifth Avenue, and eager for a little European polish."

Gabrielle's laugh of delight at the American's candor turned to concern as Mrs. Walfort struggled for a few moments with a dry cough; she soon conquered her affliction, but it returned at intervals, not troubling her much by the look of it. Despite her claim that they had come to Europe for "a little polish," Mrs. Walfort's diction and manners would not have disgraced a duchess, and even her American accent was less strident than that of most of her countrywomen—those I had met, at least.

After a short while, Dederick excused himself. Once the door had shut behind him, Mrs. Walfort let out a sigh and turned to me.

"What a handsome boy. Is he married?" She laughed, and I wondered what expression was on my face. "Oh, I'm sorry. I suppose I'm being impertinent, but in New York I'd have known the marital or courting status of just about any young person I met; we matrons are expected to inquire. As I told Mrs. Dermody in my note, I make no bones about being in London for the express purpose of getting my daughters presented at court, and they're bent on doing a little husband-hunting during the Season since Paris has turned up nobody suitable. Whatever the outcome, a London summer Season will make them fashionable to their friends back home; and if Lord Hastings represents the standard of aristocratic Englishmen, my girls are going to be in raptures." She made a somewhat rueful grimace. "Time is running out, you see. Ellen is twenty-three and Lucy twenty-one. They've been reading about the English aristocracy and are determined to see it for themselves; just one Season, they say, and then back to the States if they don't succeed."

"My nephew is not married nor yet engaged." I answered Mrs. Walfort's question; her garrulity and frankness were amusing me, and I was highly intrigued by this stroke of fate. "And since you ask about a 'standard,' I may as well tell you he's more handsome than most. Many men of our class lack chins or wits or both; that's what comes of marrying amongst ourselves." I grinned. "How the Scott-De Quincys—that's my family, you understand—have managed to remain good-looking since the Norman Conquest is a mystery, to ourselves as much as to anyone. Except for occasional misfits like myself, we are known for being tall, blond, blue-eyed, and having what people call the 'Scott-De Quincy air.' My nephew is a good example of the pedigree."

Gabrielle's brown eyes were dancing with amusement as she listened. "Lady Helena's being unfair," she said as I finished speaking. "There are plenty of nice-looking boys to be found among the English gentry. They spend an extraordinary amount of time outdoors—they ride and hunt and fish all day—so they generally have muscles and fresh complexions enough to recommend them to any young lady of taste."

"Well, that doesn't seem too bad. We saw some dreadful specimens in Paris." Mrs. Walfort shrugged as Gabrielle and I dissolved into laughter. "Well, it's true. I don't want them marrying old men; I'm not *that* ambitious. Marcus and I are simply indulging our girls' fancies as we've always done, although Lucy thinks she may remain a spinster and look after us in our old age. My children are extremely fond of making plans."

"I have *that* to look forward to," Gabrielle said to me.

Mrs. Walfort's expression changed. "But you are in mourning too, Lady Helena. I do hope nothing I've said upsets you. I sincerely pray you haven't lost a child."

I shook my head. "My husband, almost two years ago. I have no children. I'll be out of full mourning by the end of next month."

Mrs. Walfort proceeded to express her sympathy for my bereavement very prettily, during which time Dederick returned.

"I've learned that English gentlemen are fond of the outdoors," Mrs. Walfort said to him once he was seated. "Is that the case with you, Lord Hastings?"

I had time to realize she was getting our titles right at the first shot—she was clearly not as new to society as she might claim—before Dederick launched into an enthusiastic description of his outdoor pursuits, clearly happy to be on familiar ground. He had covered the joys of salmon fishing and moved on to the grouse season when the recollection of his aborted journey to Scotland clearly dawned on him, and his face abruptly assumed a blank expression. He looked at me for help, and I took the hint.

"My sister has taken the lease of a country house and estate that used to be known for raising pheasants," I explained. "Lord Hastings will have his own birds before long, and there are some very old arrangements with other landowners in Broadmere over which land can be borrowed for hunting and shooting. It's not far from where I live." I smiled at Mrs. Walfort. "My house is near Littleberry, quite close to Mrs. Dermody."

"Splendid." Mrs. Walfort's smile, quite beautiful, lit up her heart-shaped face. "Then we may see you. One of our projects is to spend regular time at the coast, as we all miss Newport dreadfully, and I hope to take a house near Mrs. Dermody for a few weeks. We are all connoisseurs of cliffs and beaches; we loved Normandy and Brittany for the scenery, although not quite so much for the dreadful ragtag of people at the watering places. We prefer fishing boats and solitude to yachts and flirtation."

Her cough overcame her; when the fit had passed, she leaned back as much as her bustle allowed, sighing.

"I'm sorry. This cough is such a nuisance. I caught a cold in the spring and just can't shake it off. Marcus is simply frantic about it. He's taken me to see the best physicians in Paris, and they assure us there are no alarming symptoms, but—" She spread her hands. "That's part of the reason for our plan to get as much sea air as we can—to make the most of living on an island. Marcus wants to go south for the winter—have you been to Tuscany and the Riviera? So lovely—but the girls think bracing cold is more healthful."

"I love to ride down to the sea myself." I laughed. "There's certainly some bracing cold on the marshes near my home. My mare doesn't like it quite as much as I do."

This gave Dederick a new way to enter the conversation, and for a while we discussed the vagaries of horses; Mrs. Walfort clearly enjoyed being on horseback. This left Gabrielle out somewhat—my friend would rather walk than ride—but she soon, inevitably, mentioned Sir Geraint. The house he had established close to the sea at Lower Broadmere was naturally attracting visitors, and Gabrielle, herself a talented artist in ceramic painting, was one of them.

"Are you the Lady Helena who's having a set of paintings made by Sir Geraint for her drawing room?" Mrs. Walfort's bright eyes brightened further. "Gabrielle, you've been holding out on me. You know very well Marcus will want to meet Lady Helena now." She turned to me. "My husband adores art and music. I've lost count of the paintings he bought in Paris, and there were two violins he said were very important; and the first thing he did when we arrived in London was visit the galleries. He now owns two huge paintings of Sir Geraint's." She shook her head in mock despair. "It's all being sent back to New York. I'll have to have the ballroom, and probably all the other reception rooms, redecorated to show it all off."

I blinked. Here, then, was an example of the fabled Americans who were invading Europe, taking its treasures back to their homes like Vikings after a raid. I began to wonder where the Walforts' money came from.

Dederick's expression had, regrettably, turned supercilious at the mention of the famous artist who had caused us so much trouble. "Mama's not exactly thrilled to be living just a mile or two from Sir Geraint." He drawled out the words, then clamped his lips together in an all-too-obvious effort to refrain from mentioning the summer's scandal.

"It doesn't matter," I said, seeing Gabrielle flush very slightly at having introduced the topic. "It's my fault anyway, for agreeing to the commission and not refusing to continue with it after what happened. Sir Geraint has set up a studio at Edenholme specifically for the Nightingale paintings." I shrugged, looking straight at Mrs. Walfort. "Anyway, I suppose you know about my sister Odelia. As my father always said, we Scott-De Quincys have weathered quite a few episodes of notoriety in the last eight hundred years, and I suppose this will pass too."

"Eight hundred years." Mrs. Walfort breathed out the words, and I blessed her inwardly for seizing on the one point in my remarks that would not lead to a discussion of my family's recent history. "You make me feel like a complete come-from-nowhere. Even in New York, which we consider old, you only have to claim two hundred years of family

history—of the right sort—to be our version of the aristocracy. I'm rather proud of both of our families—Marcus's and mine—being rooted in the Dutch settlers because that sets us apart from all the newer arrivals." She smiled. "As Marcus says, people just can't help looking for social distinctions."

"I thought the aristocracy in America was based on money," Dederick said.

"Not entirely—not in New York, certainly, especially among the older families." Mrs. Walfort turned to him. "But it's hard for them to compete with the fortunes people are making, and there are those—Mrs. Vanderbilt for one—who are just buying their way in. My problem is that I sympathize with the old families, even though they don't consider us one of them since we were all just farmers before my late father-in-law moved west to Wisconsin in the thirties and started the iron foundry."

"So iron is Mr. Walfort's business?" My curiosity was, I hoped, about to be satisfied.

"Stoves." Mrs. Walfort shrugged, a pretty movement that accentuated the cut of her beautiful clothes. "I'm not going to hide from you, Lady Helena, that our money comes from stoves. It was Marcus who saw the potential for making real money and persuaded his father to move back east—and now he has a mail-order business that covers much of the country. 'A Walfort stove will never let you down.' Marcus's stoves are, if I may boast a little about my adorable husband, the best in America, and, who knows, perhaps one day the best in England too. Now, can you still be friends with us?"

"I told you she'd be a breath of fresh air." Gabrielle spoke softly enough that only I, sitting close to her, could hear.

I shrugged in my turn. "There are only two generations between my late husband and money from cotton. Money has to come from somewhere, even if we're supposed to pretend it doesn't matter."

"Precisely." Mrs. Walfort sounded triumphant. "And there's a great deal to be made from stoves."

"Then let's agree to drop all awkward subjects." I smiled. "If you really want to meet Sir Geraint, I'd be happy to make the introduction if you come to Sussex. I will tell him I want you to see the Nightingale paintings."

The rest of the visit to Kensington Square went splendidly, and by the time we left, I felt I had made a most interesting acquaintance I would be happy to see again. In fact, I was positively curious to meet the husband and daughters of such a brilliant, forthright creature.

16
DOING WHAT GOOD ONE CAN

We returned to Whitcombe House the next day. The train to Hastings was crowded, and Dederick appeared unhappy, all the gains in his spirits over the last three days seemingly lost. I deduced the presence of a brandy flask somewhere on his person by the faint bloom of alcohol in the air, but since our carriage also contained two old ladies and a middle-aged gentleman with a malodorous beard, I couldn't question my nephew. In any case, he didn't, as far as I could see, sip from any flask as we traveled south, spending the journey staring morosely and silently out of the window.

Perhaps Rampling had the brandy, I thought. The valet had taken a second-class ticket, so Guttridge, who usually traveled with me, did likewise, murmuring to me she might engage Rampling in friendly conversation and gather "clues" to the events on the other, fateful train.

"Well, that was a waste of time," she informed me when we were changing trains at Hastings. "He gave me the slip. He was so kind in finding me a place in a second-class carriage, and then he shut the door on me, saying there wasn't room and he'd rough it wherever he could find a seat. He's got a first-class ticket for the train to Littleberry, but that's only half a dozen stops."

And indeed, although this time there were only the four of us in the carriage, it was Guttridge and I who made small talk. Dederick appeared to be dozing, while Rampling's attention was firmly fixed on a sporting paper he had purchased. He smiled and answered us willingly if we directed a question or remark at him, but always in such a way as to put an end to any further conversation.

It was a relief to me to be home, and I said as much to Dederick. Having left Guttridge and Rampling to do their jobs of unpacking our trunks and making sure our rooms were in order, I encouraged him to walk with me on the terrace.

"I hope you'll be comfortable." I smiled up at my nephew. "I intend to spoil you a little, you know."

I slipped my arm into his, half expecting him to find some excuse to break the contact between us, but he tolerated the gesture and even made some murmur that might have been thanks for my solicitude. We walked in silence for a few minutes, and some color came back into Dederick's face as the sea breezes played over us, still soft and bearing some warmth since it was only mid-September.

"I always feel better when I come back here," I remarked, holding my face up to the afternoon sun. A dark cloud, almost purple, over Broadmere and a tang in the air suggested we would soon have rain, but for now the distant sea sparkled with reflected sunlight. The dip of the valley below us was a medley of bright grassy fields, dotted with sheep, and the darker greens of trees and hedges; the River Ealy and the ditches that drained the valley bottom reflected the cloud-streaked sky, being rather full as there must have been a storm. It was my home, and I wanted

Dederick to see it as I did, a sanctuary from the world and its problems.

A flurry of motion and a volley of high-pitched barks signaled Scotty's arrival. It pleased me to see Dederick making a fuss of my terrier, who, after greeting me rapturously, stood still for an entire minute to allow my nephew to scratch behind his ears. In further token of his delight in seeing us, Scotty then deigned to remain near us instead of darting off to investigate the dirtier parts of Whitcombe's grounds. The three of us walked on amicably, and Dederick's face became less immobile as we talked quietly. Soon I decided to broach the subject I had been mulling over for some days.

"Would you talk to me soon about what happened that day?" I asked. "I'm not being nosy. Guttridge and I are concerned the police may not treat you fairly, and since we have a little experience in—well, I suppose you might call it investigating—we think we could at least try to work out what might have happened."

I watched Dederick's face fall, saw his hesitation, and held my breath, but after a few moments he nodded. "I don't imagine I can tell you all that much, but I suppose it would be all right to talk to you. You don't gossip, do you? Mama says you're remarkably close-mouthed about other people's business."

My eyebrows rose; I wasn't sure if, coming from Blanche, that was a compliment or not. "I will keep everything you tell me in strict confidence," I assured Dederick. "Except for telling Guttridge, but she's as silent as the grave. She's my—actually, I'm not always sure if I'm not *her* assistant." I laughed. "In any case, we work together well, and it would be to your advantage to involve her."

"All right," Dederick said after we had walked a few more paces. "You know, at first I thought that talk you had with me last month was the most horrible thing that had ever happened to me—before Bow Street. I swore I'd never talk to you again." He pushed his curls out of his eyes as he looked down at me. "But actually, you didn't scream—Mama screamed and cried like anything—and now I can see you didn't—you don't—treat me like I'm dirty, the way the police did." He could not quite suppress a shudder at the memory.

"That's not because I condone what you've done," I told him hastily. "But, well, I suppose I've seen too much sorrow and learned too much about life's complications to want to do anything but attend to my own conduct and do what little good I can. Goodness, that sounds rather pious, doesn't it?" I breathed out a laugh. "But I don't want to judge you, Deddy. You're unhappy, and I want to help. And on that subject, I do wish you wouldn't drink so much."

"I only had a nip or two today, *Auntie*." Dederick actually smiled, the "Auntie" a playful response to my use of his pet name. "You know, it's dashed strange having an aunt who's only three years older than oneself, and a deuced pretty aunt at that. But I rather like it when you talk like an aunt."

"Four years older," I corrected him for the second time. "So you'll try to leave the brandy alone for a while? I can promise you excellent coffee when you need a stimulant and company whenever you need it. I'll even ride out with you if you can bear to go at Sandy's pace; she's rather lazy, but I'm fond of her, and I never was one for galloping. Why don't we go to the stables later, and you can see if any of my horses suit you?"

"Oh, I'll send for my own beasts—they're in Hampshire. If you have room in your stables for one or two of them, I'll send the others to Hawthorn Hall. Mama said she has a groom now." The affected drawl was back, but I decided I simply wouldn't mind it. "I've got a couple of very decent mounts for country hacks and an excellent pair of hunters for proper sport." He looked out over the valley, over which a mist was spreading as the rain advanced toward us, with the experienced gaze of a sportsman. "It's interesting countryside. I imagine there's some fun to be had here after all."

"When shall we talk?" I asked. "I'd like it to be soon so that your memory is fresh."

"Not today." Dederick stooped to disentangle a plant that had somehow become stuck to Scotty's tail, murmuring endearments to my dog as Scotty growled at him. "I'm tired to death. You can have at me tomorrow."

He looked up at me, an odd expression on his face; was it shame? "I promise I'll keep my drinking within reasonable bounds. They say it's the mark of a gentleman that he can hold his liquor, but I think I've been overdoing it lately."

"THERE NOW."

The long day was drawing to its close, and Guttridge had just finished tying a neat bow in the ribbon around one of my braids. "You're all ready to retire, my lady."

She gave a quick tweak to one of the curling papers in my front hair and moved away from me, pulling her notebook out of a pocket. "I've been thinking about what we could do to help his lordship."

"He's willing to talk to me, at least." I climbed onto my bed, watching as Guttridge found her page. "Perhaps just me; he's rather skittish."

"Well, that can't be helped." Guttridge produced a pencil and licked the sharpened end, resting her notebook on the corner of my dressing table. "The *most* important thing is to find out who was on that train and the order of events. We're in the dark till we know the story, and the papers aren't saying. There hasn't been a thing about Lord Arthur for days."

"Names won't be easy if it was a large party. Would *you* know the names of everyone at a house party you'd been invited to?"

The withering glance Guttridge gave me assured me she would, but she merely said, "The more people we can ask, the better our picture of that day will be. You must try to speak to Rampling, my lady. He can't refuse to talk to you, can he? Especially if you get his lordship to agree."

"Still no luck in engaging him in conversation in the servants' hall?" I asked. Guttridge had told me she was going to try during the servants' dinner and in the quiet period afterward, when neither she nor Rampling would yet be needed to help us prepare for bed.

"Oh, he's friendly enough, and all the maids are smitten with him." Guttridge made a derisive noise in her throat. "But he doesn't spend a lot of time chatting in general company. He seems to like making small talk with the men about prize-fighting and where the best beer is to be found, that kind of thing. The sort of man who doesn't discuss serious things, I'd say. He's very polite and obliging with the women if they speak directly to him, and he smiles a lot, but he doesn't flirt much. I suppose that's for the best in a strange household, and quite sensible. I don't like those menservants who break hearts everywhere they go."

"I know what you mean." I stretched out my legs on the bed, enjoying the freedom of just a nightgown around me. "I don't suppose anyone downstairs is interested in Lord Arthur's death either."

"Only in a general way when it happened." Guttridge turned back a page or two in her notebook, reading what she'd written previously. "Littleberry folk aren't generally much interested in what happens outside the parish. To them as never travel, you may as well be talking about Timbuktoo."

I sighed; all the investigating was down to me, it seemed. "I suppose I must talk to Rampling. Will it seem odd if I'm taking notes? I'll have to—I'll never remember the names, given I don't know anyone in that set. I barely even bother to read the court circular or the society pages, now I don't host house parties."

"The investigator takes notes; that's the way of it," Guttridge said firmly and then spoke as she wrote: *Ladyship to talk to lordship, and Ladyship to talk to Rampling.*

"And after that, what will we do?" I shed my dressing gown, slid under the turned-down sheets, pulling the coverlet up to my waist, and tried to settle into my pillows.

Guttridge considered my question for a moment, her pencil poised. "I'll try to find out a bit more about Mr. Rampling," she said. "He may have made some friends in Littleberry when he was last here. He likes beer, so he'll have drunk in a public house or two. He's a suspect after all."

"Is he?"

"Everyone's a suspect till we can establish their alibi." Guttridge assumed the superior air of an expert talking to a novice. "Even his lordship." She looked at me, pursing her lips. "Hasn't that occurred to you, my lady?"

"I don't like to think about Lord Hastings as a suspect," I confessed.

"We can't rule him out, not yet. I'm going to go through my newspaper clippings again and note down ideas." Guttridge put notebook and pencil back into her pocket and took my dressing gown from where I'd thrown it, folding it neatly and placing it on the chaise longue. She swept up the pouch containing my soiled linen, took one last look around the room to see everything was in order, and nodded at me.

"Good night, my lady."

"Good night."

But sleep didn't come easily, despite the fatigue of the day's travels. When I eventually drifted off, my dreams featured a rocking train moving unnaturally fast through a dark night. It seemed to hold the Old Bailey courtroom where Edmund Dorrian-Knowles had been tried; only the man in the dock wasn't Edmund but Dederick.

17
THE TALE OF THE TRAIN

My investigatory interview with Dederick took place in the small library. The notebook—the kind Guttridge and I used for our herbalist activities—and pencil I held in my hands made me feel a little foolish, but in the past two years I had become more disciplined about note-taking than I would ever have imagined, having been an indifferent student when young enough for a governess and Mama's despair when I grew old enough to help her. "Have you no intellectual curiosity, Helena?" still sounded in my ears when I picked up a pencil.

Dederick seemed rested and alert, although I caught a glimpse of wariness in his eyes as he made himself comfortable on a sofa. "Notes?" was his only remark as he caught sight of my preparations, aided by a small portable writing rest that usually stood in a corner of the room.

"I can help you best if I understand more fully who was on the train and so on," I explained. "In fact, why don't we start with that list?"

My instincts were right. Dederick, hesitant at first,

became more animated through the effort of recalling who was in the party traveling toward Scotland on the sixth of September. It was an impressive list. If the train had met with an accident, the British aristocracy could have lost many heads of great families. No wonder influence had so readily been exercised to stop the police from detaining the passengers.

"Servants?" I asked at length. "I presume the gentlemen brought a valet with them and the ladies a maid, almost without exception?"

"Of course." Dederick looked faintly scornful. "There were some loaders and grooms and so on as well; don't ask me who they were or to whom they belonged. They were at the back of the train, naturally."

"While the upper servants traveled with their employers?"

Dederick shrugged. "The lady's maids, I suppose. We men are just as likely to dismiss our valets. We value our privacy. There's usually some political talk here and there, some confidential, and gambling, of course. Sometimes the two get mixed up." The corner of his mouth twitched up, as if a memory had amused him.

"Where was Rampling?" I had by now filled up two and a half pages of my notebook with names. Guttridge *would* be pleased.

"He asked permission to travel with an old friend of his," Dederick said. "Remus Fleetwood's his name. I remember it because the old boy's something of a legend. One of the finest butlers in the country in his time, but he's ancient now and in ill health. The duke sends him to London regularly to consult a medical man. He was returning home to Scotland that day."

I nodded. The old-fashioned practice of caring for aging and decrepit servants was one of which I heartily approved. "Where in the train did they travel?"

"Rampling said they were in a carriage with a stove, which sounds dashed unlikely to me, but he said it helped to keep the old man warm. It was at the back of the train, I think. Behind the luggage van."

I made a note. "Did you see Rampling at all?" I remembered how the valet had made himself scarce during the first part of our journey home from London and wondered how often that happened.

"Naturally, the valets look for their masters at the stops, to see if they require anything." Dederick leaned back onto one elbow. "Difficult job—there's a lot of moving around on these jaunts. People want to say hello and all that."

"And where were you?" I tensed a little; now we were getting to the nub of the matter. I expected Dederick to become evasive, but his long eyelashes lifted and his clear green-gray gaze was directed firmly at me.

"In a compartment of my own, asleep. There were some compartment coaches as well as those American things, *you* know. Parlor cars and dining cars, they call them. The ladies were all in those, I think. Sometimes the chaps prefer a compartment for a private talk or a nap."

"And where was Lord Arthur?"

Dederick's expression took on a hint of sulkiness. "I neither knew nor cared."

His demeanor gave me a sudden idea—not a propitious one. "Had you quarreled?" That could be significant.

"Yes." The response came fast and angry. "We met before the train, in a place we know near Euston. Arthur insisted. We got rather upset with one another."

"Why?"

"Why do you *think*?" A flush appeared on Dederick's cheeks. "Because of what Arthur had said before. His threats. I told him I was sick of him and he could go to hell. I told him I didn't care; I'd just tell everyone he was lying. I told him we were utterly finished as friends."

His brow darkened. "Arthur cried. God, what an awful scene. I was glad to get out of there, out into the street, where he had to stop blubbing. I was terrified he'd start pawing at me and hanging around my neck if we stayed any longer. We'd both had several drinks by then, and I was starting to feel rotten."

"What time was it?"

"I don't know. Early. We were due to leave at ten. I remember because that's why I insisted on getting away. Too dashed early to be getting on a train, but we were supposed to stop at Edinburgh for the night and then go north to Ballater the next morning. Then they'd take us up to the estate in carriages. Those members of the prince's family and closest friends who were joining us would come from Balmoral later in the day."

I was trying hard not to be impressed, and also quite glad I didn't have to lead the itinerant life of the very grand. Going up to London on occasion was bad enough; I'd hate to only see Whitcombe for a few weeks in the year. I finished making a note about the train's intended destination before Dederick spoke again.

"Drinking early always makes me feel sick. I was rude to pretty much everyone, I suppose, and in the end they left me alone. I found an empty compartment and settled down, knowing I could sleep for a few hours and then be fit for company again. And that was it until Rampling came to tell me they'd stopped the train because Arthur was missing."

We spent the next thirty minutes going over some of the same ground again, but in the end I thought I had exhausted Dederick's memory and possibly his patience. It turned out, disappointingly, that the list of names he had given me was not entirely from his recollections since he had been half-drunk by the time he had reached the platform at Euston Station, where the train was waiting. It was more a list of people he had known would probably join the shoot. I would, perhaps, have to rely on a more sober head for an accurate list.

18
THE TALE OF THE VALET

"You're better than a police detective, my lady."

Rampling was cheerful, even jocular, and had happily listed everyone he remembered having seen or talked to during the morning in question, spelling out names to me if my pencil hesitated. I noted down the names carefully, drawing lines between masters and servants as Rampling identified who employed whom.

The valet seemed to go out of his way to be helpful and pleasant. He was also as neat and sober as any employer might wish, with extremely well-kept hands and, if I was any judge, freshly washed hair. The impression I had gained of him during Dederick's first visit was dispelled, and I began to look more favorably upon him. After all, I could hardly condemn a man for drinking a pint or two of beer, with his master's permission, after what was no doubt a tiring day.

"I'm simply trying to help Lord Hastings," I said now.

I smiled at the valet, who responded with a pleasant grin that showed white teeth. The long chin that had seemed to spoil his appearance at first became less of an adverse feature as one came to know him, and I could understand why

Guttridge had said the female servants at Whitcombe were fawning over him. I hoped he wasn't too susceptible; I didn't want trouble with the maids.

"You were traveling somewhere at the rear of the train with," I turned back the pages of my notebook, "a butler of the name of Fleetwood. Was that in a compartment?"

"In the brake van." Rampling, at my behest, had seated himself opposite me, and despite his very upright posture, he seemed quite at ease. A small smile appeared on his lips, as if the memory of the journey was pleasing to him.

"The brake van?" I asked. "I understand Fleetwood is an old man. Wouldn't he have been more comfortable in a compartment?"

"How kind of you to think of his comfort, my lady." Rampling smiled again. "I agree that some brake vans must be very spartan, but this was a nice one, with a large stove. The compartments had steam heating, of course, but they were just the ordinary sort of compartment with benches; this van had a couple of armchairs of sorts, fixed to the floor like in a Pullman parlor car, and a proper stove. The duke arranged to have that van especially; you know it was a private train, I suppose. The only places more comfortable were the Pullman coaches, and Mr. Fleetwood wouldn't have thought it proper to travel with the gentry. He was happy about the stove; he felt the cold dreadfully, as old people do."

"But it was quite a warm day."

"Yes, my lady." The valet's tone was one of patience, as if explaining something to a child. "I had to take my coat off, and I was far too warm. Mr. Fleetwood sat next to the stove *and* he needed a blanket. But he's over ninety, the good old man, and was as strong as an ox until he was eighty-five; I remember him well from my young days."

"Was it just the two of you in the van?" I asked.

"There's always a guard in a brake van." Rampling nodded

pleasantly, as though it was quite proper I should be ignorant of such details. "He usually sat in his seat near the brake, although sometimes he was at his little desk, writing in some book or the other. Logs or ledgers, I didn't inquire, and he wasn't the talkative sort. At times, he'd go into a sort of little cupboard hanging on the side of the van, if you see what I mean, to get a clear view of the whole train. That was his usual practice when we were approaching a station."

"Did you stay in the van the whole time?"

"Oh no," Rampling replied easily. "Well, Mr. Fleetwood did, mostly, but I still had my job to do. I'd nip off to see if his lordship required anything whenever the train stopped, then I'd fetch Mr. Fleetwood a hot drink from the dining car or take him to the privy, whatever was needed. He was dozing much of the time, but he'd wake up in the way of old folks, and I'd look after him. When he was awake, we'd talk, mostly about his job back in the old days when he was the best butler in the country. I always learn a great deal from talking to Mr. Fleetwood. He is an absolute mine of notions about how to be the best servant possible, and I want to be the best. I'd like to be a butler someday."

There was an intensity in his eyes now, an enthusiasm I liked. I appreciated servants who viewed their jobs as something more than just an interval before they married, in the case of women, or left to run a little business of their own. I nodded.

"Tell me about the stops."

Rampling relaxed his ramrod-stiff posture a little, crossing one long, thin leg over the other and clasping his hands around a bony knee. "Well, the first stop was at Rugby. By that time, there were plenty of passengers who left the train to use the lavatory in the station before luncheon. I helped Mr. Fleetwood to the convenience, took him back to the van, and just had time to look in on his lordship."

"And how was Lord Hastings?"

Rampling shrugged. "He'd been drinking, I'm afraid to say, and was fairly far gone." He grimaced. "I feel bad saying that about my employer, but I think you want the truth, my lady."

"I do." It hardly came as a surprise to me since Dederick had confessed to being drunk.

"I suggested it was a mite early for so much brandy, but he just swore at me."

"I'm sorry to hear that."

"Young gentlemen can be unruly at times. It's all part of the job." Now Rampling's smile was rueful, as if he were resigned to his lot. "I knew he'd soon be asleep, and I hoped his mood would improve a bit later. I'd arranged for a luncheon basket to be brought to him, and by the time I reached the compartment, it was on a bench opposite his lordship, so I brought it to his attention. Then all I had time to do was run back to the brake van before the train left. I started unpacking the luncheon basket they'd brought over for Mr. Fleetwood and me. Everyone's very considerate toward Mr. Fleetwood, given the name he's made for himself. I would like to be so well regarded."

"I can imagine. I suppose you ate?"

"We did. Mr. Fleetwood had little appetite and complained about the quality of the food, but I found it rather good. We talked for about thirty minutes after luncheon, and then Mr. Fleetwood fell asleep, so I read the papers till we reached Stafford. Oh—" He snapped his fingers, a dry, crisp sound. "I forgot to say I saw Andrew Lawther at Rugby."

I wrinkled my brow, looking back through the list of names. "Lord Arthur's valet?"

"Yes, my lady. I saw him when I was on my way to his lordship's compartment, and he said Lord Arthur was in the parlor car and had dismissed him. He was planning to stay in the grooms' and loaders' carriage till the next stop because they had some good ale." He grinned. "That's what put me in mind of him. Begging your ladyship's pardon, but since you want all the details, when the train stopped at Stafford, he needed the privy badly."

I nodded. Long train journeys were a trial since nobody liked to have to avail themselves of a chamber pot on a moving train. "Did you or he see Lord Arthur at Stafford?"

"Well, that's the thing." Rampling uncrossed his legs and resumed his upright pose, his hands resting on his knees. "Lawther was running like, and he shouted at me to look in on Lord Arthur if I could. So after I'd made sure Lord Hastings was all right—he was asleep and hadn't touched his food—I went looking for Lord Arthur in the parlor car and dining car. I didn't see him, but I thought nothing of it. He might be in the station lavatory or one of the compartments, and I didn't have time to search the whole train. It wasn't a long stop, and I wanted to visit the convenience before we left; he wasn't in there either, as it turned out."

"So you had no idea where he was?" This seemed like an important point, and I made sure to note it down carefully.

"Never had sight of him. I asked one or two of the other servants, but nobody knew his whereabouts. Still, as I said, I didn't worry. They *are* able to look after themselves, even if you sometimes don't think so."

His deferential mask was slipping a little, but I didn't really blame him. It sounded as if neither Dederick nor Lord Arthur were considerate of their valets, and Rampling's job must sometimes be a frustrating one.

"So let's go on to the third stop. Where was that?"

I felt matters were going along swimmingly and that I was conducting the interview competently, if perhaps not with the persuasive force of the police. Guttridge said much of being a detective was about talking to people, and I wasn't afraid of that.

"Crewe." Rampling's long face became more serious. "It wasn't so far up the line, but it's an important railway town, as you probably know, my lady. It's often a long stop, is Crewe; they take time to load and unload and provision the trains. We were told we'd have an hour and that the Crewe Arms Hotel was at the disposal of such of the gentry as wanted it. You might imagine I'm familiar with the place, my lady, having been north many a time with his lordship for the sport, and I knew there'd be chaos."

"Really?"

"In the sense of those lords and ladies going every which way and then having to find them all before the train could start again. You always breathe a sigh of relief once Crewe is past. Things settle down a bit after Crewe, everybody being a mite tired by then."

By now, his face was entirely serious, his mouth set and his large brown eyes grave. "And there was Lawther again, sober this time. Don't blame him, my lady; he's a good lad, really, just a bit inexperienced. He was worried to death about Lord Arthur because he couldn't find him anywhere. I confessed I hadn't found him at Stafford, and then he really started fretting, afraid he'd lose his place because he'd left his employer behind. I had to talk some sense into him; at least, that's what I thought I was doing." He shivered. "Turned out Lawther was right to worry."

"So what did you do?" I asked. I was caught up in his story, hanging on every word.

"Well, first of all, I thought we'd better make absolutely sure Lord Arthur had gone missing. That wasn't easy; like I said, there were lords and ladies everywhere. Some on the train, some in the hotel, some just wandering around, as you might say. I helped Lawther search in an orderly fashion; we had to be fast, but we looked in all the public rooms in the hotel and then worked our way down the train, asking any servant we saw if they'd seen his lordship. The quality wouldn't have thanked us for bothering *them*, so we didn't."

"How long did the search last?" I asked.

"Forty minutes, perhaps. It was nearly time for the train to go. But we were convinced Lord Arthur had vanished into thin air, so I took Lawther to see the stationmaster."

"What about calling the police?"

"We-e-e-e-ll." He pulled the word out judiciously. "You see, Lawther said it wouldn't be the first time his lordship had just decided to leave, and once he'd run to the police and been made to look a fool. Both of us knew about the quarrel with my master; we didn't tell the stationmaster much about that. We started wondering if Lord Arthur had left the train at Stafford and gone to find a train back to London or something, and we were all for not making a fuss. But the stationmaster felt differently."

"In what way?"

"He said it was more than his job was worth to ignore a missing passenger on the duke's train. He wasn't at the point of making it a police matter, but he telegraphed back to Stafford to have some of the young men out to ride alongside the line and sent his own men out from his end. They have horses they use for inspecting the track, it seems. I asked, why do that—why ride along the line? It wasn't till then I had a nasty feeling, and when the stationmaster said people had fallen or even jumped from trains, especially when there was drink taken, Lawther and I sort of looked at one another, uneasy like. We both knew Lord Arthur was fond of Lord Hastings and that there'd been some falling out."

He hesitated, running a hand over his lean torso and moistening his lips with his tongue, as if they were dry. "I don't know quite how to say this, my lady, but it's an *unnat-*

ural fondness I'm talking about. Lord Arthur's for Lord Hastings, I mean. My gentleman's a handsome man, isn't he? Like something not quite mortal is how one of the royal ladies put it, when she didn't think I could hear." He grimaced. "I probably shouldn't be saying such a thing."

"And I probably shouldn't be listening, but as it happens, I already know."

Perhaps it was surprise that produced a sudden fit of coughing, or there was simply a natural explanation; in any event, cough he did. When he had recovered, he went on: "I really am sorry to bring up the subject, but it's an explanation, isn't it? When a man's like a woman, they can become quite upset by things, and Lord Arthur—" He broke off, pulling out a handkerchief and mopping his brow. "It's really not my place to comment, and doubtless I shouldn't have said anything at all, and I hope your ladyship can forgive me and not punish the messenger, so to speak—"

"It's all right." I raised a hand to stem the flow of words. "It was brave of you to tell me what you truly thought."

Rampling took a deep breath. "Thank you, my lady. It's part of my job, knowing matters I shouldn't, and sometimes a man must choose between loyalty and principle. There are things that go on that aren't right."

"So you think Lord Arthur might have jumped from the train?"

Rampling's voice was unsteady as he answered. "They found his body about four miles north of Stafford. God rest his troubled soul." He made the sign of the cross. "He might have fallen, of course. I heard the stationmaster tell the police it's a lonely bit of country, not like to the south of Stafford, where there's more industry, all those smoky chimneys and suchlike. I've thought of Lord Arthur lying there, broken, sometimes. I've dreamed of him."

He used his handkerchief to blow his nose. I looked down

at my notebook, giving him time to compose himself before I asked, "Were there any doors found open on the train when you reached Crewe?"

I looked up to see the color draining from Rampling's face, leaving it the yellow-white of parchment. "I don't think so. Why do you ask?" His voice was faint.

"Because an absence of open doors suggests not suicide or accident, but murder."

"THE WORD 'MURDER' SEEMED TO SHOCK RAMPLING inexpressibly," I told Guttridge later. "He sort of gasped for a bit and said there must have been an open door, but he knew nothing about it. He was in the brake van with Fleetwood all the way from Stafford to Crewe after all."

"I'd like to talk to that Mr. Fleetwood." Guttridge underlined a word here and there in her own notebook, in which we had been constructing a narrative of the events of that day from the two accounts I'd heard so far.

"And so would I." I knew I was looking smug. "I asked Rampling if he would kindly write to the old man and inquire if I—if *we*—could talk to him. I think you can be present this time."

"That's outstanding work, my lady." Guttridge spoke in the surprised tone of an adult praising a rather dull child who had said something clever for once. "It's a shame we can't find a way to interview everyone on the train."

"Good heavens." I felt exhausted at the mere thought of it. "We certainly can't do that. When you think about it, being a police officer has its advantages. I'm sure the police would regard our own minor efforts as quite risible." I flicked a finger at Guttridge's notebook. "A little hobby of investigation, as Lord Arthur said. I wonder if my entire life will be looked upon as a series of little hobbies? Have we just been keeping ourselves busy, Guttridge? I'm not sure if your scheme of interviewing people has helped at all."

"It's better than doing nothing, isn't it, my lady?" Guttridge spoke briskly. "Now we have a list of just about everybody on the train. I suppose it's a mercy the royal people were coming from Balmoral. Coo, imagine if you'd had royalty on the train. What an investigation *that* would be."

Her eyes shone. I shuddered.

"Kindly rein in your overweening imagination." I hid a yawn behind my hand. "Goodness, Guttridge, I feel like I've done a hard day's work in the fields."

A slightly chilly silence reminded me I had never done a really hard day's work in my life. I accepted the rebuke, handing Guttridge her notebook with an apologetic smile.

"I'm having luncheon with my brother and his family on Sunday," I informed her. "And Captain Murray-Jones."

"I'd almost forgotten he was here, in all the upheaval." Guttridge wrapped a long ribbon around her book, tying it in a bow. "He's cut quite a dash in the town, mind you, in that fancy uniform. Handsome in the face and figure too, isn't he?"

"Tolerably." I didn't intend to give anything away with regard to Jonathan Murray-Jones. "I've bumped into him here and there. He often seems to be walking where I am."

"And of good family, with that 'Honorable' in front of his name."

"I'll show you the relationship in our family tree one of these days. A good family, as you say, but they've had a long run of bad luck and some dark stories attached to them. Our mothers were great friends, but Mama had the deuce of a time persuading Papa to let Daniel live with us."

I shut my mouth firmly; I had not intended to say so

much about the Murray-Joneses. Guttridge, sensing my mood, changed the subject.

"You been that busy these last three weeks; you've hardly seen anything of your family, have you, my lady?" she asked, rising to her feet. "I suppose at least Lady Hastings waited till we were done with Lady Odelia to bring some new excitement into our lives. The marchioness will be back staying in this house in a fortnight, won't she?"

"She arrives on the twenty-seventh. She'll stay at Whitcombe until Hawthorn House is quite ready." I too stood up, peering at the side of my hand, which appeared to be smeared with pencil lead. "There's still so much to do. I will regard tomorrow and Sunday as a brief holiday before I allow the new excitement of Lady Hastings's move to swallow me up."

19
A PROMISE OF ADVENTURE

True to my word, I spent Saturday resolutely forgetting about anything to do with Arthur Southgate-Haigh or Hawthorn Hall. I could not forget Dederick, naturally; I took him to visit friends who were keen on field sports and thus excellent connections for my nephew. I found the hunting talk boring, but I was used to that, and Dederick seemed to enjoy himself.

On Sunday, there was church, to be followed by luncheon at Hyrst. Since Jonathan was invited to Hyrst, it was only natural he should join me, Dederick, Michael, and Julia in the front pew of the gated Scott-De Quincy section, and since he was seated next to me, it was natural enough that he should offer me an arm as we proceeded, in fine processional style, out of the church after the service.

We were following Michael and Julia; Michael, as the head of the family, always went first. As usual, he had something to say about the service.

"Michael's complaining there was too much singing." Jonathan grinned. "Does he think he's talking in a whisper?"

"He always complains." I smiled back. "All music is just

noise to him. He finds the high voices of the choirboys particularly irritating."

We both laughed as an explosive "No, I don't!" alerted us that Julia had reminded Michael he always said the same thing. Behind me, Gerry tutted, and that somehow made Jonathan and me laugh more. It was an effort to rearrange my face into Sunday solemnity as I shook hands with the rector.

"Cousin of ours, the rector, isn't he?" Jonathan released me from his arm as we stepped outdoors so he could replace his busby, which bore a lofty egret feather, resembling an elongated feather duster, at the front. "Very dignified chap. Very *tall.* I was wishing I could put my hat on *inside* church so I could outdo him in height."

"I think you've outdone him in all other respects," I murmured. Indeed, a man wearing yards of braid, tight pantaloons, and ludicrously shiny boots, with a gold-encrusted sword and that strange pouch-like object called a sabretache hanging on his left side, was entirely unable to avoid cutting a dash, as Guttridge said. I felt rather conspicuous on his arm.

Jonathan did not hear me, so I continued the conversation, trying not to notice the stares and giggles of a pair of young girls who were about to get a telling-off from their governess. "The rector's a relation on Mama's side, so yes, he must be a cousin of yours too." I put my hand back on Jonathan's heavily decorated sleeve. "Mama insisted Papa give him the living. It's a very good one, as you'd imagine."

"The best places should go to the family, eh?" Jonathan's heavy chin strap moved as he grinned again. "He certainly reminds me of your father, with all that silver hair."

"Yes, he's very like." I smiled at an acquaintance who was clearly closing in on us for an introduction to my highly ornamental cousin. A little way away, Dederick was talking with our hunting friends, who had invited him to spend the afternoon with them.

We soon had an entire group of friends and acquaintances around us, separating us from Ned and Gerry as we moved away from the church to allow the rest of the congregation out. I began to feel even more conspicuous when I saw significant glances being exchanged between those ladies —and there were quite a few in Littleberry—whose mission in life appeared to be to anticipate, and sometimes further, matrimonial matches. I tried to keep my hand from resting too securely on Jonathan's arm and resolved not to allow my sleeve to touch his muscular torso. Indeed, I resolved not to think of his muscular torso.

"We'll have to wait until Alice and Annette are done talking to each and every disadvantaged spinster of good family before we can leave," I informed my cousin as the congregants began to think of their luncheon and the crowd of acquaintances thinned. "Michael will be in an absolute stew of impatience by then; he always is. The twins don't care, though."

"I don't mind at all." Jonathan's teeth showed white in his tanned face. "It's a beautiful day, and I have a pretty woman on my arm. There's Ned and Gerry heading back to Four Square, do you see?" He let go of his sword to wave his free arm.

I waved vigorously too, hoping the activity would account for the blush I was sure had come to my cheeks. Gerry, I noticed, had a particularly satisfied smile on her face as she looked back at the two of us; she said something to Ned, who laughed.

"Will you do something for me while we're at Hyrst?" Jonathan returned his attention to me as Ned and Gerry turned their backs on us for the hundred-yard walk that would bring them to their home. "If it won't upset you, that is. I'd like to see the spot where Daniel died."

"I NEVER SAW IT, YOU SEE."

Jonathan had placed my arm in his again, this time to walk through Hyrst's gardens toward its small apple orchard.

I was replete from a rather good Sunday luncheon and mellowed by Michael's sherry and a glass of wine, and the slight trepidation Jonathan's request had caused me at first had dissipated. After all, hadn't I visited the tree, both alone and accompanied, dozens of times in the last ten years? It would be pleasant to share the experience with somebody who had loved Daniel as much as I had.

"I'm surprised you didn't visit the spot after Daniel died," I said as we came to the high arch that led from the shrubbery.

Jonathan's shrug was nonchalant, but the muscles of the arm underneath my hand tightened. "The countess—do you know, I still think of your mama as the countess—refused to show it to me and wouldn't let any of the servants take me there. Gerry told me it was your mother who made sure no marker was placed by the tree. And I never saw you at all—the only soul who was right there when it happened. Your mama said you were too ill for visitors."

"That's possible," I agreed, my mind viewing the distraught girl of ten years ago as if she were another person, quite outside myself. We had entered the orchard, the breeze blowing from the sea suddenly diminishing as we passed through the arch in the hedge of neatly trimmed hornbeam, kept thick and high to shelter the venerable apple trees from gales and apple-poaching outsiders.

"Oh, that smell of apples." Jonathan halted, sniffing the air appreciatively.

I laughed. "Yes, it takes me right back to my childhood. Whitcombe receives several bushels of Hyrst apples every year, and Mrs. Foster knows to make her apple charlotte for me at least once a week until they run out. Picking must have been going on for weeks by now, but as you can see, there's plenty of fruit left."

"I feel like Adam in the Garden of Eden." Jonathan let go of my arm to reach for a ripe fruit.

"No, no—" I darted forward to stop him from picking it. "Those are better for cooking. Try that one."

I pointed to a tree laden with red-streaked fruit. We both laughed as Jonathan grabbed at a particularly good-looking apple and several more plummeted downward, narrowly missing us.

"No, don't pick them up." Once again, I interrupted Jonathan's intention. "They bring in the fattening pigs twice a week to eat the windfalls so we don't end up with wasps everywhere. Those will be bruised now and can't be kept."

"You can tell I'm not country-bred, can't you? Here—at least I managed to secure the best-looking one." Jonathan handed me the apple. He watched as I inspected it for worm holes and took a bite, then laughingly took it back and sank his strong, white teeth into the same spot. "Delicious." His smile was now decidedly flirtatious.

I waited until he had eaten the fruit—protesting, when he tried to give it to me again, that I'd had quite enough to eat at luncheon—before I recalled him to the purpose of our visit.

"It was over here, under this tree."

I led him to a lichen-spotted specimen that might have been indistinguishable from the others to nearly everyone else. It sported only a few apples high in its branches, the rest having been recently picked. For some reason, I always remembered it was the cooks' favorite for making apple jelly —probably because I hadn't touched that preserve for five years after Daniel's death. The grass below it was scattered with leaves and small pieces of twig dislodged during picking, which suddenly struck me as sacrilegious. Nonsense, I told myself, it was just grass.

"He just sort of—folded in two." Standing where Daniel's body had lain, I felt the weight of memory bearing down upon me. "He stopped—we had been running, playing like children—and frowned, then simply folded into the grass. I thought he was larking around at first. I was standing there."

I indicated a spot on the grass between the rows of trees, now trampled by the pickers, some fifteen feet away. "I was having trouble catching my breath. I sort of gasped at him not to be an idiot, to stop playing the fool, something like that, and didn't move toward him until I could breathe more easily. And then I saw."

"He was quite dead?" Jonathan bent to pick up a leaf, smoothing it between his fingers, his handsome face blank with sorrow.

"His eyes were open." I swallowed. "They were just staring at nothing. His lips were blue." I had still been smiling when I turned his head toward me, and that moment—that face—had haunted my nightmares for years after that day. "They told me later his heart had just stopped. I knew he was dead. I knew there was nothing I could do. Absolutely nothing. I screamed."

I heard my screams in my head. "I wanted to run for help, but my legs wouldn't move. All I could do was scream and scream till at last somebody came. I don't remember much after that. I think I fainted."

My life from that moment on had been a dark jumble of bad dreams. My sisters coming to see me, saying words I couldn't hear. Mama giving me remedies to calm me and help me sleep; the bitter taste of the herbs. Long hours slumped in an armchair in Mama's herb room at Hyrst, watching her intent face as she worked, sometimes helped by little Susan Hatherall with the simpler tasks because I would not or could not do them. Papa, grave and kind, talking to me about heaven. The darkness of the rooms where I brooded, the curtains closed, no longer wishing to go outdoors—I, who had lived for fresh air and mud and sand and sea.

I shook my head violently to dispel the memories, shuddering. Jonathan laid a hand, gentle as a lover's kiss, on my shoulder. "I'm sorry to make you relive that terrible moment," he said quietly. "Thank you for being brave enough to show me the place."

I took a deep breath. "It was a long time ago." The darkness had left my eyes. I could hear a blackbird singing, Michael's children playing in the garden nearby. "It was May, of course; the trees were losing their blossoms." Now I could smile again, if tremulously. "The petals were falling like snow." They had fallen on Daniel's face.

I looked up at Jonathan, feeling my smile become more natural. "After I married Justin, I brought him here to show him the falling petals. He let me talk about Daniel." Arm in arm, Justin and I had watched the petals fall, laughing as we tried to catch them, and I had felt more peace than I had known in years. Now I could almost see the years peeling away like leaves, love and pain and loss and love again, reminding me I could love anew in defiance of death.

"I'll have to come back to Hyrst and see it for myself next twenty-third of May," Jonathan was saying. "I wonder if Michael would mind if I brought something to mark the spot?" Turning away from the tree, Jonathan placed a hand under my elbow to steer me toward the far end of the orchard, where a large bench had been placed. "I don't know what—a stone, perhaps. A boulder, I mean, or a simple marker, not some ghastly carved thing. Dan wouldn't want a weeping angel."

I'd commissioned a weeping angel for Justin's memorial, but Jonathan wasn't to know that. "What a good idea," I said as I sat down on the long, high-backed bench. "Are you planning to come back to England often?"

Jonathan seated himself in the other corner of the bench, crossing one leg over the other. "I think I may return to England for good," he said. "I like India well enough, but I feel I've exhausted its possibilities, so to speak. Besides, it's only by good luck I've managed to avoid being killed by cholera or snakebite or just by a native with a grievance. I've seen plenty of chaps succumb to diseases you've never heard of in England. Bad diseases that end in an unpleasant death."

He grimaced, running a finger over the elaborate gold knots of his sleeve insignia. "Many chaps stay because of the luxury—when you're not in the field—the servants and so on, but that's never been an attraction for me. I've always preferred to have something to do, and I haven't let myself get soft and lazy like some fellows do. I think you either fall in love with India or you have to leave her in the end. Maybe I was in love with her for a few years, but I'm out of love now."

"Perhaps you're just old enough to be thinking of settling down?" I suggested.

"Probably." The white teeth showed again in his bronzed face. "Dashed if I know how I'll go about it, though. I haven't got enough to live like a gentleman. Despite the stories, we don't all come back with sacks of gold and jewels given to us by some grateful maharaja. I could get a job in the India Office, perhaps; they say you don't have to spend too much time actually working when you're in the Civil Service. I speak and write several native languages quite well, so they'd want me, and besides, Papa was a friend of Lord Kimberley, so I have a way in. Then I could be free to pursue the things I really like."

"And those are?" But I had a good idea.

"Adventure. New experiences. India seemed to offer so many, but I've done them all, dash it, apart from a few that are almost certainly injurious to one's health or sanity." He smiled. "I've always craved adventure."

"As did Daniel. He was so envious when you left. He always said we'd conquer the world together when we were married. After all, neither of us had anything to lose. He made me feel I could go anywhere in the world, but in the end I moved just a mile away from my family home." I shrugged.

"It's not too late." Jonathan stretched an arm along the back of the bench, his fingertips a few inches from my shoulder. "You have no husband or children to hold you back. Women travel, you know."

"But I don't think I'm that Helena anymore. Although, in fact, I've had some adventures since Justin died."

"Ah, yes." Jonathan tipped his head back to look at the sky, an action that tossed his thick mane of blond hair around rather attractively. "You're a lady detective now, so the papers say. Well, why can't you travel and be a lady detective too?"

"Because I want a home . . . and a child. Children." I felt the familiar longing, which always seemed to manifest itself somewhere in the pit of my stomach. "My own family. I was too young to feel that way when Daniel was alive, but then I married and that hope began to grow in me, and now it matters more than I usually care to admit. I'm ready to settle down—almost desperate to do so. I thought I'd found that sense of being rooted with Justin, but it was taken away from me. It's when the thing you really need is taken away that you truly understand how much you need it."

"I suppose you need a man to achieve your aims." Jonathan returned his gaze to me, his bright blue eyes intent. "Of course, men are always more inclined to wander than women."

"My father was so often absent from home that I grew up thinking it was the usual way of things, but now I realize I don't want to be left behind as Mama was. It made her what she was, perhaps—she was in charge of her own life, often in charge of Hyrst for all practical purposes, and—"

"—and was a force to be reckoned with. I remember." Jonathan raised his eyebrows, his expression ironic.

"Looking back, I don't think she was very happy." I frowned. "I don't believe having just Mama there was good for me and Michael. Children need a father in the house, even if they spend much of their day with nursemaids and so on. Papa was marvelous when he was home, but he did rather come and go."

"Well, he was a peer; doesn't Michael sit in the House of Lords, just the same?" Jonathan looked puzzled. "Men are simply more active in the world than women."

"But Michael regards any time spent away from his wife and children as a loss. He 'does his duty to the country,' as he puts it, but he never spends days and weeks away for sport or friends the way Papa did. He's a surprisingly domestic creature." I laughed. "How odd I should view Michael, of all people, as the paragon of steady fatherhood." I smiled as I heard Annabelle Alice's voice, high and clear on the breeze, raised in objection to something one of her brothers had done. "The children mean everything to him, and they know it. He may not be endowed with much natural kindness, but he's a wonderful example in his own way."

"My Papa was almost never at home, as you know."

Jonathan sighed. "Perhaps I spend my life figuratively looking for him." Then his expression changed, and he laughed. "Look how maudlin we're becoming." He gestured down the rows of trees toward where we had been standing. "It's this place."

"Yes," I agreed. "I often find myself musing over the past and the future here. Look at all the things I've told you, and we barely know each other."

"And all the things I've told *you*." Jonathan rose to his feet. "It's odd, since I've never lived here, but Littleberry and the Scott-De Quincys feel more like home and family than anything I've ever known."

For a second, he seemed to hesitate, but then the carefree smile returned, and he turned away from the apple-laden trees. He held out a hand to me, almost pulling me up from the bench. "Cousin Helena, I suspect there's more adventure in you than you know. You've proved that since you were widowed, haven't you? You've simply been under the influence of quiet country domesticity for too long, and I'm just the man to shake you out of it."

"Really?" I matched his insouciant tone. "Cousin Jonathan, perhaps *you* could learn something from this country domesticity. Weren't you just talking about a post in the Civil Service? What could be steadier than working for Her Majesty's government?"

"Hmmm." He narrowed his eyes as he settled my hand on his arm, resting his fingers on mine for a little longer than was necessary. "You make a good point. Here's my bargain: I will encourage you to regain your sense of adventure, and you will help me find which direction I should take in this funny old country. Maybe I should start by looking for a rich wife to make all the other adventures possible."

We both laughed and were as merry as cousins should be as we walked toward the sound of the romping children. But from time to time that afternoon, I caught a look from Jonathan that had something positively assessing in it. Was I the rich wife he had in mind? And had he introduced the subject of his craving for adventure so he could make it plain what he was offering? My feelings on both points were unclear to me.

20
THE TALE OF THE BUTLER

"Well, here's another disruption to our lives." I waved the note I had just opened at Guttridge. "So much for quiet domesticity. And with Lady Hastings's arrival rushing toward us with—I was going to say the speed of an approaching train, but given the circumstances I think that's rather a tactless turn of phrase. Consider it amended."

"With Lady Hastings's arrival so near," Guttridge suggested. "We still have a week, my lady. What's the disruption?"

I looked up at Guttridge, who was casting an eagle eye around the morning room for any signs of carelessness in the new little under-housemaid who had been "given" the room as a trial; apparently, she was showing early signs of aptitude for her job. "It's from Fleetwood, the butler. All embroidered with many elaborate expressions of respect for the Scott-De Quincys in general and myself in particular. He says he's on his way to London again for a medical consultation—the duke *does* look after him well—and given the shortness of time for correspondence, he proposes to present himself at

Scott House tomorrow morning at ten thirty precisely, hoping I can receive him there. If able, might I wire him at the above address to confirm my presence, failing which, it's no trouble because the distance isn't great and his medical appointment isn't till two o'clock."

"Tomorrow?" Guttridge sounded indignant.

"He's quite precise about it being Tuesday, tomorrow, and not any other Tuesday. He concludes with many additional expressions of his humility and respects to my exalted self, et cetera. The address, of course, is the duke's London house. I imagine he also has the use of the ducal carriage to take him to Scott House and back, don't you?"

"I wouldn't be surprised." Guttridge lifted an ironic eyebrow. "Does he really expect you to go up to London at a moment's notice?"

"He apologizes profusely for that; apparently these arrangements are to suit the duke's convenience, which naturally outranks mine." I grinned. "It *is* what we wanted after all. Can you manage to get us up to Scott House early tomorrow morning?"

Guttridge managed. By nine thirty in the morning, having traveled from Whitcombe on the milk train, I was comfortably ensconced in Scott House's parlor, which had been unsheeted, cleaned, decorated with fresh flowers, and enlivened by a small fire, mostly, as Guttridge remarked, to take the damp off.

The doorbell clanged at ten thirty precisely, the housekeeper showing in a man who must once have had the build of a prizefighter. He still retained an impression of massive shoulders, and the dignified air of a man whose orders had been obeyed for decades, but age and infirmity were inexorably cutting him down. I had arranged for the most comfortable armchair to be placed by the fire for him and watched as he settled himself into his seat with a groan.

"I thank ye, my lady." He looked with satisfaction at the ponderous old room with its William-and-Mary furniture and Flemish tapestries. "I haven't seen this house since, oh, it must be your grandfather's time, when I was a footman. How is the present earl—that would be your brother, Michael, I think, my lady? I hope he's keeping well."

"He's in excellent health, thank you." I smiled at the old man, who was wheezing gently but keeping himself as upright as possible with the aid of a heavy stick. "He spends most of his time in the country. I'm afraid this house doesn't get much use these days."

"With Lady Odelia gone." He nodded, clearly not behindhand with the news. "Well, my lady, you'd like to ask me some questions?" He frowned slightly as he looked at Guttridge, who had seated herself by the writing desk, on which she had spread her notebook. "You and Miss—?"

"I'd like Guttridge to stay," I told him. "She will take notes."

The old man coughed significantly but made no objection to what probably struck him as a peculiar arrangement.

"Well, my lady, as I told the *police*"—Fleetwood's emphasis on the last word might have been a comment on my amateur status—"I never saw much of anything. I spent most of the journey at the forward end of the brake van, where there were two reasonably comfortable chairs by a stove. There was a sort of partition across, to make the area more snug, with windows high up and one in the roof for ventilation. The guard had his desk and seat by the brake in the biggest part of the van and a little extra fire for the winter, which wasn't lit. There was a contraption like a cupboard that they call an observation ducket at the rear of the van, for observing the length of the train when we were approaching the station. There was also an observation platform at the rear, open to the elements; you couldn't see it from the inside, there being no windows back there, but I saw it because I used the little privy they built there." He chuckled. "For emergencies only, the guard said, but begging your ladyship's pardon, at my age it's always an emergency. His Grace was very particular to have a van put on the train that would have everything I needed."

"You have a superb memory." This was a better description of the brake van than I'd had from Rampling.

"It's memory for detail that makes a good servant, my lady." The butler dipped his head in a small bow.

"Can you give us a list of the people on the train?" I asked. "Not that I imagine you saw much of them."

"I saw them at Euston." Fleetwood smiled a satisfied smile. "Many of them were kind enough to give me a how-d'ye-do. I've known some of them since they were babes in arms, and nearly all of them visited my pantry when they were little ones, as a treat. I was known for generosity with barley sugar and farthings."

His face softened at the memory, but he did not run off into reminiscences the way some elderly people did. He proceeded to give us an exact and careful account of all the house party guests, together with their servants, in scrupulous order of social precedence. Guttridge wrote it all down industriously; the housekeeper brought coffee, and I poured it for all of us. When I took Guttridge her cup, she was so absorbed in her task, her tongue sticking out of the side of her mouth, she barely acknowledged me.

"Of course, it would never have happened if that Lawther had been with his master." Fleetwood drew a wheezy breath. "I upbraided him about it later that day, my lady, but he swore hand on heart Lord Arthur had told him, in no uncertain manner, to 'leave him alone' and 'go back and stay with the grooms' and called him bad names besides. They didn't get on. And from what I've heard, my lady, he's skipped;

found a new employer straightaway and gone off to the Continent with him." He stopped for a fit of unpleasant-sounding coughs. "I'd have my suspicions if Lawther hadn't been spoken for by most of the servants as to where he was the whole journey long."

"Do you think there was anything suspicious about Lord Arthur's death?" I asked.

The old man thought about that for the space of some two minutes, drinking his coffee and mumbling his mouth around the taste of it, nodding in approval. "I do not, to tell you the truth," he finally said. "More likely, he jumped or just fell out due to the drink."

He looked directly at me, his expression suddenly sly beneath his heavy eyelids. "Perhaps it was providential, my lady. That boy would have ended up bringing his family into disgrace with his unnatural goings-on. There always are such things—I've seen it all in my time—but you didn't used to have all those wretched newspapers telling the whole world, did you? They should have whipped him when he was young, but the world's grown soft . . ." He tailed off into a series of coughs and breathless wheezes.

"Still, he's dead, and God rest his soul," he said when he had recovered. "I wouldn't say he was a *very* bad young man, despite his disgusting inclinations. Misled, perhaps. They all are, these days, the common people too. The menservants can be just as bad." His eyebrows, huge and bristling, drew together in a frown. "It's strange . . . I had a dream . . ."

He was silent for a moment and then shook his head. I saw Guttridge lift her eyes from her page, looking at me with a clear instruction to ask more in her expression.

"What was your dream?" I asked.

"I can't grasp it. I've tried." He lifted his stick, bringing it down on the floor in a series of soft thumps. "I can't stay awake these days, you see, not after midday. It grieves me to spend my days in such a muddle. But I'm ninety-one, my lady, if you'll believe it, and at my age a man may have an insignificant problem or two. At least when I'm awake, I can recall everything. His Grace still relies on me to teach the young men what's what."

"I imagine he does," I said. "You have a remarkably precise mind."

He nodded ponderously. "I've been lying in bed of a morning, trying to remember that day. I don't get up till seven thirty most days now, which is hard to think of after a lifetime of rising in the dark. If I'd been in my prime, every servant on that train would have known my eye was on them. Such a tragedy would never have happened."

21
MARMALADE AND LOBSTER

Guttridge and I spent all the time I could spare from Hawthorn Hall over the next two days writing up the various accounts of the day on the train; but, truth be told, Dederick's troubles receded into life's background as the days advanced and nothing else happened. We had, as we said to one another, done what we could.

Blanche's arrival at Whitcombe naturally meant that, in the ensuing days, Hawthorn Hall absorbed nearly every waking hour. Blanche became its tenant on the twenty-ninth of September, but since she did not want the discomfort of living in a house that was still being unpacked, and made such a fuss over the unpacking I was afraid the maids would give notice, in the end it was I, not Blanche, who supervised the process.

I also acceded to Dederick's request that I allow him a brief visit with his cousin Lydia since she and Sir John Durber were well acquainted with the local hunt and the shooting and fishing fraternities. It was a relief to have him gone; I suspected Dederick could not bear one more mealtime with his mother and aunt going endlessly over the contents of a house, and Blanche left me no time to take him anywhere.

When Guttridge pulled open my bedroom curtains on the morning of the fifth of October, I had been awake for at least an hour, staring at the barely visible ceiling, my mind running over and over all the small details of furniture and knickknacks, wondering if I had anything left to do at the Hall. Would Blanche be ready to move? Perhaps now I could finally visit Gabrielle Dermody, who had sent me a note several days earlier to confirm her return and invite me to tea whenever I liked.

"Good morning, my lady." Guttridge picked up my breakfast tray from the table. "Lady Hastings's maid asked me particularly to tell you Lady Hastings has ordered her trunks packed this morning. She expects to leave before luncheon, with apologies to Sir Edward for not staying to see him, but she's sure he'll understand." I had arranged for my brother-in-law Ned to eat with us, as a change from dining tête-à-tête with Blanche. "Apparently, the housekeeper sent over a note to say the kitchen is all in order and the new cook ready, and Lady Hastings can't wait to see it all."

There was an air of suppressed excitement in Guttridge's demeanor that was easily explained by Blanche's having made up her mind at last, and it infected me immediately. I sat up in bed, pulling pillows and bolster into place behind my back.

"That's excellent news." I smiled cheerfully at Guttridge as she positioned the breakfast tray over my knees. "Now I'm even more pleased I invited Sir Edward for luncheon. We can have a nice uninterrupted talk."

"Yes, my lady."

There was something in Guttridge's tone of voice that made me look up. "Guttridge, are you really that excited about Lady Hastings's departure? It's true, it'll be wonderful to resume our lives, and we have three whole days before Lord Hastings gets back, so we can award ourselves a small holiday." I thought about the prospect of complete freedom to do what I liked. "I suppose it *is* rather exciting."

"It's not just that, my lady." Guttridge bent to pick up the coffeepot.

I felt a qualm. "For heaven's sake, Guttridge, don't beat about the bush. If it's something that's going to disrupt our lives all over again, I should know about it straightaway. It's always best to take one's medicine in one gulp."

I picked up a piece of toast as Guttridge concentrated on pouring coffee and adding hot milk. I lifted the lid off the marmalade pot, sniffing appreciatively at the sharp fragrance of bitter orange before starting to heap it on the buttered toast. "Thank you, Guttridge. Now, out with your news. Don't make me wait a second longer."

Guttridge stepped back from the bed, her dark eyes gleaming. "Doctor Fortier is back in Littleberry, my lady. And he's not alone."

I exclaimed in annoyance as a blob of marmalade fell off my toast, which I was holding at the wrong angle. I was grateful for the distraction since my heart had given an enormous thump at Fortier's name. I fumbled the toast back onto the plate, getting marmalade on my fingers, and grabbed a spoon to scoop the sticky jam off the counterpane. I was waiting, I realized, for Guttridge to say the words, *He has a wife and child with him.* That must be what she'd been dying to impart.

"He brought a lady with him." Guttridge gently took the spoon out of my hand and gave me a napkin; I was getting myself and the counterpane stickier every moment. "The widow of his cousin, it seems, with a son. It was all round the town yesterday, they tell me, that he's going to marry her, but

I'm not so sure if that's truth or rumor. Why don't I bring a flannel for your hands, my lady?"

"I'd prefer to drink my coffee while it's hot."

I picked up my cup, concentrating hard on sipping my café au lait slowly and not letting any shred of feeling show on my face. My fingers were unpleasantly sticky, but the coffee was perfect, and drinking it gave me time to calm my jumping pulse. Guttridge, eyeing the mess I'd made, did not leave as she usually would, but stayed nearby to help me when I asked.

"The cousin and her son are staying with the Dermodys," she informed me. "Monsewer Fortier has taken the house opposite, the one that's been empty since old Mr. Herbert died. It's in apple-pie order, they say, and Mr. Herbert's niece is ever so glad to find a tenant she knows to be of good character. You can't be too careful with tenants."

"True. Mrs. Dermody will be so pleased to have her brother back safely," I said. "Now Lady Hastings is leaving, I'll make plans to accept Mrs. Dermody's invitation to tea and meet her cousin. How nice to have someone new in Littleberry."

The sharp glance Guttridge gave me suggested I hadn't fooled her for a moment, but she just nodded. I finished my last sip of coffee and put down my cup.

"I ought to get on with getting bathed and dressed, so I can see if Lady Hastings needs my help." I looked at my abandoned toast with a slight feeling of revulsion, sighing as I realized some marmalade had also fallen on my nightdress. "Guttridge, breakfast in bed is not always the luxury they make it out to be."

"Yes, my lady."

"I have indeed seen Fortier."

Ned put a lobster vol-au-vent on his plate, spooning over a generous helping of the sauce the footman held out to him. "In fact, I spoke to him about the hospital. Did you know he's taken a house of his own? The old Herbert place."

"I've heard." I took a small bite of lobster, watching as Ned dealt efficiently with his food.

"I suppose he's inherited enough from his father to live in his own house." Ned wiped lobster sauce off his bushy mustache. "More room for the Dermodys in their place now, eh? The rooms in that house are large, but not so numerous, and those children are growing fast. They'll need more space."

"But don't they have new guests?" I asked.

"Oh yes, the cousin." Ned shrugged. "A widow; French, of course. I think I saw her and her boy in the High Street. The lady was rattling away in French to her son, and none of it particularly complimentary to Littleberry, I believe. I got the impression she doesn't like England much."

That notion cheered me a little. "I imagine it's difficult, settling in a new country."

"Settling? D'you think she'll stay?" Ned grinned. "I can't see *her* enjoying a Littleberry winter."

I was becoming more and more intrigued, but Ned changed the subject. "Don't you want to hear the good news? Fortier is very interested in my proposition that he take a leading role in the hospital. Of course, he says he needs to think it all over before making any sort of commitment, but he looked like a man who'd been given a gift. I say, Helena, are you sickening for something? You're barely touching your lobster, and it's quite delicious."

I felt myself grow a little pink and cut into my vol-au-vent. "I probably ate too much breakfast." That was a lie. "It certainly would be wonderful to make some progress with finding doctors and nurses and so on, now the foundations are being dug. It makes it seem real to see all that activity at the top of Whitcombe Lane."

"Mmmm." Ned chewed industriously before continuing. "Fortier told me he moved into the Herbert house so he could have a proper consulting room and a separate space to operate; that room in the pottery's hard to keep warm in winter and cool in summer. He still intends to devote most of his energies to doing his rounds as before, to ensure the poorer people actually see a doctor in the first place. I told him the point of the hospital is to give ordinary folk somewhere to go when they can't be easily nursed at home and that we've consulted some London surgeons about how to equip a proper operating amphitheater, so we can train our own men. Ah, you should have seen his face when I mentioned *that*."

"I wish I'd been there. Although I don't imagine you'd have talked business in front of me."

"Why on earth not, my dear? After all, you donated the land, and you're one of our biggest subscribers. I don't see why a woman shouldn't be consulted on managing important matters. I always ask Gerry's advice. She loves giving it." He laughed. "Ah, that's better—a little animation in your face. You *are* all right, aren't you? You look a mite anxious."

"It's all this rushing around after Blanche." Another lie; Blanche had been remarkably well-behaved all morning. "So Dr. Fortier isn't planning to move to London now he's inherited a house there?"

"Not he." Ned laid down his knife and fork with a sigh of satisfaction. "I asked him, and he said he'd had enough of London to last him a lifetime. He was looking forward to an afternoon's proper riding, says the London parks were far too tame for him. Thank you."

This last remark was addressed to the footman who

removed his plate and would have earned a reproving glance from Gerry, but Ned didn't hold with treating servants as if they weren't there. The mingled fragrances of roast duck and spiced damsons were on the air now, and I tried to summon up some appetite. I was certain Ned would go home and tell Gerry I was sickening for something. And then Gerry would walk up the hill to Whitcombe for tea, to see for herself . . . But I was in perfect health, wasn't I? Except, perhaps, for my heart.

22
AN AFTERNOON'S RIDE

Ned was always busy, and I never expected him to linger after luncheon. Now Blanche had left, I had little to do. In the normal course of things, I would have gone to the herb garden or the workroom, but instead I wandered out onto the terrace to enjoy the sight of the sea, now brilliant turquoise under a sky from which the morning's clouds had vanished.

It was the constant demands on my time by Blanche, no doubt, that were making me restless. Not that I resented my ever-present family—far from it. I turned to look at my huge house, its brick walls mellow in the golden October sunshine, and breathed a prayer of thanks that for me, surrounded by people I loved, widowhood did not have to be lonely.

And yet it *was* solitary at times. Except for Mama—whom I could now visit every day without Blanche complaining *she* certainly couldn't stomach a daily visit and I would do better to keep *her* company—all the people in my life were on journeys of their own, in which I played the role of occasional helpmeet or diversion, never a constant companion. Even Thomas was busy with his tutor and his studies and helping Ned with the family business, and soon he would be gone to Cambridge.

I thought, as I had often done lately, of Jonathan Murray-Jones and his talk of adventure. Did he conceive of a wife as a partner in that adventure or as the angel of the hearth to whom he might return when his day's—or week's—or even month's—experiences were over? What kind of adventure could I share and still satisfy my own longings?

I turned back to the view of the sea, and a movement in the fields far below me caught my eye. It was the river path to Pincham, well frequented by walkers or riders who preferred a little mud to the turnpike road, with its noisy carts and carriages. The river where Justin had met his doom was high after the recent rain, glittering as it reflected the sun. Alongside it rode a large black horse in an easy, powerful canter, heading toward Pincham.

I knew that horse. I knew the rider. Watching until both horse and rider were out of sight, I turned away, pacing the terrace, feeling the imprint of bricks and gravel under the thin soles of my indoor slippers. I counted my steps carefully, the sounds of my footsteps and my breathing audible above the gentle soughing of the breeze, and when I reached three hundred, I turned again and walked rapidly toward the double doors that led into the house.

"Ask Guttridge to come up, would you?" I said to the first servant I saw. "And kindly ask Mank to get Sandy ready. I need a ride."

"We could go out to the shore, m'lady."

The lines around Mank's eyes deepened as he shaded them to look south. "The going might be better as the soil thins. Perhaps we could take the path that goes along by Scott's Folly? Then there'd only be that boggy bit by the gate."

We had spent the last half hour somewhat aimlessly hacking around the muddy paths that surrounded Whitcombe Hill, making occasional small talk about the weather, the sheep, and the recent harvest. Mank was my favorite groom, an older man who was spare in his frame and somewhat sardonic in his remarks, but somehow restful to be with. He was an agreeable companion on a ride, invariably patient with my whims and much liked by the horses.

I thought of the sea, no doubt rolling quietly onto the beach this increasingly still afternoon, and felt its pull on me as I always did, but I lifted my crop to point westward.

"No, let's take the Pincham path and get up to the high ground. We can trot around the lanes. Sandy likes it up there."

Mank said nothing, turning his horse in the direction I indicated and allowing Sandy to walk on past. The going was firm enough for me to direct my mare to trot, and we settled into a steady, unhurried pace.

The sun shone in my eyes as we headed along the river, past the irregular patch of ground, now thick with nettles, where the willow that had ensnared Justin's body in its branches had been burned. Past the spot where Susan Hatherall had given my husband a poisoned drink and where her father, Lucius, had held him down under the water. Love and loss again, just as in the orchard at Hyrst; if I lived my life out at Whitcombe, I would always have these memories with me, both the sweet and the bitter.

And then we had slowed to a walk, heading carefully uphill on the rough track that picked the surest way up what, in the time of the Romans, would have been tall cliffs overlooking the sea before hundreds of years of storms and silt had created the marsh.

We stopped to rest the horses for ten minutes when we reached the top but were soon in the straggling maze of lanes between the fields of the various small farms that produced the milk and cream for which Pincham was best known. Sandy pricked up her ears as I urged her into a trot; she liked the high hedgerows of hawthorn and briar and the well-made roads. The air was redolent of the homey smell of cows and the sharp, beery scent of hops, Pincham's other crop, now drying in the oasthouses.

The hedges, awaiting their autumn cut, were at their tallest. As I sensed Sandy beginning to tire and signaled her to walk, I began to feel somewhat closed in. Far from getting a good view of the countryside and any human life that might be there—as I had perhaps hoped—I could see nothing but hedge and lane. Only the occasional gate gave glimpses of fields or red-tiled farmhouses slumbering in the pleasant October afternoon.

I began stretching my back higher, trying to improve my view, but to no avail. Mank, whose horse was larger and who was riding astride, would have a better idea of what was happening around us, but I didn't want to ask him if he could see anyone every five minutes. Eventually, realizing Sandy had stopped—I had probably confused her by my unusual movements—I unhooked my free leg from the jumping horn of the sidesaddle and straightened the leg that rested in the stirrup, attempting to give myself a few extra inches of height.

The result was to confuse Sandy more, so she moved forward and began to turn while I was in a most precarious position. I flicked her gently with my crop to stop the turning movement and concentrated fiercely on not losing my balance as she shifted beneath me. Sandy snorted and put her ears back, turning her head to give me a disgusted look out of one lustrous brown eye.

"Sorry." As Sandy shook her head vigorously, I lowered myself back down into the saddle and looked around for Mank. The grin I was sure had been on his face a second before had vanished, but he stood up in his stirrups—how fortunate men were in not having to ride sidesaddle!—and peered around us.

"I'm wondering, m'lady, if I could visit my sister's house." He pointed with his whip down a lane that intersected with the one we were in, where a short row of cottages a quarter of a mile away housed workers from one of the larger farms. Mank's sister, a widow, watched the other workers' children and took in laundry. "I promised her I'd take off her bent door hinge next time I passed so I could take it to the smith. Perhaps you'd like to come with me—or you could talk to the doctor." He gave a jerk of his head in the opposite direction.

"The doctor?" I looked around us, sighing with frustration as, naturally, I still couldn't see a thing.

"The French physician. He's by the gate yonder, giving that horse a rest, no doubt. He'll have news from London, being lately arrived. Or else Sally would be pleased to see you and can give you some refreshment if you need it."

"She'll be busy, won't she?"

Mank's eyebrows, which were splendidly bushy, elevated in a silent reminder that a countrywoman was always busy, but he merely said it was Sally's ironing day.

"You go. I won't make Mrs. Stocks stand on ceremony when she has such a tremendous task to get through." I looked down the lane Mank had indicated, where I could just see the far end of a gate. "Give her my regards and tell her I'll come for a proper visit soon."

"I will, m'lady." Mank also looked down the lane, a sardonic expression on his lean face. "I'll take you to the doctor; you'll be safe enough with him. I won't be long at Sally's."

FORTIER, WHO CAME INTO VIEW LEANING ON THE GATE, staring at the damp dirt of the lane, looked up as we approached. His gaze, unfocused, suddenly sharpened, and he straightened himself up, removing his booted foot from its position on one of the gate's bars. Beyond him, Lucifer was cropping the rich grass of a field empty of cows, the sound of the green blades tearing under his strong teeth quite audible as soon as we drew to a halt.

"Lady Helena." Fortier's voice sounded strange to me for a moment, and then even more strangely familiar. He went to lift his hat, realized he was bareheaded, and smiled at his mistake; we were suddenly back on the friendly footing we had maintained in London. I smiled back.

Mank merely tugged his cap at Fortier as he slid easily off his horse to help me dismount. He loosened Sandy's girth a little as I placed the loop of the skirt of my riding habit over the button on its waistband, then gave my mare a gentle smack on her rump. Sandy needed no further encouragement; Fortier was opening the heavy gate, and she headed straight toward Lucifer. Mank, with a brief murmur, stepped into his horse's stirrup and pulled himself into the saddle with a graceful, unstudied effort.

"He's gone to visit his sister." I felt some explanation for Mank's abandonment of me was necessary. "I hope I'm not disturbing you."

"I'm not . . . I was just . . . Lucifer needed a rest."

Fortier muttered something under his breath as he struggled with closing the gate, which needed repairing. I laughed as Lucifer, who had turned toward us as soon as he'd heard our horses, sniffed at me and Sandy, then nibbled gently at my mare's neck. The two of them ambled off together to find the best grass.

"You're not in black," Fortier remarked. We had both remained near the gate, watching the horses.

"Guttridge had this made for me last month, and thought I should try it. After all, it's less than a month till I go into half mourning."

I brushed at the sleeve of my dark blue riding habit, rather nicely trimmed with royal blue piping and matching buttons, and then realized Fortier's own sleeve and the hat he'd hung on a fresh growth of elder sported deep bands of crape.

"But you—I'm so sorry about your father. I saw Gabrielle in London, but there was another visitor, and I never got a chance to ask: Did he suffer much?"

"I did all I could." Fortier smiled briefly. "I must thank you again for all the herbal preparations you sent me. Father always remembered it was you who provided them and was grateful. He mentioned you close to the very end. It wasn't an easy death, but he bore it with patience and dignity, and his last hours were peaceful."

"I'm glad."

Fortier just nodded, and there was silence again between us until I asked: "How was France?"

Fortier's face fell, and something inside me fell too. He turned toward the gate, grasping it hard enough to turn his knuckles white. He was going to tell me he would have to marry his cousin and it was too late.

There was a long moment during which I was aware of everything around me. The faint clinks of the horses' tack, the clamor of a family of sparrows in the hedge, small rustlings in the grass, the distant cry of a farmer herding his cows. The smells of the countryside, grass and mud and decaying leaves. I had turned toward Fortier, waiting. Ready to take my medicine at one gulp.

"Louise has agreed to pass as a widow for now," he said at last, and the heaviness inside me lightened a little. Yet Fortier's mouth tightened, and at length he blurted out, "She insists I marry her."

I realized I was trembling. "And will you?"

"I don't want to." Fortier's voice was very soft, but then he turned his head to look at me and said more forcefully, "You know what I want. I was standing here unable to think of anything but you."

My heart soared.

"I feel farther away than ever from being able to court you," Fortier continued. "Even though one obstacle—that of my financial position—has been removed. I can afford to live as an entirely independent gentleman now and still do the work I know I was born for. It has weighed heavily on me that I might have to become a society doctor just to hold my head up as a marriage prospect. But Father was better off than I'd realized. I can even keep the house in London." He gave a rueful smile. "A fact of which Louise has made much. She wants to live in London. It's not been an easy few weeks."

"I can imagine." My sympathy for Fortier was giving way to a strange clarity of purpose. The path ahead of me, so indistinct for so long, now seemed quite certain.

"And what about you?" Fortier looked sidelong at me. "I hear you have a cousin of your own in the vicinity. The brother of your Daniel. He's the talk of Littleberry for his looks and his regimental uniform."

It wasn't apprehension that was making me tremble now, I realized. I smiled. "Yes—he's handsome and charming and most definitely flirting with me."

"Hmph." Fortier turned away a little.

"I didn't say I was flirting with *him*."

I waited for him to turn back to me, and then I did what, if I had been telling the truth to myself, I'd known all day I was going to do. I stood on tiptoe to reach up to Fortier and kissed him hard on the mouth.

23
ROMANTIC RAPTURE

Fortier's gasp of surprise parted his lips, and I did not hesitate to use my advantage. I pressed my mouth closer to his and, with some difficulty because of our relative heights, wound my arms around his neck. He might, of course, cast me off, shocked at my forwardness; but I was no maiden, and if he were the kind of prig who would think me fast, well, perhaps I was mistaken in him.

I wasn't. Fortier's hands clasped my waist most satisfactorily, our lips adjusted themselves into a more comfortable position, and within a second or two we were in a close and passionate embrace, kissing each other with all the ardor I had longed for since the day in July when Fortier had kissed me, gently, in farewell.

It was—there was no other way to describe it—heavenly to have his arms around me, to relish the intimacy of our joined lips and intertwined limbs, to experience the shivers of need and love I could now allow to run freely through my body and know he was prey to similar sensations. I knew what I had craved knowing, that he was mine, and for that blissful moment, nothing else mattered.

I wasn't sure how long it was before we came to our senses, but there are limits to what you can do in a damp field by a gate open to a public road. We left off kissing each other, and Fortier gathered me to him more thoroughly; my feet were not quite touching the ground, but we seemed to be managing all right.

"I've never been so happy in all my life," was his conclusion when he recovered the power of speech. "I thought—I really thought—all was lost. That you didn't love me enough to accept me in these damnable circumstances."

He loosened his grip a little, leaning away from me and lowering me to the ground so he could see my face. "You do love me, don't you?"

"I'm not in the habit of embracing men I don't love," I said indignantly, but I could not continue as Fortier was kissing me again.

"And your cousin?" he asked after an interval.

"Is a delightful man and in need of a rich wife. Our shared history could, in other circumstances, count for much. But he's not *you*." I looked deep into Fortier's amber-green eyes, darker now with passion. "And it's you I've been falling deeper and deeper in love with these last two years. You should thank Jonathan, actually."

"Why?" Fortier, who had been about to kiss me again, drew back a little.

"He was trying to make me see the attractions of a life of adventure—he and Daniel were never made to stay still in one place—but he made me realize my adventure was you."

Fortier was silent for a few moments, his grip on me loosening. "I may be more of an adventure than you bargained for," he said eventually, his tone grave. "For one thing, there can't be any official engagement until I've freed myself properly from Louise."

"I understand."

"And before things go any farther between us, I have to explain about Jacques." Now his eyes were wide with apprehension. "I must tell you the whole story straightaway. I've been putting off the day, dreading you might just walk away from me once you've heard it. If we're to marry, you must know what you're getting into."

"If we're to marry—mmmm." I reached up to run the back of my hand over Fortier's beard, which was smoother than I expected, and smiled up at him in delight. "I like the sound of that."

"You're distracting me." Fortier arrested the motion of my hand, turning it and pushing up my riding glove so he could kiss my palm and wrist in a way that turned my insides to water. "May I call on you in the morning? I can hardly make this particular speech in a field."

"You don't have to be formal about it. Call on me when you like—as often as you like." I laughed, delighted, as Fortier's lips found the tender skin of my neck just below my ear. "I hope you'll start thinking of Whitcombe as your home because I'd hate to leave."

I pushed gently against his chest to create a little distance between us. "I think I can hear a horse; that'll be Mank. He left us alone on purpose, if I'm any judge."

IT *WAS* MANK. I WAS GRATEFUL IT WAS NOBODY ELSE TO WHOM we had to explain our presence in a field with, no doubt, flushed faces. My groom dismounted, his expression unreadable.

"Are you ready to leave, my lady?" he asked as Fortier busied himself with opening the gate. "We ought to be getting back. We've been out a long time." He glanced at the sun, which was indeed sinking toward the tops of the hedges.

"And I have a weeping ulcer to see to." Fortier turned toward the horses. "One of my Pincham patients asked me to stop by his mother's house before I went home. Lucifer! Stop your flirting and come here. It's time we left."

The enormous horse, who was standing with his gleaming black head hung over Sandy's withers in an attitude of romantic rapture, nickered gently and ambled toward us, my mare following placidly. Mank watched them, a broad smile on his face.

"So you're still doing your doctoring, Your Grace?" he asked as Fortier caught at Lucifer's bridle. Fortier's eyes narrowed.

"'Doctor' or 'sir' will do nicely, Mank. You'd be doing me a favor if you could spread the word that I don't intend to go around calling myself a duke. I can't help inheriting a title, but I have no land to back it up, and I have an aversion to looking ridiculous. Besides, I'm the republican sort of Frenchman. I deplore the violence of our recent history, but I agree with its aims. And yes, I mean to keep working as a physician. A man needs a profession."

"Yes, sir. The folk round here will be glad to hear that. They've missed you."

Mank reached for Sandy and busied himself with tightening her girth, muttering sharply at her under his breath as she resisted his efforts by blowing out her belly.

Fortier, who had similarly been making sure Lucifer's saddle was properly tightened, watched me unhook the train of my habit and then, forestalling Mank's usual role, lifted me easily into the saddle. He surreptitiously caressed my trousered leg as he arranged my skirt, grinning as I blushed, and then stepped back.

"*À demain*. Look after her, Mank."

He retrieved his hat from its branch, stuck it on his head, and in a moment was in the saddle, turning Lucifer inland toward the turnpike road and urging the horse into a brisk canter.

Mank and I trotted sedately in the same direction. "He's a good man, the doctor, for all he's a Frenchie," was Mank's comment after about ten minutes had passed. "Better watch that stallion with Sandy, though. She's going to have her heat soon."

I nodded, but I didn't feel much like talking. Sandy's ears were pricked well forward, perhaps from eagerness for her stable; as we neared the road and the going became muddier for a short stretch, I slowed her to a walk and caressed her smooth brown neck. She bobbed her head and made her long, low whinny of contentment, and I had to resist the temptation to lean forward and hug her neck as I'd done to my ponies as a child, to enjoy the scents of sweat and straw, the animal warmth, the rough feeling of the mane against my cheek.

"Yes, sweetheart," I murmured to my mare as I put her back to a trot. "I'm happy too."

24
AN UNDERSTANDING

"Do you think my hair looks quite right in the front?" I made a face at myself in the mirror. "I look different today somehow."

"It's the same as always, my lady." Guttridge's long fingers twitched the curl I had displaced so it fell right again. "Now, the jet earrings, I suppose."

"Could we go over my clothes again later?" I asked and saw Guttridge's eyebrows shoot up in surprise. "I'm worried half mourning won't suit my coloring. Is there anything we can do to brighten me up, do you think?"

I looked carefully at the reflection of my glossy light brown hair, parting the tresses here and there to be sure there were no white strands. "Perhaps some new jewelry?" I sighed. "I look dull."

"You look perfect, my lady." Guttridge sounded hurt. "I'm sure nobody could criticize you for not being well dressed."

I turned to face her. "I'm sorry. Don't think I meant to imply you're being anything less than your usual excellent self. I suppose I'm just more conscious of my looks this morning."

"Are you expecting a visitor?" An unusual expression of curiosity stole over Guttridge's face. "If you don't mind me saying so, you were quite in a dream yesterday evening, and now you seem a bit—well, 'agitated' is not quite the word."

"Oh, I think it is." I leaned my chin on my hand, staring at my regular features in the mirror. "Agitated, excited, flustered, disquieted—an entire thesaurus of emotions."

I caught Guttridge looking at my reflection and held her gaze for a long moment.

"Well, I never," my lady's maid murmured quietly. And then, a little louder: "Is it that you're expecting some gentleman to declare himself? Because a small posy, conveniently placed on a table, say, can be held against a black dress to fine effect and used to convey either encouragement or the opposite." She made motions with her hands to illustrate her point. "I could get Taylor to make you a nice tussie-mussie, if you like."

"The declaration's already happened." I turned my head from side to side, trying to catch the skin around my eyes in the best light for looking for lines. "He's not going to marry his French cousin."

I stopped fussing over my appearance and caught Guttridge's gaze again. "I hope you approve. Of course, nothing can be official until the matter of the cousin is completely cleared up."

"Hmph." Guttridge's mouth twisted, then gave up the struggle and broadened into a smile. "Well, it's not my place to approve or disapprove, my lady, but I'll allow he's a good man and a gentleman, for all he's both a French duke *and* a physician. I wish you both very happy."

And with that seal of approval, I finally gave up looking at myself and went downstairs to sort through my correspondence. I had made very little progress with that task when one of the footmen showed Fortier into the morning room.

I dropped my letters immediately, holding out my hands to him the moment the footman had left. "I've told Guttridge," I announced. "So I can't go back now."

"I've spent the entire night awake, wondering if it were really true," Fortier admitted. "I haven't told anyone. I'm supposed to be having dinner at Dermody House tonight, so I suppose it'll have to be then. I'm already starting to feel like Daniel preparing to enter the lions' den. Not for Gaby's sake, of course. She'll be delighted." He kissed my hands fondly.

"It's Louise you're worried about, I suppose."

"And Quinn. He likes you well enough, but as far as he's concerned, I'll be marrying into the enemy camp."

"Oh Lord. I hadn't thought of that." I wrinkled my nose. "Quinn Dermody will be hard to get past Gerry and Blanche too. I don't suppose the others will care all that much. I'll have Ned and Thomas on my side, I'm sure."

I raised my face to Fortier's. We seemed to be moving closer to one another, and I was beginning to anticipate, rather deliciously, a kiss. "Are you convinced of the reality of yesterday now, Fortier? All these thorny family problems have a distinct air of mundanity about them."

"I'll be quite convinced when you call me 'Armand.'" Fortier moved an inch closer. "Not that I want you to abandon 'Fortier' for everyday use." He let go of my hand to caress my face and hair, his fingertips moving over me as if learning me by heart. "'Fortier' makes me think you're addressing me as a friend or colleague, man to man, as it were; oddly enough, I find it delightful. Perhaps you could reserve my Christian name for our more intimate moments."

His hand was on the nape of my neck now, his thumb exploring the tender skin there in a way that was having an effect on my knees. What else could I say?

"Yes, Armand."

And our bodies melted together, but not, unfortunately, for long.

"Well, I suppose that was inevitable."

Michael's harsh voice naturally caused Fortier to stop kissing me and look up. He rather reluctantly released me from our embrace, and I was just as reluctant to turn and face my brother. My entire body was tingling, and no doubt it was that too quickly suppressed energy that put the strident note of annoyance into my voice.

"Honestly, Michael—"

I stopped short, realizing the odious Brandrick was just behind my brother. They were exactly the same height, so for a moment, to my passion-dazed eyes, the man almost looked like Michael's shadow.

On reflection, I supposed it was natural enough for Michael to walk into my morning room, in the morning, and expect to find me industrious at my correspondence, not kissing someone. "What do you mean, inevitable?" I resumed in a somewhat politer tone of voice.

Fortier, meanwhile, had stepped forward. "Good morning, Lord Broadmere, Mr. Brandrick."

He offered his hand to both. Michael made his usual gesture of allowing a brief touch and then snatching his hand away as if it had been burned; Brandrick shook Fortier's hand heartily, the slight smile on his face quickly brought under control.

"Good morning, my lady; Doctor." Brandrick greeted us in turn. He hesitated over "Doctor," and I suddenly knew Mank had already communicated Fortier's preference when it came to titles to the servants' hall at Hyrst, from which it would have quickly reached the land manager's ears.

Michael, of course, ignored the formalities. It was all Julia could do to get him to say how-d'ye-do to the most important people in a room, and by now the county had accepted his eccentricities. He addressed himself to me, ignoring Fortier's greeting.

"You know the definition of 'inevitable,' don't you? I mean, Odelia has been telling us all you're transparently—"

"Michael!"

I barely stopped myself from stamping my foot. In front of Brandrick, of all people. Yes, the man was Michael's land manager, not a servant, but he had started out as a *gardener* at Hyrst, for goodness' sake.

Michael opened his mouth, no doubt to say something else he shouldn't, but Brandrick stepped forward and placed some papers on my writing desk.

"Perhaps you'd like to look at these later, my lady." His voice, admittedly quite cultured with just a faint Sussex burr, was a pleasant contrast to Michael's plangent tones. "We came by to discuss my proposals for this year's breeding since it's getting to that time of year, but there's no hurry. I'll run down to Dene Farm."

He was gone from the room in an instant, leaving me to face two men of whom I was extremely fond, for different reasons. They were a study in contrasts. Michael's blond hair, blue eyes, and rather showy Scott-De Quincy looks lit up the room against Fortier's dark, short hair and neat, close-cropped beard, while Fortier's compelling amber-green eyes were the most striking feature in a face that, while handsome—daily more handsome in my eyes—did not insist on attracting attention the way the Scott-De Quincy "air" did.

Michael was about an inch taller than Fortier, and more solidly built; because of his clumsiness, he always seemed to take up more space than he actually did, while Fortier's neat, muscular slenderness was somehow far less obtrusive. Despite their many differences, I had realized, in the course of recent events, that Michael liked Fortier; that was a rare achievement since Michael's liking was not easily won. Standing together, they looked like allies, if not friends—just as well, given Fortier's next words.

"I suppose—I mean, I would like to ask you for Helena's hand in marriage," he said, a little awkwardly. "We don't intend to announce our engagement formally until I've cleared up some family matters, which I'll explain in a moment, but we have an understanding."

He held out his hand to me; I took it, squeezing his fingers hard. Michael simply shrugged and dropped heavily into the nearest chair.

"Why are you asking *me*? Helena's sensible enough—and wealthy enough, come to that—to do as she likes. I don't imagine she'd listen to me anyway. And as I was trying to say, Odelia told us she's in love with you. Helena is, I mean." He shrugged again. "She has a lot more money than you do, I think, but that's going to be the case with most men who want to marry her, isn't it? It all belongs to her for life under Justin's will, you know. He made it hard for her to sign it away."

"Fortier—Armand—has enough to live on, Michael." I rolled my eyes in exasperation. "He's asking you because you're the head of the family, heaven help us, and Mama's not able to give an opinion."

I wondered fleetingly whether Mama would have approved of Fortier and concluded she possibly wouldn't.

"All you actually need to do," I continued, "is congratulate us and welcome Armand to the family. It would be nice if you could do that. Unless you have any objections."

"I can't think of any." Michael rose and stood about four feet away from us, his desire not to have to get closer apparent from his stance. "I've always said you should marry again, haven't I? And Julia likes . . . Armand, and I listen to her, you know."

He took a deep breath and stuck his right arm straight out in front of him, his hand aimed rigidly at Fortier. "On behalf of the Scott-De Quincy family, welcome to—well, to the Scott-De Quincy family. I hope you've stopped running off to France now."

Fortier stepped forward and shook Michael's hand carefully. Michael tolerated it this time and even gave me a peck on the cheek before stepping back to his former distance.

"I—I have something to tell you." Fortier frowned. "I probably should have told you before asking for Helena's hand, in case it changes her mind."

"It won't." I put my hand in Fortier's again, and he turned and looked at me.

"You can't promise that, and I won't make you. You need to know what you're getting into."

"Heavens, now you're making me nervous."

"Can't we have some coffee?" Michael dropped into the chair again. "Ring the bell, Helena, for pity's sake."

But it was Fortier who stepped to the bell and then handed me to a seat. He was looking at me as if he feared he might never see me again.

"It can't be that bad." I reached out a hand to make sure he sat near me.

"Unless you killed someone." Michael looked at the ceiling, considering. "Or are going to kill someone, I suppose." An interested expression stole over his face.

"Michael!"

But Fortier was laughing, and my annoyance—and perhaps a tinge of fear—dissipated. "Nothing like that," he said. "I'm just mixed up in something that may change the course of history."

25

THE SHADOW OF THE PAST

At this interesting juncture, the footman entered, and I ordered coffee. The pause made Michael fidget, but to his credit he almost stopped moving when Fortier began to speak. Only the movement of the fingers on his right hand, scratching at his palm, suggested that he too might be a little apprehensive about what Fortier was going to say.

"You know we—Louise and I—brought a child to England with us?" Fortier waited for Michael's nod; of course, the news would have reached Hyrst. "A boy of thirteen. Jacques." He smiled. "Almost a man, really. He's not related to us."

"So the question is, why is he with you?" Michael nodded. "I hope you'll give me all the details. I dislike it when people assume one knows things. And don't make classical allusions. Chap in the Lords kept talking about Sisyphus when he was supposed to be talking about Egypt, and I caused a bit of a disruption when I asked him to explain *exactly* what the one had to do with the other. People were laughing."

"I will avoid classical allusions." Fortier's face remained grave, only a twitch of his mouth suggesting a contrary emotion. "Let's go back to the Siege of Paris in 1870 and a hotheaded boy—myself—who, when France declared war on Prussia, begged and pleaded to be allowed to serve his country by traveling from England to France and offering himself as an apprentice physician. I'd been studying medicine, you see, and thought I knew enough to be useful. I didn't know as much as I thought I did, but I learned very fast."

Another pause ensued as the coffee arrived. I secured an extra lump of sugar for mine, in case I needed bucking up, and watched Fortier carefully as he continued, his eyes thoughtful.

"I called on my father's cousin Louis de Maival—he did not use the name 'Fortier'—as soon as I arrived in the city, and met him and his daughters, Mireille and Louise, for the first time. It surprised me, to be honest, how—well—aristocratic they were. I mean, I knew my father was a duke, even though he didn't use his title, but we had never stood on ceremony the way that family did. It was if the *Ancien Régime* —I beg your pardon, the Old Regime from before the Revolution—had never vanished." Fortier had clearly remembered Michael did not speak French.

"It had taken me a little while to get my papers in order and secure travel to Paris, as you can imagine, and by the time I arrived, the war was going badly and the Prussians were besieging our people at Metz. The surgeon to whom I'd carried a letter of introduction advised me to remain in Paris, which was perhaps wise. Within a matter of days, the emperor had surrendered to the Prussians at Sedan, the empire was overthrown, and the republic proclaimed."

"And the empress had fled to England." I couldn't help interrupting. "That was thirteen years ago; about the time when Jacques was born?"

"Exactly." Fortier smiled. "I'm trying to get to Jacques as

fast as I can. By the time the siege of Paris began—the new republic refused to surrender to the Germans, if you remember—I was so busy as an apprentice surgeon I almost forgot my cousins. My days were long, exhausting, and more exciting than I had dreamed they could ever be."

I watched Fortier's animated face with a feeling that approached pride. I was not marrying an unadventurous man—that I already knew—but I wished I'd known the ardent boy of those years.

"I saw nothing more of my cousins till Christmas," Fortier continued. "On Christmas Eve, a messenger brought a note summoning me to their house. I admit, I went there mostly in the hope of getting something good to eat." He grinned. "Rations were short by then. But they gave me coffee made from acorns, and probably worse, and a very meager portion of food and more or less told me the family's honor depended on me helping Louise escape from Paris with a baby who had been entrusted to their care. His wet nurse had almost no milk, and besides, news of the child's presence in their house had spread, and they no longer trusted their friends and neighbors." He took a deep breath, letting it out slowly before continuing. "The baby, you see, was—they said—the direct descendant of Louis the Seventeenth, and thus the rightful King of France."

A brief silence ensued—my mouth was hanging open in astonishment—before Michael exploded.

"Stuff and nonsense!" He glared at Fortier, continuing indignantly, "By Louis the Seventeenth, you mean the dauphin, of course, who never bore that title officially. He died in captivity when still a child."

"'Stuff and nonsense' was more or less what I said." Fortier shrugged. "I didn't believe a word of it. I didn't want to leave Paris either. Despite the dangers of the siege and the scarcity of food, the work I was doing fascinated me . . . and I was embroiled in my first romance." He smiled at me, a little apologetically. "But my cousins believed the story implicitly, and somehow I found myself at the Gare du Nord, climbing into the basket of a hot-air balloon with Louise, a baby boy, several sacks of mail, and a man whose name I never learned. It was New Year's Eve."

"A *hot-air balloon*?" Now it was my turn to rise halfway out of my seat with incredulity. If it hadn't been for the undoubted existence of Louise and a thirteen-year-old boy, I might have taken Fortier for a fantasist or worse.

"Hot-air balloons weren't that unusual during the siege." Fortier's face was so grave I sat down again, feeling a little ashamed of my unbelief. "I used to cheer when I saw them in the skies over Paris because each balloon meant some vital correspondence or papers had escaped our besieged city, sometimes even an important passenger. I never knew how my cousin Louis arranged passage for us on one of those marvels. The wonder of seeing the buildings below us become smaller and smaller almost made me forget my reluctance to leave Paris." He smiled, but it wasn't a happy smile. "Louise was terrified."

"Hardly surprising." Michael, who as a child had been so terrified of heights he was scared to mount a horse, looked disgusted.

"We never saw Louis or Mireille again. They were both dead by the time peace was restored to Paris, but we didn't know that for months; of course, nobody knew how to find us."

"What proof do you have of the child's parentage?" Michael, clearly not interested in the fate of Fortier's cousins, leaned forward. "Were you given any tokens by which he could be identified?"

"Nothing. Nothing but a story." Fortier's mouth twisted. "I understand some form of proof made its way to England by a process that took years and involved some ten people, at least five of whom met untimely ends."

"Which might suggest there's something in it." Michael looked interested.

"I'll admit Jacques bears some resemblance to the engravings of the royal family Louise collects." Fortier sighed, nodding his thanks as I handed him his replenished coffee cup. "We were told nothing. Perhaps that was deliberate, leaving us as innocent pawns of a conspiracy of—who? My cousin Louis was probably the only person who could have told us, and he was dead."

"Was the baby given the name Jacques at birth?" I asked.

"He had no name when he was entrusted to us." Fortier drained his cup and rose, pacing the room. "No papers. Nothing."

"But he was important enough for someone to arrange passage for him on one of the precious balloons," Michael said.

"Exactly. With two idiotic innocents who thought they were the heroes of a Dumas novel. At least I did." Fortier's gaze was upon me. "He continued to be important enough for strangers to appear on Louise's doorstep occasionally in the ensuing years. Once with a most useful false record of the child's birth. We have long thought the date might be correct."

I frowned and saw Fortier's expression change to apprehension, but my question was a practical one. "Why didn't you bring Louise and Jacques to England before now?" I was thinking about Fortier's trips back and forth across the English Channel. "Surely, that would have been better than leaving them for long periods while you were in England? And perhaps safer for Jacques."

"Not necessarily." Fortier's answer came swift and vehement, and I saw that Michael was also shaking his head.

"England has always been where those opposed to whatever regime is current in France gather their forces."

"The Revolution made France unstable, and it's been that way ever since," Michael said. "If you want an argument in favor of a sound monarchy, you only have to look at the French; in every crisis, there are at least two parties behind the door waiting to seize power. The present republic probably won't last long."

I held my breath; that was exactly the sort of thing Michael would say at the dinner table, usually provoking an argument. My brother, a highly intelligent man despite his inability to read or write, had an excellent grasp of politics but absolutely no grasp of diplomacy. Yet Fortier just shrugged and went on with his story.

"Our balloon landed a few miles north of Le Mans, and our guide put us on an ancient diligence traveling toward Rouen. He was very keen to dissociate himself from us, I believe. The journey north was dreadful." He shuddered. "I don't want to tell you what it was like being strangers in the countryside with a starving baby when the whole country was turned upside down by war and defeat. I'm surprised Jacques survived. I'm amazed neither of us had our throats cut and that only some of our money was stolen. We eventually found sanctuary in the village of Clouville, about twenty miles from Rouen, where nobody ever guessed at the link between the name Fortier and my illustrious ancestor the Duc de Maival. Louise spun a tale of a secret marriage and flight from enraged parents as an excuse for our presence in the village, and then, when I insisted on returning to England, to avoid looking like an abandoned wife she came up with the story that I had enrolled as a ship's doctor. She has a talent for elaborating a convincing narrative." He grimaced. "I do not. But neither have I ever had the callousness—or self-preservation, perhaps—to walk away from a woman who had no other male relatives and a little boy who soon began to call me 'Papa.'"

"So you kept going back," I said. "To keep them safe."

The smile that Fortier gave me as he seated himself again soon vanished as he slumped low in his chair, supporting his head on his fist as if wearied by telling his tale. "For the first few months, Louise counted on being reunited with her father and sister, and she barely protested against my return to England, the more so since my father was sending her money to live on. It wasn't until we learned of the death of my cousin Louis that I began to feel the trap closing around me." He smiled briefly at me again. "As you so perceptively say, Helena, from that point on I felt responsible for their safety. Yet Louise was no helpless fool; by the time Jacques was three, she had recovered her entire inheritance from her father, purchased a small manor house just outside Clouville, made some wise investments, and woven a convincing web of stories around herself. I simply had to appear from time to time to reassure the people of Clouville I had not abandoned her and Jacques. I despised the pretense, but what else could I do?" His face softened. "And I grew to love Jacques."

"And nobody came to claim him?" I asked.

"Good point." Michael sounded surprised that I had thought of this question before he did.

"Louise has received no visitors in connection with Jacques for the last five years." If possible, Fortier looked even more glum. "I believe she has begun to see herself as Jacques's sole protector. And now I have a title that could be useful to her. She appears to have abandoned her sworn intention to retire to a convent one day in favor of the fantasy of elevation to the position of foster-mother to a king."

"So *that's* why she wants you to marry her," I said, suddenly enlightened.

"She won't admit to it." Fortier let go of his hair, leaving it sticking up at an odd angle. "Her argument is that I've pretended to be her husband too long for her to marry anybody else—but she didn't *want* to marry *anybody*. Not until she realized Father was dying." He thumped the arm of his chair.

"Then you shouldn't have proposed to Helena." Michael sounded highly indignant on my behalf.

"He *didn't*." I realized as I said it that Fortier had, in fact, never proposed to me, and in the same instant I dismissed the thought as entirely irrelevant. "I forced the issue. And then you came in and found us kissing, and he did the correct thing and asked for my hand." I took a quick breath and continued before Michael, who had opened his mouth to argue, could speak. "And as you've already pointed out, I can marry whomsoever I want."

"I did say that." Michael looked around the room as if seeking somebody to appeal to; his gaze settled on Fortier, the only other person present. "But *you* said Helena could change her mind. You see, Helena, it's not too late to find a different husband."

"Oh, good grief." I buried my face in my hands. I would count to twenty; I would *not* start shouting at my brother. But my mood changed when I realized Fortier had crossed the room to me, kneeling at my feet.

"He's right," he said simply. "And I'm so very sorry I didn't tell you this whole story before, Helena."

"I didn't give you a chance to tell me." I felt suddenly weary. "But, Fortier—"

"I don't want you to say anything now." His voice strengthened. "You may feel quite differently once you've thought it all through. All I ask is that if you conclude you don't want to walk into this particular adventure, you tell me as soon as you've made up your mind."

THERE WAS SOMETHING ABOUT THE LINE OF FORTIER'S BACK AS he walked out of my morning room that made me think of a man going to the scaffold. I understood instinctively that he was torn between the inability to cease showing his love for me now that I had broken through his reserve—or iron self-control—and the inability to make his own needs a priority, as most men would even if they had to find an excuse to justify their actions. I would have to make this decision for myself.

I looked at Michael. My brother was unusually still, staring into the middle distance with a heavy frown of concentration. Was he committing everything to memory, or had he—as he so often did in the House of Lords, according to Julia—found a flaw in Fortier's story?

"I'm not going to give him up," I said after a few minutes' silence during which I came, with little effort, to my decision.

"I know." Michael straightened in his seat, still frowning. "This is a highly complicated matter. Do you know who died in August?"

"Who?"

Michael shifted his gaze so I received the full effect of his blue glare. "Does the world beyond Whitcombe not exist for you?"

Have you no intellectual curiosity? I took a deep breath. "I was very busy with Blanche in August," I said steadily. "And I have absolutely no idea what you're talking about."

But Michael had lapsed into silent thought again, and I knew better than to pester him for an answer. If this person who died was important to me, he would tell me in his own good time, and I had plenty of thoughts of my own to occupy my mind. Most of those thoughts were about Fortier. I would write him a note. After all, he had asked me to let him know as soon as I had decided.

A light rain pattered on the morning room windows, and I imagined Fortier walking through it. Or riding? But he had not been dressed for riding. He had walked up from the town, after a sleepless night, because he loved me and was afraid I would turn away from him.

Michael's grating voice interrupted my reverie. "You've walked into a difficult situation."

I had my answer ready. "I sometimes feel my life has been a collection of difficult situations. Especially since Justin died." I smoothed a hand over the black skirts I would only be wearing for three more weeks. "But I'm learning I can deal with whatever arises. My heart is too deeply involved, in this case, to do otherwise than marry Fortier."

"I know," Michael said again. "I do wish you wouldn't talk about your heart, though. It's such a nebulous concept because clearly you're not referring to the organ in your body. Why can't people be more precise?" He rose to his feet. "I'm going to find Brandrick."

"But Michael—"

"I can't explain it all to you right now." Michael glared at me. "I have a great deal of thinking to do and will have to have some things read to me, and it's difficult because I can't tell people why I want those things read, so it will take time."

I felt a sudden, unexpected wave of relief that Michael, at least, appeared to want to be my ally in what was apparently going to be rather a large adventure. "Very well," I said to my brother. "At least I know I can rely on you to be discreet."

"Obviously." Michael moved his cup and saucer back to the tray, and I winced at the sharp *chink* of china as he performed the action with his usual lack of grace. "If I find it necessary to say anything—to people in the government, you know, because you must realize this may be important—I will talk to Fortier first. To—Armand."

"He doesn't mind 'Fortier,'" I said to Michael's retreating back. I was definitely starting to feel happier. Indeed, the joy of the early morning was returning to me. "I'm absolutely on tenterhooks to meet Louise and Jacques now. Is that ridiculous? Especially as I can appreciate that Louise will have every reason to dislike me as soon as Fortier—Armand—tells them all we're going to marry. Which he will, once he hears from me."

"It's not ridiculous for you." Michael stopped at the door, turning to face me. "For you, it's always the people who matter. The . . . the . . . *emotions*." He twitched. "I've observed some people are like that, men as well as women. They don't *analyze* the way sensible people do."

"Yes, Michael, dear." For once, I did not feel annoyed with my brother.

"Hmph." But Michael shut the door more carefully and quietly than he was wont to do.

26
CHRISTIAN CHARITY

I wrote a note to Fortier, sending it to his house as I didn't know where he would be. I'd have to get used to that, I thought, since I was marrying a busy man. My note was couched in the most affectionate terms.

He must have had a long day of work since his reply did not arrive until I was about to join Thomas for sherry before dinner. It simply said: *I love you. A.*

I set off for church the next morning with a light heart, which became even lighter when I saw Fortier sitting in his usual pew toward the back of the nave with Gabrielle and Quinn Dermody. There were no strangers with them. It was highly likely Louise and Jacques would attend mass at Littleberry's newly built Catholic church.

When the service was over, I made sure I remained near the door. It was a while before I saw Gabrielle, elegant in a new black dress, but she spotted me straightaway and clasped my hands in hers.

"Armand told me." A squeeze of the hands and a smile of suppressed excitement accompanied her whisper. I shook hands with Quinn Dermody and held out my hand to Fortier, who kissed it.

"Will you have tea with us tomorrow?" Gabrielle asked. "You must meet my cousin and her son." She glanced at Fortier. "Armand has said he'll come. I've also invited India Walfort—do you remember her from London?—and her family since they all speak French quite well. They've just taken a house in St. Leonard's-on-Sea for a few weeks." She lowered her voice. "We thought it would be less awkward if we introduced you to Louise in company. Quinn will be there to glower at her if she misbehaves."

"Does she misbehave often?" I looked up at the tall Irishman.

"She has a tongue that could slice a cucumber." Quinn raised a black eyebrow. "Her hatred of England is only exceeded by her low opinion of the Irish, and she thinks we're bringing the children up badly." He grinned. "I'll make sure Mariette and Constantin are there as company for Jacques."

Gabrielle gave her husband a challenging look. "It's no wonder she's bad-tempered with you provoking her. I will glower at *you* if you misbehave."

"How did she take the news?" I asked Fortier, as quietly as I could.

"Badly." Fortier looked at his sister and brother-in-law, and I saw in their faces a reflection of his own rueful expression. "She didn't exactly make a fuss. After all, I'd told her more than once that I loved you." His lips twitched upward in answer to my smile. "But she did everything she could to make it clear she regarded this as a temporary development —a bout of insanity on my part. Still, it was a relief to have the moment over and done with."

"Have you told your sisters?" Quinn was looking over my

head to where, I knew, various members of my family were gathered.

"No." I looked up at Fortier again. "I'm not really ready to do that until we decide to make our engagement public. They'll only think they can persuade me out of it."

"It certainly won't please Lady Geraldine." Quinn's low rumble and significant look, followed by a polite bow of the head, made me turn to see Gerry, holding Ned's arm as he talked to a fellow wine merchant, staring in our direction. "She'll have something to say all right once the cat's out of the bag."

A qualm assailed me. Gerry's face was carefully immobile, her regular features arranged in their usual expression of cool superiority, the face of a woman who had ruled the upper reaches of Littleberry society since before I was born. But I could see her disapproval in the rigidity of her stance, the way her fingers were digging into Ned's sleeve. It must have been quite uncomfortable for him, but I knew he would not ask her what was wrong until they were alone. The cat was possibly halfway out of the bag already.

I ARRIVED PUNCTUALLY AT DERMODY HOUSE THE NEXT DAY but found the Walforts were there early, as was Fortier.

"Quinn took Cousin Louise and Jacques for a carriage ride, along with Mariette and Constantin," Gabrielle murmured into my ear as we embraced. "He promised to return late so you and Armand could spend a little time together, but it appears our Americans have other ideas. Still, you'll like them."

She was right. I took to the Walfort girls immediately; they were well educated, well read, and lively, with a naturalness of speech and movement that, although very free and easy compared to English ladies of the same age, never seemed hoydenish or out of place. Their dresses would be the envy of the county, and as for their hats—it really was about time I visited Paris again.

The young ladies were also most pleasing in form. Ellen, the eldest, was tall and very slender, like her mother, with the same dark red hair and blue eyes, and the world would no doubt judge her the beauty of the two. A considerable beauty, in fact.

Yet I found her face a little immobile, and after a while it was Lucy whose looks pleased me the most. She was shorter and rounder of face and figure than Ellen; her eyes were a lustrous dark hazel, with an abundance of thick, black lashes. Her hair was also dark, thick, and curly. Her best feature was her smile, the sweetest I had ever seen.

She undoubtedly took after her father, who had the same fine eyes, almost too sensitive for a man, and curling hair, the latter being well streaked with gray and cut short. He was clean-shaven, revealing a mouth that always seemed ready to smile and a deep dimple in his chin, and the overall impression I received was that of a very kind man.

It didn't take me long to decide I liked Marcus Walfort as much as the women of his family, perhaps even more. He was a quiet man, possibly in consequence of having such a talkative wife, but whenever he spoke, what he said was worth listening to. He clearly possessed a well-stocked brain; his ideas on art, literature, and music were plainly the result of extensive looking, reading, and thinking, not just derived from the opinions of others. Tall and solidly built, he had not run to fat, being fond—as a chance remark told me—of rowing and sailing, indeed any activity that involved water.

Our talk eventually came round to the following Season, the topic being introduced by Mrs. Walfort, who told us they were considering taking a house in London for the summer.

"Mrs. Dermody told me you have a house in St. James's," she said to me, "and that it's been in your family for the best part of two hundred years. You must expect us to be impressed. Fifty years ago, there were cattle wandering along Fifth Avenue."

"You don't have to go back two centuries to find cows grazing in St. James's Park, and our cities are much older than yours." I smiled at Ellen Walfort, who had come to sit near her mother; the two of them made a pretty picture together, the youth of the one not detracting from the elegance of the other. "In any event, Mrs. Dermody is not quite accurate. Scott House belongs to my brother. But it's certainly been there a long time, and Lord Broadmere doesn't use it a great deal, so my sisters and I stay there when we wish to visit London."

"Is St. James's the most fashionable part of London?" Ellen wound her slender fingers into her mother's; I found it charming how affectionate and demonstrative the Walforts were with each other.

"Not really." I considered Ellen's question. "Not anymore. Exclusive, perhaps. If you want to be fashionable, you might look at Belgravia. I'm the wrong person to ask; our kind of family makes a point of not being fashionable, if you see what I mean. And we have such an old London house almost by accident. We haven't had a great deal of luck with houses. Our castle fell down the cliff hundreds of years ago, and the last time we built a really large house, it burned down. The ruin's still there; do you ride? I could show it to you, if you want. The local people call it 'Scott's Folly.' If either of you sketch, you'd find it a picturesque subject."

Ellen's fair brow was furrowed. "Are you saying we shouldn't try too hard to make an impression?" She turned her bright blue gaze on me. "It matters a great deal to me what kind of impression we make. This is really my one and only attempt at being presented at court and doing the Season, as I hear you English say. Lucy doesn't care so much —do you, Lu?—but I feel I'll be too old by next summer. And there's so much to learn. In Paris, they care most about your dresses and table manners and *esprit*—wit—but the English seem to turn everything we've learned there on its head."

"Be who you are, Birdie." Marcus Walfort, who had been talking to Fortier, broke off what he was saying to turn to Ellen. "You have nothing to be ashamed of."

"There's absolutely nothing wrong with dresses, wit, and table manners," I assured the beautiful young woman. "Manners are generally a good idea, in my opinion."

I caught a grin from Fortier before he once more attended to what Mr. Walfort was saying. "I agree with your father," I told Ellen. "Be who you are. You appear well equipped to take a place in society."

"But she shouldn't be too impressed by the titles, should she, Lady Helena?" Lucy Walfort came to sit on the other side of Ellen, stroking her arm. "Even if they mean more here than they did in Paris. Why, Ellen turned down a count and a baron in Paris—both awful old men. I'm sure the count was wearing a corset." She frowned. "A lady we met on the steamer from France said English country houses are cold and the winter weather is simply worse than anything you can imagine. All damp and gray instead of our lovely New York snow." Her lips curved up prettily. "I think the countryside around here is charmingly cozy, and so wonderfully green, but we'd do well to see it in winter for ourselves before Ellen steps foot into a ballroom. She dances divinely, by the way." She kissed her sister's cheek. "It'll be a lucky man who snares her."

A clatter of feet and a burst of laughter announced the arrival of the two eldest Dermody children, who spilled into the hallway amid a breathless mixture of French and English babble. With them was a boy who must be Jacques. Mariette brought the boys to a halt with an imperious wave of the hand, as effective as a regimental sergeant-major, and once they were still, she led them into the parlor.

"Bonjour, mesdames, messieurs." She made a curtsey and then switched to English. "I'm sorry we're late, Maman. We had such a delightful ride—all the way out to the sea—and watched the shrimp fishers at their keddle nets for a while. Jacques likes the sea, don't you?"

She turned to the taller of the boys, who, like Constantin, was making a polite bow to the assembled adults.

"I do," he replied. "I was never on a ship before we came to England, but I was not sick."

Jacques pronounced the words carefully, in heavily accented English, and then asked Mariette in French whether it was all right to mention seasickness in company.

He was standing close to me, so naturally I held out a hand to him. "Monsieur, your English is admirable. I am Lady Helena Whitcombe."

Was he really a descendant of kings? Although only thirteen, Jacques already exceeded my height by several inches. He was heavy of body and feature and somewhat plain. His light brown hair was wispy, his nose showed signs of wanting to become too large, and his light gray eyes were a little too prominent. A few pimples detracted further from his looks. And yet there was a good deal about him that was pleasing, mostly a matter of expression and mobility of feature, particularly the intelligent, kindly light in his eyes. I liked him immediately; of course, I was always disposed to like children.

"Milady." He kissed my hand, his other arm tucking automatically behind his back, like a courtier. "I have—had—a tutor in France for the English language. It is difficult, but I will learn faster now." He turned toward Fortier. "Monsieur is teaching me also."

I saw the sadness in Fortier's eyes and understood they had schooled the boy to stop calling him Papa. When, I wondered, did they tell him the people he had loved as parents were not related to him? Did he know who he was supposed to be?

"The English language is ridiculously complicated." The lady who had entered the house on Quinn Dermody's arm spoke in French. "Goodness, how I've been tormented by that terrible gale howling around us the whole time we were out. Jacques, you are untidy. Armand, will you introduce us to the guests?"

She used the formal *vous* toward both Fortier and Jacques, as was the usual practice in noble French families. She was, as Fortier had suggested, decidedly aristocratic in both bearing and speech. Also, she was considerably prettier than I had imagined, with pale blond hair and light hazel eyes that were now trained on me with an expression in which curiosity and dislike mingled alarmingly.

Introductions duly took place. Fortier adopted the strategy of introducing us in the order in which we were placed around the room, so my formal introduction to Louise occurred somewhere in the middle. She favored me with a regal nod, which I returned in kind; after all, I was the one with the title. Louise seemed a little puzzled by the Americans, who all spoke passable French, especially Ellen, who appeared to have been studying the language assiduously.

The adults seated themselves, the three children asking permission to go look for the younger Dermody siblings. I would have to find some way of getting to know Jacques, not because of the story surrounding him, romantic and farfetched as it was, but because I felt deeply sorry for a child deprived of his parents at birth and then a second time by reason of who he was supposed to be. And, truth be told, the fact that this boy had known Fortier as his father drew me to him.

Was Louise as ignorant of English as she pretended to be? I rather thought not, but if the conversation lapsed into English, she showed irritation. She also had a way of taking something somebody had just said and making a comparison that inevitably began, "In France . . ." in a manner that quickly became irritating. Fortier was wonderfully patient with her; I was not so sure I could be.

Eventually, the conversation came round to art, and I supposed it was unavoidable that Marcus Walfort would mention Sir Geraint Dorrian-Knowles and his much-vaunted set of Nightingale paintings. Despite the shadow cast over the Dorrian-Knowles family and my paintings by Edmund's execution for murder, the Nightingale series had continued to be mentioned in the journals, and Mr. Walfort was eager to know how the work was progressing.

"I believe the emperor painting is nearing completion," I answered. "That's the centerpiece, the one where the emperor sits in his throne room listening to the Nightingale. It was the first one Sir Geraint started."

And also the one most viciously attacked by Edmund. As he had promised, Sir Geraint had worked fast, almost feverishly, on painting a new version that was strikingly similar to the original yet indefinably better; most noticeable was that there was now more emotion in the faces of the emperor and kitchen maid.

"He works on the paintings in rotation," I explained. "I understand he likes to leave the previous days' work to dry thoroughly before continuing. He's often in London, working on preliminary studies for the figures he's using for the other paintings. He sometimes works with artists' models, and they are usually to be found in London."

And he no doubt also visited his wife Millie, who was still being nursed in an asylum in Hampstead Heath.

"I visit Sir Geraint's studio at Lower Broadmere regularly," I continued, "so I've seen enough of the work to know all the pictures will be marvels of complexity and symbol. His masterpiece, as he himself claims. For myself, I'm delighted he's incorporating so many details from the countryside and the shore around us."

I had forgotten to speak French since I was addressing Mr. Walfort directly. Louise listened with pursed lips and then spoke—in her own language, of course.

"Your sister Odélia"—she pronounced the name the French way—"also puts the flowers of the countryside into her paintings, does she not? I have read about *her*." The degree of disdain she put into the last word was no doubt carefully calculated. "In France, a mistress may be thought of as an asset to a man. We are more realistic than you English, who choose to pretend such things are not happening until you are forced to admit it is so."

She sniffed delicately, as if there were a foul smell under her nostrils. "Some families make a specialty of supplying mistresses. But then, I am a guest—I am an outsider—and there are young, unmarried ladies present, so I will say no more. Remember, *mesdemoiselles*, Christian charity means we must always strive to think the best of others."

She sat back with a significant look at me and then at Fortier. I saw India Walfort's brow furrow slightly and the corners of Louise's pretty mouth curl in apparent satisfaction. Had she just hinted I was Fortier's mistress? I felt my cheeks pinken, and Louise's eyes brightened.

Gabrielle was also frowning. I could not see Fortier's

expression from where I sat. Quinn Dermody unfolded his long legs and stood up.

"Such an interesting conversation." He spoke in English, exaggerating his Irish brogue, and clapped Fortier on the shoulder. "But I'm a working man and can't sit here all day listening to you ladies gossip." He looked pointedly at Louise as he said the word *gossip*. "Neither can Armand, I'm thinking. Is your new operating room finally ready, my brother? You can show it to me before I go down to the pottery."

I could now turn and look at Fortier. To my surprise, he was smiling directly at me. "Would you like to see the room too, Lady Helena? After all, you're a patroness of Littleberry's new hospital, and you must learn more about how surgeons work. Lady Helena has donated the land for our future hospital," he said to the whole company, "and is a generous subscriber to a building that will be a great asset to the poor of our parish. A great example of Christian charity indeed."

"How wonderful." India Walfort nodded in approval. "That's the kind of charity we like in America. I miss my charitable work. You must tell us all about it, Lady Helena. Perhaps we could subscribe to the hospital."

This was pulling the serpent's fangs with a vengeance—a concerted effort to shut Louise out and show her that her insinuations had no power. And they were quite right. I too must show how little I cared for her attack on my good name.

"I'd be delighted to tell you," I said. "Perhaps you would like to meet Sir Geraint at the same time? He's such an interesting man." I included all those present with a gesture. "You must all come. You know, I would love to give a dinner for Sir Geraint, to which you are *all* invited. I'll introduce you to some of my family as well."

General exclamations of delight followed my announcement, and the party began to break up amid many shakings of hands and a long, close embrace between me and Gabrielle. We did not leave Louise out; in fact, I could have sworn the Walfort girls were making an extra fuss of her on purpose, giving her very little chance to say anything untoward as Fortier, Quinn, and I took our leave to go see the operating room.

"Will you really invite Louise as well?" Fortier asked as the three of us stepped into the darkening afternoon, shivering slightly at the rather too fresh breeze blowing in from the sea.

"Of course." I tugged my gloves more firmly into place. "I'm a Scott-De Quincy, after all, and need to remember we're not easily intimidated. Your cousin may have flustered me for a moment, but with your help, I can brazen it with the best of them."

27

THE ART OF PLANNING A DINNER

"Sir Geraint? Really? Why?"

Blanche, who was looking very comfortable as the châtelaine of Hawthorn Hall, paused in the act of pouring tea. "And why aren't you inviting Gerry and Michael?"

"Politics," I said firmly. "If Michael is at the same table as Quinn Dermody, he's bound to start an argument about the Irish Question. I've already spoken to Julia; she agrees with me it's best to keep them apart if we can."

I had also let Julia into the secret that they would one day be related by marriage to an Irish radical. Michael, probably the most discreet man I had ever known, had said nothing to her about Fortier asking him for my hand in marriage. I was not quite ready to tell my sisters, trusting I would find the right moment.

"Neither Michael nor Julia speaks much French," I reminded Blanche, "and the Fortier cousin seems to want to speak nothing else. And Gerry and Michael would disagree with Quinn Dermody about most local matters. So will you, of course, but you don't argue for the Tory interest with nearly as much tenacity. Besides, it would be unfair to invite

Dederick and not you, and I absolutely want to invite Dederick. If you want to come, that is," I said to my nephew, who was busy scratching Scotty's belly. My dog was upside down on Dederick's lap, looking quite ridiculous with all four legs splayed out.

"I'd love to, but why me?" Dederick looked up, his hands stilling. "Not that it won't be good to have something to do." He yawned and stretched; Scotty, sensing he would no longer be pandered to, rolled himself upright and came to sit by me.

"Because I have two young ladies to entertain, and I want to give them some young men to talk to. So there'll be you, Cousin Jonathan, and Thomas."

"A varied selection of English manhood?" Dederick snorted. "Jonathan in his regimentals, and perhaps Thomas can fascinate us with his Latin declensions and biblical Greek and Hebrew."

I ignored him. "As for Sir Geraint, I can't keep employing—well, that's not really the word—one of our greatest living artists and not entertain him, even with all the awkwardness. It's time I began inviting him to the house again. He seems able to leave all personal feeling aside when it comes to his profession, so I don't think he'll say anything embarrassing. And who knows? He may get a commission from the Americans out of this dinner, and it would be churlish not to give him the opportunity when they're so very keen to meet him. I have the impression the Walforts are fabulously rich."

I had not mentioned the Walforts' wealth to Blanche so far, and now her gaze sharpened. "You say they have two daughters?"

"Yes, and they want to be presented and do the Season. The eldest seems very keen. Both are very presentable in all meanings of the word. The eldest girl is quite a beauty."

Dederick made a face. "Beautiful young ladies are usually too full of themselves."

"I think you'll find this one isn't, although they're both remarkably confident for unmarried women. Americans seem to expect more from their daughters than the English do. They've been well educated, for a start."

"Bluestockings." Dederick yawned again. "But possibly a solution to our problems, eh, Mama? I'll do my best with them, and even if they both fall in love with Cousin Jonathan, only one of them can marry him. Maybe I can have the other."

"You can be quite charming if you wish." I was getting the measure of my nephew. "Even though you talk nonsense *en famille*. At worst, it will be good practice for talking to rich Americans when you go wife-hunting in the Season."

"Why must you have the Dermodys at all?" Blanche pushed out her plump lips in a pout. "That dreadful man."

"He has better manners than many of our county friends and is certainly better read than most of them. At least he can make conversation on subjects other than land or sport." I was determined not to be persuaded to change my guest list one whit. "The Americans are Gabrielle's friends, so I must invite her, and I can hardly leave her husband out. And Dr. Fortier knows rather a lot about art, which I hope will be the chief topic of conversation."

"Well, I know why you're inviting *him*."

Blanche looked smug. I felt a small thrill run through me, as I so often did when Fortier's name came into the conversation. If only Blanche knew.

"And there's one more thing," I said. "I will be out of black. Do you realize the twentieth is the anniversary of Justin's death?"

"Of course I do."

I wasn't at all sure that was true, but I let it pass. "So I will be in half mourning by the twenty-third. Not that I chose the date on purpose."

28
BOCCA BACIATA

Perhaps I had not been completely truthful with Blanche about my decision not to hold my dinner until the twenty-third. Guttridge and my dressmaker between them had come up with a lavender evening gown so entirely marvelous it demanded to be aired for the first time in company, particularly if that company included one's future husband. I had to wait until we could seize a few moments alone together for his reaction, but I was not disappointed.

"I've waited a long time to see you in a dress like that," was Fortier's comment as we emerged from our initial kiss.

"Mmmm." It had been a long kiss, and I was still somewhat distracted. "It becomes me, doesn't it?"

"Most certainly. I particularly like some aspects of it." Fortier, who had not yet seen me in evening dress, was engaged in kissing the skin that the low neckline revealed.

"Stop." I pushed him away gently, my skin tingling. "I must get back. The hostess can't go missing for long; people will put two and two together."

Fortier sighed. "If you must. I have to say, I've never before appreciated the advantages of a large house for stealing moments like this." He kissed my lips again, briefly and gently. "I feel as if we never get a chance to be alone."

"I know." I squeezed his hand and stepped away from him, hoping by the time I rejoined my guests I wouldn't look as thoroughly kissed as I felt. "But let's be practical—please." I smiled at his grimace of frustration. "I've put you halfway down the table. You'll be taking Louise in, and I've seated her opposite you."

"I wish it were you."

"So do I." I took another step back to forestall any further demonstrations of affection. "I'm giving an arm to Sir Geraint—it seems only right since he's the guest of honor—but he'll be at the other end of the table. I'll be able to see you better than I can see him."

"Inwardly, I'll be gazing at you adoringly. My *Bocca Baciata*."

I would ask him what that meant on another occasion. And one day, I reflected as I hurried away, I would be able to look down the table and see Fortier at the other end of it, taking his place as my husband. Right now, I was on my way to give Mrs. Eason a no doubt needless instruction about the Walforts' rooms as an excuse for my absence; the Americans were staying overnight to avoid having to travel back to St. Leonard's-on-Sea on this late October evening.

I returned to the Great Hall, which was brilliantly lit and enlivened with a good fire, to find Fortier drinking sherry with the other guests, discussing Littleberry business with Thomas as if he'd never slipped away to meet me. Jonathan, who greeted me with a lift of his glass and a cheerful grin as I arrived, had attached himself to Ellen in my absence, and Dederick had joined them; the two men were vying with each other to be charming and amusing. Ellen was responding with smiles and laughter, yet her face gave little away.

The rest of the company was gathered around Sir Geraint. We had already visited the drawing room, where, in the golden glow of its newly reinstated chandeliers, the renowned painter had given an impromptu talk on his vision for the room's decoration. As always, Sir Geraint seemed completely at ease; not for the first time, I wondered how a man who put so much emotion into his paintings could have so little himself. Perhaps he used it all up in his art.

"We are summoned." I smiled at Sir Geraint as Dunnam appeared in the Great Hall to announce dinner.

"Then I obey." Sir Geraint was accustomed to dining at Whitcombe but had not done so since Edmund's arrest; now, he gave me his arm with a slight bow, as if the long months since he last ate at my table had never happened.

"Do you not think English food is far inferior to what one can obtain in France?" The remark came from behind me, in French; I did not have to turn round to know it was Louise who had spoken. I caught Gabrielle's eye as she passed me to take her place in the line and saw the brief flush on her cheeks at her cousin's rudeness, but I simply rolled my eyes at her in a gesture of humorous resignation.

"I think it depends on the cook." That was India Walfort's voice, so it was to her Louise had addressed the remark.

"Of course, many English employ French chefs. Does Lady Helena employ a French chef?" I was sure Louise had pitched her voice at exactly the right timbre and volume to be heard by me, if not all the company.

"Decide for yourself." Those were Quinn Dermody's sardonic tones in his excellent French. "But be sure of your verdict; you may well not get another chance to judge the matter."

I looked behind me briefly to be sure all fourteen of us were in place, seven men and seven women, and was pleased to see Louise looking annoyed at Quinn's implied threat. Fortier appeared to be stifling a grin.

I had given the seating arrangements some thought, so as to surround Louise with people who could be relied upon to speak French with her; Quinn would be on her left since he was the best guarantor of her good behavior. I had not wanted to put the Irishman anywhere near Blanche lest either of them waxed political, so Jonathan sat next to Blanche, opposite Ellen, who was next to Dederick; this, I reflected, had been a happy choice, seeing how well Ellen had been getting on with both young men. Dederick and Blanche were on my right and left, respectively, being my two highest-ranking guests, and I had put Mr. and Mrs. Walfort at the other end of the table so they could make the most of Sir Geraint.

A polite guest's obligation was to make conversation, not to remark on the food, but I was well aware Mrs. Foster had outdone herself and everything, from the *soupe à la reine* through to the *boeuf à la jardinière*, roast goose, and boiled fowls in oyster sauce, was flawless. Quinn Dermody ate with particular relish, a faint grin on his face whenever he looked to his right to see Louise patently enjoying her portion.

Even better, Louise, who had been visibly taken aback by the size of Whitcombe House from the moment she arrived, occasionally lost the thread of the conversation through gazing at the portraits on the dining room walls, contemplating the heavy Georgian silver that graced my table, or watching—possibly counting—the servants. She, of course, chose to attribute her lack of understanding to another cause.

"But I cannot follow all this English," she complained in French to Fortier. "It is an ugly language at the best of times, but when they are all talking together—" She shrugged expressively. "Do you not think it is rude to invite people and then speak in another language?"

"I don't think everyone here speaks French, so in whom does the rudeness reside?" To my surprise, it was Blanche who leaped to my defense—in French; Mama had employed French nursemaids and governesses for all of us. "I know for a fact that my son, *the marquess,* has enough French to read a menu and flirt with a shopgirl, but he did not have my advantages with respect to a thorough education in the language. My late husband, *the marquess,* did not wish me to hire French servants the way my dear mama did, as it was his belief Frenchwomen were trouble."

The way she emphasized *le marquis* and the smile with which she accompanied her words were a sight to behold. Clearly, she might criticize me in private, but she, like Gerry, would allow no criticism of her family in public.

"Your mother says you flirt with French shopgirls," I heard Ellen ask Dederick quietly. "Do you?"

The two of them seemed to have struck up an amiable rapport, and Dederick's answering grin was unusually friendly and carefree. Ellen had clearly discovered that the key to Dederick was not to be awestruck by his title and gloriously good looks, but to adopt a brisk and teasing tone and ignore the sharper side of his tongue.

At the same moment, Blanche was pointedly asking Jonathan if he spoke French. Our cousin laughed and shrugged, causing the chain and gold braided cords that decorated the front of his dress uniform to ripple and catch the light from the candles.

"Yes, but I'm dreadfully out of practice, Lady Hastings. There wasn't much call for French in Lucknow. I can follow a conversation well enough, but you won't catch me waxing eloquent in the language." He smiled winningly at Louise. "Perhaps the *chère madame* could help me improve my command of the language of Molière. Although I have heard you speak English too, Madame Fortier, in such a charming accent that I was quite smitten. I've been waiting to hear it again."

"Maybe the duke—Dr. Fortier, if you insist—could be your interpreter." Blanche was smiling again; it worried me she was smiling so much, but perhaps this was her strategy for fending off an attack on her family. "You must be very fond of your cousin, Doctor, to have spent so much time with her in France."

My heart jittered at the question, as clearly there was almost nothing Fortier could say in answer without embroiling himself in awkward explanations. Mercifully, a burst of laughter from the other end of the table caused the heads of those seated near me to turn in that direction.

"I'm sorry." Marcus Walfort smiled shyly. "I was telling Sir Geraint the anecdote about how Mrs. William Astor made a pretense of believing I had come to sell her a stove when her husband introduced us. And how Mrs. Cornelius Vanderbilt the Second invited us to an important reception at her house on the strength of the insult. The Vanderbilts, you see, are new money, like us. I was trying to explain New York society to Sir Geraint. I've invited him to come and see for himself one of these days, as our guest. He would be a sensation in America."

Exclamations of agreement followed, and the conversation became more general. I could see Lucy Walfort and Thomas getting on well; I had asked Thomas to take Lucy into dinner since they were the junior members of the party. I breathed a sigh of relief as Fortier asked an intelligent question about the Pre-Raphaelite Brotherhood in general and

Dante Gabriel Rossetti's early work in particular, and with the arrival of the dessert and ices I could relax a little and listen to Sir Geraint's long reply. I felt only slightly disconcerted when the great artist mentioned a painting called *Bocca Baciata* as having caused a stir for its sensuality.

"IS THAT AN ITALIAN DICTIONARY I SEE IN YOUR HANDS?"

Fortier smiled as he entered the small library. The night being moonlit, several of my guests had gone out to the terrace to see the sea in its silver glory, while others had repaired to the green drawing room, where coffee was being served. Now everyone was well fed and occupied, I had decided to pursue an errand of my own.

"I thought I'd look up what you and Sir Geraint were talking about." I paged through the dictionary, frowning at the unfamiliar language. "Where is he, by the way?"

"Still on the terrace with the Walforts, looking at the sea and talking philosophy. So do you know what *Bocca Baciata* is now?"

"I don't even know how to spell it." I laughed. "It seemed a bad idea to ask Sir Geraint about it at dinner because I was afraid it might mean something louche. Does it?"

"It means *the kissed mouth*." Fortier came to stand close to me. "As Sir Geraint said, it was the title of a somewhat provocative painting by Dante Gabriel Rossetti. But the reference is to the *Decameron*; it comes from the tale of a woman who has already had lovers. 'The mouth that has been kissed does not lose its good fortune; rather, it renews itself just as the moon does.'"

He smiled, touching my lips gently with a finger. "When I applied it to you, I was thinking how lovely your lips looked after I'd been kissing you. But it could equally refer to your having been married before." His fingertip strayed to the embroidery of my dress along the neckline. "Love is renewing you." Now his touch was warm on my collarbone. "You don't mind that I don't put you on a pedestal, do you? That I love you as a flesh-and-blood woman? I'm afraid you'll find me quite direct when it comes to the physical realities of life. I deal with them every day after all."

His voice had become soft and intimate, and it was doubtless the physical realities of life that were causing my heart to pound and my head to swim. But a movement caught my eye, and I stepped away from Fortier as Louise and Jonathan entered.

Louise looked more cheerful than usual, although her face resumed its lines of discontent as she realized Fortier and I were alone together. "I *say* you," she remarked pertly—and incorrectly—in English to Jonathan, presumably meaning she had been talking to him about us earlier. Of course, she, unlike my own family, knew the truth of it. Had she revealed our understanding to Jonathan?

"I'm sorry I left the gathering," I said. Whatever my feelings, I was the hostess of this dinner and knew my part. "I just wanted to look up the meaning of something Sir Geraint said. I'm afraid my knowledge of art is woefully deficient. Fortunately, my late husband and his father collected a fine reference library." I held up the dictionary, which was still in my hands.

"We've been exploring your house." Jonathan turned around to get a better look at the small library, tipping his head back to view the blue vaulted ceiling with its painted lozenges depicting writers of antiquity. "I can't get over how grand it is; every time I see a new room, I'm impressed all over again. Far grander than Hyrst. When was it built?"

"Seventeen twenty-two." I had told the story of my house many times before during house parties, as there were always some curious visitors. "Justin's grandfather bought it from the Botelers sixty years later. It's rather a sad story; the only Boteler son ruined himself gambling and tried to rescue his fortune by smuggling, only to be killed one night out on the marsh. Justin's grandfather was a recently created baronet and saw the opportunity to surround himself with a suitable mode of living, ready-made, as it were. He bought the place lock, stock, and barrel."

"I knew a chap called Boteler." Jonathan tugged at an earlobe. "Killed by cholera on our march back to India in '79. Cheerful as you'd please in the morning, dead by nightfall." He shuddered. "But why am I talking about such horrors when I have a beautiful woman on my arm?" He reached for Louise's hand, securing it under his braided sleeve as he spoke. "Now we've rooted out you two scholars, come and join us in your lovely room with all the portraits. Is that really Cousin Thomas's domain? He's a lucky man."

I turned to follow the pair as Jonathan tilted his head to listen to Louise, who was speaking to him in broken but passable English. Fortier claimed my arm.

"I'm glad to see Louise has made a friend," he said quietly to me. "It should improve her temper a little."

"She's lonely, I'm sure." I smiled up at Fortier. "You know, with the Walfort girls, Louise and Jonathan, and my niece Maryanne coming back from Shropshire—she's decided the young man she'd been hoping to marry is a loss—and Thomas and Dederick, we could get up quite a few outings and gatherings to cheer up the winter. If Gabrielle and I put our heads together, we can surely keep everyone entertained from now till Christmas."

"I adore the way you enjoy looking after everyone."

Fortier squeezed my arm into his side. "I hope you'll include me in these entertainments."

"I adore the way you never presume." I felt a thrill of joy run through me. "Don't worry—I'll invite you to everything, whenever you can spare a few hours from your work. Then surely we can find some time for each other without interruptions."

29

LOVE AND SOCIETY

"I've been enjoying myself as much as anyone these past three weeks," I told Gabrielle in mid-November. "For me, society always used to mean Justin's friends, who were several years older than me, and visiting with my sisters. It's wonderful to have a whole group of friends closer to my own age."

I moved to the window of Gabrielle's garden studio and looked out. "Although I love being with children just as much. It's good to have Petey back from school, and he gets on so well with Jacques and Mariette." Thomas's younger brother, released from Westminster early because of an outbreak of influenza, was playing quoits with the other children in the Dermodys' sizable garden. "Don't you just adore the noise and chatter of children?"

"Mmmm." Gabrielle was concentrating, busy applying glazes to a huge stoneware vase. "You're very happy—that much is obvious. But you're in love with a man who loves you, so who wouldn't be happy?" She smiled, not looking up from her task. "Armand certainly is."

"It's rather hard to hide love." I left off watching the children and went to sit by the fire; Gabrielle's studio was cold. "It seems to be in the air, especially with Jonathan flirting with all the women." I smiled. "Even me. Armand says he'll turn into a jealous lover if he has to keep watching Jonathan paying me compliments, but I know that's a jest. He's too good-natured to be jealous, and besides—we're sure of one another." The thought warmed me more than the flames crackling in the hearth.

"Jonathan flirts as he breathes, without thinking of the process." Gabrielle puffed out a laugh. "He's going to find it hard to settle on just one woman. Now, if you want my opinion, which you may not, Thomas is showing signs of developing a *tendresse* for Lucy. And maybe, just maybe, Dedrick is fond of Ellen's company, although it's hard to tell with those two." She straightened up, kneading her back with her fists.

"Lucy spends more time with Maryanne than she does with Thomas," I pointed out; my niece Maryanne, seemingly undaunted by her failure to find herself a husband in Shropshire, had become a constant member of our little group. "Those two are becoming firm friends. Thomas has his studies, and of course he doesn't ride and can't go on long walks. That leaves him out of some of our outdoor excursions, which I think is a great pity, but he won't let me find a solution that makes him different from the rest of us. I sometimes think he pretends to have more work than he actually has because he feels he's a hindrance." I sighed.

"Dederick doesn't always join us either." Gabrielle removed her apron and came to sit near me, putting out her hands to the flames to warm them. "Does the marchioness object to our outings? Or does he too have something else to do?"

"He goes to London to visit his club. He misses his London life."

I had not told Gabrielle—had told nobody—about Dederick's night at the Bow Street police station, so I couldn't confide in her how much his absences bothered me. Supposing the police realized he was breaking the agreement I had made with them on his behalf? I had asked Dederick to promise me he was not going anywhere other than his club; he had done so readily, and I believed him. Besides, he always took Rampling with him, and it was only one night in the week. He would return the next day by teatime, cheerful and comparatively sober. Blanche said she couldn't order him to stay at home, and I supposed she was right; and since he no longer lived at Whitcombe, I could hardly supervise his comings and goings.

"I'm finished for the day." Gabrielle removed the linen sleeve protectors from her dress. "I never expect to have much light this time of year, but this must be the darkest November I've ever seen. Still, you wait till I've fired that." She waved a hand at the vase. "I'm trying to recreate the unearthly twilights we've been having—to build a sort of record in ceramics. I'll do more of them if I can find a buyer for this one."

"Sir Geraint is painting the sky too." I had visited the artist's studio two days before and seen several studies in watercolor of the recent remarkable sunsets. "He says he wants to use the more brooding effects for the sky of Death's garden."

The skies had drawn us all outdoors every evening it wasn't raining, to watch the virulent greens, the strange copper tones, the streaks of magenta, the peculiar blue light, and the lurid reds tinting the undersides of the clouds as if they'd been dipped in blood. I knew the aurora borealis could be seen in the far north of the British Isles, but this was something different and had provoked a considerable correspondence in the newspapers.

"I should visit Edenholme tomorrow to compare impressions," Gabrielle mused. "I'd like to spend more time at Sir Geraint's house; he seems to receive so many visits from the sort of people I like to talk to. Will you come with me?"

"No, thank you. Once you start talking to artists, I'm always left out of the conversation." I laughed as Gabrielle raised her hands in a comically rueful gesture of acknowledgment. "Taylor says it's going to rain, and I'm determined to have a quiet morning tomorrow. I'm awfully behind with my correspondence."

30
AN ENGLISH WINTER

The wind was already blowing a fine, icy rain across Whitcombe's windows when I awoke the next day. I kept my resolution to pass an industrious few hours while Scotty, happy to have me to himself, snoozed by the morning room fire.

I wrote a lengthy letter to Odelia, in which I admitted Fortier and I had an understanding. Knowing she'd bristle at the implication she might gossip if I asked her to keep my secret, I imposed no demands upon her, but I told her we had made no announcement, not even to our other sisters. I knew it wouldn't be long before we had to face that particular fence, but that would mean explaining Louise and Jacques, a thought that daunted me and made me procrastinate telling the truth.

It was Thursday, and I was "at home" to callers, but I didn't anticipate seeing anyone, given the weather. By the afternoon, the rain had strengthened and changed from vertical to horizontal as the wind grew wilder. I could see clouds nearly touching the top of Whitcombe House, sullen dark gray clouds with a bluish tinge, and wondered if we would soon be enveloped in fog.

I was surprised—and pleased since I'd had enough of hard work and solitude—to hear the crunching of wheels on gravel at three in the afternoon. We were showing visitors to the main library—I did not want to disturb Thomas all the time—so it was to that room I repaired, telling one of the hall boys to take Scotty outside for an airing. Within a very few minutes, a footman stepped in to announce Mr. and Mrs. Walfort.

"A wonderful surprise." I held out my hands to the Walforts, whom I had seen so often in the past weeks that we were becoming friends. "I didn't think anyone would be brave enough to come out in this."

I kissed India and shook Marcus's hand heartily, ushering the two of them to seats near the roaring fire under the massive black marble mantelpiece. "What are Ellen and Lucy doing?"

"Writing their letters." India laughed. "I insisted. They lay about all morning, and I wasn't going to give them another excuse to put off their correspondence. But it's the girls who are our main reason for coming to see you."

"I'm intrigued." I waited until the footman had withdrawn, with instructions to have coffee and sweetmeats brought up, before speaking again. "There's nothing wrong, is there?"

India began to speak, but her dry cough interrupted her. In recent weeks, I'd sent her our preparation of marshmallow root, thyme, and ivy, which had helped, but the cough was not yet banished. Marcus watched her struggle to calm the spasms, a worried look on his face.

"I'm sorry. Changes of air always set me off." India smiled weakly. "Which brings us rather neatly to the point of our errand. My London physician is adamant I shouldn't stay in England over the winter."

"I want us to travel south immediately." Marcus allowed Scotty, who—damp but thoroughly toweled, to his evident disgust—had come in with the footman, to sniff him. "We must find the sunshine, wherever it may be in this benighted November, so India can sit in it."

"I'll concede I never imagined the sky could be as dark and gloomy as it is here." India also greeted Scotty, who, the formalities concluded, gave her hand a brief lick before heading for the warm marble flagstones in front of the fireplace.

"November is always a miserable month in England," I admitted. "And no Thanksgiving to enliven it. Perhaps that's why we're beginning to make so much of Christmas. This year it seems worse than ever." The footman had closed the curtains over the library's long windows to shut out the Stygian gloom, and the noise of the rain had dropped to a quiet pattering, broken often by the howls of the wind.

"My sister Odelia is in Rome at the moment," I said. "Perhaps you could go there? She writes that it's nearly as warm there now as it is in summer here. I can always write an introduction for you." I grimaced, remembering Odelia was tainted with scandal. "If you'll consent to meet her, that is."

"I rather like the sound of Lady Odelia, to be truthful." Marcus's smile lit up his face. "I saw one of her paintings—a Lady of Shalott—on sale in a gallery when I was in London on Tuesday and had it shipped to New York for my study. We'd be delighted to make her acquaintance."

"Perfect," I said. "I'll add a note about you to the letter I've just written to her. Would you like a general recommendation as well? It might help with the English community in Rome or wherever else you go. There always is an English community if the spot is picturesque or particularly healthy.

As a nation, we're fond of travel." I glanced at the window as a gust of wind hit it, making the curtains move despite the fact everything was carefully closed. "You know, sometimes I understand Odelia's dislike of the country in winter too."

"Americans are also very fond of travel." India watched Scotty sniff the shoes of the footman, who was depositing a large, heavy tray on the table. "I expect we'll encounter quite a few people we already know, but your recommendation would be welcome; the English don't always mix with us. We'll find a pleasant villa for entertaining. Our house in St. Leonard's is adorable, and very cozy for the four of us, but if we ever decide to spend a long time in England, we'd have to build something."

She looked up at the library's ornate, double-height ceiling and the deep gallery along its inside wall. "This is our idea of a suitably sized house, but I understand finding a country house in the right spot, not already occupied or falling down in disrepair, can be difficult."

"I'm glad you like Whitcombe." I was getting used to the way India talked, as if money were no consideration whatsoever. "Will Ellen and Lucy travel with you? We'll miss them terribly."

"Well, that's the thing." Marcus sipped his coffee, watching the footman close the door. "The girls don't want to leave."

"Lucy says she's in love with England," India explained. "She's never been fond of moving around. She says she's just not enough of a cosmopolite to bear the sort of people we'd meet in the popular places."

"And Ellen wants to live through an entire English winter before she decides whether marrying an English gentleman is a good idea." Marcus smiled. "She says no title will be worth being miserable in the country all winter."

"They say we could simply keep the house in St.

Leonard's and let them live there," India said. "After all, they're both grown women and can manage the servants by themselves. But—"

"But you've come to ask if I might consider having them to stay at Whitcombe." I laughed, interrupting India in my eagerness.

"Is it terribly forward of us?" India asked. "After all, we haven't known you long."

I laughed again. "When one has a house like mine, offering room in it to people one likes comes quite naturally. Whitcombe was made to be filled. Of course I'll have them; in fact, the prospect of having two lively girls around the house at Christmas is delightful. It will help me too; having younger people around is just what I need now I'm out of my first mourning. I'll make sure Ellen and Lucy see plenty of county life, and I'll rack my brains to try to introduce them to people who are likely to be up in London for the Season next year."

India looked at her husband, who breathed a deep sigh of relief. "Thank you," he said. "They'll have an allowance, of course, and should be able to order any clothes they need from Paris. Their measurements are recorded at Worth and all the shops young ladies seem to require."

"*That* will cause quite a sensation." I smiled at the Walforts. "You do realize, don't you, that unmarried English ladies don't usually get dresses from Paris? Unless they are considerable heiresses, and then usually only for the Season, the exception being if they're wealthy in their own right through some accident of inheritance. The gentry spend all their money on the son and heir, first and foremost, and then on helping the other sons into a position in life."

"Yes, I've noticed." India raised her eyebrows. "In fact, from what I've seen, the daughters of the English nobility get the poor end of the deal. Very little education, if you'll forgive me for saying so, and little in the way of real society until they're debutantes."

I nodded. "And then they're expected to marry as soon as possible and produce heirs, which is the point of the process. Land needs heirs to inherit and look after it, and the younger sons are needed for the army and the church. Any girls who don't marry are burdens on their parents and, eventually, their brothers."

Michael was still paying Odelia an allowance. At least the twins earned their keep by ensuring Hyrst was kept in order, leaving Julia free to concentrate on her children and the county.

"Americans—our sort of Americans anyway—value their daughters." Marcus had a smile on his lips, but his eyes were serious. "That's not just because of the usual family bonds of affection, although we seem to have more of that than many English families, no doubt due to your habit of handing your children over to nursemaids, nannies, and boarding schools. To us, a girl is an asset in society, and we try to equip them with everything they need to succeed. We invest in them, and we keep them close."

"An English girl of my class gets training rather than education," I said. "One needs to know how to run a large house and how to manage guests, how to draw a little and paint a little, play and sing a little, not look a fool on a horse, talk sensibly about the land, and support the politics of the gentry, which are inevitably of a conservative character." I was positively laughing now as I summed up my own training, all directed toward the exalted aim of becoming a wife and the mother of future aristocrats. "A married woman often has considerable social duties, especially if her husband's in politics or involved in the running of the county."

I was enjoying discussing Englishness with these Americans; I had never really thought about our way of life before. "In the winter, there's sport, which means house parties, and one can't really bring children to those, so one leaves them with Nanny. And, to be perfectly frank, a marriage made for dynastic or financial reasons isn't always a close one, and sometimes it's better to keep the children away from the consequences. Married couples often pursue . . . diversions."

"Good heavens." India's eyebrows, as red as her hair, rose again. "You *are* frank."

"If one or both of your daughters is even thinking of marrying into our nobility, it's best you—and most importantly, they—understand all the implications." I was thinking of Dederick at that moment, giving my words a certain gravity. "*We* absorb the rules from a young age, and it all seems natural enough to us, but even then one sees young women unhappily married to much older men, who may already have had a mistress for years, simply to look good at the dinner table and supply legitimate heirs. Their misery drives them to enter into liaisons that end up bringing them more heartache than joy. I'm very happy to help Ellen and Lucy aim for the nobility, if that's their ambition, but I would hate to see them walk into a marriage blindfolded when they, perhaps, have different expectations of the married state."

"So would I." Marcus looked quite stricken. "You make me want to take them back to New York straightaway. We had a taste of that world in Paris—too many noblemen looking for rich wives. Did you know they even travel to our country for the purpose? And we, of course, are no end impressed by their titles. It always strikes me as odd that a country founded on democracy is so impressed with these relics of feudalism." He grinned. "Begging your pardon, of course. I didn't mean to imply you were a relic of feudalism."

"But New York is just as bad." India did not seem to appreciate her husband's attempt at levity, turning to him with an expression almost of pleading. "The old families resent us, and now there's all the nonsense about Mrs. Astor's four hundred. We're the wrong sort of money for New York society, and I don't know if I can bear to do as the Vanderbilt ladies are doing and just *force* my way in. I don't have the stomach for it, yet the alternative is to leave our girls out in the cold." She looked quite distressed.

Marcus, whose kind face reflected his wife's emotion, sighed heavily. "When I was a boy, I had such joy at the idea of making a fortune. I relished the challenge and dreamed of giving the beautiful young lady I had my eye on every luxury." He rose and went to stand by his wife, taking her hand. "But wealth brings its own problems, I suppose. We came to Europe to broaden our horizons and, now that our choices are no longer narrow, must grapple with finding the right path."

Marcus lowered himself, quite easily for a tall man, so that he could look into India's face. "Ultimately," he said, "we can only be loving parents who advise. We can't make our daughters' decisions for them. They're not children anymore."

"No, they're not." India's smile, and voice, trembled a little. "But a mother can still worry, can't she, Helena?" She appealed to me. "Ellen has gotten it into her head that she'll soon be too old to make a good marriage. She's so . . . *driven.* She takes after my husband in that respect." The hand in his visibly tightened, its slender knuckles whitening. "She wants to make the perfect marriage and follow the dreams she has in her head—that mysterious little head that's always making plans she keeps to herself. I don't think even Lucy knows all of them. But Lucy has inherited your sweetness, my darling, and will do everything she can to help her sister."

"You see, Helena?" Marcus stood up as easily as he had crouched down; this was clearly not a man who spent all his time at a desk. "You're taking on a lot. Not just the daily care of our daughters, but your presence at a time when they're making perhaps the most important decisions of their lives. I hate having to split the family like this right now, but—" He seemed to lose the ability to speak, merely looking at me in mute appeal.

"I'll do my best for them." It was a responsibility I had not in the least anticipated, but somehow I could see it had fallen to me for a reason. "Believe me, I do understand why you would prefer not to leave the girls to their own devices this winter, and neither do I think forcing them to travel with you when it's against their plans is a good idea." I smiled at India, who was dabbing at her eyes with a handkerchief. "Go and find the sun in good spirits. I'll keep your children safe."

31
NOT IN AGREEMENT

"Mr. Walfort is clearly a man of action," I said to Mrs. Eason the next afternoon as she supervised the arrangement of the three rooms—two bedrooms and a sitting room—she was getting ready for the Walfort girls' all-too-imminent visit. "When I agreed to host the young ladies, I never imagined we would have only two days to prepare. I wonder if this is a shock to them as well?"

"Oh, I imagine they'll survive it," said Mrs. Eason stolidly. She had been housekeeper at Whitcombe since Justin's father's time, had doubtless dealt with every possible whim of the gentry, and was imperturbable when it came to sudden instructions. "Their poor maids must be going frantic packing trunks."

"At least they'll be able to close up the house at leisure." I watched as Mrs. Eason bustled off to talk to the carpenter who was repairing a door, then nodded at a footman who was carrying a chair into the sitting room, indicating with a flurry of my hand he should put it where the housemaid was pointing and not bring his own opinions into the matter.

Heated by that small exercise of power, I further satisfied my urge to do something useful by straightening a picture.

"Yes, Robert?" A movement caught my eye, and I turned to see the head footman had stepped inside the door.

"Mrs. Fortier is in the library, my lady. She insists on seeing you."

My first reaction to the name was, regrettably, tinged with a sort of possessive jealousy that had seized me more than once since I had met Louise. I would never be *Mrs.* Fortier, of course; Armand would have to put up with me being announced as Lady Helena Fortier since I had no intention of giving up my courtesy title. Still, it stung to hear Louise announced this way.

Her family had, according to Fortier, called themselves "de Maival," and Louise had only decided on "Fortier" as a *nom de guerre* when they were spending their first night out of Paris in an inn, relying on the fiction of being married to eke out their precious money by sharing a room. The situation must have been difficult, particularly in the presence of a screaming baby who had to be found a wet nurse, but I'd wondered more than once if there had been an ulterior motive in Louise adopting her cousin's name. And then I would scold myself for inventing possessive fantasies—surely, she was thinking of not letting Jacques fall into the wrong hands at the time, not of trapping Fortier into marriage?

My second thought, as I walked without hurrying along the corridors that would eventually lead me to the right staircase, was relief I was wearing such a smart dress, of a gray that caught the light like pewter.

"Good afternoon," I said in French as I entered the main library, where Louise was bending her slender neck back under her hat, which was trimmed with a thick length of green ribbon, trying to see as much of the enormous room as possible. "How may I help you? Or is this merely a social call?"

We knew each other rather better by now after three weeks of including Louise in the outings and activities Gabrielle and I had arranged. She had begun to speak English with Dederick and Maryanne since neither of them had French; when Thomas was present, she ignored him completely. But she would only accept correction of her English from Jonathan, on whom she bestowed most of her smiles.

With Fortier, she adopted the possessive half-indifference of a long-married wife, expecting him to assist her where help was needed and issuing opinions and orders as if she were used to him obeying her. He, being a good-natured creature and courteous to a fault, simply did as she asked. If Louise's intentions were to make me feel more like a mistress than the woman Fortier was courting, she didn't always succeed, but sometimes her barbs stung me, especially when she referred to people and events in the Normandy village where she and Jacques—and occasionally Fortier—had lived.

"I thought I would come and see you alone." She left off constructing a mental inventory of my library, letting her long lashes fall on her soft cheeks as she brushed at an unseen speck of something on her green dress, on which pink roses rioted and which was trimmed with pink ribbon in a way that made me long for a little more ornament to my half mourning. Fortier had told me she was three years his senior and that her thirty-fourth birthday was approaching, but her appearance was still youthful, and she clearly followed the latest fashions, as any self-respecting Frenchwoman of means would.

"What a pleasure." I moved to the side of the vast fireplace to tug at the bellpull. "Do please sit down."

Louise chose the sofa opposite the fire; I, not quite as at ease as she looked, opted for a somewhat upright chair.

"Your people were trying to tell me something about you being upstairs," Louise said once she was seated. "Were you resting? I did not understand most of the words."

"They were probably trying to say I was not at home—in the sense of receiving callers." I smiled to take the sting off my reply; one should never make a guest, however unexpected, feel unwelcome. "I wasn't resting, quite the opposite. Ellen and Lucy will stay with me for a few weeks, and I wanted to make sure they will be comfortable."

"They did not say." Louise's tone showed her surprise.

"India's doctors have ordered her abroad for her health, and Marcus acted on their instruction very quickly. They will go to Dover tomorrow afternoon and make their way south slowly. They'll be stopping in Paris for a few days to see their friends, then staying in Marseille with some other Americans, and thinking all the while about making Rome their winter home."

"Your sister is there." Louise's lips curled upward.

"Yes." I put a great deal of unconcern into my answer. "Marcus has purchased one of her paintings and is keen to meet her."

The inevitable arrival of a footman with a tray stilled her words, but her lips continued to curl, and dimples formed in her cheeks as if she were amused by some thought. I poured coffee with a steady hand; by now, I was used to Louise's way of dropping references to Odelia into the conversation.

"How are you getting on, living with the Dermodys?" I eventually asked, once it became clear Louise was not ready to say what was on her mind. She did have *something* on her mind, I was sure.

"The house is too small." She pursed her lips prettily.

"Was your house in Normandy a large one?" I asked.

"Oh . . . no . . . not so large." Louise smiled. "But there were just the three of us. It was a happy home."

I could think of absolutely nothing to say to that, so I fell silent, sipping my coffee and staring at the gloomy gray twilight through the window. Louise too was silent for a while, but when she finally spoke, her tone was firm.

"I do not want to continue to live in Littleberry." The long lashes lifted, the hazel eyes reflecting the fire's flames as she stared at me. "It is a cold, damp, and disagreeable place, your Sussex. When my house in Normandy is sold, Jacques and I will move to somewhere I like. And Armand will move with us."

My heart thumped in alarm, but I knew Louise by now. "Is that his promise or merely your intention?"

"It is his duty. He has ruined me for others by pretending to be my husband, and nobody with a Christian conscience could claim otherwise. Father Clement agrees with me." This was the Catholic monk who presided over her church in Littleberry. "You must let him go."

"I will not." I kept my voice cool and even, yet I couldn't stop the flush I felt rising to my cheeks. "You lived together like brother and sister; don't try to tell me a different story. Has every unmarried man who has a female servant or a sister or, yes, a cousin living with him to keep his house ruined that lady? We'd have to prosecute a quarter of the country."

"But I was not living with him to keep his house." The small, superior smile again. "He was living with *me*, in *my* house. As my husband. As the entire village of Clouville will testify."

This, to be true, was a thought that had often entered my head, but I had shied away from it, sidestepping as a horse does when it comes to an obstacle that makes it nervous.

"He won't leave me," I said. "We're going to be married."

"I see no signs of a betrothal." The little smile was becoming quite annoying. "Or is it that he has simply taken from you what a wife should give to a husband? With your money, you are well placed to be a mistress. You can enjoy him and yet be independent of him. I know you are rich."

"I'm not his mistress. We've never—we will wait until we're married."

Fortier and I had somehow managed to snatch some brief time together, but he had never taken advantage of the fairly obvious fact I found him hard to resist. He was determined, he told me, to do the thing properly, but now it occurred to me he might be trying to avoid "ruining" me—if such a word might apply to a widow—in case he could not free himself from Louise. I was absolutely sure of his love, but this blasted woman was making an excellent case.

"How sweet." Louise's eyes narrowed. "So you refuse to give him up?"

"Of course I do." I wasn't sure what expression was on my own face, but I suspected it was not a pleasant one. "What did you imagine—that I would simply give you Armand because you said he was yours? We're not in the nursery squabbling over a toy. You'll have to do better than that."

"Oh, I shall."

Louise dabbed at the corners of her mouth with her napkin, then dropped the linen onto her half-empty cup of coffee so that it bloomed with a wet brown stain. She rose to her feet in a smooth, elegant motion. "I am not without friends."

She was almost at the door before I found the strength in my shaking legs to propel myself up from my seat.

32
A FEAST OF TROUBLES

The Walfort sisters, a little subdued at first by the sudden departure of their parents, quickly recovered their high spirits. The day of their arrival was Blanche's birthday, and I sent my sister a copious tribute of hothouse flowers accompanied by a note to tell her of Ellen and Lucy's change of residence. Her reply included an invitation to luncheon on Sunday, *and do bring the dear girls*. Naturally, I accepted.

I did not tell Fortier about Louise's visit. My first instinct had been to run to him; she had upset me considerably. Yet a little reflection led me to the conclusion that until Louise acted on her threat, it was merely a threat, and repeating our conversation to Fortier would not help matters. He did not attend church that Sunday, having been called, so Gabrielle told me, to a stillbirth in Littleberry's slum district. I was determined that when I next saw him, I would not let any trace of Louise's troublemaking disturb our happiness.

Sunday saw the five of us—Blanche and Dederick, the Walfort sisters, and myself—in Blanche's dining room, eating a splendid meal prepared by the new cook I had found her.

Blanche had invited no other members of the family, and by the attention she was paying to Ellen, I detected an ulterior motive behind her invitation.

"You're fortunate to find my son in the country," she told Ellen while we were drinking sherry, waiting for luncheon to be announced. "I'm fortunate too—a happy mama—to have him here. Usually at this time of year, he's at—Blenheim, isn't it, Dederick?" She smiled at his nod, looking as satisfied as a cat with a particularly succulent-looking fish on her plate. "He *has* been kind to me this year, to help me settle down in Sussex. Missing the sport for my sake."

"I shouldn't think you miss standing outside in the rain," Lucy said to Dederick, her eyes sparkling. She was placed so as to have an excellent view of Ellen and Dederick, who were seated next to one another, and seemed to enjoy the sight of them together as much as Blanche did. They made a handsome pair, Dederick's pale blond curls an attractive foil to Ellen's bright hair and creamy skin, set off by a pale yellow dress sprinkled with small pearls.

"Oh, I don't know." Dederick, who was in a mellow mood, gave a carefree smile. "They say there's no such thing as bad weather, only inappropriate clothing. It's surprising how much water a tweed suit keeps out. There's nothing more invigorating than standing in a good trout stream on a misty November morning. I remember when the duke . . ."

And he embarked upon a story that kept us all entertained until luncheon had begun—assuming one enjoyed a fishing story, and when one was in the presence of country gentlemen, one learned either to enjoy it or pretend one did.

"So does the Duke of Marlborough own Marlborough House?" Ellen asked as we finished the fish course. "That's the name of the house that the Marlborough House set meets at, isn't it? Or am I completely wrong, and it's just one of those British traditions?"

"No, it's a real house, and it has given its name to our social set, but the duke no longer owns it." Dederick put down his knife and fork. "Marlborough House has been used, on and off, as a royal residence for decades and has been the Waleses' London home since the sixties. With the Queen reluctant to take an active part in society since the death of the Prince Consort, it functions as a kind of second court."

"A more sophisticated one." Blanche had had a glass or two of wine and was, for her, positively merry. "I'm afraid Her Majesty has a rather bourgeois approach to amusement. She believes in family *gemütlichkeit*."

"Coziness," Dederick drawled by way of explanation. "She can sometimes seem more like a fussy aunt than the ruler of an empire."

I nodded, remembering my own presentation, the matronly little Queen leaning forward to salute me as her "cousin," as she called all the old nobility. I'd poked fun at her when I was back at Hyrst with Daniel, but then I had only been sixteen.

"The Marlborough House set revolves around sport, which is of little interest to the dear Queen." Blanche was in her element. "Do you understand the sporting season in England? No? Dederick, perhaps you can explain."

This gave Dederick an excellent opportunity to shine with a series of explanations and anecdotes that, with various interruptions and comparisons from the Walfort girls, who had clearly experienced a similar sort of society in Newport, ensured the conversation tripped along splendidly until the fruit and cheese were on the table. Dederick, I found, could be very entertaining; he knew so many people that even I was fascinated by his tales about grandees whose names and engraved portraits were to be seen in the political and society columns of the newspapers. Justin had been similarly knowledgeable, but he had, as he told me before we married, decided to retire from the hurly-burly of society, and I had been quite happy with a quiet life at Whitcombe.

"Must you have a long line of noble ancestors to be invited into this—well, it sounds a little like a club?" Ellen leaned forward, clearly enthralled.

"Not nearly so long as you'd think." Dederick raised his eyebrows at her in a show of hilarity, his expression animated. "The Prince of Wales is nothing if not a man of the world. Of course, many of his guests are drawn from our nobility, but he likes actresses and opera singers, Jewish bankers and American robber barons just as much. You're never quite sure whom you might meet, but when you see them at his table, you know they will be accepted everywhere."

"Such odd combinations." Blanche was laughing now. "I remember being seated between an Indian prince and a peculiar man who had somehow made a fortune with oyster shells. He kept calling me 'your marquess-ship.' Francis had to rescue me later; he wouldn't leave me alone!"

Her droll expression, as much as her words, gave rise to general laughter, and I had the pleasure of seeing my fussy, often pompous sister glow like a young girl. She had not seen as much of society as she'd wanted because of Francis's ill-health, and the evident pride she took in even this small anecdote touched me. Was Odelia perhaps simply envious when she'd teased her over her ambitions?

"Yes, there are some oddities, but one gets used to it." Dederick nodded. "You might find a brewer from Manchester or a French princess at the table. If the prince finds you interesting or useful, it doesn't matter who your father or grandfather was."

"Less snobbish than much of New York society, then."

Lucy glanced at Ellen. "But still quite exclusive in its way, I imagine?"

"It depends." Dederick was peeling an apple with precision, letting the long, thin coil of peel slide over his fingers. "Obviously, everything goes on by invitation. There are many cliques within the set, and people come and go. There's the matter of age too. Those of us who are nearer to the prince's sons' ages aren't as close to the center of things as some of the older chaps. The prince is over forty after all. But he's fond of the pretty wives of the younger men."

"To look at, I hope," Lucy said with a small frown.

"Of course." But Dederick's smile said otherwise. "Sometimes it amuses His Royal Highness to keep company with us young fellows. He says laughing at our antics and our talk keeps him youthful."

"What about his own children?" Ellen asked. "Do they join in?"

"Not really allowed." Dederick cut a piece off his apple and chewed it. "They're set apart, as it were, since they need to make dynastic marriages. The princesses are pretty, but they are carefully chaperoned."

"And the young princes are lately returned from a long naval tour of the empire," Blanche added. "No doubt it's been good training for them."

"And kept them out of trouble. One hopes." Dederick met his mother's fond gaze with innocent-seeming eyes. "The prince often refers to the importance of staying out of trouble. He's particularly keen we conduct ourselves with honor on the sporting field or at the gambling tables."

He would be. I had my own opinions on His Royal Highness's sense of morality, but I supposed it was better to impose some rules than none at all. I selected a sugar plum, nibbling at it as Dederick talked, watching his face and Ellen's. I didn't think he was striving to impress her—the anecdotes he was telling seemed to flow quite naturally—but, hard as she was to read, I detected a warming toward Dederick as he talked, his handsome face alight with genuine pleasure.

We all laughed so hard at one particular remark that the footman who entered had to speak again, more loudly this time, to make himself heard.

"Two persons insist on seeing you, my lady," he said to Blanche, his gaze flicking to Dederick. "And your lordship." He coughed. "They are waiting in the entrance hall."

"We're not at home to any *persons*." Blanche frowned. "Particularly on the Sabbath. Tell them to leave a card explaining their business and come back tomorrow."

"I don't think I can, my lady." A hint of red appeared on the footman's cheekbones. "They are persons of the detective police. From London. They've traveled down in a carriage."

THERE WAS A SILENCE LASTING A FEW MOMENTS BEFORE ELLEN and Lucy both exclaimed in innocent surprise. Their words formed the background to a tableau I would long remember: Blanche and Dederick frozen in place, their faces, flushed by food and wine, paling to a sickly yellow. The paring knife Dederick had been holding must have slipped; a tiny bead of blood blossomed on one finger, dark against the pale skin.

I was facing the door, so it was I who first saw the two men in ordinary black overcoats and bowler hats, looking for all the world like a pair of upper servants on a day out, loom up behind the discomfited footman. Behind them, distressingly, were two uniformed policemen. The knowledge of how Littleberry gossiped made it worse that the two policemen were members of our small town's constabulary.

"I'm afraid you have to be at home to us, my lady." As he

removed his hat, I recognized the heavily mustachioed detective we had seen at Scotland Yard. "Good afternoon, Lord Hastings."

Dederick had put down knife and apple and was sucking at his cut finger in some annoyance, but now he looked up and started violently in recognition. His hand moved convulsively toward the small, sharp fruit knife on his plate.

"I wouldn't do that, my lord." The detective's voice was very soft, but the two uniformed men behind him tensed as if ready to spring forward, their expressions showing their nervousness at having to deal thus with "the Family." Dederick pushed his chair back and stood up; all four men took a step toward him.

"You didn't even wait for us to come out and meet you," Dederick said incongruously. His gaze moved to Ellen. All the wariness that had melted from his face as he'd entertained us seemed to settle back upon him like a mask.

"We prefer what you might call the element of surprise." The detective smiled, an expression I remembered all too well from Scotland Yard—not a pleasant smile. "It's astonishing what people do when they're given a few minutes to think."

"I wouldn't hurt anyone." Dederick looked at the knife again.

"But you might hurt yourself, and we can't have that either." The detective's voice was perfectly unemotional. "Even a pretty silver knife like that can slash a throat. Some people prefer it to a noose. Begging the pardon of the young ladies."

He had not appeared to look around, but the tiny bow he made—still watching Dederick intently—seemed to take in all those present.

Blanche made a small noise in her throat as Lucy screamed. The young girl stifled her reaction by clamping a hand to her mouth; Blanche stood up, her chair falling backward to the carpet. She was shaking.

"You will state the purpose of this intrusion immediately." Her voice was a thread of sound, her eyes like two blue stones. The sight jerked me out of my own inaction, and I rose and moved—carefully, so as not to cause the policemen to do anything untoward—to stand by Blanche, my arm around her waist. I could feel the tremors running through her body.

"I'm here to arrest Lord Hastings, of course." The detective smiled his tiger's smile. "On suspicion of unlawfully killing Lord Arthur Southgate-Haigh on the sixth of September last. Also on suspicion of unlawfully killing Mr. Remus Fleetwood on the seventeenth of November last. To wit, yesterday."

"Fleetwood's dead?" My voice sounded strange in my ears. "Fleetwood the butler?"

"Oho." The detective exchanged a look with his colleague. "Lady Helena Whitcombe appears to know *immediately* who we mean. Yes, my lady, Fleetwood the butler, who somehow ended up under an omnibus on Pall Mall at two thirty yesterday afternoon, very near the Carlton Club. Lord Hastings was at the club; you can't deny it, my lord." His eyes crinkled at the corners. "You were in London in contradiction of our little agreement, weren't you? You also can't deny Lord Arthur was in your compartment in the train, can you?" A jeering note was creeping into his words. "It took us a while to work that out. Slow at times, the detective force, but we're very thorough. Like the mills of God, we grind exceeding small."

"He was with me." Dederick looked as if he were going to be sick. A smear of blood, presumably from his finger, marred his starched white shirtfront. "At least I think I remember him being there. I was so drunk."

"Not asleep, then?" The other detective spoke at last, at the same time reaching into a pocket.

"No—yes—asleep—unconscious—God, I don't know." Dederick's voice was frantic. "I'm not even sure it was an actual memory or some kind of dream. I think I'd drunk the entire bottle of brandy." Dederick looked around at all of us, his eyes wild. "I remember Arthur crying. He was always blubbing. Standing there, pleading with me." He drew a shuddering breath. "But I didn't push him off the train, I swear. I didn't hurt him. I would never. I've never hurt anyone in my life."

The second detective had produced a small notebook and a pencil and was scribbling industriously. Dederick's cheeks were wet with tears, although he wasn't sobbing. Ellen had moved to Lucy's side when the younger girl screamed, and they were clinging to each other; both were pale, and it occurred to me they had never witnessed trouble in their short, sheltered lives.

I was holding just as tight to Blanche, who was shuddering violently. I knew what was in her mind: the noose. I had a horrible impression my sister's bladder had failed her and fervently hoped she wouldn't have to move from the spot she was in and betray her shame to the men on the other side of the room.

Fortunately, Dederick showed more pluck than I had perhaps expected. He straightened up and nodded at the police detectives, his voice firm.

"I'll come with you. I know I'm innocent. You can't harm me if I've done nothing." He swallowed. "Where will you take me?"

"Bow Street." I saw Dederick grow paler, but the senior detective nodded in his turn, seemingly approving of Dederick's bravery. His colleague scribbled. "We'll have to put handcuffs on you once you're in the carriage, you understand, as a precaution, but we won't do it here in front of everyone. These constables are just here to make sure you come with us quietly, like a good gentleman."

"I'll make sure you have everything you need—lawyers and such—and whatever comforts you're allowed," I assured my nephew. "Don't worry, Deddy. I'll take care of your mother."

I looked at the footman, who was still standing, stony-faced, by the door, and summoned up the tone I needed. "Get my coachman to take the young ladies back to Whitcombe and tell him to bring Guttridge back here. Get somebody to take a message to Dr. Fortier in Littleberry that Lady Hastings is ill. But first tell Lady Hastings's maid to attend her here. Nobody else is to come. I want the staff kept in the servants' hall until I come downstairs."

I turned my attention to the Walfort sisters. "Girls, leave us, please. I'll return to Whitcombe once I've taken care of my sister." I forced a smile. "Please don't be distressed. This is all a mistake."

"Thank you, Aunt Helena." Dederick took the five steps needed to place him near the small group of police officers before turning to face Blanche. "I'm sorry, Mama."

And then they were gone somehow, all of them, and Blanche was sinking to the carpet, a heartrending wail escaping her lips at long last.

33
THE JOLLY FOX

"She's sleeping," I said as I closed the door of Hawthorn Hall's drawing room, where Fortier and Guttridge sat by the fire in quiet conversation. "Thank you, Armand. I was afraid for her."

It was the first time I'd called him by his Christian name in front of Guttridge, but it didn't seem to matter.

Fortier rose from his seat and pulled a settee closer to the hearth. As I sat down, he seated himself next to me, taking my hands and chafing them gently.

"You always seem to get cold at moments of crisis." His tone was mildly teasing, but his fingers, strong but delicate of touch, rested on my wrist for a few moments. "But you're not going to faint. Your pulse is excellent."

His hand encircled mine, warm and wonderfully comforting. "Miss Guttridge, would you mind arranging for some tea?" he asked. "For all three of us, of course. We'll save the revelation of this particular family secret, about which, incidentally, I know nothing, for when your mistress is warm and comfortable."

"You should call me just Guttridge, sir." Guttridge rose to

locate the bellpull. "I'm not sure I know the complete story neither."

"I'll tell all once the tea's served," I said.

I gave way to temptation and rested my head on Fortier's shoulder, noting how Guttridge's face softened as she sat down again. She would give me no trouble over Fortier. Much had changed since she'd told me he was the sort that couldn't be trusted.

Darkness had fallen by the time I had done relating the whole story of Dederick, from Blanche's admission of their problems, to the excruciating conversation I'd had with Dederick about Lord Arthur, to the interview Guttridge and I had conducted with Remus Fleetwood. At one point early in my narrative, Guttridge took a breath as if she wanted to say something, but she subsided and I did not stop.

"Where's Rampling?" Fortier frowned. "Does he know his employer's been arrested?"

"It's his half day," said Guttridge, who was putting the remains of our tea in order. "I already asked about him—in fact, it surprised me the police didn't ask to take him too, to talk to him, but perhaps that will happen later. He's an upper servant, so he won't need to come back early."

"We'll have to talk to him." I rubbed my eyes, realizing how tired I was. "I'll have to stay the night, Guttridge, but don't worry—I'll borrow one of Lady Hastings's nightdresses for tonight and have them make up the chaise longue in her room. Could you be here very early tomorrow morning with some clothes? I've telegraphed to our family's lawyers, and I imagine it'll be I rather than Lady Hastings who speaks with them once they get here."

"Of course, my lady." Guttridge hesitated. "But . . . about Rampling . . ."

Fortier sat up a little straighter. "You wanted to say something earlier, didn't you?"

"Yes, sir. I thought of it when her ladyship was telling us about Lord Hastings having what you might call a perverse inclination. I only put two and two together just then because of a remark my young man made to me yesterday evening." She pursed her lips. "We went for a nice walk."

"Silas knows something?" Fortier raised his thick black eyebrows. Of course, he would know Guttridge's swain from the pottery, where until recently he'd had his consulting room.

"He just gave a sort of hint." Guttridge made a moue of disapproval, causing her long nose to twitch. "Our walk ended in the Bird in Hand, and he drank a pint too many, if you ask me. He's usually more discreet."

"What did he say?" Fortier asked.

"I think he meant Rampling could be a—a lover of men too." Guttridge sniffed. "I won't tell you exactly what he said, because his language was rather colorful due to the drink, but I believe his meaning was that Rampling's promiscuous, even with the quality." She looked at me significantly.

"*Not* with Lord Hastings," I said fervently. "Please don't tell me that." If it turned out Dederick had been lying to me, and about Rampling to boot, any hope of my nephew marrying Ellen Walfort would be dashed—because I would prevent it.

"We'll have to ask Silas exactly what he meant." Fortier's expression was eager, interested. "Before we take any steps regarding Rampling. Guttridge, could you fetch Silas to my house tomorrow? Before you go to Lady Helena?"

"After," I said indignantly. "As long as Blanche has recovered a little, you'd better not leave me out of it."

"It was a horrible night," I told Fortier the next morning. I had arrived at his house very early; by tacit consent, we ensconced ourselves on the sofa in the back parlor, where Fortier was in the habit of dining and receiving visitors. He had converted the largest room at the front into a small operating theater, used the other front room for consultations, and had made the smallest room into a study. I had not yet seen the bedrooms.

"But Lady Hastings is fit to be left?" Fortier slipped an arm over my shoulders as I rested my aching head on his chest.

"Banham is with her, and somebody from Piper, Wiggins, and Showell should be along later today; it will comfort her a little, I think, to have some practical, legal advice," I said. "I've given Banham strict instructions on how to brew more lemon balm tea when she wakes and to send for me if necessary, but Blanche is in a deep sleep now. She woke twice in hysterics; she had terrible dreams about Dederick on the gallows."

I yawned. "It was a good thing Guttridge brought our bag of what she calls 'fainting cures' along with her when they fetched her yesterday. I brewed us lemon balm tea to lift Blanche's mood and sprinkled plenty of lavender oil around her bedroom to calm her, but most of the time I talked." I sighed. "Poor Blanche. It's odd, you know; I was so small when Blanche married Francis and left Hyrst that I feel I hardly know her, but now I've spent the entire night in her bed. It helped to keep her calm to have me there."

"So you've had barely any sleep." Fortier kissed the top of my forehead.

"Mmmm. I like your house." Another yawn stretched my jaw. "Will you mind terribly living at Whitcombe? It's so cozy here."

Fortier's chest moved in a brief laugh. "Why should I

mind living in my beloved's enormous house? I can always keep this one for consultations anyway. I have no burning desire to live above my shop, as it were; in fact, I don't really care where I live as long as you're there." Another movement of laughter. "Whitcombe will certainly be convenient for the hospital if I accept Ned's offer."

"True. And perhaps even you will be glad to get away from the smell of carbolic on occasion. Although I'm getting accustomed to it." Fortier's operating room was scrubbed down after every use, and weekly if it hadn't been used, and the resinous and somehow leathery fragrance of the carbolic soap permeated the room where we sat, or rather, reclined. The immense mulberry tree that dominated the walled garden was visible to us, its bare branches waving in a way I found oddly protective; the sounds of Fortier's servants going about their morning tasks reached us through the open door, and the fire crackled quietly.

"Will you turn your house in Kensington Square into a surgery too?" I shifted my position, enjoying the subdued prickles of unsatisfied desire our closeness was inflicting on me, both torment and anticipatory delight. The smell of Fortier's cologne was enough to make me want to put my hands on him despite my tiredness and the contingencies of the day, but Guttridge would arrive soon with Silas, and so I contented myself with breathing in the scent of him and thinking about our future together as an antidote to my fears for Dederick and Blanche.

Fortier's arms tightened around me. "I have an absolute horror of inadvertently starting a London practice. No, *ma belle*, I'm determined to be a country doctor. When we go to London, I intend to be just another gentleman, albeit one who attends the meetings of the medical societies. I plan to keep the house pretty much as it is; unless you have plans for it?"

Fortier moved, trying to see my face. "The house will be yours as well after all. Our London residence, if you don't object to Kensington Square."

"I have no objection to it; why should I?" I smiled. "It's a lovely house."

"It's not an aristocratic part of London." Fortier settled back down into the corner of the sofa. "Professional men, artists, writers, that sort of resident. Some doctors and a school."

"I can bear to mingle with the middle classes." The idea of strolling around Kensington arm in arm with Fortier struck me as a way in which I might actually enjoy London. "As I've said before, it appears to have worked for Gerry. I'd thought of buying a London house so Michael can use Scott House undisturbed, at least till O comes back to England, but I'd be perfectly happy with your father's house. Your house."

"Our house." Fortier's lips found my neck, but then he lifted his head. "That's the door knocker."

I sighed, sitting up as Fortier rose to his feet and followed his housekeeper, who had bustled into the hallway in response to the rap on the front door. His house had no other entrance, being tightly squeezed between its neighbors, like many Littleberry dwellings; his servants would probably come in via the garden, but all visitors, high and low, were greeted at the door.

Deprived of the warmth of Fortier's body, I took a moment to yawn and stretch and steel myself to the labors of the day. I could hear Fortier greeting Guttridge with his usual courtesy and her reply; a more boisterous tone in Fortier's voice then suggested he was shaking Silas's hand. The sound of a pleasant voice, a light tenor softened by the Sussex burr, caused a prickle of excitement; at last I was going to meet Guttridge's "young man." I rose to my feet, readying myself for the moment.

Guttridge greeted me with a smile as she entered the parlor. She was followed closely by a thin man of medium height with a mop of light brown curls, thinning over a high forehead. His large hazel eyes were his best feature, and taken as a whole, he had a pleasing appearance. We shook hands, smiling at each other in recognition; I had certainly seen him here and there in Littleberry, and there was always a certain fellow-feeling in acknowledging the shared bond of dwelling in the same little town despite our different stations in life.

At Fortier's behest, Silas took a seat on the sofa I had recently vacated, with Guttridge beside him; Fortier and I repaired to the room's armchairs, but not before Fortier had shut both door and window to prevent the servants from hearing our conversation and added another log to the fire.

"Bertie says I must tell you about Gid Rampling," Silas said as soon as all these preparations were complete. "And that I must leave nothing out." He looked at Guttridge, who nodded, while I bit my lip to stop myself smiling at hearing her called "Bertie."

"I'll try to remember everything, my lady, sir." Silas looked at me and Fortier in turn. "Bertie says it's important and I should be as honest as if I'd taken an oath in the dock. So I will, for Bertie's sake, and I hope you won't mind hearing it." He cleared his throat noisily, as if nervous, but plunged onward without waiting for us to reply. "You see, sometimes I go to the Jolly Fox."

He paused as if this detail were significant, and then, seeing neither Fortier nor I reacted, continued. "I see that doesn't mean much to you." His lean cheeks took on a tinge of pink.

"It's a public house, isn't it?" I asked. "Near the shipyard." Littleberry had dozens of public houses, mostly very small, but except for two or three coaching inns of the better sort and two very low taverns of ill repute, they were exclusively the domain of men, and I had no reason to know them.

"That's right." Silas nodded. "It's popular with artisans of the better sort, and the beer's good, and I go there more for the company than anything else." The flush on his face deepened. "Mostly. But for some, the Fox is a meeting place. For men with certain tastes."

"I see." I kept my tone neutral.

"I often go out for a drink in the evening, my lady, owing to how Bertie doesn't have a lot of time off and I can't abide sitting in my room by myself. Well, my lady—sir—back near the end of August, I'd been in the Fox talking to some of Sir Geraint's workmen about the carvings and so on they're doing at Whitcombe, but they pushed off to their lodgings and I thought I'd have one more pint. I was sort of staring into my glass, not really wanting to go back home and wondering if I should walk down to the sea, when a man came and sat at my table. That was Gideon Rampling, turns out."

He stared down at his hands, which were finely shaped, if a little roughened by his work as a painter and mold maker at Quinn Dermody's pottery. "He was pleasant enough, and I didn't mind talking, but after a bit I could tell he wanted . . . you know . . . and I wasn't keen. It took him a while to get near the point, and then it took me a while to let him down gently because there was something about him told me he might turn nasty if I said the wrong thing, and by the end of it we'd both had a bit too much to drink." He rubbed nervously at a cut on his palm with one finger. "We sort of left it—me and him—*it*—at 'not today, but maybe one day,' and we were still friendly, and he got boastful."

Silas looked at Fortier, his expression anxious. "He wanted to show me he was somebody, I reckon. To make me see I was missing out on a good chance." He swallowed and wiped the injured hand across his mouth. "He said—or he hinted, but he'd been drinking, as I said, and it was more a boast than a hint—that he had a lover with a title when circumstances allowed. I could see he was a valet by his clothes, so I believed him."

Fortier and I looked at each other. Guttridge had been right; this could be significant. I was becoming more interested in Silas Horniblow by the minute; now I'd had time to listen to him, I realized he was more intelligent than I had at first assumed. He would be an odd man out at the Dermody pottery; most of the pottery workers I'd seen around Littleberry, women as well as men since women's small fingers were valued for fine work, were unlettered, cheerful, irreverent people who cared little for their work beyond the money it provided. This man was something more than that: a thinker. Furthermore, he was not using dialect words, speaking with precision as if he was accustomed to making an effort to improve his speech.

"You're brave to admit to that conversation," I said as gently as I could. "Be assured no trouble will come of it for you."

"Yes, my lady. Thank you, my lady." He relaxed a little. "Rampling wasn't talking loud, even if he had drunk a drop too much. You've got to be careful, see, especially a man like that with a good position in life. He'd risk a great deal if he made the wrong move or told the wrong person." He blushed again. "I think he really liked me."

"Did he say anything about his lover?" Fortier asked. "Anything that could identify him?"

Silas frowned, blinking rapidly as he thought. "Only about the gentleman crying easily. He was poking fun a bit at the toffs, begging your pardon. Trying to make me laugh. He did too, but only because I'd had a drop. I almost said something about Bertie working for the quality, but I'm glad I held my tongue. It doesn't do to gossip."

He looked sideways at Guttridge. "That's all, Bertie. It really is, and I hope you're right about no trouble coming for me out of it."

"Not from my lady; you've had her word," Guttridge said stoutly. "And you know the doctor, don't you? They just want to be sure of your evidence."

"I have just one more question." Fortier smiled reassuringly at Silas. "Did you get the impression this lover was in the past or the present?"

"The present, definitely." This time, Silas's answer came quickly. "It's funny, I can still see the smile on his face, trying to charm me and maybe make me want him more for being popular with other men." His lip curled a little.

"Have you seen Rampling since then?" Fortier asked.

"Oh yes." Silas nodded. "Once or twice in the Jolly Fox, once or twice in the town. We're on nodding terms, friendly, but not like we'll stop and talk. I think his mind's been elsewhere lately."

And with that, there was little more to be learned from Silas, who, moreover, had to get to work. Guttridge accompanied him to the door; I heard the sound of a kiss, but an affectionate peck rather than anything lover-like. I had to admit, meeting Silas had increased rather than satisfied my curiosity about this friendship.

"Thank you, Guttridge," Fortier said when she returned. "And thank Silas again from us, won't you? As Lady Helena said, it was brave of him to admit so much."

"I know all about it, in case you're wondering." Guttridge had brought in my coat and hat; depositing the latter article on the sofa, she moved behind me to help me with the coat. "He's not—well, not *very* that way inclined. It's just a weakness he has, and he only gives in to it every so often. He's a good man." One corner of her long mouth turned up as she moved in front of me to position my hat. "And very discreet. Keeping company with me helps to stop gossip about him, and I like being with him. He's clever and kind and a good friend, and I'm resolved not to marry, so clever and kind does me just fine."

34
LADY HELENA'S INVESTIGATIVE BLOOD IS UP

I returned to Hawthorn Hall to find Blanche eating toast. She was very pale, with dark rings around her eyes, but the fact she was eating lifted the cloud of anxiety that had descended on me as I traveled toward Broadmere.

I sat on the bed to embrace her, being careful not to unbalance her tray. "Is there more coffee?" I asked. "Or perhaps I should ring for some more? It smells delicious." I had not taken the time for breakfast.

"You could, I suppose." Blanche took the lid off the coffeepot and peered into it. "I can't get the taste of the concoctions you gave me last night out of my throat. I wouldn't let Banham give me any more of that horrible tea. Still . . ."

Her gaze met mine, devoid of the usual expression of defiant superiority. "You were trying to help, and you did, and I'm grateful."

"Of course I want to help. I'm your sister."

I put my hand on hers, glad when she turned it over so the palm was upward, and clasped my fingers. "Would you be able to see whoever Piper, Wiggins, and Showell send on your own?" I asked. "I hate to desert you, but there's something that's very much on my mind, and I simply must return to Whitcombe—"

"Is this because of your Americans?" The sharper note was back in Blanche's voice. "Now they've seen Dederick arrested, they'll doubtless want to leave Whitcombe. Is it already in the papers?" She paled a little more. "I suppose Gerry knows."

"I have no idea. And, to be honest, I have no intention of taking the time to find out. There's something I need to verify, which is why I want to go back to Whitcombe, only I had to come here first to see how you were. I'll write a note for the solicitor so he has the facts of Dederick's arrest —in case you can't remember—and the questions I have about whether we can see Dederick and so on, but there's something else I need to think about. Is Rampling still here?"

"Rampling? Why?" Blanche frowned. "I don't know where he is. Banham said he wanted to speak to me about something—probably wants to give notice—but I couldn't possibly. I must look an absolute fright."

I sighed, realizing the man from Piper, Wiggins, and Showell was going to have a hard time of it whenever he turned up. No matter; I needed to get back to Whitcombe, and I needed to find a way to have Rampling attend me at my own house.

"I'll go look for Rampling and send Banham to you at the same time." I got off the bed. Blanche made a face.

"The man's probably lazing around in the servants' hall. I don't like the creature—and now Dederick is paying his wages for no work."

"He may be quite distressed, Blanche." Or he may not, and after what we'd heard from Silas, it seemed important to ascertain Rampling's mood. And there was something else of which I needed to make absolutely certain.

"I need your opinion," I said to Blanche, who was pouring herself the remains of the coffee without offering me any. "Do you suspect Rampling may have a preference for men?"

The question took Blanche by surprise; she coughed on her toast, draining her cup to stop the coughing before she spoke.

"I know he has, the horrible beast. Dederick said Rampling once dared to make an approach to *him*. He should have dismissed the man on the spot, but—there." She let her hands fall onto the coverlet in a gesture of helplessness. "My darling boy must have believed it would be better to retain the filthy creature's loyalty than risk him gossiping. Why do we give these people such power over us?"

"Because we're too lazy to do things for ourselves." I leaned against the bedpost, gesturing toward her breakfast tray. "Here, since I'm going to the servants' hall, I'll take that down."

"It's not laziness." Blanche's eyes had recovered their accustomed coldness, and she clutched at her tray as I bent toward it. "It's a matter of keeping up the dignity of our class and providing employment to those God has placed below us. You certainly *won't* carry a tray downstairs. The very idea."

"I'm so glad you're feeling better." The expression on Blanche's face lightened my mood for a moment. "I really ought to get back to Whitcombe. I'll find Rampling, send Banham to you, write a note for the lawyers, and then go home."

Rampling was not in the servants' hall. A few minutes' conversation with the Hawthorn Hall domestics elicited the information that, having failed to secure an interview with Blanche, he had taken the train to Eastbourne to visit the tailoring establishments, with a view to purchasing a few items he thought Dederick might find useful. So much for Blanche's insinuation that he would be idle.

Perhaps his absence would work in my favor. I left a note for Rampling to say that, Lady Hastings being unwell, I would try to resolve any problems he might have. Would he kindly come to Whitcombe when he returned, even if the hour were late?

I spent another twenty minutes answering the questions of the Hawthorn Hall staff, reassuring them that all would be well, giving instructions on looking after the solicitor when he arrived, and asking Banham to do her best to make sure her mistress was ready to receive that gentleman. I had to repeat everything at least once—a group of anxious servants was remarkably hard to deal with—but at last I was free to go.

The journey home gave me time to reflect. I had been brought up to regard any perversion of nature—or biblical instruction—as wicked, sinful, shameful, something to be whispered about but never spoken. I had barely understood the whispers until I had married Justin, but my late husband's views were broad and generous. He, like Daniel before him, had talked about questioning what I had been taught to be true. And then there was the biblical instruction to "Judge not, that ye not be judged." Should I not question my own judgment with respect to Rampling? Did I, like Blanche, judge him already as a "filthy creature" and "horrible beast" because of what Silas had told us? Why was I so ready to consider the possibility that Rampling was a murderer when I could not do the same with Dederick?

There had to be something more, was my conclusion. I needed evidence—and I thought I might have it, slender as it was. But the plan growing so vaguely in my mind could be a dangerous one.

My thoughts swirled, endlessly returning to the same points of departure and divergence, as my carriage descended the steep road from the promontory on which Broadmere had been built in the time of bad King John. They blinded my eyes to the flat, muddy lanes, straggling hedges, and brimming ditches of the marsh's edge as the coachman whipped up the horses, following a road that had been under the sea when the ancient Romans had arrived. But by the time we turned inland again, heading for Littleberry and Whitcombe, I had resolved to bury my prejudices and look only at the evidence. After all, Guttridge and I had taken careful notes. We only knew a fraction of what the police must know, but for Dederick's sake, we had to do our best with that small knowledge.

I arrived at Whitcombe to find Ellen and Lucy in the green drawing room with Thomas, blond and curly and red heads close together as they scrutinized the morning's papers. Lucy, who sat nearest the door, heard my footsteps before the others did. She sprang up immediately and flung herself at me, her lovely eyes brimming with tears.

"Is Lady Hastings all right?" she sobbed into my shoulder. "I thought she would die on the spot; I swear I did. Poor thing—poor Dederick—and after everything your family went through this summer. Ellen and I were up half the night praying for all of you."

Ellen, who was rising to her feet, showed evidence of the night's vigil in her pallor and tear-reddened eyes. My heart went out to both of them.

"Bless you for not rejecting us as a collection of inbred, immoral half-wits." I hugged both girls to me, putting out a hand to Thomas as he rose more slowly and came to join us. "I thought you might be on your way to the Continent by now, to find your parents."

"We wouldn't dream of deserting you." Ellen kissed me on the cheek. "If I weren't so worried about Mother's health, I'd write straightaway to her and Father and *order* them to come back and help you. Father always says you must never decide about a person until you understand them, and their circumstances, thoroughly."

"I was just thinking along those same lines about someone else," I admitted. "But on no account must your parents return. I've already wired our lawyers in London; that's all the help we need at the moment. And my sister is recovering from her shock, thank you." I smiled at the two young ladies. "I'm just sorry I might have to absent myself from your company for a little while. Will you be all right?"

"Oh, we have Thomas." Ellen turned to my nephew, slipping a hand through his good arm. "When we got back yesterday, we were frantic, but Thomas was marvelous. He's going to make the most wonderful pastor one of these days."

Thomas lowered his eyes modestly at this praise, but I could see he was practically glowing with happiness inside. As soon as I could, I drew him aside and asked him to keep the Walfort sisters busy for the evening and then sought the peace and solitude of my morning room. I needed to think.

It wasn't long, though, before Guttridge appeared, as always aware I needed her before I even knew it myself. Her first question was purely practical.

"Are you hungry, my lady?"

"Completely hollow inside." It wasn't until then I realized I'd missed both breakfast and luncheon. "I assume the household routines haven't collapsed in chaos just because I'm not paying attention to them, and everyone else is fed? Including yourself?"

"We've all eaten, thank you, my lady. Do fried soles with melted butter appeal? With apple fritters to follow? Mrs. Foster can have those ready for you in ten minutes."

My stomach gave an embarrassingly loud growl. "I will be ready in five. And Guttridge, do you know what time the train from Eastbourne arrives at Broadmere?"

"The next one will be there at 2:50, my lady. Then 3:30, I believe. Would you like me to find a timetable?"

"Yes, thank you." Left alone, I jotted down figures on a piece of blotting paper. Rampling could take anything from twenty to thirty minutes to walk from Broadmere's station, which was in the valley, up to Hawthorn Hall. Then he might spend anything from thirty minutes to an hour at the Hall and then perhaps take another thirty minutes to get to Whitcombe, assuming he found a mode of transport other than walking. Considerably longer if he walked, but the earliest I might expect him would be in just two hours' time. I must not delay any longer.

"Guttridge, could you please come back in five minutes to collect a note for Dr. Fortier? And ask Mrs. Foster to have some more apple fritters ready, in case he's hungry. And coffee when he arrives, plenty of it, for both of us. And would you please bring me our notes on the case? I'll read them as I eat."

FORTIER ARRIVED AN HOUR LATER. I HAD A SECOND SERVING OF apple fritters while he ate his way steadily through a large amount of plain buttered crumpets, washed down by black coffee.

"I want to talk to Rampling alone," I told him. "But I don't want to *be* alone, if you get my drift. I've been receiving people in the other library"—we were in the small library, seated by the fire—"and you can easily hide in one of the reading bays in the gallery. You'll have a good view of where we'll be sitting, and you'll hear everything perfectly without being noticed. I think Rampling will be more at ease if it's just me he's talking to."

"But then it'll be you who has to broach the question of his lover." Fortier looked a little shocked.

"All the better, because he won't be expecting a lady to embark on such a subject." I felt pleased with that argument. "He thinks I know nothing of such matters; he himself said to me, when we spoke before, that the fondness between Dederick and Lord Arthur was what he called 'unnatural.' Disingenuous, don't you think?"

"Almost calculating." Fortier pushed his plate away.

"Exactly." I had by now based my opinion of Rampling on our written notes, not on my prejudices. "He was play-acting, I think. Pretending he was shocked, pretending he was sorry to have to shock *me*."

Fortier thought for a moment. "It would, of course, be a familiar strategy for him to act as if he found such things shocking, so nobody would suspect they applied to him too. If you had to go through life hiding such an important facet of your character, with the stakes as high as they are, you too might become a habitual dissembler."

"You're very fair-minded. I adore you more every day."

"Keep your mind on your task, Lady Detective." Fortier blew me a kiss. "So I'm to hide in the gallery and do what? Rescue you if you scream?"

"Well, that, obviously. I'm not really sure what you're going to do, exactly. I just know I want you to be there. My aim is to catch Rampling in a lie."

"Oho." Fortier nodded toward the two notebooks I had balanced on the arm of my chair. "Lady Helena's investigative blood is up. Isn't Guttridge terribly put out you're not including her?"

"Probably, but I have to do this alone. I want Rampling to feel he has the upper hand. Now, let's wash our hands and so forth and make ready. He might be here soon."

35
MAGNETIC FORCE

"It's good of you to see me, my lady."

Rampling's smile caused two deep dimples to appear on his lean cheeks rather appealingly. Indeed, the man had what the poet Donne called "magnetic force." Had he been born into a higher station in life, he might have done well in Parliament.

"I didn't think it was fair to leave whatever matter you wish to discuss unanswered," I said. "I don't believe Lady Hastings will be in any state to talk to you for a few days."

I was standing, since Rampling had expressed himself reluctant to sit down in my presence, and I didn't want to crane my neck to look at him. "Besides, I'd like to go over your account of that day on the train again, if you please. You were such a good witness; I'm keen to listen to you again. But your business first." I smiled in a way I hoped looked encouraging.

"I wanted to ask permission to visit a friend in Wiltshire since I'm not immediately needed," Rampling said. "I know I ought to be here waiting for his lordship to come home, but this arrest has unsettled me horribly. I keep thinking I should be in London, but I would have to ask her ladyship to pay my board and lodging there, and I don't imagine for a moment she'd want to do that. It's my impression she doesn't like me much, truth be told."

"So you wish to take time off instead?"

"Well, yes." The large brown eyes held a sincere expression. "I have a friend in Salisbury I haven't seen for some while. We were footmen together and still write to each other. I've also thought of going up to Leeds, which is where I grew up, to see if I can find my brothers and sisters and make amends. I wanted more out of life than they did, you see, and we fell out when I was young." He shrugged one thin shoulder. "But that depends on how fast I go through my savings, and I may be on a fool's errand there." He smiled. "I could just stay in Salisbury, where I'm sure of a welcome."

"And how long would you be gone?"

"A month at the most, and I'll come back immediately if needed, of course. I pray Lord Hastings will be released soon; naturally, I do."

"Naturally." I thought for a moment. I somehow doubted Rampling would return from his trip to Salisbury, if that were really where he intended to go. And the conversation I wanted to have with him might render all of this nugatory in any case. Still, the better course might be to seem to agree and put him at his ease.

"Very well," I said. "I'm sure that in the circumstances, I can speak for Lady Hastings, given her indisposition. Now, would you please sit down? You're keeping me standing since you're too tall for me to look up at you from a chair."

"As you wish, my lady."

Rampling seemed amused at this reminder of the physical differences between us; well, it was all to the good if he thought of me as a weak and ineffective little woman. He waited for me to seat myself in an armchair before taking a position on the settee opposite the fire, crossing his legs as he leaned back comfortably, now seemingly perfectly at ease in my company. Good.

I risked the tiniest flick of the eyes upward as Rampling looked down at his nails, which were neat and shining. I couldn't see Fortier, but I was sure he could see me, and Rampling too. No sigh or rustle betrayed his presence. If he were to move, it was possible we'd hear nothing above the chinks and crackles of the wood burning and settling in the vast fireplace and the intermittent gusts of wind from the sea hitting the windows and moaning around the stonework.

"Remind me, now, of that day on the train," I said.

I had chosen my armchair because it was where I had secreted the two slim books in which Guttridge and I had made notes. It was one of a pair of chairs upholstered with Turkey carpets in the days of Justin's grandfather; someone had fashioned extra covers for its arms out of small rugs, which formed a convenient hiding place.

Rampling smiled indulgently. "Well, my lady, I was in the brake van with Mr. Fleetwood, God rest his soul." He crossed himself. "Us and the guard, of course, who would move around from his seat by the brake to his desk or go into the little viewing box, as he needed to do, while Mr. Fleetwood and I stayed by the fire. We talked a bit, and sometimes Mr. Fleetwood would doze off, but then he'd wake up and we'd talk some more. Old people sleep light, I find."

"Just so. And there were three stops? What happened at each one?"

Rampling interlaced his well-kept fingers. "First stop, I looked in on his lordship, but he was drunk and swore at me to go away, so I did. I saw Lawther—Lord Arthur's man—who told me his master was in the parlor car and had dismissed him to the servants' carriages, where he was quite happy to have a drink with the grooms and loaders." He made a face, as if he disapproved of this arrangement.

"But you never saw Lord Arthur."

"Well, no, but I had no reason to doubt Lawther's word. The parlor car was where most of the gentry gathered, there or the dining car, to be sociable. The compartments were there for anyone who wanted peace and quiet or privacy." He laid a slight emphasis on the word "privacy" and accompanied it with a worldly smile, as if to say he knew well I'd understand the desire to be private. "I'm sure the police took evidence from guests who'd seen Lord Arthur in one of the Pullman cars."

"I suppose so."

But I wasn't, in fact, at all sure just how much the police had learned from the exalted travelers since most of them had dispersed not long after the discovery of Lord Arthur's body. And just how observant were people who were eating, drinking, conversing, and playing cards? I had enough experience of house parties to know that card players, in particular, were heedless of what went on around them.

"And at the second stop, you looked in on Lord Hastings again?" I asked.

Rampling nodded. "Yes, but he was asleep. Lawther was in a hurry for the WC, and a little under the weather, so he asked me to find his master and see if he needed anything. I set off to search for Lord Arthur, but I couldn't find him. I assumed he was in the station lavatory, or moving around from place to place, and I'd just missed him. It wasn't that long a stop, and I didn't have time to look everywhere, so I got back to the brake van."

I nodded. "The third stop?"

"A long stop at Crewe. I saw Lawther again, and this time he was worried because he couldn't find Lord Arthur. So I helped him look, and when we couldn't find the gentleman, we told the stationmaster. Which led them to finding his body, poor soul."

"Very concise," I remarked. "In fact, far more concise than when we last spoke, if memory serves."

"I can give you details if you wish, my lady."

"I may wish. Tell me—when you were in the brake van, could the guard see you?"

I watched Rampling's face carefully, noting the compression of his lips and the very slight paling of them. "He was busy, like I told you," he said, more slowly than before. "But there would have been almost no time he wouldn't have seen me. Us."

At the very edge of my vision, I caught a movement, as if Fortier had stood up, and thanked heaven Rampling was facing toward the fire. I knew Fortier had suddenly seen what had been in my mind for the last few hours. Emboldened to make my next move, I slipped a hand underneath the stiff piece of carpet protecting the arm of my chair and brought out our notebooks.

"I find that hard to believe." I opened Guttridge's notebook, which contained a fuller and tidier version of my own notes, and turned its pages, running a finger over the neat lines of script. "When you told me about the brake van before —*and* this time—you omitted to mention the partition between where the guard sat and where you and Fleetwood were sitting. You never mentioned the privy of which Fleetwood availed himself. You *did* mention the observation ducket, though."

I looked up from my page at Rampling, whose expression had become less relaxed. "Fleetwood had an impressive memory, given his frailty."

"May I see what you've written down, my lady?" Rampling rose and took a pace or two toward me, the smile back on his face. "It's easy to forget what someone's told you."

"That's why I gave you a second chance to tell me." I smiled back, although having this tall man looming over me made me feel unaccountably nervous. "But I didn't forget. Guttridge and I went through my notes and the conversation I had with you several times, straight after our talk. Guttridge wrote out the version I'm reading now."

"As I'm sure you recall me saying, my lady, you're better than the police." Rampling laughed, yet his laugh wasn't entirely convincing. "But remember that I was always with Mr. Fleetwood."

"He was asleep much of the time," I countered. "Even so, there was a memory bothering him, as I'm sure you know. He thought it might be a dream but couldn't dismiss it from his mind." I took a deep breath. "Did he see something? Or hear something? You and Lord Arthur talking. The sound of footsteps and the door opening and closing as you showed Lord Arthur out onto the observation platform."

"That's daft." Rampling's laugh became louder. "Then the guard would have been watching. I'm sorry, my lady, but you can't just make up a story that fits what you'd like to be the facts. It's far more likely Lord Arthur went looking for Lord Hastings, and Lord Hastings pushed him out of the compartment in a fit of drunken rage."

"But how?" I had been over that possible scene several times in my mind. "Compartments just have a narrow space for one's legs between two benches and a door either side with a sliding window. To get out, one has to wait for the guard to open the door or struggle to push down the window and lean out to work the handle. All this whilst attempting to overpower one's victim? I doubt Lord Arthur would have been willing to be pushed out."

"He might have opened the door himself, threatening

suicide, and then Lord Hastings pushed him. Or he might have jumped, and then Lord Hastings just closed the door."

"And pretended it never happened? My nephew would have to be a master dissembler, and I somehow don't think he is."

"Or he overpowered him with a punch to the jaw and shoved him out. Lord Arthur was a slight man, not much good in a fight, I'd have said."

There was a conscious look in Rampling's eyes and a subtle, unthinking curl of his fist on which I was not keen.

"And you accuse *me* of making up stories?" I sat up as straight as I could, wishing I could see behind Rampling to the gallery. "Lord Hastings is in good health, but he's hardly a hulking fellow. It's not easy to manhandle someone who's unconscious. Believe me, I've had to deal with more than one unconscious guest after dinner, and one needs at least two footmen, sometimes three."

Heaven be praised, I thought I had a glimpse of a movement in the gallery above us. I made a huge effort to keep my eyes on Rampling's face.

"And besides," I said, ready to play my trump card, "I have a further theory. I think Lord Arthur had another lover on the train." I stared the valet straight in the eyes. "You."

A tremor ran through Rampling's thin frame, and he took a step closer to me, his hand twitching. I was still seated; I had perhaps a moment when, if I were quick enough, I could at least try to escape him. But a voice from above made Rampling whirl around.

"Don't hurt the lady."

Fortier spoke clearly and precisely, not shouting, but with a great deal of authority. His hand clutched the gallery railing; I could see the whiteness of his knuckles and the lines of tension in his body.

"I wasn't going to hurt her, sir." Rampling's voice, a little high and breathless now, had a touch of wheedling about it. "I was just shocked by what she said. Where did you get such a terrible lie from, my lady?" He turned back to me.

I shrugged. "Gossip. Littleberry's known for it."

"A lady like yourself shouldn't listen to gossip. Who told you?"

I saw Fortier disappear into the darkness at the far end of the gallery, then reappear as he descended the spiral stair. He was hurrying.

"Because *somebody* must have told you," Rampling said, taking a step back from my chair as Fortier approached. I felt a wave of relief.

"You're clearly going to deny it." Fortier moved so he was face-to-face with Rampling. The valet was the taller of the two, but much narrower in build, especially in the shoulders.

"I don't need to deny anything." The smile had returned to Rampling's face. "Gossip is just gossip. Sticks and stones." He stepped back a pace or two, distancing himself from us.

"But it might make a difference to Lord Hastings, don't you see?" Fortier asked, his expression as pleasant as Rampling's. "And so might Lady Helena's other conclusions. In English law, guilt must be established beyond any possible doubt, so anything that throws doubt on the accusation against Lord Hastings may save his life. Lady Helena has raised some interesting points, and tomorrow she will, I'm sure, communicate those points to the right quarters. The case against Lord Hastings is beginning to look less likely."

He turned a little so he remained directly opposite Rampling, stepping slightly in front of me. "If I were you, I wouldn't leave Littleberry straightaway. To do so just after this conversation may suggest guilt."

"I'll consider that advice, sir." Rampling's face gave nothing away now. "But it's late, and time I left you. Good night, my lady."

"THAT WAS REMARKABLE," FORTIER SAID ONCE WE WERE QUITE alone. "*You* were remarkable. But by God, I'm glad I was here."

"So am I." I was trembling very slightly. "Were you actually going to jump from the gallery if he got any closer? I thought for a moment you were."

"So did I." Fortier grinned. "My protective instincts were winning out against the voice of reason, which was telling me a man with a broken leg would be no help to you."

"It would have been thrilling to see you jump."

I wrapped my arms around Fortier, leaning my head against his chest. "Like seeing you knock Edmund Dorrian-Knowles unconscious with a punch."

"I nearly broke my hand on that occasion, if you remember." Fortier spoke into my hair. "If it's a romantic hero you want—"

But his voice failed him, and his remark was lost. By unspoken consent, we turned our embrace into a long, close, and very passionate kiss.

36

LIKE TO DIE

It was no surprise to me I had trouble getting to sleep, especially after relating the complete tale to Guttridge, who took notes. I awoke very late on Wednesday morning, a little surprised Guttridge had not been in to rouse me from my tardy slumber. I rang the bell.

I was even more surprised when the bell was answered not by Guttridge, but by my housekeeper, Mrs. Eason, carrying my breakfast tray. This was so unusual—why not a maid if Guttridge were busy elsewhere?—I was quite taken aback. Had the normal serene running of Whitcombe suddenly turned on its head?

"Where's Guttridge?" I naturally asked.

"Down at Wellington Gardens, my lady." In another departure from routine, Mrs. Eason set my tray firmly on the table instead of bringing it to my bed.

"Where Silas lives?"

I said the words innocently, but as soon as I pronounced them, a horrible idea assailed me. "Something's happened to him, hasn't it?"

"Yes, my lady." My housekeeper's normally smooth and

placid face creased into lines of distress. "They found him in the twitten behind the cottages when he didn't come to work this morning. Terribly beaten—like to die, they're saying. Bertie—Miss Guttridge, begging your pardon—ran out of the house without her cape, went straight to the stables, and commandeered a carriage."

"Sensible." I threw off sheets and counterpane and scrambled out of bed. "It's like Guttridge not to lose her head entirely."

"It is, my lady. She even thought of telling the coachman to go by Dr. Fortier's house first, to waste no time in getting the doctor in case nobody had thought to summon him. The carriage has just returned, empty."

"Very well." I turned as I reached the connecting door that led to my dressing room and bathroom. "Never mind my breakfast. Send a maid to help me get ready, and tell the coachman we'll be off as soon as I'm decent. Even if Guttridge doesn't need my help, she's going to get it."

I SET OFF IN WHAT LOOKED LIKE THE BEGINNING OF A NASTY storm. The wind had begun to rock my carriage with fierce, roaring gusts; an icy rain beat against the windows as the horses carefully picked their way down the steep road toward Littleberry.

And then we were down in the town, the ponderous old warehouses by the tidal river giving us brief shelter from the worst of the wind, before we struck out again toward the point where the river swept round in a broad curve on its winding course to the sea.

"You'll have to go on foot with James, my lady, to have any hope of reaching the cottages." My coachman had brought the horses to a halt, twisting round to speak through the flap behind his seat. "The river's flooding, and the new road's not safe. James will take you round by the twitten."

"Stay near here in case I need you, but see if you can find shelter for yourself and the horses if you can," I ordered and, haste seeming more important than ceremony, had James the footman lift me down onto the road instead of taking the time to let down the steps.

I gave the parcel containing Guttridge's outer clothing to James and clung to his arm as we proceeded, noting the way the river was lapping ominously at the earth bank protecting the dwellings in this low-lying part of Littleberry as we splashed along the muddy footpath set some three feet higher than the road. The spot, optimistically called Wellington Gardens but with little of the garden about it, would have been a depressing place at the best of times, but in this unusually dark November it was positively bleak. Only a few straggling patches of rank grass and a dispirited young tree dignified the approach to the "cottages," in reality a row of terraced workers' houses built in the '20s. Beyond the short row of buildings was waste ground; only the square outline of the Strict and Particular Baptist Chapel lent a small touch of solid respectability to an area that definitely needed improvement. No wonder Silas was reluctant to return to his lodgings after work. I followed James doggedly into a narrow passage between two houses, my face wet from the icy rain and my skirts already soaked and muddy.

"I might have known I'd see you here, my dear." The voice of my brother-in-law, Ned, emerged from the rain behind me. "I've been dashing around getting a general search for the attacker in place; we can't just leave it to our tiny police force. Jonathan's been helping me."

Allowing the footman to go on ahead, Ned held out a protective arm as I negotiated some slippery cobbles. "I happened to be on my way to Fortier's house when I saw him leaving with Guttridge. He told me Silas had been badly beaten, probably by Dederick's valet, of all people. I hope you can explain that to me."

"I can." I followed James into a narrow hallway, smelling of kippers, that felt even smaller once Ned had joined us. "I have the horrible feeling this is all my fault."

"Ah." Ned removed his top hat, grimacing as water cascaded from the brim, making the damp floor even damper. "I went straight to Hawthorn Hall, and the man's gone. I had to wake Blanche." He made a face. "She said the man went to Whitcombe late yesterday afternoon and never came back to Broadmere, and then she complained strenuously about you interfering and making things worse. You know the sort of thing. She was making such a fuss that when I got back to Littleberry, I let Gerry have the carriage so she could go to her."

My heart was in the process of sinking to my galoshes when a door near us opened, revealing Fortier. His face brightened.

"Helena—thank God. Ned." He reached out a hand to Ned, who shook it. "Helena, please tell me you came in a carriage. I'm furious with myself for letting yours go back to Whitcombe."

"It's here," I reassured him. "Or at least it's a little way off. The road's flooding."

Fortier clearly noticed James for the first time and spoke directly to him. "Can you manage the other end of a stretcher?" He smiled briefly as James nodded, then returned his attention to Ned and me. "I need to get Silas to my house straightaway. Guttridge and I have improvised a way to carry him."

"That bad?" Ned asked as we moved to allow Fortier to reach for his greatcoat, which was hanging from a hook on the wall.

"His spleen is badly damaged." Fortier was fastening his coat rapidly. I thought I could hear Guttridge's voice in the room behind him, talking softly in a rapid monotone. "I have to operate." He dropped his voice to a murmur. "It was a vicious attack, and to be honest, I'm worried. Even if the operation goes well, there's a high risk of infection and other consequences after a splenectomy. We may soon be hunting for a murderer."

I HELPED GUTTRIDGE DON HER CAPE AND HAT AS FORTIER AND the footman, with some assistance from Ned, began carefully maneuvering Silas out of the house on the ladder Fortier had padded with blankets to serve as a stretcher. As soon as she was dressed, Guttridge picked up Fortier's medical bag, clutching it to her as if it were a life preserver on a sinking ship. Her face was haggard.

"I'll kill 'im." Her Cockney accent was breaking through her normally correct speech, her wide mouth set in an angry line. "So 'elp me, if I get 'im in front of me, I'll swing for 'im. Did you see Silas's face?"

I nodded dumbly. Silas's head was an ugly mess of blood and bruises, both eyes swollen shut. The arm that lay upon the blanket covering him was also bruised, as if he had attempted to defend himself.

I put my arm around Guttridge. She was taller than me, and she had the bag in her arms, so the gesture was ineffectual, but it elicited a nod of the head and a twitch of the lips. I thought she might be fighting back tears, but in a moment she too was gone, following Fortier and James as they disappeared into the narrow twitten with the makeshift stretcher between them.

There would be no room in the carriage for Ned and me,

so we retreated into Silas's room, viewing the cramped quarters with some dismay.

"I thought the Dermody pottery workers were better paid." I could see the room was carefully arranged, with a bed in an alcove and a tiny table at the other end, surrounded by shelves containing books and artist's materials, but it looked damp and smelled of drains.

"They are." Ned began pulling bloodied sheets off the bed. "Silas's wages are higher than most too, due to his skills, but he gives most of his money to his family. That's how many of the common folk make ends meet; they help each other." He grinned at me. "Come along, Helena. A bit of work won't harm you, and it'll keep us warm."

He was right. There was nothing much we could do except bundle up the bedlinen and mop the floor, since the rest of the room was clean enough, but even that task filled the time. Ned found a bucket in the hallway and filled it at the pump in front of the cottages, although, as he said with a laugh, he might have filled it faster by leaving it out in the rain. The upstairs rooms were clearly occupied; I could hear the desolate sobbing of a woman, a child wailing, and somewhere in the vicinity a man and woman were shouting abuse at each other. Ned and I talked as we worked, and I explained the events of the previous afternoon.

"Rampling's disappearance makes it all pretty conclusive, eh?" My brother-in-law groaned as he straightened up, eyeing the pile of sheets and the bloodstained mattress with distaste. "I wondered why Fortier was so certain it was he."

"I betrayed Silas to him, I think." I shut my eyes briefly, remembering Rampling's expression as he asked me who had gossiped. "If he dies . . ."

"Don't think like that." Ned, who had known me since I was born, put a fatherly arm around my shoulder. "We have to pray he lives—and I will see what I can do about his lodgings. Quinn can probably help."

"And I'll send my people round with a new mattress and bedlinen." I forbore from saying, "If he lives."

"That's the spirit." Ned's arm tightened. "We can help Silas best by giving Rampling's description to the police; you'll need to come with me as I don't know the man." His bearded chin lifted as a knock sounded at the door. "Let's hope that's James, come to tell us the carriage is back."

IT WAS INDEED THE FOOTMAN, WITH A WARNING THAT THE river was overtopping the earth bank and could soon reach Wellington Gardens. The impending disaster had clearly impinged on the consciousness of the neighborhood, and by the time we were trotting along the path with a clear view of the water beginning to spill over the inadequate flood wall, several men were organizing themselves to get people and belongings up to the higher floors of the houses. It became evident that Silas—if he lived—may not have a room to return to.

We, at least, had a carriage, but any hope of reaching the town by the faster lower road was gone by the time we arrived at it. My coachman took the slow, circuitous route upward through a series of ill-made, steep lanes that led to the higher ground where the marsh ended, with frequent stops as we encountered spots where the storm was washing the surface of the road away or creating quagmires of mud on the more level ground.

It was a while before we reached the former turnpike road that led past Whitcombe Lane. I had a glimpse of the scarred land and piles of dirt and clay that represented the future foundations of the new hospital before we began our slow descent back down into the town by the landward side.

"I'm dreading what we may find," I admitted to Ned as the carriage lurched onward through the gale. "If Silas has died . . ."

"I know." Ned grasped my hand in his large one; our gloves were damp, but I could still feel the warmth of him through the layers of leather and wool. "And I feel bad about abandoning Wellington Gardens in a flood, but our priority has to be catching Rampling. I will deal with the flood defenses and the state of those houses later—if they don't get washed away—but first, the hunt."

His brown eyes, normally so benevolent, held a glint of ferocity. "Here we are on the cobbles; we can make a little speed at last. A quick stop at Fortier's to find out the state of things, and then on with the chase!"

"He's still alive."

I'd seen Fortier's face in the window, clearly looking out for us, and it was he who opened the door as my carriage drew to a halt outside his house. I closed my eyes briefly in response to his words, giving thanks for Silas's survival.

"When I saw you waiting for us, I thought the worst," I admitted as Fortier stood back to allow Ned and me to enter his house. "Did you operate on him?"

"Of course. With Guttridge as my assistant. She wouldn't have it any other way." Fortier smiled. "A remarkably brave woman, that. She's nursing him now, and she's sent for one of his sisters. And for Tilda to bring half the contents of your herb room from Whitcombe. *And* she's sent orders to Whitcombe for Mrs. Foster to send broth for when the patient starts to recover. She may bring him through this by sheer force of will."

"Surely, you haven't had time to do all that." I glanced at the window but could get no clue as to the hour of day from the dark sky and sheeting rain. "What o'clock is it?"

Both men removed their watches from their waistcoat pockets and opened the dial covers. "Three thirty." Fortier spoke first. "I was beginning to wonder if some accident had befallen you on the way."

"The flood befell us." I pushed back the damp hair from my forehead. "It clearly took us far longer than I realized to get to you. Will Silas live, do you think? Is he conscious?"

"He's had two brief moments of consciousness since the operation." Fortier glanced toward his consulting room, from which I deduced the patient must be in there in some kind of temporary cot, with Guttridge in attendance. "He hasn't spoken. He's been trying to open his eyes, and that gives me hope. I'll have to get back to him soon, although there's not much I can do for him at this point. He needs nursing, careful observation, and sleep."

"Not murder, then—not at this moment." Ned was looking out of the window, clearly impatient to be doing something. "Wounding or causing grievous bodily harm with intent to murder, though."

"Life imprisonment." Fortier nodded. "If we can catch him."

"And this is all my fault." My heart was heavy in my chest. "I put it into Rampling's head that it was Silas, didn't I?" *Interfering and making things worse.*

"You did your best not to." Fortier touched my cheek. "But I don't suppose it would have taken Rampling long to discover Silas had come to my house, knowing what Littleberry's like. We didn't make a secret of his visit. And your plan to interview Rampling again was a clever one. Perhaps

I'm to blame too, for letting him leave instead of going to the police immediately."

"But we didn't have sufficient proof—just an idea," I said. "And now we may have our proof at the price of Silas's life or health." I thought of Guttridge again, and my voice broke.

"Stop it, Helena." Ned's low growl prevented what would probably have been an outburst of tears on my part. "Nobody's to blame but Rampling."

"That bastard." Fortier's eyes were dark. "I've seen the results of many beatings, but rarely one as violent as this. He meant to kill."

"So let's catch him." Ned shut his pocket watch with a snap. "Will you come with me to the police station to give a full description of the man, Helena? Fortier's needed by his patient's side, and I don't want to lose any more time."

"I'll go wherever you want." The fierce desire to act ignited in me at last, burning away all traces of blame and regret.

"Good. Let's hope the search party has something to report." Ned began tugging on his damp gloves. "*Somebody* must surely have seen Rampling leave Littleberry."

37
A TICKET TO DOVER

It took just minutes to reach the police station, but I was grateful for my carriage to keep us out of the howling gale and the rain slashing horizontally through the air. My horses and servants had been exposed to the weather for hours, so after a brief consultation with Ned, I dispatched the lot of them back to Whitcombe to get warm and dry. We could hire transportation if necessary.

"Jonathan!" It cheered me to see my cousin in his field uniform, sharing the warmth of the station's fireplace with a group of other men while yet more volunteers sat around on assorted chairs, on tables, or on the floor. All were in various degrees of dampness and wreathed in a fug of tobacco smoke. Some rose to their feet as I entered; most of them greeted me in some way since, as one of "the Family," I was known to practically everyone in Littleberry.

"No luck, then?" I went straight to Jonathan, acknowledging the greetings as I threaded through the throng of men. "Ned brought me here to give an accurate description of Rampling since I've probably seen more of him than most of you. I don't suppose you have any clues as to where he might be?"

"The description will certainly be handy." Jonathan pulled a chair one of the volunteers had vacated closer to the fire and urged me into it. "It's dashed difficult to find a trace of someone who's not well-known in the town, especially in this kind of weather. Even in a tiny place like Littleberry, there'll be places to hide. We've quartered the town fairly thoroughly, but it can be hard to find a resourceful man who wants to stay hidden. Take it from an officer who's led more than one search in his career."

"And the railway station's been watched?" Ned, who had followed me, spread his hands out to the fire with a sigh of satisfaction.

"Just as you ordered, although they stopped the trains at two because of flooding along the coast." Jonathan shrugged. "We've checked all the livery places; nobody has hired a horse or cart or carriage of any sort so far today. The commercial travelers are all waiting it out in the public houses till the storm abates."

"What about early, before the alarm was given?" Ned asked. "He may well have taken an early train." He frowned heavily.

"Thought of that—eventually." Jonathan smiled cheerfully. Of course he did not know Silas, so to him the whole exercise must seem like something of a game. "As I said, the trains aren't running, so your stationmaster's coming up here with his ledger to tell us about the early passengers."

"He'll certainly be able to rule out most of the travelers," I said. "Mr. Sinden knows everyone in the town, and except for his mealtimes, he's always on the gate."

"So I've heard." Jonathan nodded enthusiastically. "I've gathered the men here for a bit of a rest and a bite to eat while we review Sinden's ledger and gather our strength for another push. The Royal Oak will soon be here with beer and pies. I'll send a party out to Broadmere in case he's skulking around near Hawthorn Hall; some fugitives stick close to home on the assumption everyone will be looking farther afield."

"Good man." Ned's expression lightened, and he thumped Jonathan on the shoulder. "Army training, eh? Always feed the troops. I could do with a pie myself."

Mr. Sinden was a quicker man than his drooping eyelids and mustache, and his lazy Sussex speech, would suggest. He arrived, water streaming from his oilcloth cape, in time to partake of the refreshments from the Royal Oak, and I had the interesting experience of eating a warm pie from a piece of waxed paper, washed down with half a pint of ale. The inner man—and woman—satisfied, most of the volunteers set off into the storm to search Broadmere for the first time and Littleberry for the second, armed with the detailed description of Rampling I had provided.

This left a small group, kept back for contingencies, to form an audience for Mr. Sinden. "I can give ye names for most an the marnin's passengers," the stationmaster said slowly as he opened up the bulky ledger he had carried up to the police station under his cape. "I matched up my memory with times and tickets and wrote them all out purty for ye, Jacob."

He nodded at the station sergeant, who had joined us in the bare, but reasonably warm, room. "Ye'll know most an them yourself, I rackon. So will Mayor." He looked at Ned, who smiled briefly in agreement.

Mr. Sinden handed the list to the sergeant, who automatically deferred to Ned by passing the sheet of neatly written names, times, and destinations to him. Ned ran a blunt, thick finger down the lines; he knew most of the inhabitants of Littleberry by name and often knew their business too.

"Hyde, Feldwick, Langton . . ." He looked across the table at Jonathan. "Clerks traveling to London. They won't get back today, poor fellows." He read some more. "A handful of men known to me, all respectable." He huffed out a laugh. "Lade, Callow, and Henty left early this morning; they're probably out on business that's *not* respectable, eh, Jacob?"

"Can't stop them on a suspicion, or we'd be all day asking questions," the sergeant replied laconically. "Much good may it do them in this drench."

"Is that all, Sinden?" Ned asked the stationmaster.

"All I can give a name to." Mr. Sinden made a twirling motion with his finger to indicate Ned should turn the sheet over. "There was three foreigners."

By which, of course, he simply meant strangers. He would have distinguished anyone who did not appear to be English as a "Frenchy," whether they were from the plains of Africa or the Russian steppes.

"One an 'em, bound for Ashford, sayed to me he was a 'dairy expert.'" He pronounced the last two words in an exaggerated imitation of university speech. "Gooin' round talking to farmers 'bout the milk prices, travelin' from Pincham into Kent."

"And the others?"

"Naun sing'lar." Mr. Sinden shrugged expressively to emphasize his statement that there was nothing out of the ordinary about the other two men. "Single ticket on the 7:30 to Hastings, ticket through to Dover on the 8:10. Return."

"Dover." Several of us spoke at once, and I hastened to explain to Jonathan, who was looking a little blank. "Passenger steam packets don't travel out of Hastings. They've never been able to build a suitable harbor."

"Ah." Jonathan nodded. "Would he have had time to get all the way to Dover before the line closed?"

A chorus of voices affirmed that possibility, but it was Ned's growl that dominated. "There's no doubt about that. We have to pray he didn't have time to board a boat, but I don't think so. The storm began building at around nine o'clock this morning, so sea conditions must have been unfavorable for a crossing by the time the train arrived."

A movement at the door interrupted our conference. Murmured greetings of "Doctor" made me turn around to see Fortier shedding water off his greatcoat.

"News of Silas?" I asked, my heart beating fast. Had Fortier arrived to tell us Silas had died? But to my relief, he smiled.

"Only good news. He's stable, and Miss Guttridge insists I leave her to nurse him." He shook Jonathan's hand on his way to the fire, hanging his heavy coat on a hook near the hearth. "I have her full agreement to join the chase. I think she'd be leading it herself if she could bear to leave Silas." His expression became somber. "She says it's just as much my business as hers, and she's right. Striving to mend the damage that b—that blackguard has done makes it my business."

Nods and grunts from the men signified their agreement. One volunteer swore volubly and descriptively to illustrate what he might do to Rampling when found until a punch on his arm from his neighbor reminded him of my presence. I hid a smile; the men were clearly unused to involving a woman in their deliberations, but I had arrived with Ned, and therefore nobody had questioned my right to be there.

"A return ticket to Dover, though," said Ned after rapidly explaining to Fortier what we suspected. "That doesn't suggest flight. The single ticket to Hastings, now . . ."

"He may have bought a return ticket to throw any pursuers off the trail." Fortier made himself comfortable in his chair, crossing his arms and leaning back. "Mind you, the ticket to Hastings could serve the same purpose. If I were running from trouble, I wouldn't make it obvious where I was going; I'd set off in the opposite direction and then double back. Besides, I know from my own travels that there are many smaller ports where you can pick up a steamer to France—although I'll admit the crossings are fewer and farther between, with much smaller boats where it's harder to hide yourself in a crowd."

"Or he could have headed inland," I said. "He may not have taken a train at all. If he'd set off during the night, he could be miles away by now, even on foot."

"What a pessimistic lot you are." Ned shut the ledger with a bang. "Jacob, will you telegraph to Dover with Rampling's description? We have time, thanks to the storm. He won't be able to board a boat for a while."

"And to Hastings, just in case that single ticket was Rampling." Fortier pushed his chair back as he stood, its metal-shod legs screeching on the flagstone floor. "But you're right, Ned. Dover's our best bet, and assuming we won't catch him there is the best way of making sure we don't." He paused, frowning. "But that means we have to get to Dover before the storm abates and they start loading the steamers."

"No trains," Ned reminded us. "It's a day's ride by carriage. And are you sure you can leave your patient?"

Fortier began pacing in the space by the window. "I'm never entirely sure I can leave a very sick patient, but I do it all the time out of necessity. My instincts, and Albertina Guttridge, are backing me up in this case." He turned on his heel. "Lucifer can cover forty miles in a day, and we're used to riding out in bad weather. Patients don't time their ailments according to the doctor's convenience."

That remark elicited smiles and nods. Jonathan rose to

stand by Fortier. "The army doesn't worry overmuch about the weather when it issues orders either." He clapped Fortier on the shoulder. "Two are better than one, as the saying goes, and I can easily get the horse I've been using for rough riding. He's a big beast who covers the ground well. So why delay?"

Jonathan's deep Indian tan had faded somewhat, but his teeth still showed white against brown skin as he laughed cheerfully, as if they were planning a pleasant outing on a sunny day. "I could do with some exercise."

THE RAPID DEPARTURE OF THE TWO MEN PROMPTED THE remaining volunteers to decide for Hastings, which, being only twelve or so miles distant, might be reached by road even in the storm. They left the station conversing loudly, leaving me and Ned—neither of whom would expect to be invited along on such an excursion—alone with Mr. Sinden and the sergeant. The room seemed very empty.

"Of course, he could be anywhere *but* Dover." I sighed in frustration.

"People are surprisingly predictable, m'lady." The sergeant scratched his chin, producing a rasping noise. "He'd know there's a good chance of getting a steamer at Dover, hiding in the crowd. And it's the quickest route to France, and what better place than the Continent to disappear?" He pushed the chair he had just vacated under the table. "I'll send a few telegraph messages. Mr. Sinden, can you do the same to all the stations you can think of? The more eyes we have looking for him, the better. I'll just make a copy of the description her ladyship gave us for you."

"Do you want to go back to Fortier's house to help look after Silas?" Ned asked as I rose to my feet.

"I *want* to go to Dover." As I said the words, I realized how frustrated I felt, trapped into inaction by the accident of being born female. "I know what Rampling looks like, just as Fortier does. I could spot him in a crowd. Why do I have to be left behind?"

For a moment, my imagination conjured up the fantasy of riding through the storm on Lucifer, astride on the great horse with Fortier's arms holding me close. Then common sense intervened to point out Fortier had already left; he would need his arms for riding; I would slow Lucifer down; and finally presented me with a highly undignified picture of how I would actually manage astride in a bustle dress. Despite my annoyance at being abandoned like an unneeded parcel, I suppressed a giggle. Ned didn't notice.

"I understand, my dear." My brother-in-law sighed heavily. "If only I were twenty years younger. But I can't ride that distance at any speed these days, even on a perfect day for riding. I need help to get on and off a horse now."

"I've always needed help." I slipped a hand under Ned's arm. "At least I have since I started wearing long skirts. How infuriating that there are no trains. Wouldn't it be wonderful to beat Fortier and Jonathan to Dover?"

"It would be splendid," Ned agreed. We fell silent, watching as two of Littleberry's police constables—the same two who had arrived at Hawthorn Hall with the London detectives—entered the waiting area just outside the room where we stood. One of them was complaining loudly that the storm would stop him getting his daily letter from his young woman, and his companion was teasing him about his lovelorn state.

"Wait." I turned to face Ned, slipping my hand out from his elbow and resting it on his waistcoat. "Have you ever known the weather, however bad, to actually prevent the post from being delivered? The General Post Office has a reputation for being undaunted by almost anything you can name. How do they manage that?"

"A mail train," Ned crowed, grasping my hand and kissing it. "There's a chance they may still be running, to Ashford at least; the line's all inland from here. And the weather can be quite different even ten miles inland, so we can't assume the lines from Kent to the coast aren't working."

"Mr. Sinden?" I turned toward the stationmaster, but he was already nodding slowly, a smile appearing under his drooping mustache.

38

THE HEROES OF THE HOUR

It being late November, darkness had fallen by the time Ned and I descended from the postal train at Ashford, accompanied by the two police constables who had been involved in Dederick's arrest. But we had luck with the boat trains at Ashford and lost little time embarking on the final leg of our journey. Ned and I, crammed into the corner of a full compartment, both dozed off as the train chugged and whistled its way through Kent, only slowing as we neared the coast, and it became apparent the storm had not yet blown itself out.

"You, my dear, are a genius." Ned, his spirits revived by his nap, grinned cheerfully as he helped me descend onto the platform of Dover's town station. "Did you get any rest?"

"I've never slept so well on a train." And indeed, the morning's exertions had apparently tired me enough to make the clattering, rattling ride feel like the rocking of a cradle.

"Now, where would our two constables be?" Ned replaced his hat on his head and suppressed a yawn with his hand.

"If we stay here, they'll have to walk past us. The second-class carriages are farther back."

I gazed at the crowd of dejected passengers, some of whom were learning for the first time that the trains would not be running out to the pier until the authorities at Dover were satisfied the storm had slackened enough to allow the steamers to depart. It was going to be a long and uncomfortable night for most of them, but for us, the storm was a symbol of hope.

I smiled at the two middle-aged ladies who had sat opposite me; one of them had complained of feeling sick as soon as we left Ashford, and my memories from before I dozed off were of anticipating the worst happening and becoming slightly nauseous myself as a result. That lady was now chattering cheerfully, but I did not like to inquire whether she felt better because she'd *been* sick or simply because she was no longer on the train.

Ned was waving at the police constables, causing the two ladies to look at him rather sharply, but they were moving off, ushered toward the gate by the railway employees, by the time the two policemen reached us.

"We think we should go to the Lord Warden Hotel, Sir Edward," one of them—the one who had been hoping for a letter from his beloved—said to Ned. "I grew up in Dover, so I know that's where most people would end up at one time or the other in weather like this."

"And we need to talk to the stationmaster, in case Rampling's been hanging around the station," said the other.

"What about the pier?" I asked. "Will there be anyone there?"

"They don't let the trains run down there unless the boats are able to dock," the first police constable said firmly, but then he seemed to reconsider the question and shrugged. "There's always a few people make their way down there, mind. You can order people to stay put till you're blue in the face, but there's always some who don't listen and go out to shelter under the promenade, thinking they'll be first on the steamer." He sniffed contemptuously. "Idiots. Getting wet and cold's the most likely, of course, but the pier can be dangerous in a storm. You don't understand the sea unless you've lived with it."

"That's where I want to go." I looked at Ned. "If he's here, he's been here all day, and he must realize we'll be looking for him. I know I couldn't stay in a crowd, wondering who might be looking at me. I'd want to hide, but I'd want to be near the boats so I could take the first opportunity to get aboard. At worst, we'll be able to choose a good spot to watch the people getting off the trains from the town station, just in case the constables are right and he's stayed in the town."

"How long do you intend us to stay out there?" Ned's eyes widened. "It's pitch dark and still raining and blowing a gale. You'll get soaked."

"I'll stay there all night if necessary." I was rarely angry with Ned, but frustration and determination to get my own way on this point made my voice shrill. "I feel responsible for Silas, Ned. I *know* I put the idea into Rampling's head that Silas talked to us. Not only do *I* know it, Guttridge knows it." I sniffed hard, swallowing to steady my voice. "If she could be here, she'd have commandeered a hackney and be on her way to the pier by now. Stop treating me as if I can't manage a night in the cold."

The three men looked at one another, and Ned shrugged. "Very well, my dear. I'll find a cab."

"I'll do that, Sir Edward," the first constable said. "I know my way around here." He looked at me. "You do understand, my lady, that we have to make inquiries in the station and at the Lord Warden first. It's our job to be thorough." He nodded sympathetically. "But we'll come to the pier as soon as we can."

"It doesn't seem so bad."

The wind pulled the hood of my cape off my head and tugged at my hat as I craned my neck to look up at the great pier, essentially a high wall onto which an overhanging shelter had been added with a promenade on the top, to give a magnificent view in the good weather. The cab had brought us to where a steep flight of steps led up to that promenade; beyond it, the dark cavern of the long shelter was studded with the feeble lights of small lamps.

A regular booming sound and the constant noise of rain and wind made it impossible to hear anything else. I had to shout into Ned's ear to make myself understood.

"The wind doesn't seem so bad here because we're in the lee of the gale," Ned bawled back at me. "Do you see the lamps? I'm sure the police were right about there being people under the promenade. Let's start walking along this part."

"He might be *on* the promenade," I yelled back and darted toward the steps that formed part of the wall. I was impatient to be doing something—anything—to find Rampling after a day that seemed to have consisted of one wait after another. Once I was at the top of the high wall, I would have a better view, and the wind really didn't seem so bad now.

I heard Ned call, but the wind took away his words, leaving just a vague sound. I was much shorter than Ned but considerably younger; I climbed the steep stairs as fast as I could, pulling myself up by the railing, heedless of whether he was able to match my pace.

I had never before appreciated how long the pier was. Justin and I had sailed from Dover on our honeymoon voyage to Paris five years before, but we had simply descended from the train and strolled to the first-class gangway, our attention on the blue sea and each other rather than on our surroundings. Now, as I climbed higher, the lighthouse's restless beacon illuminated a vast, broad structure, angled round to the left. Down below, under the promenade, specks of light were moving restlessly or hanging stationary in the darkness, betraying the presence of people waiting for an early chance at a good place on the steamers.

As I reached the promenade, I realized there was a high, thick wall on my right; I would have to stand on tiptoe to look over it. The booming noises were louder now, and when I licked my lips, I tasted salt. Waves must be breaking at the base of the wall, perfusing the air with a saline mist.

Boom . . . boom . . . boom . . . I shrieked as a particularly high wave sent a shower of ice-cold salt water over my head, knocking my hood off and sending my hat sideways so the pin pulled painfully at my hair.

I yanked out the hatpin. Naturally, this meant I lost my hat, which went sailing upward into the darkness before I had a chance to grab it. I pulled my hood back onto my head and used the hatpin to secure it, but the wind, which by now was taking my breath away, set the edge of my hood into a rapid flapping motion that stung my right cheek repeatedly and painfully.

An exceptionally powerful gust caught me, and I staggered to the left, dancing in the effort to keep my balance.

"Stop being a bloody fool!"

A large hand seized my arm and swung me round to show me Ned, bareheaded and patently angry, resembling a large and aggressive bear in the uncertain light.

"What do you think you're doing?" he roared at the top of his voice. "Can't you see the wind could catch your skirts and blow you over the railing?"

Another wave broke over us, larger this time, and I gasped. Ned shoved me toward the railing on the harbor side of the promenade, and I clung to it, my wet gloves slipping on the icy metal.

"Down. *Now.*"

One did not disobey the Mayor of Littleberry when he used that tone. I hastened back to the stairs, descending carefully, step by steep step, making sure I put my foot down firmly each time. The descent seemed far more slippery and precarious than the ascent had been.

The lower level of the pier felt like a haven of calm and quiet after the fury of the wind above. Ned steered me under the roof created by the promenade, near to where a lamp hung unattended, his expression still furious—until I pulled off my hood, whereupon he began to laugh.

"What in the name of all that's holy did you think you were doing?" he gasped once he could speak. "I'm sorry to laugh, my dear, but you should see yourself. I don't suppose I look much better. I'm sorry I swore at you."

"I'm sorry I was a bloody fool." I swept my sodden hair back from my forehead and hugged my brother-in-law, comforted by the woolly solidity of his thick coat. "Now you've lost your hat too, and you don't have anything at all for your head. Gerry's going to be so cross with me."

Ned clapped a hand on his head, grinned, and disappeared back out into the darkness, returning with his top hat, which he jammed into place. "I had the sense to drop it at the foot of the stairs. Besides, your sister really ought to stop behaving as if I'm feeble just because I catch the occasional cold."

"I was just trying to see if Rampling were up on the promenade," I said.

"He'd have to crawl along it or be driven mad by the wind," Ned pointed out. "Now, why don't we do the job we came here for instead of gallivanting around? I suggest we walk calmly and sedately under this shelter, arm in arm, as if we've just grown tired of waiting at the hotel and gone for a stroll. If you keep your hood on, nobody will notice the state of your hair." He laughed again. "As we go along, I'll make discreet inquiries."

"Why aren't the steamers closer to the quayside?" I asked, realizing I could see the lights of three packets bobbing queasily on the water some twenty yards away.

"So they don't get wrecked against the stonework, I imagine." Ned waited for me to arrange my hood, then took my arm. "They're probably moored on a chain. Do you know, I think the storm is calming a little. We've been lucky this time; the pier's suffered enormous damage twice in the last few years. The promenade once came down completely in a storm."

I said nothing, but it wasn't the cold making me shiver as I looked up into the darkness above our heads. We walked on in silence for a few minutes, passing small knots of men, most of them with pieces of luggage at their feet, most of them smoking pipes or cigars. Ned asked questions as we passed them, but nobody admitted to having seen a man of Rampling's description. They answered curtly, their attention riveted on the steamers; whatever business was taking them to the Continent, it was clearly something they were impatient to get on with.

I understood the feeling. "We're not going to find him, are we, Ned?" I asked as we reached a part of the platform where no men stood. "He'll get away, and I'll have to face Guttridge with *that* news as well."

"Don't give up hope." Ned patted the hand that rested on his arm. "Who knows? Rampling may have given us the slip altogether and gone to one of the other ports—Folkestone, for example—but the police and port officials there will all have his description. He may still be caught without our intervention." His bushy beard moved as he smiled. "Not everyone can be the hero of the hour."

"Talking of heroes, I'd feel better if I could see Armand and Jonathan."

"Mmmm." Ned squeezed my arm into his side. "You're going to marry Fortier, aren't you? It's probably time you admitted as much to your family, given most of us already suspect it."

"What does Gerry think?" I had no need for my eldest sister's permission, of course, but I had been wondering.

"Oh, she's furious." Ned laughed. "Mostly about the 'low connections' you're entering into, by which she means Quinn Dermody. Now she's realized Mrs. Dermody is a duke's daughter, she's torn between the urge to pay a call on her and her own aversion to Quinn."

"Oh dear."

"She'll come round. I've pointed out more than once that Dermody's a perfectly respectable owner of a thriving business, not really so different to me."

"Poor Gerry, she tried so hard to introduce me to 'suitable' men." I smiled. "I wish I could have liked one of them, for her sake."

The shout that went up from a group of men near us drowned out my words. The men began removing their hats and waving them at the rocking steamboats.

"Ah, they're firing the boilers," Ned said, pointing at the thready plumes of dark smoke, visible against the faint lights of the town, beginning to emerge from the stacks of two of the vessels. "Won't be long now. They'll have to disembark all the poor souls who've been waiting on the boats. Can you imagine the kind of crossing they've had?" He shuddered expressively.

"And then they'll bring the trains up, and there'll be hundreds of people." I sighed in despair, trying to make out the train tracks I knew must be on our left. "Won't they get off the trains on the other side of the tracks? Will all the steamers be letting off and taking on passengers at once? You know, watching is far more complicated than being a passenger. When one's boarding, one just does as one's told."

Ned squeezed my arm. "If I know anything about travel, the lines will move slowly and we'll have a chance to look. They'll bring more lights too when boarding starts. You're right, though; we need to be on the other side of the tracks. See that lower bit there, the mooring for smaller boats? Why don't we shelter by that collection of huts beyond it? We can stay out of the gale there, and it's barely raining anymore."

It wasn't, but there was an icy tinge to the wind, more obvious away from the shelter of the promenade. I was starting to feel cold as well as hungry and thirsty; Ned was shivering, despite his earlier bravado.

We were quite close to the lighthouse by now. A strong smell of the sea was in my nostrils, and I could hear a monotonous lapping noise as the small waves of the harbor hit the side of the pier. We huddled close to the huts in silent dejection. This part of the pier had a number of stout wooden buildings and, it seemed, a great many coils of rope lying about to stumble upon in the dark. I began to long for the arrival of the trains, for lights and people, even for an unsuccessful end to the chase, as long as it ended.

What trick of vision alerted me, I never knew. I was becoming half-mesmerized by the beam of the lighthouse lamp, sliding in stately silence over pier and waves, throwing weird shadows around as it swept by, a dance of light and dark that soon became monotonously familiar. My teeth were chattering, my eyelids beginning to droop with fatigue; and then one shadow went the wrong way, moving toward a set of railings that led to the stairs at the far end of the promenade. Recognition slid neatly into place in my exhausted mind.

"Rampling!"

I would not have believed I could shout so loud; some power that did not appear to be part of my body tore the cry out of me. Ned, who had been as still as a stone beside me, jumped violently and looked wildly about us. I tugged at his wet coat, pushing and pulling him at once to get him to look in the right direction. "It's him! It's Rampling! There, can't you see?"

I dodged around a rope coil and ran toward the shadow. It was a futile chase—I could never have caught him, even if my soaked skirts and cape did not hamper me—but I saw him hesitate for a moment and forced my legs to go faster, my breath sobbing on the wind. Ned must have been somewhere behind me; perhaps it was the sudden sight of the two of us that caused Rampling to lose his head and run, not past us down the pier, where he would probably have had room to elude pursuit, but toward the stairs.

There were people by the stairs, emerging from the deep shadows the lighthouse beam never touched. Two men, one dark, one blond, both instantly recognizable as the lighthouse beam swept silently above them.

"Get him!" I shouted, and I could hear Ned shouting something too. Farther down the pier, I heard a police whistle, making my heart leap. "Get him!" I was still running, and my voice was diminishing to a croak.

They got him. He hesitated again, and when Jonathan threw his weight at him, I heard a loud grunt and the satisfying smack and plash of a man falling onto wet flagstones. They had fallen into darkness, and I only had the impression of a heaving mass, slightly darker than the surrounding dark; all further sounds were lost in the wind.

I didn't stop running. Only seconds passed before I was close enough to make out the sound of Jonathan's voice.

"That's the barrel of a Webley-Kaufman service revolver you can feel, old man. I might want to reconsider moving about so much, if I were you. I've seen what a mess these things can make, and I'd hate to have it go off by accident and get your insides all over the place." Then, after a few more moments: "That's better. Are you all right there, Fortier?"

"Just fine." Fortier's voice emerged from the writhing mass, which, as I neared it, resolved itself into two men kneeling and one on the ground, more or less underneath the others. "Could you get off his neck, Jones? I think you may be asphyxiating him. I'm not in this to kill anyone, no matter how I feel about him."

"If you insist." Jonathan moved, but very slowly. "You remember about the revolver, don't you?" he asked Rampling. "And besides, I believe the police may be coming. Are you still alive?"

The answer was a stream of profanity. Rampling was clearly alive. I had come to a halt, out of breath, my chest heaving, taking in huge mouthfuls of the damp and very cold sea air. Men rushed past me, and I watched as Rampling was hauled to his feet between the two police constables, one of whom opened the side of a dark lantern to inspect him. He looked unhurt in the feeble yellow light, barring a nasty scrape that ran down his cheek.

"Let me see him." Fortier was on his feet, running to catch up with the policemen, who were starting to tow Rampling back down the pier. Jonathan stepped toward me, grinning as he replaced the revolver, which he had hidden behind his back as the constables approached, in its holster. "Probably shouldn't be waving this about, uniform or no uniform, but it came in handy, didn't it? Cousin Helena, how on earth did you get here?"

"Postal train," I said briefly, still a little winded. Jonathan laughed and caught my hands in his.

"What a marvel you are. I could kiss you—shall I kiss you? Perhaps not in front of Ned."

Fortier had turned back, having clearly satisfied himself Rampling had no serious injuries. I could see him fairly well now; lights were appearing, and I realized a train was approaching, slowing to a halt some twenty feet from where we stood. I could no longer see Rampling or the policemen. I let go of Jonathan's hands, turning toward Fortier, but the latter spoke to Jonathan first.

"Damn it, man, you could have injured someone. I told you we didn't need a firearm."

"Took the bullets out." Jonathan pushed a hand under his cape to rattle a pocket. "I'm not fool enough to get court-martialed before I take leave of the regiment. I knew he wouldn't know the difference. But don't you see who's here? She commandeered a postal train. Isn't she a wonder?"

"I spotted her a while ago. That's what I was trying to tell you." Fortier stepped forward to push a strand of wet hair off my cheek. "You look more like an urchin than a Scott-De Quincy at this moment." I couldn't see his face—the lights and steam of the train were behind him, outlining his lithe figure—but I could hear the smile in his voice.

"And you?" I asked him as the lighthouse beam caught him, showing me he was completely soaked. He was bare-headed, and rolling around on the flagstones had not improved the state of his clothing.

"Get used to it. I often look like this by the end of the day." His voice changed, becoming sterner. "That was utterly insane, running after Rampling like that. What did you think you were going to do in the outrageously unlikely event you'd caught him?"

"I didn't know you were there. I had to do *something*—"

"—supposing he'd hurt you?"

"—why didn't you give us some sign you were there?"

We were talking over each other, and then we both stopped talking and began laughing. Fortier gathered me into his arms, lifting me off my feet.

"We didn't say anything, my darling, because we didn't want to give ourselves away. We've been tracking him for hours, crawling along the promenade so he wouldn't see us, communicating in signs like a couple of deerstalkers. He hid himself when he saw you and Ned. You distracted him for long enough that we were able to get close. Jones is right—you *are* a wonder."

We began laughing again, hugging each other, and matters might have become more romantic if Ned and Jonathan hadn't also burst into laughter and reminded us of their presence.

"That's the way the land lies, is it?" Jonathan said as Fortier let me go. "Ah, well. I was beginning to suspect it anyway." He shook Fortier's hand vigorously. "Congratulations, old man. And congratulations to you, dear cousin, who, alas, will never be more than a cousin to me. May I kiss your cheek?"

"Of course." I submitted gladly to a cousinly embrace.

"We had a good day's hunt, didn't we?" Jonathan said to Fortier. "Let's go make sure the horses are all right, and I'll see if there are any rooms for the night at the Lord Warden. I'm confident I can talk them into giving Helena a room, and we men can bunk up together if we—"

He stopped as Fortier and I said, "No!" in unison.

"I want to get back to my patient," Fortier said. "I'll need to find another horse, but the stables should have one that will do. If necessary, I'll ride all night."

"And I have to get back to Guttridge." I put my arm through Fortier's.

"Whatever we decide to do, let's decide it indoors." Ned's stentorian voice rose above my words. "I, for one, am craving hot food and drink and a fire. I hate to admit it, but I'm feeling my age."

39
SYMPATHY AND ENCOURAGEMENT

"I'm sorry, Ned."

I had woken so late at the Lord Warden Hotel that I felt decidedly sheepish when I finally found Ned in the parlor. I had thought I'd never sleep, but then, as day was breaking, I had closed my eyes and opened them two hours later.

"I feel ridiculous not being able to dress myself properly without a lady's maid." I sat in the chair opposite Ned. "I must look a fright." Unsurprisingly, I was hatless, and my clothes, although no longer damp and soiled since they had spent the night in the large hotel's laundry, felt all wrong. "I kept tripping over the nightdress they gave me, and the mattress had a huge depression on one side I was constantly falling into. I should never have let you persuade me to stay."

"What would you have done? Gone with Jonathan and the horses?" Ned rose to give me a kiss on both cheeks, his beard scratching my skin. "He left at dawn, they told me. I don't suppose anyone's found your reticule?"

"I suppose it's at the bottom of the harbor." I grinned; I had had to borrow the money from both Ned and Jonathan for the various telegrams I had sent, and it had become a joke between the three of us that I kept thinking of more to send. The first had been to Messrs. Piper, Wiggins, and Showell, telling them the real murderer had been arrested and instructing them to press for Dederick's release without delay. Then there was a carefully worded and encouraging telegram to Blanche, one to Gerry to assure her Ned was in good health, one to Thomas to let him and the Walfort girls know we would return the following day, and, for good measure, one to Guttridge to apologize for my absence.

"Do you need breakfast?" Ned asked.

I shook my head. "They brought me coffee and toast. Could we leave by the first possible train? You'd better send another telegram to Gerry once we've ascertained which one we'll be on and ask her to bring your carriage. You know, in novels, the heroines just seem to flit from place to place without any trouble. It's rather disappointing to realize this kind of adventurous travel is fraught with inconvenience and chores."

GERRY WAS WAITING FOR US AT THE LITTLEBERRY STATION.

"Now, you're not going to start fussing over me," Ned growled as he followed me up the carriage steps.

Gerry had clearly been about to do exactly that, but her words of reproof turned into a sort of breathless squeak as her husband enfolded her in a bear hug, planting a smacking kiss on her mouth.

"That's better." Ned settled himself back into the velvet upholstery, a smug expression on his face. "I'm perfectly all right. In fact, I slept marvelously well. All that fresh air and exercise."

"Yes, I heard all about it from Jonathan." Gerry arched her

eyebrows in her inimitable fashion. "He seems to have found it all most amusing. He told me to tell you, Helena, that he went round to Dr. Fortier's house to find out how that man Horniblow is. Apparently, he seems very likely to live and is taking a little broth. He has spoken a few words and appears to have all his wits."

"What a relief." I felt my shoulders sag as if a weight had rolled off them. "Rampling injured him horribly, Gerry."

"So people are saying. I intend to go round there myself later. Cook is putting together a basket of delicacies suitable for invalids, and I'm bringing ten yards of good linen as a gift for Horniblow's sister, as well as two jars of this year's marmalade, which is excellent. Ned is very fond of it."

She ran a tentative finger over Ned's coat, which had been well dried and brushed but looked as if it might be beyond saving. "I don't know Horniblow or his sister, but I'm told she's a good woman and her children attend the Sunday school at the quay, the one for the fishermen's families."

She continued in the same vein while Ned, accustomed to his wife's ways, took the opportunity to fall into a doze. I listened with half an ear, only interrupting when I realized we were heading straight to Whitcombe.

"We're going the wrong way, Gerry. I must look in on Silas—and Guttridge."

"You're going home." Gerry smiled her elder sister's smile. "It's all arranged. Guttridge will be there to look after you."

"I hardly need looking after." I tried not to sound petulant. "Guttridge must barely have slept, and she should stay with Silas."

"Her place is with you. It's Horniblow's sister's place to nurse him. She is a married woman and his sister; Guttridge is a spinster."

She looked at me significantly. I rolled my eyes.

"So the gossips are wagging their tongues already?"

"Of course not. The man's badly injured." Gerry sniffed delicately. "But it doesn't do to give people grounds for talking, and Guttridge is a sensible woman."

"I suppose you sent her a note." This was usually how Gerry imposed her will on the women of Littleberry.

"Of sympathy and encouragement, naturally. I heard she took your carriage to Wellington Gardens."

"Guttridge has my permission to take anything of mine when she needs it."

"Hmmm." Gerry arched her eyebrows again. "They're not our *friends*, Helena. Even the best of treasures, as I'm sure Guttridge is, are not of our class. What a funny little thing you are. And while we have a moment to ourselves, what about this man Fortier?"

"Leave her alone, Gerry." I did not know how much Ned had heard; he definitely sounded sleepy.

"I leave Helena alone entirely too much," Gerry said indignantly. "Now, Helena, dear, are you *sure*? Don't pretend not to know what I'm talking about. He is more suitable than I originally thought; I'll grant you that. But I've heard a very distressing rumor about his cousin—or cousin's wife, surely? Since she has the name Fortier—that he has compromised her in some way, so that not marrying her would be immoral. If not illegal."

She raised her hands as I opened my mouth—to say what, I didn't know. "Now, I don't pretend to be in possession of any facts, and wagging tongues can be malicious. But where there's smoke, there's fire, and there *is* smoke, Helena. Fortunately, the child does not resemble him in any way."

"Leave her alone." Ned's eyes were wide open now, and there was a scowl on his face I rarely saw there. "I'm surprised at you, Gerry, repeating scurrilous gossip like that. I don't believe for a moment Fortier's the type of man who

would ruin and then abandon any woman, and would he have brought her to England if that were his intention?"

Gerry looked taken aback, but it wasn't like her to let her husband get the upper hand for too long. "I'm simply looking out for Helena's interests."

"And so am I. And so is Michael, and neither of us has raised any objections to Fortier, have we?" Ned's beard jutted forward as he stuck out his chin obstinately. "For once, Geraldine, you had better let the heads of the family take charge. You of all people should know that occasionally, just occasionally, the men have the right of it."

Gerry flushed; I, who had no idea what Ned was talking about, had up till then been simmering like a pot about to boil over, and my words might have been far more heated if the spectacle of my beloved sister and even more beloved brother-in-law fighting over me had not filled me with distress. When I spoke, my voice sounded very small.

"Don't quarrel. Could we talk about this another day, Gerry? Please?" Preferably when I had Fortier by my side; but in any event, I didn't want a fight with Gerry.

Gerry breathed deeply, drawing herself up to her full height, but said nothing, turning her head toward the window so the profile once considered the most distinguished in the county—now weakened a little by advancing years, but still beautiful—was outlined clearly against a background of white and gray clouds. Ned bestowed a sympathetic smile on me and then, clearly far more tired than he would admit to, gradually lapsed back into a doze.

I spent the rest of the drive to Whitcombe looking out at the rain-soaked fields and muddy road, wishing heartily that Louise "Fortier" could vanish from the face of the earth.

40
LOVE AND COMPLICATIONS

Gerry kissed me goodbye when we arrived at my house, insisting on taking Ned straight home and not allowing him to leave the carriage. I was given, metaphorically speaking, a little like a parcel into the hands of Dunnam, Mrs. Eason, and Guttridge.

Guttridge, who had fully recovered her professional demeanor and cheerfulness and clearly felt optimistic about Silas, whisked me off to my private rooms immediately. Insisting my clothing was still damp and the hotel undoubtedly infested with fleas, lice, and bedbugs, she subjected me to a hot bath and a thorough hair-washing as if I were a puppy who had rolled in something noxious.

The indignity of this forced pampering dissipated as I, freshly washed and coiffed and attired in a new dress of beautifully soft mauve wool, entered the green drawing room to find Ellen and Lucy Walfort, Thomas, and his sister Maryanne engaged in a lively game of spellicans. The three young ladies were watching Thomas as he skillfully extracted one of the highest-valued ivory sticks, shaped like a spear with a wavy blade, manipulating the hook deftly with his good left hand.

"You'll drop it—you will!" Maryanne was clearly trying to put her brother off his stride, but Thomas completed his maneuver to cries of encouragement from the other two players. His handsome face was alight with happiness as he looked toward the sound of the opening door, only to fall a little when the three girls leaped nimbly to their feet and ran to greet me, leaving him to lurch awkwardly up from his seat at the table. But he was a good-natured man; the smile returned, and he came to hug me with as much enthusiasm as the ladies.

"Here you are at last. What slowcoaches you and Papa are!" exclaimed Maryanne. "Dr. Fortier—he says we must call him Armand—was here at eleven o'clock to tell us all about your adventures, and Cousin Jonathan is back at Four Square. He sent a note asking if he could come to tea, and Thomas said yes. Of course, I'll have to get home well before dinner to cover Papa with kisses and tell him how doughty he is. He'll need some appreciation once Mama's done with him, because naturally she's been fussing about him running off on adventures as if he's half his age." She mimicked a simper at the other girls. "I can go home with *Jonathan*."

"The hero of the hour." Lucy's eyes danced as she mimed adoration with fluttering eyelashes and hands clasped before her breast. "Helena, did you actually *see* him jump on that villain? Armand's description of the scene was absolutely thrilling."

"I saw every moment." I seated myself on a sofa, beckoning Thomas to sit by me. "It wasn't quite as spectacular as you imagine. For one thing, it was dark. Ned and I were wet and cold, and as for the other two men, well, 'drowned rats' doesn't begin to describe them."

"But they did ride across the marsh in the storm, didn't

they?" Ellen's beautiful face was unusually animated. "How brave they both were."

"They did, and I'm not trying to undervalue their actions." I smiled at Ellen. "I don't know when they arrived at Dover—I forgot to ask them last night—but they stalked Rampling by crawling along the top of the pier with the waves breaking over them and the wind howling like a pack of demons." I forbore from explaining exactly how I knew how bad conditions were on the promenade.

"They arrived about an hour before you did, Armand said." Lucy spoke from the table, where she had returned her attention to the spellicans, considering their positions carefully, her chin resting on her folded hands.

"When did he leave Whitcombe?" I asked. "Wasn't he exhausted? He must have ridden half the night." I was disappointed, to say the least, not to see Fortier, although after Gerry's words, I supposed I should be grateful for time to collect my thoughts.

"He stayed till noon, but he was too busy to eat luncheon with us." Maryanne stretched and yawned in a manner that would have earned a scolding from her mother. "It seems he had more patients to see. He didn't look all that tired."

"Ah, these men of vigorous constitution." Lucy looked up from the small pile of ivory sticks in front of her. "Thomas, aren't you going to play again? You have more points than any of us, and I want to get my revenge."

Thomas pushed himself up from his seat and took the hook in his hand but played badly, sending several of the spellicans sliding to the floor.

"I'll get them." Lucy slid from her chair.

"I c-c-c-c-can do it." Thomas's voice held a note of ice, the word *can* forced out with greater effort than usual.

By the time Thomas had completed the ungainly maneuver, both of them were flushed, but whether from embarrassment, anger, or, in Thomas's case, physical effort, I couldn't tell. With so many sticks lost from play, the game was ruined. Thomas, with a rueful smile, began returning the spellicans to their wooden box.

"Here's Cousin Jonathan." Maryanne tripped lightly over to the new arrival under the watchful gaze of the full-length portraits of Justin's ancestors. "I'll ring for tea, Aunt Helena."

Jonathan was resplendent in his dress uniform, the gold lace bars across his chest making it look even broader, the tight-fitting pantaloons and tall boots accentuating his height. He removed his sable busby cap with its high white plume and set it carelessly on the writing desk covered with Thomas's books; I noted he had not handed it to the footman so he could make his entrance in full fig. Having presumably given up trying to impress *me,* was he now aiming his affections at one of the other ladies?

Or perhaps his aim was simply to revel in the attention due to a hero. He kissed the hands of all the ladies, including mine, and shook the left hand Thomas held out to him. Thomas joined in the round of congratulations and then retired to a seat, watching as the ladies asked questions and Jonathan, evincing as much modesty as was possible in the circumstances, repeated what they had no doubt already heard from Fortier. He referred to me occasionally for clarification or affirmation of his tale, and I answered in as lively a manner as I could. But my eyes were on Thomas, and my heart was breaking a little.

"I don't think Lucy's all that fond of Jonathan," I said to my nephew once Jonathan and Maryanne had departed home to Four Square and the Walfort girls had gone upstairs to rest before dinner.

"Do you suppose Jonathan actually c-cares for either of them?" Thomas asked. "Or is it you he aspires to? He seemed rather k-keen at one p-point."

"He's given up on me." I couldn't stop a broad smile spreading across my face, however concerned I was about Thomas. "Armand and I rather forgot ourselves yesterday evening after all the business with Rampling." I shrugged happily. "We're in love, you know."

"I know." Thomas lowered himself to the sofa to sit next to me, putting his good arm around my shoulders. "That much has become fairly obvious. Only that dunderhead Jonathan has been too wrapped up in himself to notice. Has Armand p-proposed marriage to you?"

"He asked Michael for my hand." I giggled at the memory. "Michael actually behaved himself—in the end—and welcomed him into the family. We just haven't made a proper announcement yet because there are complications."

"The French c-cousin?" Thomas nodded. "She does rather resemble a c-complication. I think you n-need to grasp the n-nettle and make an announcement, Auntie Helena. It's time you were formally engaged." He kissed my forehead. "For what it's worth, I'm d-delighted. Your happiness cheers me up."

"And your unhappiness makes me sad." I drew away from Thomas a little so I could look into his face. "It *is* Lucy, isn't it?"

"Since the moment I first saw her." His expression was bleak. "I've always told myself I would avoid any attachment till I was in a p-position to k-k-keep a wife and family in c-comfort. I thought I m-might eventually marry a nice, plain woman from my c-congregation, the sensible sort who didn't mind marrying a c-c-cripple to escape spinsterhood."

He closed his eyes, and when he spoke again, his voice shook. "And so what happens? I fall head over heels in love with a beautiful, clever, talented woman—the most perfect woman I've ever seen—and so far above me in eligibility and fortune that I don't have the faintest chance with her."

He removed his arm from my shoulders and turned away in a vain effort to hide the moisture darkening his lashes. "So now my perfectly reasonable plan is smashed to pieces. It's idiotic, I know; I'm only twenty-five, and I shouldn't expect to marry until I can support a wife. I've never understood why people elope before, but now I do. I lie awake at night with everything in me screaming that I want a wife *now*. I want *her*. Now."

"Oh, Thomas." I put a hand on his shoulder, the best I could do as he was still turned away from me, fumbling in his pocket for a handkerchief. I knew my nephew as such a good-natured man that I often forgot the depth of feeling behind his sanguine exterior.

"I'm sorry." Thomas drew a deep breath and turned back to me. "I could at least behave like a man. It hasn't helped to have Jonathan here, reminding us all he can fight and ride and stride around in that ridiculous uniform while I play children's games. I'm angry—not at him, but at *this*." He put his good hand under the elbow of his withered arm, lifting it into view.

"*This* doesn't make you less of a man." I caught his twisted right hand in mine, caressing it. "And do you realize you said all of that without stammering?"

"I n-n-n-n-n-n-n—I *know*." Thomas ejected the word with furious force, and for a moment he looked strikingly like Michael in one of his tempers. He took a deep breath. "It's anger—s-strong emotion. It's happened before."

"The anger's from your Scott-De Quincy side, I think. Although your father was angry at me for a few moments yesterday, and I was quite impressed." I smiled at the memory of Ned calling me a bloody fool and was glad to see an answering gleam of humor light up Thomas's beautiful blue eyes. "Perhaps it's that anger, that imperious desire, that will help you win Lucy's heart. If you always hold back for fear she may reject you, how will she know how much you care? She does like you; that's plain enough. It's easy to spot when a man repels a woman—physically, I mean—and I've never seen that when she's with you. Rather the opposite."

"She's being kind. She's a generous soul." Thomas used his good hand gently to detach my grip from his crippled limb. "Like you. Think of all the obstacles to such a union, Helena. Would a woman of her b-background and education ever be happy in a c-country vicarage, thousands of m-m-miles from her home?"

"Why don't you ask her?" I said. "What do you have to lose by making your feelings plain? Isn't it better to know now if she doesn't want you than to live with false hope?"

Thomas smiled sadly. "I'd rather live in hope. At the m-moment, it's all I've got."

41
PLANS FOR THE FUTURE

Three days passed peacefully. Although I felt a pang of worry every time I looked at Thomas, I had to admit he hid the pain of love well. In any case, I was often at Fortier's house, visiting Silas in Guttridge's company.

"I'm better cared for here than I've been since I was a child." Silas, now housed in Fortier's back bedroom, was still extremely weak, but cheerful and talkative, although his speech was still hindered by his injuries. "Your salves are wonderful, m'lady. My face hurt so much I thought I couldn't bear it, but now look at me, talking away. My sister reckons it's a miracle cure."

"It's just arnica, with one or two additions of our own." I smiled at Guttridge. "We've given Dr. Fortier several jars of it for his surgery. Your looks are improving daily, although I must admit the bruises are a most interesting range of colors. A bit like the sunsets we've been having."

"Here, don't laugh." Guttridge paused, a gobbet of arnica salve on her finger. "You'll split that lip again. Keep still." She anointed his right cheek liberally; Fortier had sewn the torn skin up neatly, and the effect was rather piratical, but the inflamed flesh was subsiding into something that looked far more normal.

"He has an excellent ability to heal." Fortier spoke from the doorway. "You've got a sound constitution, Silas, although living at Wellington Gardens wasn't good for you. I don't think you'll have to go back there. I've spoken to Mr. Dermody, and the mayor is raising the question of the flood protection for those houses with the council. When you leave me, you'll go to better lodgings."

Smiling at Silas's expressions of gratitude, Fortier and I, by tacit agreement, descended the stairs to give Guttridge a few minutes alone with her friend.

"It's this kind of case that needs a nursing hospital the most." Fortier led the way to his study. "Fresh air, clean linen, and nourishing food do much to improve health, and comfortable surroundings lift the spirits; it's astonishing to what degree a patient's mental state promotes healing." He lifted a sketch from his desk. "Have you seen this? It's your hospital."

"Not mine." I gazed, entranced, at the drawing of a pleasant, rambling building that resembled a large manor house, its upper half hung with the traditional red Sussex tiles like fish scales. "It's Justin's, if anything. It will bear his name even when I cease to do so."

This reminder earned me a kiss, but Fortier was too eager about his subject to extend the dalliance.

"I suggested a terrace," he said, running a finger along the smaller inset drawing of the building's rear elevation. "The terrace at Whitcombe inspired me, given the land slopes away exactly the same way. In the front, I hope one day there'll be a pretty garden for patients to sit in the morning sunshine, but it's the back that'll have the most therapeutic value."

"Because of the view." I nodded. "And the sea air. Standing on my terrace always invigorates me somehow."

"Exactly. I see the terrace as being laid out a little like a seaside promenade, with plenty of seats. Not too grand, to put the patients at their ease. We'll have a women's and a men's side of the hospital, of course, but I'd like the terrace and garden to be places where the patients can meet and talk and see their families."

I smiled. "I like to hear you say 'we.' So the decision is made, is it? I thought Ned was making rather a point of shaking your hand after church yesterday."

"Yes, I've agreed to his proposal, and what's more I'm going to be on the board of governors." Fortier looked pleased. "I just hope the rest of them won't object to me."

"Why should they?" I scrutinized the drawing again, feeling a thrill of anticipation and excitement. "May I borrow this until tomorrow, to show the others?"

"You may." Fortier dipped a pen in ink and wrote neatly in one corner: *The Whitcombe Cottage Hospital, Littleberry*. "There, the finishing touch. Are you going home now, or paying calls?"

"It's too early for calls. Besides, you don't know, do you? Dederick has been released."

"He has?" Fortier's face lit up with delight. "When?"

"At dawn. He sent a telegram to Blanche straightaway, and she sent me a note. I suppose he'll go straight to Hawthorn Hall. I wish I could see their reunion."

I HAD TOLD THOMAS ABOUT BLANCHE'S NEWS AT BREAKFAST, so by the time Guttridge and I arrived at Whitcombe, he had passed it on to Ellen and Lucy. The two young Walforts were waiting for me, in a state of high excitement.

"Would it be presumptuous of us to ask if we could give a party for Dederick one day soon?" Lucy asked. "We're awfully good at parties. Not that you're not, of course, but you have a great deal more to do than we have."

"And anyway, we want to make it a Thanksgiving, of sorts," Ellen added. "We'll go to church on Thursday and offer our prayers of thanks, just as we'd do if Mother and Father were here, but we'd like to postpone the celebration for a few days to give Dederick time to become comfortable at home again. Would it be all right if we talked to Mrs. Foster about food?"

"Our American traditions will be a bit strange to all of you, we know." Lucy smiled gaily. "But what better subject for Thanksgiving than a prisoner being set free? Will you let us?"

"Of course. You must treat Whitcombe as your home. I hope you won't miss your parents too much on Thursday."

"Oh, we miss them every day." Lucy's smile faltered a little. "But Father writes so cheerfully of Mother. I'm glad she thinks the sunshine's doing her good."

"And we'll have *such* a lot to write them about." Ellen put her arm around Lucy's waist. "We'd already started a long letter about the exploits of the Investigating Lady and her gallant friends; you'll be a legend in America soon—you'll see. Now we have to tell them about Dederick and how right we were to have faith in him."

At that moment, a footman stepped in to announce Lord Hastings, who I sincerely hoped had heard Ellen's last sentence. As Dederick—quite neatly washed and dressed, given the circumstances—walked in with a shy smile, my cry of delight was followed by louder exclamations from both of the Walforts, who, despite their excitement, considerately held back to let me embrace my nephew.

"I thought I'd come here first and ask for your carriage, Aunt Helena," Dederick said after the first joyful moments were behind us. "At least . . . I mean . . . I walked up from the station and wondered if you might kindly allow me to go home in your carriage." He looked down at the mud that clung to the sides of his shoes. "And perhaps lend me a shoe brush or whatever it is one uses. I want to look my best for Mama."

"I'll get Robert to valet you properly." A thought struck me, and I frowned. "You'll need a new valet, won't you? I should have thought of that before. Shall I write to the agency on your behalf, or do you have someone in mind?"

"Do please help me." Dederick shrugged. "I didn't choose very well last time, did I?"

"It's not your fault," I hastened to reassure him.

There was a slightly awkward silence, but then Ellen spoke. "Would you inquire about a lady's maid for us at the same time, Helena?"

I tensed a little; were they thinking of leaving after all? Lucy, always the more intuitive of the two, put a hand on my arm.

"There's nothing wrong with your hospitality," she said with a glance at Ellen. "It's just we read somewhere it's usual to have your own maid if you're hoping to be presented during the Season. Would that be all right? It wouldn't upset your servants?"

"She'll have a lot to do," Ellen added. "We'll have to think about ordering our dresses before too long. It should perhaps be a London maid—a young one with a genuine interest in fashion. We want to make our mark."

"And there's so much to learn," said Lucy. "We want to understand the etiquette completely. We're dreading we'll make a silly mistake and say something wrong to the Queen or call a duchess 'Your Grace' instead of 'Duchess'—the kind of mistake Americans often make. We know this Season will be a turning point for us."

"You see, we've been talking about this a lot." Ellen looked shyly in Dederick's direction. "There are two likely outcomes. The first is that I—or Lucy or both of us—receive a proposal from a suitable gentleman. We know Father's money—our marriage settlements—will come into play, but for my part, I want more than just a transaction. I'd rather accept nobody than accept the wrong man."

"And if Ellen stays in England, I shall too, to look after her once Mother and Father return to New York." Lucy's eyes twinkled. "But if all else fails, we plan to go back to New York together as young ladies who've been presented at the Court of St. James and refused noble suitors. That'll give Mother the satisfaction of impressing the Four Hundred."

"And if we go back home, I'll marry—well, there are two or three men to choose from." Ellen looked more beautiful than ever as she blushed. "Men I knew when we were children, who still write to me asking when we're coming back. They've all got plenty of money, so I know they want me for myself." Her eyes widened a little, self-mocking. "I'll have to marry soon, or everyone will consider me an old maid."

"But listen to us, talking about ourselves again." Lucy turned to Dederick, who was smiling at the exchange, and I wondered fleetingly whether Ellen had introduced the topic on purpose. Was she simply trying to put Dederick at his ease by taking the attention away from him, or was she letting him know the terms of her engagement in this husband-hunting enterprise?

"Are you truly free now, Dederick?" Lucy was asking. "We've missed you so much."

"They said so." Dederick pushed back his curls, which had grown rather too long since I had last seen him. "They wouldn't tell me much, to be honest. Last night they came and asked me all sorts of questions all over again, and at first I thought I was for it. But then they said the fellows at the club had given me a—what-d'you-call-it?—an alibi, for Fleetwood, and then they told me about Rampling." He shook his head. "I've had a lot to think about overnight."

"You poor lamb," Lucy cried. "I don't suppose you even want to talk about it."

"Not much—now." Dederick looked down at his feet again. "Maybe not for a while, but if I do want to talk, it'll be with you, my friends." He raised his head, his hair almost hiding his eyes. "But I say, if you want to know everything about society, why not consult me? If I don't know something, Mama will. She's a stickler for getting it right. It was hard for her at first, you see, even as an earl's daughter. She was just a girl when she married, and the people Papa knew were very grand."

The young ladies exclaimed in delight at Dederick's offer and began to make a fuss of him in a way I believed he rather liked, but soon he turned to me.

"Aunt Helena, can we get Robert to shine me up now? Mama's probably sitting at home with the train timetable, trying to predict when I'll get there." He smiled at the girls, all his former charm restored. "I promise I'll come to visit as soon as Mama can bear to let me out of her sight."

I SENT A PASSING MAID TO LOOK FOR ROBERT AND LED Dederick upstairs. "You can use the room you were in before," I told him. "If you need fresh linen or anything, I may be able to find something of Justin's. I still haven't gone through everything in his old dressing room."

"I'll be all right." Dederick held the door of the bedroom open so I could precede him, shutting the door behind us. "I say, Aunt Helena, do you think I might have a chance with Ellen? I do like her. If I have to marry, and Mama keeps saying I do, I'd rather it be someone I trust." He looked a little embarrassed. "I can't say I'm head over heels in love with her or anything like that. Not yet. But I've had time to reflect; Mama always says the most important thing is to feel I can be friends with my wife."

"The most important thing is the truth." It was perhaps a bit harsh in the circumstances, but I wasn't sure I'd get such an opportunity again. "You have to be truthful with Ellen and eventually with her parents. About Lord Arthur, that is. I imagine Mr. Walfort will want to know about your financial situation too. He doesn't seem like a fool to me."

"Nor to me." Dederick pushed his hair back. "I'm afraid the thing about Arthur might lose me whatever chance I have, though."

"That's a risk you have to take. It's all going to come out anyway, you know. They'll put Rampling on trial, and you're bound to be called as a witness, and there'll be yet another scandal. I just hope you won't have to join Odelia on the Continent."

"So do I." Dederick shuddered. "I'll definitely have to stay away from Marlborough House for a while."

He leaned back against the windowsill, his pale blond hair gleaming against a background of gray clouds. "I'm going to have to behave like a saint for quite some time. Oddly enough, I don't really mind." He smiled. "It's been almost a relief not to be constantly addling my brains with drink and spending money."

"Almost?" I laughed.

"Entirely, then. I don't suppose I'll be capable of living like a prig when I go back into society, but at least I've learned something."

A peacock somewhere on the terrace below shrieked into

the silence that hung between us for a moment, and I watched Dederick's smile vanish. "Believe me, Aunt, whatever happens, I'm terrified of getting mixed up with men like Arthur again. I mean, I understand—sympathize—with them, but I've seen things now." His young face was suddenly grim. "There've been things over the last few weeks I can't even talk about. I've learned that when you have a weakness punishable by law, it gives other men—who have far more of vice about them than poor Arthur ever did—power over you. There may always be a part of me—" He flushed deeply, looking away, his lips compressing for a long moment. "But I'll make sure nobody ever sees that side. Ever." His voice had grown hard.

"I'm sorry." And I really was.

"Yes." He gave me a tight smile. "Well, it's an unforgiving world we live in. Except I know Mama will forgive me, and you do too, don't you?"

I shook my head, denying the need for forgiveness rather than the forgiveness itself. "There's nothing to forgive. We're all allowed to put the past behind us once we've repudiated it."

I stepped over to put my arms around my nephew, and felt his head rest on my shoulder for just a moment, his hands pressing me to him for a second before he let go as footsteps sounded in the corridor. "You'll come to Hawthorn Hall with me, won't you?" he asked.

"Of course." I turned to smile at Robert as he opened the door. "I wouldn't miss this for the world."

42

LOVING ONE ANOTHER

While Robert was making Dederick presentable, I went to the morning room to write and then hurried to the stables with a hastily scribbled note, wanting to be absolutely sure it left Whitcombe before Dederick did. I entrusted it to Mank, asking him to ride straight to Hawthorn Hall and insist on putting the envelope into Blanche's hands himself. I was sure Dederick was right about Blanche keeping vigil and wanted to spare her every moment of worry I could.

We reached Hawthorn Hall to find Blanche waiting for us on the steps of the carriage entrance, swathed in furs against the growing cold of the darkening day. Thanks to my note, the reunion between mother and son was perhaps a little more dignified than it would have been if we had simply arrived unannounced, but it was still very touching to see the two of them locked in a close embrace, whispering words of love to one another. Neither wept in front of the servants, but I was sure they had to work as hard as I did to prevent the tears from coming through.

Blanche looked much older than the woman who had

swept into Whitcombe in August, demanding I help her. She had lost flesh, and it didn't suit her, nor did the new lines on her face, nor the pallor from spending too much time indoors. She shed a few tears once we were alone, but Dederick fairly soon excused himself on the grounds that he was quite exhausted and needed to rest before dinner.

"Do you think he looks unwell?" Blanche wrung her hands as the door closed behind her son. "Oh, Helena, supposing he's picked up some disease from that ghastly prison?"

"He'll be all right," I said. "He's young. A few rides will set him up and bring the color back into his cheeks. It's you I'm worried about." I reached over to pat her hand. "You need looking after, with all the shocks you've had. I intend to visit often and invite you over to Whitcombe a great deal, and now perhaps you can see more society. Ellen and Lucy are keen to come to the Hall. Dederick has promised to help them understand our ways better, and they'd welcome your advice. They're set on doing the Season."

"I suppose that would be a pleasant occupation." Blanche smiled faintly. "It would be like launching daughters into society, wouldn't it? I always wanted daughters. I was wildly happy to have given Francis a son and heir, but I never stopped being sad there were no more babies. *You* must understand that feeling."

"I do." It seemed churlish to resent the reminder of my childless state. "I'll pray as hard as I can that you not only get a daughter-in-law you love, but as many grandchildren as your heart may desire, and several of them girls."

We both laughed, of course, but I wasn't just joking. I had come to realize how little Blanche had in life beyond her family. Perhaps even her constant carping about money wasn't the self-centeredness I took it for, but simply the desire to live in the style of a marchioness for the sake of the son who was everything to her.

"Of course, I may never get the chance to help the Walfort girls." Blanche's expression changed. "We may have to hide away during the Season and wait it out till the next." Her brow furrowed in distress. "I'm dreading the scandal, Helena. Even though Dederick won't be on trial, and I don't have the words to tell you how grateful I am for that, there will be a trial, won't there?"

"I suppose there'll have to be." I felt a sense of dread myself at the prospect of standing up in that witness box again, being stared at by dozens of men judging me for daring to "investigate" a matter properly left to the police.

"I'm so afraid of what will happen," Blanche said. "The newspapers made such a fuss about Odelia. When Dederick told me about Lord Arthur, I started imagining how those beastly men of the press would treat my boy, and soon it'll actually be happening."

She drew in a deep, shuddering breath. "I know I can be horribly critical of others' mistakes myself. I've always been ambitious, you see, but I've always been afraid, and it makes me sharp. Now I'm facing the consequences of my ambitions, aren't I? If I'd kept Dederick closer, perhaps he'd never have done . . . what he did."

"I'm not so sure." I remembered the look on Dederick's face when he had begun to tell me there would always be a part of him attracted to men. "Perhaps some men are just made differently. It was what Justin thought, and he'd had a great deal of experience of the world."

"The Church and the State say otherwise." For a moment Blanche's eyes were chips of blue ice. "They say it's a sin and a crime. They'll always say so."

"I hope people will excuse Dederick because of his youth." I moved closer to Blanche, wishing to comfort her. "And, look—if there's a scandal, we'll weather it together, as Scott-De Quincys. Stare them down, as Papa always said."

"Papa was a man." Blanche's voice was bleak.

"Yes, and people always look more kindly on men than women, and on the beautiful and well-bred most generously of all." I squeezed her arm. "Dederick will recover from this. He has a great deal of promise in terms of looks and health, he's more intelligent than I realized, and this experience seems set to make a better man of him. Try not to worry. Try to look forward to sometime in the future when all these difficulties are behind us."

"When I can feel safe." Blanche's voice was a mere thread of sound. "Francis made me feel safe—from Gerry's and Mama's criticisms, from never having enough money to go out in really good society, from the threat of ending up a spinster, as Alice and Annette were clearly bound to do."

She smiled, but it wasn't a cheerful smile. "For nineteen glorious years, I felt as if I almost had enough. If I'd had more children, and more time with my darling husband, I might have felt the . . . the empty space inside of me was full at last. But Francis died, and I went back to not feeling safe. I knew somehow I wouldn't marry again. All the glory had passed to you, the bride of the richest man for many miles around."

"I don't see happiness as something that slips away from one person to settle on another," I said. "Besides, Justin and I only had three years." And how short they seemed now.

"But you have money of your own now. So much money."

"I inherited Justin's fortune because we didn't have children. I think you know how much I'd have liked a child of Justin's, even just one. You're so blessed to have such a beautiful, healthy son."

For a moment, we stared at each other, and then I held out a hand. "Shall we agree to just love one another? After all, we're neighbors now as well as sisters. We don't know each other nearly as well as we should, but now we have a chance to change that."

Blanche held out her hand in response, and as our fingers folded together, I saw her shoulders relax.

"We must talk about my paying the rent for Hawthorn Hall at Candlemas," she said. "My house in Tunbridge Wells is let for more than I thought it would fetch."

"You don't have to do that."

"I think I do." Blanche squeezed my hand. "I'm still terrified, Helena. The trial . . . the papers . . ."

"I know."

"But you're all here to protect me. My family."

And for a little while, at least, the sister I hardly knew felt like a friend.

43
VIOLENT MEN

"Are you hiding from all the upheaval?"

Fortier, who was cultivating the very pleasant, if a little indiscreet, habit of visiting me at least once a day, grinned as he entered my morning room to find me busy at my desk. Through the door, which Fortier left chastely open, drifted sounds of strenuous activity, punctuated by the Walfort sisters' lively voices and the occasional burst of laughter.

"Yes," I admitted. "Watching my dining table being dismantled was the last straw, although I concede Ellen and Lucy were right about the room being perfect for dancing. It's far bigger than I realized now the furniture's been taken out."

I tipped my chin up so Fortier could kiss me; that delightful task accomplished, he made himself comfortable in an armchair.

"Justin and I never held dances," I said and then bit my lip. "I'm sorry. I don't know how you'll be happy in this house if I'm always talking about Justin." I looked guiltily at the photograph on my desk.

"Nonsense." Fortier, who was dressed for riding, stretched his boot-clad legs out comfortably. "I'm perfectly aware I'm marrying a widow. In fact, I've been to Sir Justin's grave to ask for his approval."

He spoke with such perfect gravity and sincerity I wanted to fling myself into his arms, but there was that open door. "I love you, you know," I said instead.

"I know." Fortier smiled. "And don't you dare hide away that photograph or any portraits of Sir Justin that hang in this house. I refuse to be jealous of a dead man. Now, what excuse did you find for not remaining to help with the party preparations?"

"A very valid one." I held up the letter I had been studying. "The agency has sent me the details of four possible valets for Dederick, and since he'll be here soon, I thought I'd better read it through first. Are you joining us for luncheon?"

"Can't," said Fortier briefly. "I'm on my way to a broken leg that's not mending well. Do you have any dried nettle, comfrey, or boneset, by the way?"

"Plenty of all three."

"Excellent. I shall, with your permission, plunder your workroom before I leave. How is Dederick?"

I shrugged. "Well enough. I think he's been taking the tonic I prepared for him. He's going to stay to help Ellen and Lucy. Maryanne is here as well."

"So I saw. She appeared to be knee-deep in tablecloths. I hear they're going to put the buffet table in the Great Hall."

"Correct." I rested my chin on my hand, as always delighted to see Fortier making himself at home. He had always seemed at ease in my house, I reflected, and now to my no doubt partial imagination, the house seemed almost to be embracing his presence. "Ellen and Lucy found all the card tables in the attic and are having the piano brought down; did you know Lucy's very musical? The housemaids have been helping them make new tablecloths, and we're all going to eat comfortably in small groups. Then they've planned some sort of entertainment to inform us about the traditions of an American Thanksgiving, after which those who wish to will dance, and those who'd rather eat and talk will be well accommodated. It's a little topsy-turvy compared to the English way of doing things, but they're certainly inventive hostesses. I can't believe they've managed all this in a week."

A movement at the door interrupted me; Dederick had arrived. I smiled at my nephew, who, like Fortier, had clearly ridden over to Whitcombe, as he entered the morning room, bringing the fresh air of the outdoors with him as well as the scents of horse and leather. "Goodness, you're cold," I exclaimed as his lips touched my cheek. "Taylor says we'll have a frost tonight."

Dederick shook Fortier's hand and then, to my surprise, turned back to close the morning room door. "Is there something wrong?" I asked.

"Would you rather I left?" Fortier began to rise from his chair.

"No, don't." Dederick shook his head. "You helped save me; you should hear this. I've just had a visit from Orlando Showell, the chap who's been helping me with my defense."

"His name is not unknown to me," Fortier said gravely but with a hint of amusement in his eyes. Sir Orlando was a very well-known Queen's Counsel, famous for defending the nobility in court.

"There's been what he calls a development." Dederick sat on the sofa, perching on the edge rather than making himself comfortable. "Personally, I'd describe it as a thunderbolt. I'm glad Mama was out."

I looked at my nephew carefully, noting the heaviness in the rounding of his shoulders and the downward curve of his lips. “Bad news,” I said; it was a statement rather than a question.

“Yes. In a sense. Although . . .” Dederick looked up at the ceiling for inspiration and then directly at me, his gray-green irises pale in the weak winter sunlight that brightened the room. “I can’t think of a way to break this gently, Aunt. Rampling is dead.”

“Heavens.” I whispered the word, seeing my astonishment reflected in Fortier’s eyes. “How?”

“Found hanged in his cell.” Dederick frowned, and I saw Fortier’s thick black brows draw together. For my part, it was the memory of Lucius Hatherall hanging from a beam in his kitchen ceiling that reared itself before my eyes, unpleasantly vivid. I swallowed against a bad taste in my mouth.

“Did he hang himself?” Fortier asked.

“Showell said that was his first question too.” Dederick had hunched himself together, his wrists on his knees, his hands dangling in a gesture of dejection. “The evidence appears to be inconclusive. The thing is, though, he confessed to both murders—Arthur’s and Fleetwood’s—last night.”

Dederick raised his head a little to look at me; his face was white and strained. “Showell’s not satisfied the confession was voluntary.”

“There’ve been enough questions asked in the newspapers about the use of coercion by the police,” Fortier said.

“Yes.” Dederick glanced at him. “Well, after the way they dealt with me, I can well believe it. According to Showell, Rampling was all set to use exactly the same defense of *corpus delicti* that Showell was preparing for me. In both deaths, there were no injuries that couldn’t have been caused by a simple fall and no witnesses to Rampling pushing either man. Nothing that would shout ‘murder’ to a jury.”

“So Rampling’s lawyers would have argued for a verdict

of not guilty by reason of lack of proof that murder was committed." Fortier nodded. "And they'd quite possibly have succeeded. Once you've convinced a jury there's any doubt, they're unlikely to hang a man."

Dederick's Adam's apple bobbed as he swallowed hard. "So why would Rampling confess if there was a chance he could get away scot-free? I wouldn't have." He took a deep breath. "I would have held out against any and every accusation—until I no longer could. I wondered, and Showell agreed, if the only way they could extract a confession was by force. An interrogation that became too rough. Showell's intention is to make discreet inquiries."

"Which will probably result in nothing." Fortier looked disgusted. "Do you have a copy of Rampling's confession?"

"Not yet. Showell insisted on reading it and is having the police make an exact copy." Dederick rubbed his forehead as if his head ached. "He took notes. The essence of it is Rampling found poor Arthur in my compartment when he looked in on me at Stafford. I was unconscious. Arthur was crying."

Dederick's voice broke, and several moments passed before he regained control of himself. "Rampling said the crying upset and angered him. Arthur was babbling on about Endymion—*you* know, the chap who chose eternal slumber as a way of keeping his looks," he said to me in response to my puzzled frown.

I didn't know, but I nodded anyway; Dederick seemed eager to get the business of telling done and was already speaking again. "Arthur used to tell me, all those years ago at school, that he loved to watch me sleep." His cheeks flamed. "I didn't love him, and that thing with the letters upset me a great deal—all those threats to make a public fuss—but God, he didn't deserve to die because he loved *me*."

His head sank even lower, and I saw a single tear drop to

the carpet, but after a few more moments had passed, he straightened up, his face pale but emotionless. "Rampling was jealous, but he hid it. He persuaded Arthur to come with him to the brake van—to comfort him, he said. Rampling could be very charming when he wanted to."

I nodded. "I noticed that. There was something quite appealing about him, wasn't there? And if he was already Lord Arthur's lover—"

"Arthur would have trusted him." Dederick sighed deeply. "They got into the van a couple of minutes before the train was due to leave, when the guard was absent. Rampling had managed to cheer Arthur up, and they were even laughing. All an act on Rampling's part, I suppose."

"Was that when they woke Fleetwood?" I asked. I had never met Lord Arthur, so in my imagination he was just a shadowy figure, but I could almost see Rampling, as if the scene were being played on a stage—the easy joviality, the appearance of being willing to please. Had they whispered together? Embraced, perhaps. Stifling their laughter like schoolboys, perhaps stumbling into the partitioned area where Fleetwood dozed, and the old man in the armchair opening his rheumy eyes for a second, uncomprehending, as sleepers usually were when suddenly aroused. A moment that had cost him his life.

"I don't remember that part." Dederick shook his head. "If Showell gives me a copy of the confession, I'll see what it says. Or better still, I'll give it to you—you can read it and burn it, for all I care. I don't want to see it." He shuddered. "I want to put it all behind me."

"And Rampling confessed to pushing Lord Arthur—from the observation platform, I suppose?" Fortier asked. "He must have taken him out there to hide him from the guard. Did he say what happened?"

"Only that he pushed him." Dederick flicked his blond

curls back from his forehead, a little impatiently. "Showell said that particular part of the confession is very badly recorded, to the point where he, if he'd been defending Rampling, would have built many an argument in favor of the confession having been extracted by force. But he *did* confess—and also confessed to pushing Fleetwood under that omnibus on Pall Mall."

"Convenient," Fortier said quietly.

"I suppose so." Dederick shrugged. "Showell says whatever the truth of the whole dirty mess is, he has no doubt whatsoever that I'm completely exonerated as far as the police are concerned." He was silent for a few moments. "In any case, he's reluctant to press too hard for an inquiry into Rampling's death, in case my name comes into it."

"A fine family lawyer." Fortier, always sensitive to any implication that the aristocracy used its position to shield itself from harm, glowered, but he said the words quietly and gave me a half smile, albeit with a cynical twist to his lips.

Dederick did not answer, and we all fell silent, each one of us immersed in our own thoughts. A loud bang and a shriek of laughter came from the dining room, but none of us reacted to it. I was thinking of the violent men I had encountered over the last two years—Lucius Hatherall, who had held Justin under the water to save his own daughter from an accusation of attempted poisoning, and Edmund Dorrian-Knowles, driven by his mother's despair to murder one mistress and attempt to murder another, my own sister. Love turned to violence, and here it was again, an ugly distortion of what the Bible taught us was the greatest of all virtues.

And then realization struck; I felt the force of the relief of it run through my body like a galvanic shock. My hand flew to my mouth.

"There won't be a trial." I looked at Dederick. "Will there?

If there's no defendant, there can't be a trial. There won't be a scandal."

"So Showell says." Dederick did not look like a man who had just been reprieved from social disaster. "He said I could pretend none of it ever happened. I wanted to kick him."

"That's damned brutal." Fortier's voice was soft, but his expression was still thunderous.

"Yes, well, he's that bluff sort of man who doesn't appear to have a sensitive bone in his body." Dederick shrugged. "Perhaps the law has hardened him. And I don't think he likes me anyway, knowing what he does."

Another moment's silence ensued, and then Dederick shrugged again. "To Hades with him. I don't suppose he'll have reason to visit again. Aunt Helena, will you come with me when I tell Mama?"

"Of course." I rose to lay a hand on my nephew's shoulder; Dederick responded with a brief smile, and I felt again the new warmth between us. "Will you say anything to the others at luncheon?" I asked him.

Dederick shook his head slowly. "Not yet." He murmured the words again, very low. "Not yet. And I'll do my best to make sure Mama doesn't . . . well . . . gloat over the fact that I'll escape a scandal. Not that I think she will." His expression softened. "This whole business has changed her somehow."

44
ROSES FROM THE SOUTH

Ellen, Lucy, and I were up before dawn on the day of the Thanksgiving party, rejoicing when the sun rose serenely from behind the black tree-studded outline of the hills to the east of us, limning them with a golden light that made the sky above appear deep blue.

It had become much colder. By the time we had eaten an early breakfast, the gardeners had finished heaping fresh pine boughs onto the terrace beds from which the frost-blackened dahlias had been removed; their sharp, resinous scent filled the cold air and delighted our senses as we ventured outdoors to ensure everything looked perfect.

"Real winter weather at last." Ellen put her arm through mine as we looked out over the frosty fields. "I'm relieved to see England can manage a decent spell of cold after all those dreary gray skies. I hope some of the guests will want to take a turn out here."

"Oh, the ladies will enjoy the opportunity to show off their furs." I smiled up at the American girl, whose bright hair seemed to gather the sunlight into it and reflect it back in a myriad of colors, as sparkling as the frost. "And I daresay it'll be even colder just a few miles inland."

"Yes, the sea changes everything. That's how it is in Newport." Ellen turned to me, her blue eyes bright. "Why don't we take one last look at the Great Hall and then start on our toilettes? I'm longing to see you in your Parisian dress."

"So is Guttridge. You'd think I was a debutante again." I grinned. "She's made full use of the addresses she copied out of your Paris notebook."

"Do you always let her choose your dresses?" Lucy, who had been chasing Scotty away from the pine boughs lest he defile them, joined us as we began walking back toward the house.

"I do, rather." I laughed. "I've never cared much for clothes. I was Mama's despair. Once I was finally engaged to be married, she told me she would hire a lady's maid with enough force of personality to ensure I would be dressed to match my station despite myself. And she did, of course, although Guttridge has had a struggle against my preference for dressing like a plain countrywoman." I looked down at my mauve dress, of which I was becoming quite enamored. "She appears to be winning."

"She has excelled herself with your ballgown." Lucy's tone was teasing. "Our dear Doctor Fortier is going to faint with joy when he sees you."

"I rather suspect it's all for his benefit anyway." I felt a faint blush rise to my cheeks, but with the Walfort girls living in my house, Fortier's wooing of me was something of an open secret between us. "His stock has risen immensely with Guttridge since he saved Silas's life. She plans to decorate the deepest part of the neckline with some pale pink rosebuds Taylor has been cosseting in his warmest greenhouse." I felt my blush grow deeper. "She tried the effect yesterday, and if anything they draw attention to—well—"

"—to your very pretty figure." Lucy's laugh was merry. "I saw exactly that effect illustrated in the *Revue de la Mode*, so you'll be quite up to date."

"And my diamonds have arrived," I said. Guttridge had sent to the bank for the diamond parure Justin had given me on the last Christmas we spent together.

"Diamonds." Ellen breathed a sigh. "The glory of the married woman. I think I'd look rather well in diamonds."

"You may try mine on." We had arrived at the Great Hall, brightly decorated for the feast. "Well, ladies, to work; after all, we have a great deal to be thankful for."

"We do indeed." Ellen touched my arm gently. "I am thankful for you, Helena."

"And I am thankful that I am at *last* going to see you dancing with Armand Fortier." Lucy took possession of her sister's hand, towing her toward the staircase. "And perhaps Ellen will dance with Dederick *and* Jonathan, and I—I will drink punch and talk to every single one of our guests. We'll show these English aristocrats how to have a good time."

"I FEEL LIKE I'M IN A HOTEL." GERRY FLICKED A FINGER AT THE elaborate menu card that stood proudly in the middle of our small table, nestled in an ingenious arrangement of red and gold chrysanthemums from my greenhouses, sprigs of rosemary from the gardens, and sprays of glossy red rosehips from the hedges in Whitcombe Lane. "Still, Mrs. Foster has done very well, considering the inconvenience. Some dishes are peculiar in their conception, but I must say she hasn't failed in the execution." She smiled at me. "And I must congratulate you on your toilette, Helena. That décolleté suits you very well."

"It's marvelous to see you in dresses like this again, my dear. And the food's absolutely delicious." Ned took another bite of the creamy lobster stew we were all enjoying. "The menus are splendid pieces of work. Did you make them, Helena?"

"You ought to know I'm not that gifted with the pen." I laughed. "Ellen's penmanship is superb, and Lucy decorated the cards. They've made cards to guide us through the entertainment too, and Lucy is going to sing and play for us. I hadn't realized, until they had the piano brought down from the attic, how musical she was. Ellen plays and sings well enough, but Lucy has real talent."

"What shining stars these Americans are." There was the faintest hint of sourness in Gerry's tone. "I'm glad Maryanne is out, otherwise those girls would entirely eclipse her next year. They will make splendid marriages."

I avoided looking at Thomas, who was seated opposite me, silently consuming his meal. The look on his face as he had watched Lucy practice the pieces she had chosen for the afternoon's entertainment had been such a struggle between soaring pride and frustrated love I had wanted to shout at him to tell her—*tell her!*—but not for the world would I reveal his secret, even to his loving parents. Even though I was almost certain Ned would be on my nephew's side, ready to make some provision to allow him to at least propose to the girl. No, Thomas was going to let Lucy walk into the London Season without a word passing his lips and possibly lose her to some less-deserving man.

I did not reply to Gerry, instead taking a sip of the kirsch punch in my cup; it was not strong. I had noticed our American guests were less fond of inebriating themselves than my countrymen. I let my gaze stray to the table where Fortier sat with Quinn, Gabrielle, and Louise and saw his gaze directed toward me; I looked away quickly, my heart beating faster with the imminent prospect of dancing with Fortier for the first time.

"I HAVE WAITED A THOUSAND YEARS FOR THIS MOMENT. THAT dress is astonishing, and as for the roses . . ."

"Guttridge's idea."

"I will thank her later."

Fortier's grasp of my hand was light but firm as he led me out into the middle of the floor, around which a few of the tables had been arranged into small groups. Those unwilling to dance could enjoy the music and the sight of the fifteen or so couples who had stepped onto the floor as the conductor announced "*valse générale*" and the first slow introductory notes of a waltz drifted through the air, setting the tune for the dancers and allowing us to take up our positions and talk a little to our partners.

"Ah, Strauss. 'Roses from the South.'" Fortier's eyes lit up as he recognized the music. "It's a good choice. New, but not so new that nobody knows it."

"Do *you* know it?" It struck me suddenly that Fortier had a life outside Littleberry, where he perhaps danced—in London, perhaps in France—with other women. I tightened my grip on his hand the tiniest amount; Fortier felt it and returned the pressure.

"I do, *ma belle*." He smiled. "Even I don't work *all* the time."

"I don't know it. It's been too long since I danced. You'll have to help me through it."

"As long as you can reverse—"

"—I can."

"Then we will go along nicely." Fortier waited as I found

the hidden loop to hold up my dress's long train, bowed as I curtseyed, and performed the sometimes awkward maneuver of ensuring we were in the correct starting position with easy grace. He was not wearing signs of mourning—men were never expected to do so for long—and to me there was no man in the room better dressed, even Dederick. Was Dederick on the dance floor? I hadn't even noticed. I felt blind to everyone else around us.

"I'm dreadfully out of practice." I suddenly felt my breath grow short.

"You are the most beautiful and the most graceful woman in the room."

It wasn't true, of course, but I could feel the warmth of our joined hands through our gloves, and his hand on my back was steady, his touch light but reassuring. The introductory music was drawing to a close. I took a deep breath, gazing up at the man who was to be my husband.

"That's better." Fortier smiled again, his splendid eyes holding mine. And as the first lilting notes of the waltz sounded, my feet automatically did the right thing, my heels rising inside my dance slippers to make my steps quicker and more graceful.

The music was glorious, and I began to relax, a smile spreading across my face as I learned that Fortier really did know how to dance. Love was renewing me, he had said, and as I followed him through the intricate composition, so full of delightful changes of tone and mood, I felt light and new, a freshly minted bubble floating on the air.

"A thousand years, and it was worth it," Fortier breathed as the music slowed for a second or two, and then we were off again, turning and floating, and nothing else in the world mattered.

45
A WARNING

The low winter sun was a circle of glowing red, sinking rapidly behind the far-off headland amid a blaze of pinks and oranges, reflected sumptuously by a calm sea of blue-tinged gray. In the two days since the party, the mercury had dropped considerably; this day's dawn had brought a hoarfrost that had persisted into the afternoon.

My gardeners had strewn gravel on the terrace so I could take my walks with Scotty, but I had no wish to venture out into the frozen world outside Whitcombe. Everything was white; long ice crystals grew upon every surface, turning the trees in the valley to confections of sugar, strange and ghostly under the darkening sky. Not a breath of wind stirred the silence. Even the birds had deserted the heavens, no doubt seeking warmth in some safe roosting place. My toes and fingers ached pleasurably. I would only stay out for ten minutes at the most, enjoying my last look at the sea for that day.

The house too was calm, restored to its usual self after the excitement of the party. Ellen and Lucy were at Four Square with Maryanne, and Thomas was down at Ned's warehouses by the muddy shore of the tidal river. They would be back for supper. For now, I was content to be alone, looking forward to my solitary cup of tea and modest slice of cake in the small library as a reward for braving the icy air. I could no longer hear Scotty, who was probably looking for rabbits on the hillside.

"Well, I'm not going down to the lane to look for you," I murmured in the direction in which my dog had vanished. "I'm far too well dressed to risk falling."

I hugged my new Parisian pelisse to me, feeling the soft fur tickle my cheek. A simply marvelous hat had arrived at noon to go with it, and I had decided to try it all out, proceeding in stately and fashionable solitude as if I were a drawing in a fashion plate. Would Fortier like it? I had discovered that one's attire was far more interesting when he took notice of it. Those roses, now . . . what a success *they* had been.

A volley of barks from the front of the house informed me I was wrong about Scotty's whereabouts. He had taken to watching the lane recently, hoping for Fortier, Dederick, or Jonathan, all of whom he liked, and I thought perhaps he had spotted a visitor drawing near. I smiled in anticipation; at this hour, it was most likely to be Fortier.

It wasn't difficult to deduce from the changing note of the barks, rising from deeper-pitched challenge to Scotty's frantically high yelp of welcome, that I could well be right. I turned toward the house, a smile upon my lips.

It *was* Fortier, taking the short flight of steps up to the terrace two at a time, gravel crunching under his feet. Scotty raced ahead of him, for all the world as if Fortier had asked him to lead him to where I was, wagging his plumed white-streaked tail enthusiastically as he slowed to a halt by me.

"Thank you, monsieur." Fortier nodded to my terrier, who responded with a brief *ruff* and went to sniff among the pine branches, hoping no doubt to catch a shrew or a vole. "Good afternoon, *ma belle*. That's an awfully becoming hat."

He moved swiftly to press a kiss on my mouth but did not linger over the salute. I looked at him closely.

"Not more bad news." I reached out a hand to Fortier.

"One of the many, many things I love about you," he said, enclosing my fingers tightly in his gloved hand, "is the way you notice how people are feeling. I am feeling angry and despondent for a reason that concerns you closely. It's not a disaster." He turned his head to smile at me. "At least now I'm with you, it doesn't feel like a complete disaster. Come; the sun has almost gone, it's cold, and I was hoping you'd offer me tea. I'll tell you all about it once we're warm and fed. It can wait that long."

"Of course we can have tea. I was about to anyway. Ohhhhh . . ." I sighed in frustration as Scotty raced off in the opposite direction, barking at something. "I'll send a footman to call him when it gets dark. He's no fool; he'll come to them and even let them wash him in return for a few scraps from the kitchen."

Guttridge, with her usual uncanny prescience, entered the conservatory just as we stepped through the door from the outside. She helped me shed my new hat and pelisse with greater care than I would have taken and provided me with a pair of soft slippers to replace the warm boots I had been wearing. Fortier shucked off his greatcoat, then, noticing the state of his boots—he had probably taken Lucifer round to my stables—unbuttoned his gaiters and used the bootjack by the door to remove the offending articles.

I followed him as he padded through Whitcombe's lofty corridors in his everyday jacket, riding britches, and a pair of serviceable wool socks that had darns in both heels. The intimacy of the sight made me both smile and sigh for the day when he would come back to Whitcombe in the evenings as to his home . . . back to me . . .

We had reached the small library before Fortier groaned in annoyance. "The letter—I left it in my coat pocket."

"It will be safe in Guttridge's care, whatever it is," I assured him. "I'm sure she's brushing your coat out herself. I don't think you have any notion what a favorite you are with her now."

"I'll go get it." Fortier turned around.

"I'll ring." I laughed, heading for the nearest bellpull. "Bells and footmen are far more practical than searching for someone in a house like this. You're going to have to learn you can't do your own fetching and carrying anymore."

Within two minutes, a footman appeared, and I instructed him to fetch Dr. Fortier's coat. It arrived, freshly brushed, soon after, and tea followed a minute or two later. Five minutes later, the fire had been built up, I had poured the tea, and Fortier and I were ensconced in armchairs by the hearth.

"What luxury you live in, my darling." Fortier took a hurried sip of his tea before burrowing his hand into the pocket of the coat that lay across his lap. "Ah, here it is. Not exactly the best of news." He dropped the coat unceremoniously beside his chair.

I stared with avid curiosity at the black-bordered envelope, noting the fine quality of the paper. As Fortier extracted and unfolded the equally black-bordered sheets of paper, I saw the black crest in the corner. A crown surmounted it. It certainly wasn't the royal arms of England.

I set down my cup and stepped to Fortier's side, trying not to block the light as I gazed at the regular lines of writing with their curly *d*'s, long strokes across the *t*'s, and tails at the end of nearly every word, as if the writer had been reluctant to put down their pen. It was written in the French language, and under the crown was a device of back-to-back capital *E*'s.

"The Empress Eugénie?" I guessed.

"The same."

"Writing to *'Monsieur le duc.'*" I stared at the salutation. "She clearly hasn't heard you're not interested in using your title. Why is she writing to *you*?"

"Oh, she knows well enough I won't adopt the title. It was *'Cher monsieur et ami'* when she sent me her condolences on Father's death." He handed me the sheets of paper. "You may as well read it."

"You know each other?" This was a side of Fortier I hadn't suspected.

"My father was an ardent Bonapartist, remember? His admiration for Napoleon III cooled somewhat when the late emperor began making war all over Europe, but until we left France, he was a regular visitor at the Tuileries. He sometimes brought us children with him."

"You're full of surprises." Of course, to most English observers, Napoleon III had been an adventurer who had used his uncle's famous name to seize and retain power in a most irregular fashion, but for almost two decades, until his empire had collapsed in the flames of war, he and Eugénie had ranked on a par with the crowned heads of Europe. She was still a great friend of our own Queen . . . I read on.

"Je tiens à vous avertir . . ." I breathed deeply. A letter starting with the statement that the writer was about to warn the recipient of something was definitely not the best of news. It was, I noted with a corner of my mind as I read, the prose of an intelligent, socially astute woman who wrote letters often.

"What does she mean, she has intercepted Louise's correspondence?" I frowned as I reached the first sentence of significance.

"That also worries me." Fortier's mouth had a cynical twist. "It means she probably knows about Jacques and that the three of us are being spied on. But I shouldn't be surprised. She had an entire court in exile under her roof in Chislehurst in the '70s, and they would naturally be interested in anyone who might pose a threat to her son's chances of becoming emperor. The game I have been playing for the last thirteen years has high stakes."

"But her son is dead . . ."

"There are other claimants." Fortier shrugged. "But the main import of the letter isn't politics. Keep reading."

The writing was clear and legible, and it wasn't long before I arrived at the nub of the matter. I felt my palms grow damp.

"Louise can't really do that, can she?" I looked at Fortier in dismay.

"Apparently, she can." Fortier reached up to caress my arm. "In France, one has to prove actual harm, which is difficult, but Louise is taking full advantage of her change of domicile."

"But—an action for breach of promise?" My voice sounded high and breathless, and indeed the idea of Louise suing Fortier in a court of law did rather take my breath away. "Have you ever promised marriage to Louise?"

"Of course not." Fortier looked worried, but his tone was dry. "I suppose the argument against me would be that I acted in such a way as to suggest I would marry her someday. Including, as you know, living with her—albeit occasionally—under the pretense I was her husband."

He has ruined me for others by pretending to be my husband, and nobody with a Christian conscience could claim otherwise. I heard Louise's voice again, aristocratic, sure of herself.

"She told me as much," I said and saw Fortier's eyebrows rise.

"She talked to you about it?"

"She came to see me the day the Walfort girls were moving in." I did my best to smile at Fortier. "I'd almost forgotten about it, to be honest, what with Dederick's arrest and the business with Silas and Rampling. There's nothing like a threat of hanging and a brewing scandal to distract one's attention."

"And you didn't think it important enough to tell me." Fortier pulled me down onto his lap, wrapping his arms around me.

"She told me to let you go. I said I wouldn't. For me, that was the end of the matter."

I felt Fortier's lips seek mine, and for a few moments we forgot ourselves, but he ended the kiss too soon, picking up the letter from where I had let it fall. "Keep reading."

I sighed and turned the page, then squeaked as I read my own name. "An action against *me* for alienating your affections? Good grief, is such a thing even possible?"

"I believe alienation of affections is a valid action at English law." There was a hint of amusement in Fortier's eyes now. "If I *had* entertained any affections for Louise beyond those of cousinly regard, you would certainly have alienated them. I have eyes for nobody else."

"In what way is this not a disaster?" I felt a little sick.

"It's just a threat." Fortier kissed my cheek. "Litigation isn't easy, and it's costly. To be honest, for me the bigger problem is what Eugénie says next. Keep reading."

I worked my way down the neatly written lines, frowning. "She finds herself obliged to inform 'certain other interested parties' of this development, but her deep affection for you prompts her to give you this warning." I looked at Fortier. "What other interested parties?"

"Precisely. I wish I knew. This is the first inkling I've had that the empress even knows about Jacques, and now here's an indication she's been communicating with others about the matter." He frowned ferociously. "The more I think about her words, the more I find myself wondering exactly how many fingers are in this particular pie. I find myself wondering who, exactly, is spying on us. I find myself wondering if she will tell me the answers to these questions and advise me what best to do. I will definitely have to go to Hampshire to see her." He drew in a breath. "This letter suggests she is willing to help me."

"Because of her deep affection for you?"

Fortier's stomach gave a growl that was most inappropriate to the occasion. He leaned forward, managing to grasp a buttered teacake with the tips of his fingers. "I'm sorry," he said with his mouth full. "I haven't eaten since breakfast, and I can't hold out any longer. Would you like some?"

"I know better than to come between a starving man and his prey." Fortier's calmness in the face of this impending catastrophe soothed me. I leaned my head into his shoulder to allow him to eat more easily. Two teacakes later, he spoke.

"The empress likes me." He licked his fingers, the napkins being out of reach. "Father always said I won her heart by playing so nicely with the prince imperial when he was just a baby and I was four years old. In any case, she has written to me every year on my birthday, even after we moved to England and Father abandoned the Catholic Church."

"When *is* your birthday?" I was taken aback to realize I didn't know.

"The seventh of August." He kissed me, tasting of butter and cinnamon.

"Really?" I wrapped an arm around Fortier's chest, holding him tight. "How odd. On the seventh of August, I received the letter from Blanche about Hawthorn Hall, and I sat in the drawing room looking across the Channel and thinking of you. You seemed so far away from me then, in every sense of the word. Is it terribly selfish of me that my biggest worry is that you'll go away from me again?"

"Yes." I could feel Fortier's laughter as he caressed my hair. "But *my* biggest worry is also that I'll go away from you, and a worry shared is a worry halved. Or something to that effect. What shall we do, *ma belle*?"

"Let me think."

For a few minutes, there was silence between us. In fact, the whole world seemed wrapped in silence; I could hear no noises either outside or in the house. Just the beating of Fortier's heart, strong and regular. As steady as the beat of music. I closed my eyes, remembering that two days ago we had danced and that I had surely never felt more joyous. I seemed to be groping for an answer that was just out of reach. What should we do?

And then I knew. I raised my head from Fortier's chest, but his words cut across mine.

"I think—"

"We should—"

We both stopped, surprised. Fortier motioned for me to continue.

"Before we do anything else, I think it's high time we announced our engagement," I said. "Let's do it very soon, before Louise has a chance to make mischief in public. This warning of the empress's has given us an advantage, and we're almost duty bound to take it."

I straightened up so I could see Fortier's face. The expression of delight on it was so radiant I wanted to shout for joy, but I bit my lip and waited for him to speak.

"I was about to plead with you for the very same thing." He kissed my hands. "I've been worrying about putting you into a . . . a false position, especially since the party. I don't imagine anyone in Littleberry is unaware we're in love by now. Gaby said we were entirely adorable dancing together —and very obvious."

"We did dance well together, didn't we?"

"So shall we follow the Duke of Wellington's example and say 'publish and be damned' to my dear cousin Louise?"

"Well, it isn't quite in the same context. But I must admit, not being honest with my sisters about you is becoming something of a strain. I think if all this nonsense with Louise is going to come out into the open—and I'm sure it will—it should be because we're no longer hiding our love." I sobered a little. "If she wished, Louise could create quite a sensation over your cohabitation by bringing actions against the two of us. Even if she didn't win the court case, the mud would probably stick, and heaven knows my family doesn't need another scandal. I would far rather get ahead of Louise by announcing our engagement."

Fortier frowned a little. "It wasn't cohabitation, at least not in the sense I think you mean. I swear—on my father's grave, Helena—I never slept with her. I've never even kissed her beyond a cousinly kiss on the cheek."

He threw the letter and its envelope onto the tea tray. The empress had clearly dipped her pen before writing her signature, and "Eugénie," with its looping *g* and down-slanting tail on the final *e*, stood out as starkly as the letter's black border against the gleaming silver.

"Don't worry." I ran the palm of my hand over Fortier's neat, glossy beard. "I believe you. If you had taken Louise to bed, you'd behave differently toward her. But you can't prove a negative, except by having Louise medically examined, I suppose, and I can't see you insisting on that."

"No." Fortier shuddered.

"So it's not going to be easy if she carries out her threat." I held his gaze. "But if she does, she will be fighting the two of us, working together."

"Oh, most wonderful of women." Fortier rose to his feet, lifting me up, and wrapped his arms around me, pulling me close. "The very worst aspect of this blasted letter was the thought that I would be dragging you into trouble. I'm not even sure we can actually marry if there's a breach of promise action against me."

"Possibly not." My head was against Fortier's chest again, my voice muffled. "We certainly won't be able to put up the banns if Louise is likely to declare a just impediment." I freed myself so I could speak more clearly. "Not much hope of an actual wedding until we've straightened out this mess."

"There's always a special license." Fortier looked hopeful.

"Yes, but . . ."

"You'd rather marry in your own church with all your family about you and the rector all smiles."

"Of course I would. In any case, we're getting ahead of ourselves. The point is not *when* we marry, but that we make it clear we intend to marry. We must state our intentions before Louise has a chance to act. Since you've already asked Michael for my hand, I'll have him place an announcement in *The Times*—well, I'll write it and get him to send it—and we'll have some kind of dinner to ensure Littleberry knows we're marking the occasion."

"Perhaps we could ask Gaby and Quinn to host us at Dermody House." Fortier's expression had lightened considerably. "Not nearly as grand as Whitcombe, I know, but since we'll be shocking your family by marrying into it, I feel it's time we extended some hospitality to them. And Gaby's studio has a marvelous floor for dancing."

Fortier expertly changed his grip on me into the correct position for a waltz, steering me out into the most unencumbered part of the room. "I was so angry with Louise when I received this letter this morning, you can't possibly imagine.

But I've had a whole day of riding and work to think about the matter, and I'm grateful to her."

"Grateful?" I couldn't help laughing; Fortier was leading me into a very lively waltz step.

"Grateful." Fortier reversed with such vigor that the flames in the fireplace leaped in the draft as my skirts swung round. "I've been holding back, fretting about everything; Gaby always accuses me of being far too deliberative. But when faced with a challenge like this, my blood fires and I immediately want to take the battle to the enemy. I intend to have an engagement ring made that will shine on your finger as a clear challenge to Louise. I refuse to allow her to think for one moment that she can drive us apart."

He stopped, looking down at me with an expression that was both tender and somehow rather stubborn. "It really won't be easy, Helena."

"It was never going to be easy for the two of us to join together." I smiled. "Even now you've revealed yourself to be a duke. *And* the friend of the most celebrated woman in Europe; that will certainly impress Blanche. But after the last two years, I suspect we have wit and courage enough to face every obstacle that threatens to separate us."

It was ridiculous that I should feel so lighthearted with such storm clouds gathering above us, but I wanted to sing and shout. Somehow this unexpected turn in Fortier's own family drama—so much grander and more story-like than mine—had pushed us over the final obstacle to moving from an understanding to an engagement. Yes, perhaps I too could be grateful to Louise.

"When I go to the empress, you'll come too, won't you?" Fortier was saying. "As my fiancée, of course. I think she'll like you."

"Of course." I grinned. "Another challenge to dear Cousin Louise."

"To the devil with Louise." To my surprise, Fortier suddenly sank to his knees, looking a little incongruous in his stockinged feet. "There is only one woman in my heart, mind, and soul, and that's you. Lady Helena Whitcombe, will you marry me?"

"I thought you'd never ask."

The Scott-De Quincy Mysteries

A reluctant lady sleuth finds she's investigating her own family . . .

Lady Helena Investigates
Lady Odelia's Secret
Lady Ambition's Dilemma

Lady Helena Whitcombe, twice unlucky in love, is bereft when her husband's corpse is found floating in the river at the foot of their opulent estate. But when mysterious French physician Armand Fortier tells her he doesn't think Sir Justin's death was an accident, Lady Helena begins a new life as Sussex's "investigating lady" and soon finds herself unearthing a trove of bewildering family secrets. Go to www.janesteen.com/insider or scan the QR code below for news and offers on future books.

The House of Closed Doors series

The House of Closed Doors
Eternal Deception
The Shadow Palace
The Jewel Cage

Nell Lillington is a heedless, cosseted seventeen-year-old when she chooses not to reveal the name of her baby's father. In 1870s Illinois, such a decision has far-reaching consequences, and Nell finds her path to happiness strewn with murder. Join Nell as she struggles to reconcile love, independence, and respectability in these engrossing Victorian mysteries—great clean reads that will keep you entertained for hours. Get the first book for free by signing up for Jane's newsletter at www.janesteen.com/insider or scan the QR code below.

FROM THE AUTHOR

Dear Reader,

I hope you enjoyed reading *Lady Ambition's Dilemma* as much as I enjoyed writing it. I'm an indie author paying bills by doing what I love the most—creating entertainment for other people. So my most important assets are YOU, the readers, without whom I'd just be talking to myself. Again.

My promise to you is that I'll do my best. I'll research to make the historical background to my stories as accurate as I can. I'll edit and polish until the book's up to my (high) standards. I'll give you a great-looking cover to look at, and I'll make sure my books are available in as many formats and in as many places as possible. I'll keep my prices as low as is compatible with keeping my publishing business going.

What can you do for me? If you've loved this book, there are several ways you can help me out.

Let me know what you think. If you go to www.janesteen.com, you'll see a little envelope icon near the bottom of the page. That's how you contact me by email. I'd love to hear what you thought of the book. Or find me on Facebook, Threads, Instagram, or Goodreads.

Leave a review. An honest review—even if you just want to say you didn't like the book—is a huge help. Leave it on the site where you bought the book, or on your favorite reader site.

Tell a friend. I love it when sales come through word of mouth. Better still, mention my book on social media and amplify your power to help my career.

Sign up for my newsletter at www.janesteen.com/insider. That's a win-win: my newsletter is where I offer free copies, unpublished extras, insider info, and let you know when a new book's coming out.

And thanks again for reading.

Jane

AUTHOR'S NOTE

"It's so hard to tell with the French." Julia sighed. "All those years of turmoil. Republic, empire, monarchy, republic, empire—where are we now?"

"Republic, silly . . ." — *Lady Helena Investigates*

I make no apologies for allowing some French history to creep into my narrative, although I'm not going to explain at this point who died in 1883 and why that person's death mattered. Suffice to say that I've been scattering bread-crumbs about Fortier ever since he first appears, because I knew his story was going to be a big one, and the Scott-De Quincys are fluent in French for a reason.

I was delighted when the word "Ruritanian" surfaced during the beta read of this novel, because I absolutely love a Ruritanian romance. And I like nothing better than a really big story—think *The Scarlet Pimpernel, The Prisoner of Zenda,* or even *A Song of Ice and Fire* aka *Game of Thrones*. The movie of *The Prisoner of Zenda* (the 1952 Stewart Granger version) was a particular influence on me, since it was a favorite of my mother's, who was probably the person most responsible for my interest in historical fiction. They always seemed to run old movies on Sunday afternoons when I was growing up; the historical subjects, WWII movies, and Hammer horror movies were my delight then and my inspiration now.

So when I set out to challenge myself with a series that had a large cast, almost all of whom I've now introduced, I also intended to bring in an element of fantasy based on real history, and what better history than the turbulent state of France in the nineteenth century? By the time you first meet Lady Helena, France has had two empires, two monarchies, and three revolutions in the last hundred years, and although the republic founded in 1870 did in reality last until the Second World War, in the 1880s this was by no means a certainty.

There is so much scope for fun and games in this very real history of the nineteenth century, during which France also became one of the key European powers and a big player on the global scene. This was an era when Europe was at the center of world politics and power; America had only just begun to flex its economic muscles properly and was far from being the dominant force it became in the twentieth century.

London was the largest city in the world throughout most of the nineteenth century, and the most important; Paris ranked third in size behind Beijing, and vied with London for global influence. The British, French, Germans, and Dutch were all engaged in grabbing land and power all over the globe, causing changes that are still affecting us today.

England, interestingly, was the premier place of refuge for French citizens who would rather avoid political trouble at home, including various members of various royal and imperial families, some waiting for an opportunity to claw their way back into power and some quite content to live as wealthy private citizens. And the French weren't the only populations whose aristocracy found a more convenient home in England than in their own countries, not to mention an opportunity for those of the highest rank to marry their children into England's ruling dynasty, then almost certainly the most powerful in the world. The European aristocracies learned each other's languages, traveled to each other's countries, and until the World Wars of the twentieth century formed a huge European political/dynastic/cultural network that also had its eye on the rest of the world. That's the background I'm working against.

I also intended, and still intend, to give you the tropes of a historical mystery series, blended with a large dash of family saga and, as you've probably guessed by now, more than one romance. No small ambitions here! Keeping the balance between the small scale and the large is my biggest challenge.

Another thing I should mention about 1883 was a shock that was literally felt around the world. From May to October of that year, the Indonesian island of Krakatoa underwent huge paroxysms of volcanic activity, peaking on 27 August with an explosion so massive it was heard nearly two thousand miles away, and a pressure wave that went around the globe three and a half times. It resulted in a volcanic winter and months of spectacular sunsets in the northern hemisphere, famously thought to have suggested the background to Edvard Munch's celebrated 1893 painting The Scream. It also killed over 36,000 people, including the entire population of a nearby island.

I have left the Scott-De Quincys rather indifferent and uninformed about these particular events on purpose, to reflect the fact that although there was some attention given to them in the illustrated papers in September, they were hardly headline news for long, and it wasn't till December that the British seem to have become really interested because of the dark skies and strange sunsets they were having. Dare I say how typically British it was to care more about our weather than far-off tragedy? But even now, distant disasters play out more as a background to our lives than as an important event, until they disrupt our own little worlds. And perhaps that's just a survival strategy.

I hope that by now you're looking forward to 1884 as eagerly as I am. My cast is (almost all) in place, my bread-crumbs are strewn, and the plot lines are multiplying. It's go big or go home time, and I have some huge reveals in store. Start guessing . . .

ACKNOWLEDGMENTS

After a great deal of preparatory work in 2022, *Lady Ambition's Dilemma* was no more than a synopsis when I sat down to start the serious work of plotting and writing on January 1, 2023. The discipline I had to exert to write three drafts in a year didn't just affect me, so my first thanks are to my husband Bob, for helping out with the rest of life.

Then come my publishing team: Kate Burgess, Leander Couldridge, and Ellen Hills. The steady work that all three of them put in helps me keep the publishing side of this writing venture going, and I am hugely grateful for their reliability and patience.

The book itself was greatly improved by input from my beta readers. Brandi Coffey, Hilarie Berzins, Jacomien Zwemstra, Jenna Matheson, Kristen Tate, Leslie McKinnon, Marta Tetzeli, Regina Newman, Sheila Matthews, and Shirley Stephens, thank you so much for all the help you gave me! I know I never let you refer back to the previous drafts, which must be frustrating at times, but I hope you can spot some—many—of your suggestions in this final version.

When it comes to turning the text I end up with into the various editions—ebook, print, and audiobook—that will be bought or downloaded by readers, I can't do it without a professional copyedit, for which I must once again thank Jenny Quinlan. The gorgeous cover owes its existence to Rachel Lawston and Alexandra Allden, while Elizabeth Klett narrates in a flawless Lady Helena voice and produces crisp, clean files for the audiobook version. All of these professionals are wonderful to work with and I'm so proud of what they help me achieve.

And last but not least, Susan Kings and her team at Kings Accounting are there year-round to help me run my publishing business and ensure I pay my taxes. I particularly value the advice and the magic phone calls to the right people whenever there's a hitch.

ABOUT THE AUTHOR

The most important fact you need to know about me is that I was (according to my mother, at least) named after Jane Eyre, which to this day remains one of my favorite books. I was clearly doomed to love all things Victorian, and ended up studying both English and French nineteenth-century writers in depth.

This was a pretty good grounding for launching myself into writing novels set in the nineteenth century. I was living in the small town of Libertyville, Illinois—part of the greater Chicago area—when I began writing the *House of Closed Doors* series, inspired by a photograph of the long-vanished County Poor Farm on Libertyville's main street.

Now back in my native England, I have the good fortune to live in an idyllic ancient town close to the sea. This location has sparked a new series about an aristocratic family with more secrets than most: *The Scott-De Quincy Mysteries.*

I write for readers who want a series you can't put down. I love to blend saga, mystery, adventure, and a touch of romance, set against the background of the real-life issues facing women in the late nineteenth century.

I am a member of the Alliance of Independent Authors, the Historical Novel Society, Novelists, Inc., and the Society of Authors.

To find out more about my books, join my insider list at www.janesteen.com/insider (can also be reached via the QR code below). Below that are various links to my social media, where you will get to know me and my books better.

facebook.com/janesteenwriter
bookbub.com/authors/jane-steen
goodreads.com/janesteen
pinterest.com/janesteen
threads.net/@janesteenwriter
instagram.com/janesteenwriter

Made in the USA
Monee, IL
01 April 2024

56176877R00229